DARE TO DANCE

The Maxwell Series - Book 4

S.B. ALEXANDER

Raven Wing Publishing

Dare to Dance
Book Four: The Maxwell Series
Copyright © 2016 by S.B. Alexander
All rights reserved
First Edition: September 2016
E-book ISBN-13: 978-0-9969351-5-9
Print ISBN-13: 978-0-9969351-6-6

Visit: www.sbalexander.com
Editor: Red Adept Editing, www.redadeptediting.com
Cover Design by Hang Le: http://www.byhangle.com

This is a work of fiction. Names, characters, places and incidents either are the product of the author's imagination or are used fictiously, and any resemblance to locales, events, business establishments, or actual persons-living or dead-is entirely coincidental.

Adult Content Warning: The content contained is the book includes adult language and sexual content. This book is intended for adult audiences 17 years of age and older.

DEDICATION

To anyone who has struggled in life.

DARE TO DANCE PLAYLIST

- "Dancing On My Own" by Calum Scott
- "In The Dark" by 3 Doors Down
- "Let Your Tears Fall" by Kelly Clarkson
- "The Fighter" by Keith Urban
- "Here Without You" 3 Doors Down
- "Out Of My Head" by Theory of a Deadman
- "We Don't Have To Take Our Clothes Off" by Ella Eyre
- "Heart Of A Champion" by Nelly
- "Collide" by Howie Day
- "Careless Whisper" by Seether
- "Slow Dancing in a Burning Room" by John Mayer
- "Tightrope" by Kelly Clarkson
- "Whiskey And You" by Chris Stapleton
- "Waiting for Superman" by Daughtry
- "Over You" by Daughtry
- "When I Was Your Man" by Bruno Mars
- "Stay" by Rihanna
- "In My Daughter's Eyes" by Martina McBride

PROLOGUE

RUBY LEWIS

You'd filled that hole inside my life
With things I thought I needed.
As fast as you had hooked me
Was as fast as you retreated.

Did love become a transient thing
To transfer at your will?
All you took from me that day;
It leaves me empty still.

You were the sun that ruled my sky,
Now no more exists.
You plunged me into darkness
With my hatred and my fists.

Perhaps it would've helped
If you'd not left me broken-hearted.
I'd kill for the half dignity I had
When this all started.

But that was then, and this is now.
I'm fighting to stay whole.

I'll forget the way I loved you
And that part of me you stole.

Your face still haunts my memory
So I let it settle there,
'cause it serves to stoke my anger
And reminds me not to care.

So pull your chair up ringside
And you'll see a thing or two.
The dancing that I'm doing,
Yeah, it's now because of you.

CHAPTER 1
KROSS

The rolling green lawn of Greenridge Academy spanned both sides of the private high school. I drove down the winding road that led to the large campus of buildings scattered around the property.

"Boy, does this bring back memories," my brother Kody said from the passenger seat.

Some memories I didn't care to remember. Kody and I, along with our brother Kelton, had spent our sophomore year at the academy. Everyone at Kensington High thought we'd been shipped off to a military school. Greenridge was far from military, although the atmosphere had sure seemed like it at the time. Regardless, our old man had been furious about all the fights we'd been in at Kensington High during our freshman year. The final straw had been the fight with Kade's enemy Greg Sullivan. Kody and I had beaten the boy to a pulp.

"So, is this guy good?" Kody thread his fingers through his thick black hair.

"We'll see." My boxing coach, Jay Crandall, sent me to Greenridge to check out an up-and-coming boxer who just happened to be a student there. I wasn't exactly jumping up and down for joy to revisit the place, but I wanted to get paid. While I built my boxing career, I was working for Jay at the gym, helping to train and coach members.

I parked in a visitor's space, studying the century-old structure that was the anchor of the campus. The graying stone façade reminded me of a castle, complete with two corner towers, red pointed peaks, and a large portico. The beauty of the campus wasn't the main building but the surrounding mountains, the dense trees, and manicured rolling lawns that seemed to go on for miles, lending a cozy feeling to the property. The environment was a stark contrast to the cold classrooms and sterile halls of the school and dormitories.

The year I'd attended was a time of firsts, lasts, good, bad, and everything in between. But mostly, I'd been angry with my father for disrupting our lives, for separating us from Kade and our barely lived in home in Ashford, Massachusetts, only to move us into a dorm that felt like a prison.

The double wooden doors of the main building burst open, and students filed out as though someone had disrupted a hornet's nest.

"Best part of this school was being close to Mom," I said as we watched the throng of students disperse in all directions. Mom had been in a mental health facility not far from the school.

Kody unstrapped his seatbelt. "I thought for you it was Ruby Lewis."

"I guess." Back then, Ruby had been a refreshing ray of sunshine. The moment I laid eyes on her, the anger I held firm slipped to the wayside. We bumped into each other after school one day, not paying attention to where we were going. I'd been reading a text from Kade, and she'd been looking for her keys in her purse. I tried to speak, but my tongue wouldn't move. All I could do was stare at her like a boy who had just discovered girls for the first time. Maybe I had. Up until the tenth grade I hadn't paid much attention to girls. I didn't care to. Girls had always chased my brothers and me, probably because they thought triplets were hot or something. They ogled at us and giggled when they passed us in the halls at school. After a while, I got tired of all the attention, especially if the girls interrupted our conversations. That was a norm for girls during lunch in the school cafeterias. But Ruby was different, shy, not to mention beautiful with her shiny auburn hair, porcelain skin, and blue-green eyes. As cheesy as it sounded, I seriously thought I had run into an angel.

"Whatever happened to her?" Kody asked.

I inhaled the air of the truck, which was stinky thanks to Kody's burps of garlic and onions. "Not sure."

We'd dated for five months before I had to move back home to

Ashford. Then I lost touch with her. Actually, I ignored her repeated calls. I'd gotten spooked when she told me she might be pregnant.

My old man had explained the birds and the bees to all us boys. "Protection," he'd said. "Not only to prevent pregnancy, but sexually transmitted diseases."

I'd heard him, but I hadn't listened. Ruby and I got caught up in the moment. Even though she later conveyed to me that she'd finally gotten her monthly girl thing and wasn't pregnant, our relationship changed, or rather I changed. It was as if that one incident had been a wake-up call to real life, and I hadn't been ready to deal.

Kody nudged me. "Are you taking a trip down memory lane?"

I chuckled. "You could say that." I opened the door of my truck. "Let's go." I didn't need to think about Ruby, although I had wondered over the years, and more lately, how she was doing. Part of me wanted to apologize for being a dick. Another part of me wanted to see her. She had to be more beautiful now.

The cluster of students quickly dispersed as Kody and I started for the path behind the school that led to the gym.

Kody stabbed a thumb toward the main entrance. "Aren't we supposed to check in at the office?"

"Are you still obeying school rules? You're not in high school, dude." The last thing I wanted to do was run into teachers who might remember us. Kody and I hadn't been good students that year.

Kody fell into step with me. "Worried about Mrs. Munoz?"

"I made amends with her. Remember? I wrote I was sorry a hundred times for calling her a witch in Spanish. You concerned about Ms. Sharp?"

"I do want to apologize again."

I raised an eyebrow. Mandy, Kody's girl, had died a few months before we started at Greenridge. So Kody had more of a chip on his shoulder than I did. "You don't think she's forgiven you for breaking her nephew's nose?"

He shrugged. "I wouldn't if I was her. But I do remember she was hot." His grin was mischievous. "It's only been four years. I believe she's probably, what, twenty-seven now?"

If she were still teaching there, I wouldn't mind seeing if she was still curvy with long legs and shapely breasts. "Are you into older women?"

"Dude, they know what they want. Besides, they're not up for a serious relationship." Most of the girls screaming his name at Rumors when he sang and played the guitar were college age, and most were on the hunt for a steady boyfriend.

"Tell me more, brother," I said.

He laughed. "Another time. We got company."

Two high-school-age guys swaggered out of the gym as we approached. One was stocky, and the other was tall and lean.

"Hey, you're here to see Liam," the stocky dude said a little excitedly. "You're Kross Maxwell."

Kody and I exchanged a surprised look. We expected girls to get all giddy, but not the guys.

The tall and lean dude extended his hand. "I'm Miles. I've seen most of your bouts. I hear you're trying to sign with Gail Freeman. Man, hottest promoter in the country." He waggled his eyebrows.

I smirked as I shook his hand. Not only was Gail the best boxing promoter around, she was definitely a sexy lady. Her physique aside, she was picky in her selection of boxers to sign. Their records had to be almost perfect. She rarely gave a second look to boxers with several losses.

"You're a legend, Bro," Kody said.

Maybe I was a legend at Greenridge, but I had work to do if I wanted to sign with Gail. Out of nine bouts in three years, I'd lost once, and that loss had come last week. My head was up my ass, which was one reason I'd gotten knocked out. However, the main reason was because my footwork had been sloppy. I was still irritated with myself. "Liam inside?"

"He's in the ring," Miles said.

"Come on," Stocky Dude said. "We're going to be late."

They walked off as two girls glided toward them.

I pulled opened the side door, which led into a hall. The warm air breezed over me.

"I'll meet you later." Kody slapped me on the back. "Wish me luck."

"Don't get us thrown out." Back in our day, the principal had threatened to suspend us and would have done it if it weren't for my father smoothing things over.

Kody shuffled backward, his blue eyes alight with pleasure or mischief or both. "I'll be sweet."

Normally, I wouldn't be worried. Kody wasn't Kelton, who would have had the teacher splayed out naked on top of her desk. But after our conversation a minute ago, I was learning a new side of my brother. At twenty years old, Kody was slowly opening up to dating. He sure had his pick of the litter when he sang his brooding songs. Or maybe he had been dating for years. I had never seen Kody with a girl, though. It didn't matter. We were adults. So what if he got caught with his pants down.

I ducked into the gym, and memory lane came screaming back—in particular, Ruby and I making out behind the bleachers. Actually, this was the place where we had both lost our virginity.

A familiar voice cut through my brain. "Come on, Liam."

Blinking away the image of Ruby and me naked on a mat, I padded across the hardwood floor. My boots thudded, sounding hollow above the grunts and groans coming from the boxing ring center court.

I sidled up to Coach Scott, who stood a head shorter than me. "Which one is Liam?"

Both boys were the same height and same build. It was hard to decipher the differences since they were wearing helmets. But one did have blood around his bottom lip.

"You're late," Coach said without breaking his attention away from the ring. He still had gray hair, although it appeared he'd lost some on top. "The one with the busted lip."

Coach hated when people were late for anything. He reminded me of my father, who despised the same thing. The pet peeve was a product of both of them being ex-military. Regardless, I would be wasting my breath if I gave him the excuse that traffic out of Boston was brutal. His response would be, "not my problem."

The two boys in the ring jabbed and punched, dancing around each other, bobbing every now and then.

"Liam reminds me a lot of you. Look how quick he is on his feet." The gruffness in Coach Scott's voice changed to a more pleasing tone.

I agreed with him. Liam's footwork was smooth, which would please Jay all the more. "His partner doesn't look too bad." The boy knew how to keep up with Liam, throwing some direct jabs to Liam's face.

"So, what happened at your last fight? You rarely get knocked out." Coach Scott crossed his arms over his chest. "Liam," he shouted. "Don't let Chip ruin that pretty face of yours."

Liam was tiring, which wasn't surprising for his boxing style. He was what the industry called an out-fighter. Out-fighters, like the famous Muhammad Ali, were regarded as the best boxing strategists since they knew how to control the fight. Liam was still learning, and therefore, tired easily from all the footwork, much like I had when I first started.

"Bad night," I replied. I hadn't been sleeping well. It had all started several months ago when Kelton had gotten the scare of his life. He'd thought he was the father of Chloe's baby, an ex-girlfriend of his. It was then that my sophomore year reared its ugly head, hence the reason Ruby was in my thoughts nonstop. Kody wanted to make amends with a teacher. I had the urge to do the same with Ruby, and maybe more.

After about thirty minutes of making mental notes on Liam's style, I said good-bye to Coach Scott. I had to get back to Boston to train a client. I also wanted to make one stop before Kody and I got on the road.

"You don't want to chat with him?" Coach Scott asked.

"I don't need to. Liam looks good. His footwork is quick, and his style will appease Jay."

Frankly, it was a wasted trip in my book. Jay could've brought him down to the gym in Boston if it weren't for the meeting he had with Gail Freeman. Jay also didn't want to get the kid excited until he knew for sure.

After a few more minutes of chatting with Coach Scott, I made my way out, texting Kody and told him it was time to go. When I got to my truck, Kody was waiting for me with a shit-eating grin on his face.

I pressed the key fob, and two beeps sounded. "I take it you found Ms. Sharp."

"I gave her my number," Kody said as he climbed in. "My image of her was spot on. She's curvy, stacked, and sexy as hell."

I choked as I slid behind the wheel and started the engine. "Maybe I should be hanging out with you more often." I could get into dating a woman who didn't want to sink her claws into me, like the girl I was dating seemed to be doing. Penelope wanted my nuts in her hand at every turn. The sex was great, but I was building my career and didn't have the time or the interest in a steady relationship. I'd already lost one fight because my thoughts were on a girl.

I wheeled out of the parking lot.

"You get plenty of attention at your fights," Kody said. "Besides, Penelope isn't doing it for you?"

"I'm not ready to settle down with the picket fence, wife, and kids." I wanted someone who didn't complain about a broken nail or whine about having to watch a football game.

"I feel you, Bro." He fiddled with the radio, tuning into a country station before he sat back. "Wait. The highway is the other way."

"I have to do something first." Since I was in the area, maybe I could catch Ruby at home, or at least get her number from her parents. Not to mention, I needed to get her out of my head, especially with an upcoming fight. I couldn't lose another one. Not with a signing deal with Gail Freeman looming.

Orange and red colored leaves floated to the ground along the tree-lined street. Fall was in high gear. Before long the branches would be bare and covered in snow.

"Care to share?" Kody asked.

After I'd told Kelton my little secret months ago, I tossed it aside. I didn't see a need to blast the news that I'd almost gotten Ruby pregnant to Kade or Kody. But every time I saw Chloe, who was now almost nine months pregnant, I thought of Ruby.

I glanced from left to right, looking for a yellow house among the variety of two-story colonial homes that dotted the street. "Don't freak. Two weeks before we moved back to Ashford, Ruby told me she thought she was pregnant." I counted to three.

Kody lowered the volume of the radio on my second count. On three, he said, "What the fuck! You're just telling me this now."

"Chill. I didn't see a need to bring up the subject. But since you're with me, you should know just in case she bolts out of her house and attacks me." I braked at a stop sign. "And she wasn't pregnant. It was a false alarm."

"God, Kross. That's good news. So why do I get the feeling you're not happy? Did you want her to be pregnant?"

"Fuck no." I wasn't happy because I might come face-to-face with the woman I'd left hanging. A woman who'd called me several times sounding frantic, and whose calls I'd ignored. A woman who probably wanted my balls between a nutcracker.

Family was everything to me. I wanted my own one day, but at sixteen, no way. Even now at twenty years old, I was still too young to start a family. "But I was a dick. I didn't return her repeated calls after we moved back home." I gave my truck some gas.

"Come on, man. We were sixteen. How were you supposed to act? You were scared."

Maybe I was scared, but I was also confused. Too much had changed—my sister Karen's death, Mom moving into a mental health facility, moving from Texas to Massachusetts. Then no sooner had we gotten used to a new school in Ashford before we were plucked from it and forced into Greenridge Academy. Ruby had been my escape, and I'd used her. At least looking back on the situation, that was how I felt now.

"So, why the apology?"

"We were friends, and I let her down." Truth be told, she'd said she loved me. My response to her had been, "No, you don't. You think you do, but the feelings we shared won't last." It had been wrong of me to say that. I'd learned from Kelton recently that young love could stand the test of time.

"Did you love her?" Kody asked.

"I don't know. I was so confused. All I could think about when she told me she loved me were Mom's words to Kelton: 'It's infatuation. You don't love Lizzie.'"

Kody chuckled. "But that didn't stop Kelton now, did it?"

"Kelton proved all of us wrong." His childhood sweetheart had shown up in Boston several months ago, and now Lizzie and Kelton were madly in love and living together. Not that I was here to confess my love to Ruby, although I was curious how I would react to seeing her again. She had always made me feel lightheaded in a good way.

Kody scratched his head. "I sense you're not telling me everything. Do you think if you see her again, she might stir up old feelings?"

I pressed on the gas pedal. "What? No. But every time I see Chloe, I'm reminded of how much of a dick I was to Ruby. She kept calling me after we left the academy. The messages she left sounded like she needed my help. I should've at least responded to her, but the pregnancy scare and her telling me she loved me kind of freaked me out. I really just want to apologize."

A weathered, worn yellow house came into view on our right. I wheeled into a spot across the street.

"Seems to me that no one lives there," Kody said.

Compared to the meticulous manicured lawns of the surrounding homes, Ruby's home gave off an ominous vibe in the daylight. The grass was overgrown. The bushes lining both sides of the tiny porch needed a trim, and the black shutters were chipping.

I opened my door. "You want to wait here?"

"I'll stretch my legs."

As Kody and I strode up to the house, a Jetta zipped into the driveway next door. The bass of the music pounded as the driver screeched to a stop. Once the engine died, a young girl hopped out, dressed in workout gear. She caught sight of us as she hitched her sport bag over her shoulder.

"We have a looker," I whispered.

"If you two are here to rob that house, it's empty." The teenage girl raised her voice as she tucked her shiny black hair behind her ears.

"Do we look like thieves?" Kody asked.

She sashayed her curvy hips through the weeds. "Kind of." She giggled. "I'm Tasha."

Okay, maybe we did. Kody and I were both dressed in jeans, boots, hooded sweatshirts, and knit caps. Normal attire for us.

"I'm Kross," I said. "This is Kody. I'm looking for Ruby Lewis."

She eyed Kody for a beat before settling her gaze on me. "I'm sorry I can't help you. Shortly after the cops arrested her father four years ago, Ruby and her mom left."

I wracked my brain, trying to remember what her father did for living, but I wasn't sure Ruby had told me. I'd only met him once at one of her ballet recitals.

"Why did he go to jail?" Kody asked.

She lifted a shoulder. "Dealing drugs."

Kody and I exchanged a what-the-fuck look.

Ruby's messages toward the end had sounded desperate. *"Kross, why won't you call me back? I thought we were friends. I need you. I need to talk to you."*

"Any idea where Ruby might be?" I asked.

"Sorry, I don't." Her gaze lingered on Kody, who eyed me with a look that said he wanted to get out of there.

"Thanks for the info." I started for my truck, feeling more like a dick. Ruby had wanted my help, and all I'd done was hit ignore on my phone.

Kody caught up to me. "Kross, did you know her old man dealt drugs?"

"No idea. Our family had our own problems back then. And Ruby didn't talk too much about her parents. All I knew was her mom didn't work."

"Kross," the girl called. "Are you Kross Maxwell?"

I pivoted on my heel in the middle of the street then angled my head.

She jogged across the lawn and stood on the curb. "Are you the father?"

My mouth fell open. "Come again?"

She looked back at Ruby's house then at me. "Ruby was pregnant when they left."

The neighborhood narrowed to nothing—no sound, no light, just a black hole. Kody dragged me out of the street as a car sped past. My heart was beating so fast, it was bruising my ribs. I swung my gaze from a pale-faced Kody to the girl.

Finally, I shook my head. It couldn't be possible. Ruby had said she wasn't pregnant. My limbs became weak, my brain became foggy, and my tongue wouldn't move. Tasha had to be mistaken.

"So, you know this for a fact?" Kody asked.

"Sure as the wind is blowing right now," she said. "When her and her mom left in the fall of her junior year, her belly was big, and her mom told mine that Ruby was pregnant."

I thought back to when Ruby and I had had sex, counting the months. We'd had sex in May of our sophomore year. I'd moved back to Ashford in June. So by the fall of that year, she would've been at least four months pregnant. The blood drained from my face.

"Bro, maybe it's not yours." Kody's face had turned completely white. No doubt mine had too.

I shoved both hands through my hair. Kody might have been right, but my gut was telling me differently. All I could think back to were Ruby's messages. She hadn't been calling me because of her father's arrest. She'd been calling me because she was pregnant.

"According to my brother, Ruby had told him that the father was a guy by the name of Kross Maxwell." She flashed her big dark eyes at me. "Is that you?"

Either a sinkhole was beginning to form beneath my feet or the earth was shaking. Kody caught me as I swayed. *Fuck. Fuck. Fuck.* I sucked in the late October air, the cold burning a path down my throat. I was a daddy. I was a fucking daddy. I had to sit down. I whipped my head in all directions. But that only served to increase the dizziness. Kody guided me to a fire hydrant. But my body wouldn't stop listing to one side then the other as though I was on a boat in high seas. Nausea shot up to settle in my throat.

"Is he okay?" Tasha asked.

Kody tapped me on the face. "Bro?" He waved a blurry hand in front of my eyes.

I bent over and heaved. Nothing came out. I heaved again as Kody steadied me. This time, I literally lost my lunch. Sweat coated my forehead as ice sliced through my veins. I shivered. I could handle difficult situations. I'd learned quickly when my sister, Karen, died, and even more so when my mom had fallen into a deep depression. I had to in order to help my father and Kade. While Kade was consoling Kody and Kelton, I tended to my mom, especially when my old man was away on missions. Sure, I cried over my sister's death. I cried alone in my room at night when no one was around. I wanted to be strong. I'd seen how Kade had struggled with becoming a pseudo parent, and I'd had to help him.

But the news that I could be a father made me feel as though I had just been rammed in the gut by a cement truck.

"Breathe," Kody said.

I couldn't get air in my lungs. I couldn't even form words.

"Here's a tissue." Tasha's voice rose. "I'll get some water. Be right back."

"Sit," Kody ordered.

Wiping my mouth, I dropped down on the curb as the neighborhood spun around me. "I'm a fucking father." I wished I were numb. But a sharp pain throbbed inside my skull, feeling as though I was getting hit from both sides. Maybe I was taking after Kade and getting a migraine. I turned away from Kody and puked again. Man, I knew now how Kelton felt when he thought he might be the father of Chloe's baby.

"Fuck," Kody said. "I don't know what to do, Bro. Do you want me to call Kade?"

A maniacal laugh escaped me. I didn't have the first clue what to do, not when my hands were shaking and the nausea wouldn't settle. "No. This type of news is something that Kade needs to hear in person. Give me a minute. I'll be fine." Another crazy laugh broke out, only this time in my head. I was far from fine.

Tasha came back with a bottle of water and handed it to me. "I'm sorry that I told you. I thought you knew."

I downed the water, the liquid cooling the acidic burn in my throat.

"Does your brother know where Ruby might be?" Kody's voice cracked.

"I don't know," she said. "He's not home either. He goes to Boston College. I'll give you his cell before you leave."

It was time we did. I had to get out of there and away from Ruby's house. I had to find her. I just didn't know how yet.

CHAPTER 2
RUBY

A light rat-a-tat-tat of rain pelted the roof of our makeshift home made of cardboard and a tarp, while my best friend, Norma, hacked up a lung.

I touched her forehead. "You're burning up."

She sniffled as she turned on her side. "I'll be all right. It's just a cold."

I glanced at the Timex watch I'd found in a trashcan. I still had time to run to the drugstore. "I'll be back. You need medicine."

She grabbed my wrist. "We don't have any money, and you can't get caught stealing again."

It warmed my heart to know I had someone in my life who cared. I loved her for looking out for me. We were a team. We had been since we met in jail a month before. Norma had been in for prostitution. I'd gotten caught stealing food from a grocery store. I actually considered her family. My mom and dad were both in jail for selling drugs. I silently laughed at how I was on the track to join them if I kept stealing.

"I have a few dollars." I didn't have enough for cold medicine. Since our release from jail, we had done everything we could to find jobs. We'd begged for money and waddled through dumpsters for food. She had no one in her life, and she refused to go back to her pimp.

"Ruby." She sneezed. "We need that money for food."

I swiped my hand over her short, dirty blond hair. It was literally greasy and dirty, giving her hair color a darker hue. "You need to get better." She'd been sick on and off for the last week. I was worried that something other than a cold was plaguing her, but with no money, doctors wouldn't even see her.

Norma sneezed again. "How much money do you have?" She was the practical and cautious one in our friendship.

I dug into my ripped jacket and pulled out change and a dollar bill, courtesy of a nice old man who was the only one to drop money in my cup while I was begging for change earlier that day. "See. It's plenty to buy one dose of Advil, which will help with your fever."

She coughed. Her brown eyes were red and watery. "Once I'm better, I'll resume looking for a job."

I'd submitted applications at several fast food restaurants in the last month. Those were the only places I could apply. I barely had any skills since I didn't finish high school. But it was hard to communicate with a potential employer since we couldn't afford cell phones. "I need to follow up with Burger King tomorrow."

"I'll see if my pimp can hire us," she said through a wheeze.

"No way. I'll continue to live on the cold streets of Boston before I do that."

She took my hand. "Ruby, you need to get Raven back. She's with a strange family. You're her momma. She needs you."

I jerked my hand away as tears threatened. "I know, damn it. But I'm not whoring myself. Right now, she's in a good place. She has a warm bed and food in her belly. I can't give her that right now." I cursed my mom for following in my dad's footsteps. Part of me couldn't blame her too much. She was only trying to make ends meet for Raven and me. I'd always argued with her that I would find a job while she watched Raven, but she'd said bonding with a child was the most important thing for a mother.

"I'm sorry." Norma's teeth chattered. "I didn't mean to make you upset. But we've been on the streets for a month. We, you at least, have got to do something to show social services you have a steady job and an apartment."

I chewed on the inside of my cheek. "Selling my body isn't a job social services would approve of." The social worker had told me to stay out of jail, get steady employment, and find a decent apartment.

Then we could talk more about getting Raven back, which I was determined to do.

"I know that." Norma's eyes fluttered shut. "But we can make some money to put away for an apartment, and we can continue to look for jobs while we work the streets."

I angled my head. Maybe she had a fever that was making her delirious. I touched her forehead again. Yep, she was burning up. "Look, get some rest. I'm going to get medicine, and I promise if I need to steal, I won't get caught." As much as I needed to do the right thing for my own sake, I couldn't let my friend suffer. Her cold could turn into pneumonia. Or worse, she could die.

"You don't need to promise me. You need to promise yourself," she said, fading in and out of consciousness.

She was sounding more and more like my mother. Norma was only two years older than me, but she came off older than her twenty-two years, maybe because she'd run away from home when she was fifteen, and she'd been surviving on the streets since then.

I covered her with a blanket that was in desperate need of at least ten washings. "Sleep. We're in a dark, deserted alley." We'd picked that spot because we hadn't seen any other homeless people around. Besides, not many people were out in the rain. "No one will bother you. I'll be right back." Before she could stop me, I crawled out of the box, flipped my hood over my head, and dashed down the alley onto a main thoroughfare.

I jogged two blocks before the streets came alive with traffic. I passed restaurants where people were gathered, talking and laughing. I couldn't help but stop to gaze at a couple sitting at a table by the window. The two were holding hands and staring into each other's eyes. My stomach knotted as sadness sank low in my gut. I had a boyfriend once. I touched my chest, feeling for the pictures inside my jacket pocket that I carried with me at all times. Two were clear reminders of Kross Maxwell. No matter how mad I was at him, he still held a place in my heart. But high school, fun, ballet, Kross, us, had no place in my life. Thinking about the good old days would only depress me or make me angrier. I'd wanted to find him, but with how crazy my life had been with my parents and Raven, there was never a good time. Now that I was homeless, it definitely was not a good time.

Someone bumped into me. "Oh, sorry," the woman said as she gave me a pitying look before she kept walking.

Instead of spewing swear words at her, I tucked my chin down then started on my quest. Rain poured down and so did my tears. I thought about my little girl who was almost four years old and about how much I wanted to hold her right then. I wanted to squeeze her dimpled cheeks, look into her dark-blue eyes, and feel her thick black hair. *What are you doing, Ruby? You're only torturing yourself. Get your ass in gear and get a job.*

I'm trying, I screamed at my subconscious.

I picked up my pace as I traded thoughts of Raven for a plan of where to start looking when the fast food restaurants opened the next day. Burger King had the most promise. The manager was a young guy who seemed to like me by the way he smiled at me. Then I would check in with Taco Bell and a sub shop.

The drugstore sign came into view. I wiped my face with the backs of my fingerless gloves and ducked into Walgreens. The bright lights froze me in place for a second. I hated light. Light meant happy times, but it also reminded me of when I performed on stage at ballet recitals —a memory that would never become a reality again.

I squinted as I scanned the signs above the aisles, spotting the cold medicine near the pharmacy in the back of the store. I hurried down the outside aisle, away from the cashier who was ringing up a customer. I skirted a display of foil pans, boxes of pumpkin bread mix, and other items for Thanksgiving. At one time, I couldn't wait for Mom's turkey on Thanksgiving. Now, I hated the holiday that was only weeks away. While everyone stuffed themselves with turkey and said thanks for the things in their lives, I was dumpster diving for fresh scraps.

Once in the aisle with all the cold medicine and pain relievers, I searched up and down for single packets of Advil.

A short man, donning gold-rimmed glasses and a lab coat, walked up with a box of NyQuil in his hand. "Are you looking for something specific?"

I'd like that box of NyQuil. "Do you have a packet of Advil?"

"They're located at the counter up front." He placed the box of NyQuil on the shelf next to the cold medication.

Somewhere, a phone rang, then the overhead speaker announced, "Pharmacy, call on line two."

"If you need anything else, let me know." He darted out of sight.

I kept my eyes on the man in the lab coat. He had his phone to his ear, reading a computer screen. Then I put my hand on the box of

NyQuil. The price was way more than the three or so dollars I had on me.

Norma's voice blared inside my head. "Please don't steal."

I didn't want to, but she was in dire need of medicine. I looked up and down the aisle. The box of medicine seemed to burn in my hand. My heart sped up as it always did before I stole anything. Winter was the easiest time to steal since jackets and big coats could conceal most items. No one else was visible, except maybe the cameras somewhere in the store.

In lightning speed, I grabbed the box of NyQuil, slipped it inside my coat pocket, then casually strolled up to the front counter. I was careful not to run even though my adrenaline was rushing through me like the rapids at Niagara Falls. I blew out a breath, trying to calm my racing heart as I dug into my pocket and retrieved my money.

A young guy with zits all over his face smiled. "Can I help you?"

"A packet of Advil?"

The phone behind the counter rang. Zit Face picked it up. "Yes." After a second, he glanced at me, drawing in his eyebrows.

Busted. I bolted out of the store.

"Hey, stop," Zit Face shouted.

Cold air stung my heated face as I sprinted across the street. Horns blew as I almost collided with an oncoming car. Someone was yelling, but I didn't dare stop to look behind me. After running several blocks, I ducked into an alley to catch my breath. As my lungs expanded, I spotted a light seeping from underneath a door near a dumpster. A faint aroma of grease carried on the wind. I sniffed like a dog searching for his next meal, the scent pulling me deeper into the alley. The closer I got, the more my stomach growled. I peeked inside the door. Loud shouts and whistles trickled out along with heat, spice, and more grease. I licked my lips.

The sound of an engine rumbled at the mouth of the alley. I skirted a box and hopped into the dumpster, a feat I'd become extremely good at. I landed on a bag of trash and something wet. The engine noise got louder, the lights of the vehicle spraying out. I crouched lower, holding my breath. A car door slammed. Then another. Deep male voices peppered the air. *Please don't let it be the cops.*

"The fight should yield us close to fifteen thousand dollars," one guy with a gruff voice said.

"Just make sure she shows. I'll be taking your nuts if she doesn't," a deeper male voice added.

Two beeps echoed before the voices disappeared.

I poked my head out an inch above the dumpster and let out a sigh at the fact the dark-colored vehicle didn't have lights on the hood or "police" written on the metal somewhere. At the same time, the need for food waned as my mind spun with the possibilities of what I could do with fifteen thousand dollars. That amount of money would definitely be a good start to getting an apartment for Norma, Raven, and me. I climbed out and brushed off my clothes, which was futile since I lived on the streets. Not to mention, I'd just sat in all kinds of crap in a dumpster.

The dim light on the building lit up the name Firefly on the metal door that was now closed. *Damn it.* I pulled on the doorknob. Pay dirt. Shouts and whistles erupted from the stairwell that went down, although another went up. I would bet it led up to the kitchen. My stomach voted to take the kitchen route. Sometimes, cooks and servers were nice enough to hand me scraps or a loaf of bread. Maybe I could get some soup for Norma. I heard more whistles and guffaws. Curiosity was always a bitch, so I chanted "eeny meeny miny moe, which way should I go."

Another outburst of cheers rose from below, feeding my curiosity enough that I descended the stairs. When I reached the dirt-crusted floor at the bottom, a rat scurried by me. A bright light bled from a doorway up ahead, spotlighting yet another rodent. I checked behind me. Confident that no one was around to kick me out, I pushed forward toward the ruckus and onto a landing that overlooked a room below. A crush of male bodies was crammed wall-to-wall, all crowded around something I couldn't see. Their fists were in the air, waving handfuls of money. I moved closer to the railing when someone grabbed me by the shoulders.

Jumping what felt like a mile in the air, I turned with my fist ready to pummel someone.

A tall, wiry man with dark hair and dark eyes let go of me and held up his hands. "I'm not going to throw you to the wolves." His voice was gruff like the man I'd heard in the alley. "If you want to punch, then go down there." He flicked his pointy chin toward the crowd.

Fighting wasn't my scene, but if fifteen thousand dollars was up for grabs, I would sure give it a go.

He angled his head, a gold studded earring glinting off the brightness of the stadium-like lights. "Are you mute?"

I narrowed my eyes. "Thanks for the offer, but I have to go." This was a bad idea. The dude gave me the creeps.

He blocked my passage, his hands now at his sides. "Seriously, come with me. I'll even give you something to drink while you watch. Then you can leave." He sized me up as though he was interviewing me before throwing me to the wolves, as he had so eloquently put it.

I tried to skirt around him again. "My mom is expecting me home." A young woman in a room full of men wasn't a good idea, particularly excited men.

"Where's home?"

I glanced up, meeting his dark wide-set eyes. "Like I would tell you."

He dragged two fingers down his day-old stubble. "You have a name?"

"People usually do." I rolled my eyes. "Now, get out of my way."

He chuckled. "Tough girl."

I wasn't always a tough, sarcastic girl. Actually, I'd been shy in high school. But the streets had molded me into a person I didn't like, a person I would have never imagined I'd become.

He scanned my body again.

"Look, mister. I sense you're up to something, but give me a once-over again, I'll kick you in the balls."

He bowed his head and slid to one side. "You look hungry. Would you like some food?" His gravelly voice turned sweet.

My stomach growled for the fiftieth time that day. "What's the catch?"

He gave a slight shake of his head. "None."

There was always a catch, but Norma needed some soup or sustenance, and I did too. Another wave of hoots and hollers singed the air. My gaze tracked down to the active crowd, but I still couldn't see what all the excitement was about.

The wiry man followed my line of sight. "You're welcome to go down and check out the festivities."

"Do you have any soup?" I asked.

"If that's what you want."

"Actually, I'd like two plates of food and a bowl of soup to go. But I have no money." If he asked for sex as payment, I was hightailing out of there as fast as I could. I would find food in some dumpster on my way back to Norma.

He waved a crusty hand down the stairs. "I offered you food, so don't worry about the money. Head down and enjoy the show. I'll be right back."

I sized him up like he'd done to me. He wasn't a bad-looking man. I would guess him to be in his late twenties. He was dressed casually in jeans, and he had defined arms but wasn't at all broad in the shoulders. He sort of reminded me of a basketball player.

"One wrong move, and I'll kill you." I wasn't joking. I carried a small pocketknife for many reasons, including protection. I'd never used the knife though.

He grinned. "My name is Tommy, and I'm not a pervert."

I snorted. He sounded as if he was in one of those AA meetings. Regardless, I would bet he wasn't an upstanding guy. "Ruby." Once my real name was out there, I berated myself. I should've used an alias. Then again, it was only my first name.

"Well, Ruby, enjoy yourself. I'll be right back." He left through the same door I'd walked through.

I traipsed down to the melee, my curiosity pushing me forward. I plowed through fat men, skinny men, short men, and tall men, inhaling cigar smoke, cigarette smoke, body odor, and other disgusting scents.

They parted, some reluctantly, others easily. When I had a clear view of the object of their focus, my mouth dropped open. A beefy woman was beating the lights out of a girl half her size.

"Why isn't she fighting?" I asked a cigarette-smoking man on my right.

He blew out smoke. "She's afraid. It's her first time."

I waved at the brawl. "I don't get it. Why is she even fighting if she's afraid?"

The meek girl had blue streaks through her blond hair. She cowered in a corner of the makeshift boxing ring that had been formed using four metal poles and yellow police tape.

"The money," he said. "The winner gets three hundred dollars."

That's all? The two men I'd overheard had mentioned fifteen thousand, which meant that these two women were getting screwed, although three hundred was quite a bit of cash for someone in my predicament. "The fight is fixed, isn't it?" It had to be. Who would win between Hefty Girl against Meek Girl was a no-brainer in my book.

"Sometimes," Smoker Dude said, "it's not a slam dunk. Some shy girls have so much adrenaline and anger, they can beat the shit out of the larger opponents."

I suspected I could beat the lights out of someone if my life depended on it. "But someone should end this one."

Beefy Girl wore a crew cut, stood at least a head taller than Meek Girl, and had guns on her arms that mirrored Sugar Ray Leonard. She threw a punch that landed against Meek Girl's temple. I wasn't into boxing, but my dad loved to watch the sport.

"You get where you are? This is underground fighting. Only rule here is one girl has to be knocked out for the other to win."

I had the urge to jump in the middle and save Meek Girl. I wasn't by any means built like Beefy Girl. I was five foot four and on the skinny side since food was scarce these days. But between all the walking and dumpster-diving, I considered myself strong.

Beefy Girl threw a punch, connecting with Meek Girl's nose. Blood sprayed out, making me cringe.

"Do it again, Vickie," someone shouted.

Again, Vickie drove a fist into Meek Girl, this time connecting with her jaw.

I couldn't take it anymore. I barreled through the bodies to the other side of the ring. "Fight, damn it." I shouted as loud as I could at Meek Girl. "Kick her ass."

Vickie bared her teeth like a rabid dog. "Get out of here."

"Fuck off."

She dove at me. I jumped back as she tripped over Meek Girl's foot. Vickie splattered, face first onto the dirt floor. Meek Girl glanced at me, her blue eyes wide. The sound in the room died. The crowd seemed to hold their breath collectively. Some appeared mad, while others had curious looks on their faces.

Tommy ran over, grabbed my arm hard, and pulled me through the crowd. "What do you think you're doing?" His breath smelled of alcohol.

I jerked away from him when we reached the stairs. "The small girl wasn't fighting."

"So the fuck what? If she doesn't want to, then that's her choice." He pointed to a bag on the stairs. "There's your food. Now get out of here."

I crossed my arms over my chest. "You wanted me to watch. Now you're kicking me out?" I should have probably left while he was giving me a chance, but I didn't want Meek Girl to get hurt. I also wasn't afraid of Vickie, although I should have been. I didn't know how to fight. I'd watched plenty of matches with my dad, and I had even watched Kross spar when he was in the gym at the academy, but I never ventured into the ring.

Tommy ran a hand through his wavy brown hair. "You want to fight?"

I jutted my chin out. "I want in."

A wry grin broke out across his face. "You think you can win against Vickie?"

"Yeah." Not really. But I wanted the opportunity to make money. In my mind, fighting was better than selling my body. My dancing skills could prove beneficial with my flexibility. Sure, it was illegal, and getting my butt kicked regularly would definitely not look good on my resume, but Norma had a point. We had to make enough money to be able to eat and find a place to live. Then during the day, we could continue to look for respectable jobs.

He roared with laughter over the cheers and jeers. "Be here next Saturday, same time." He lifted the bag and handed it to me.

For the first time in ages, hope coursed through my veins. I ran up the stairs.

"Oh, and Ruby," Tommy called.

Stopping midway, I tossed a look over my shoulder.

"I hope you know how to fight."

I rolled my eyes. I wasn't sure why because I had no business being cocky. "You care?"

"I'd hate to see your pretty face get messed up."

I hadn't been called pretty since I'd dated Kross. "You must have blinders on. But thanks, Tommy. I'll see you soon." I left, holding onto the bag tightly. I had a week to build up my nerve. I couldn't believe I had signed up to get my face smashed in. But if I won, then all my efforts would be worth it.

CHAPTER 3
KROSS

The gym was filled with people working out on weights, treadmills, elliptical machines, and throwing their fists into punching bags.

"Kross, damn it," Jay bit out in his cigar-smoking voice. "What the fuck is wrong with you? You haven't been the same since you went up to the academy to scout Liam. You need to win your next bout to impress Gail."

For the last week, Gail and winning were the furthest things from my mind. Hell, my boxing career didn't stand a chance unless I could snap out of the fucking haze clouding my brain. I jabbed Liam. Jay had invited him down for a couple of days after I'd given the kid my thumbs-up.

"Weak. Where's your footwork, Maxwell?" Jay sounded as frustrated as I felt. "The kid is showing your ass up."

I stalked out of the ring, glaring at Jay's hooknose and baldhead. He pinned his gaze on me, and I growled in return. I had enough anger in me to kill Liam, and I didn't want to hurt him, although the kid had been tough in sparring with me. He took my punches and returned a few good ones of his own.

Jay marched up to me. "I don't want to know what's going on in your head." He tapped an arthritic forefinger against my temple. "Take time off and get your shit together."

"I'm fine. Besides, you said Gail would still give us a look as long as I kept my losses to less than three." I wasn't sure my head would be screwed on in time for my next fight, and I didn't know when the next fight was. Jay was still working on the details. Still, my head wouldn't be in the ring until I knew one way or the other whether I had a kid on this fucking planet.

"In the three years I've been coaching you, you choose now, when we're so close to signing with her, to mouth off to me?" He scratched his shaven jaw. "I'll let this slide. She called today. She has another prospect that seems to have a better record than you. She didn't like how you went down at your last fight."

I'd only lost one bout. I didn't know anyone in my circuit with a better record than me. "Who's the boxer?"

He huffed as his nostrils flared. "Reggie Stockman."

I stilled. "Fuck." Reggie and I had history. He'd been one of Sullivan's cronies who'd helped put Kody in the hospital back in the ninth grade.

"Exactly. The man hasn't lost a match since you knocked him out cold during your very first fight three years ago, which didn't count since neither of you were in the game yet."

That night was the best ever. I had gotten to legally punch his lights out without going to jail. Then he'd disappeared. Since then, I hadn't seen him. We'd been fighting in different circuits. "I can take Reggie."

Jay rapped his knuckles on my head. "Don't get cocky. Instead, get your head screwed on, because she's setting up a bout between you two." He pivoted on his heel and stomped back to his office.

Climbing out of the ring, Liam spit out his mouth guard and removed his gloves. "Reggie has four knockouts in his last four fights."

I snarled as I began to remove my gloves. "Your point?"

"There are only two boxers I follow religiously." He took off his headgear, revealing sweat-soaked brown hair. "You and Reggie. The difference between you two is huge. Reggie goes in for the kill, hard and fast. You dance and tire your opponent out. That's why someone like Reggie can't touch you. But I feel you need a wakeup call."

I contemplated bashing in the kid's face. Instead, I gave him my full attention. I wanted to hear what else Liam had to say, and he didn't deserve to get his head squashed.

He continued, sounding as if he was my coach. "Your last fight. You were a deer in the headlights. Walk into the ring like that again, and Reggie is going to tear you apart."

The kid had balls, but he spoke the truth. I had to figure out how to find Ruby or forget about her, and I couldn't do the latter. *Idiot, ask Liam. The boy goes to Greenridge.* Liam was a senior, which meant that he could've known Ruby when he was a freshman.

I'd called Tasha's brother, but he didn't know how to locate Ruby. That had only made me angrier, sadder, and more frustrated because I didn't know where to even begin to find her.

I finally got my gloves off. "Have you attended Greenridge since the ninth grade?"

He stuffed his gear into a sport bag. "Yeah, why?"

"Did you know a girl by the name of Ruby Lewis? She would've been a junior when you were a freshman."

"No, sorry. I don't." Then again, freshmen probably didn't know many upperclassmen.

"You're a good boxer. Maybe you can help out more leading up to my fight." I liked the kid. He had balls, and if he'd studied Reggie's moves, I could use him on my team.

"Seriously, dude?" His eyes flashed with excitement as he zipped up his bag. "I'd be honored."

"Clear it with Jay. I've got to run." Since it was Thursday, it was brothers' night. Kody, Kelton, Kade, and I hung out once a week, watching sports, drinking, or both.

Heading for the showers, I called Kody. "Hey, are you still coming over tonight?" I'd asked him to keep a lid on my secret until I told Kade and Kelton.

"Only if you're ready to break the news to our brothers."

"I am." I hated to keep anything from them, and if I didn't get the shit off my chest, I was going to explode. Plus, I needed to win my next fight. I'd worked my tail off to become a boxer. I couldn't throw it all away when I was so close to signing with Gail Freeman.

"Good, because it's killing me. You know they won't judge."

It wasn't about them judging me. Kelton had been supportive when I told him Ruby had thought she was pregnant. But I wasn't sure how Kade would react, although I could hear him now. "Where was your protection?"

I shrugged off Kade for the moment then quickly showered and dressed as I thought of Ruby.

Every night, I lay awake, wondering if she'd given birth to a boy or a girl. *And what color hair did the kid have? Black like me or red like her? What did she name the child? How in the fuck was I going to tell my parents? Or Kade?*

I was slipping my wallet into the back pocket of my jeans when the door creaked open.

"He was in here earlier," a guy said.

"Maxwell," someone called out. "You in here? It's Dillon, man." He came into view around a bank of lockers. "You look like shit. What happened?"

"And you look like a girl with your hair in a ponytail," I chided, shutting my locker.

Dillon Hart, badass dude, loved by women, had a heart of gold, particularly when it came to young girls who ran away from home or pimped themselves on the streets. He tried to save them all while searching for his baby sister who'd run away two years prior at the age of sixteen. I had to hand it to him. The man was planning to open a home for runaway girls. All that aside, Dillon and I had become close friends. Maybe his street connections could help me find Ruby.

"Women get their panties wet over my hair. I see you're growing yours out. Copycat."

I pushed my fingers through my thick wet strands. It had been four years since the last time I'd let my hair grow past my ears. I usually kept it high and tight, but Dillon was wearing off on me. I wasn't planning on ponytails, but Lizzie had counseled me that girls liked to play with hair. She even went as far as telling me that she loved running her fingers through Kelton's hair. I had noticed I was getting more looks with my longer style, and even Penelope had commented on how she liked playing with my hair.

"Bite me. What's up?"

He leaned a shoulder against the locker, shoving a hand into the pocket of his jeans. "I needed to beat something, and I thought of you. But I see you're heading out."

"Problems? Can't get a girl in your bed?" I teased.

"I see you're in rare form. Who pissed in your territory?"

An auburn-haired girl. My kid who I didn't know.

He grinned. "Not getting laid enough?"

"On the contrary." I didn't have any problems in the bedroom. "Trying to find a girl who seems to have disappeared."

He popped off the locker. "Tell me more." The light snuffed out in his brown eyes at the word "disappeared."

I couldn't tell him until I told my brothers. Blood always came before friends. "Look, I need some help. Why don't you hang with my brothers and me tonight? I'll fill you in then."

He nodded. "I'll pick up some beer."

I harrumphed. "Whiskey would be better."

"That bad?"

"I guess that depends on how you look at it." I couldn't get past how furious I was with Ruby that she had lied to me. At sixteen, I wasn't ready for a child, and neither was she. She didn't have to shoulder the burden all by herself, though. I would've taken responsibility. I might have been a dick for not wanting to talk to her, but for fuck's sake, I'd had a right to know. *Yeah, you would've known if you had called her back or picked up the phone, dickwad.*

I growled.

Dillon slapped me on the back. "I'm here for you."

I prayed Kade had the same attitude.

Two hours later, Kade, Kelton, Kody, Dillon, and I were watching the Patriots play Buffalo.

"You guys lucked out on this apartment," Dillon said with a mouth full of pizza.

The brownstone was a monstrosity, with three bedrooms, two bathrooms, a living room, a modest kitchen, and a dining room. I was surprised that Kelton and Lizzie had found the place. It was located close to Boston University for Lizzie and Kelton. It was close to Rumors for Kade, and it was a perfect spot for me since I could walk to the gym from there.

Kody tapped me on the arm. "Well?"

I reached for the bottle of whiskey that was on the glass coffee table. The Pats scored, and Kelton and Kade high-fived. I poured five shots as Kade and Kelton jabbered about the Pats quarterback. Then Kody muted the TV.

"You better have a good reason," Kade said with a growl.

A sharp pain gripped my stomach. I didn't need Kade in a bad mood. Not if I was about to tell him I could be a father. I could hear his voice in my head. "What did Dad teach us? Are you a moron?"

I knocked back a shot. The amber liquid burned on the way down as vomit threatened to shoot up.

Kade scowled. "Since when do you drink whiskey?"

I lifted a shoulder as I grabbed another shot. The longer I looked at Kade, the more my courage vanished and the more nausea settled heavily in my stomach. As I shifted my gaze to Kelton, I was reminded of the day he'd found out that he could've been a father. Fear had turned my brother whiter than snow. I probably had the same fucking color on my face.

Kody nudged me. "Slow down."

Dillon joined in, drinking his shot.

Kade raised an eyebrow. "What's going on? You're pale."

Kelton helped himself to a shot as he watched me.

My heart beat like a wild boxer who was throwing his fists into my face repeatedly and in quick successions. "I have something to tell you." I blew out a breath. "When Kody and I were up at the academy, I decided to drive by a friend's house." I never talked about Ruby to Kade, only because our mom had been the focal point of our family at the time. Then when I left the academy, I'd put that part of my life behind me. "Anyway, I dated this girl Ruby at the academy." I snatched the last shot of whiskey.

"If it's what you told me," Kelton said, "Kade won't kill you. Nothing came of it."

I tipped my head to the side and frowned.

"You said she wasn't." Kelton's eyes went wide. "Dude, talk."

Kade sat quietly, his gaze never wavering from mine.

My pulse pounded in my ears. "Ruby thought she was pregnant, but it turned out she wasn't. At least that's what she told me."

Kade's copper eyes formed into slits.

The room began to spin. I released a breath, then another, willing the bile to go down. My head began to hurt. Sweat coated my entire body as though I'd just finished a workout.

"Kross? Kross?" Kody's voice was faint, as though he were a million miles away instead of sitting next to me.

"Dude?" Dillon's voice was a little louder.

I jumped up and over Kody. Kade got up too. Then I began pacing even though my legs were trembling. As I swayed to one side, Kade caught me.

"Just tell them." The words rushed out of Kody's mouth.

Kade crossed his arms over his chest as I walked over to the window, away from everyone. The emotional turmoil wreaking havoc inside me was on the precipice of exploding, and I didn't want my brothers near if I lashed out. "I'm a daddy."

"What the fuck!" Kade's voice went up.

I glanced from the busy street below back to the room. Kade's eyebrows were raised. Dillon and Kelton had their mouths hanging open. Kody picked at a label on his beer bottle.

"After Kody and I left the academy last week, I wanted to see if I could get in touch with Ruby. So I went to her house. We didn't find her or her family, but we did speak with Ruby's neighbor, Tasha. During the start of Ruby's junior year, Ruby and her mom left town. When they did, Ruby was pregnant, and I'm the father."

"Do you believe this neighbor?" Kade asked.

I bowed my head. "According to Tasha, there was no mistaking that Ruby was pregnant four years ago. So that much is true. As far as me being the father, I contacted Tasha's brother. He confirmed that Ruby told him a Kross Maxwell was the father. Part of me believes him. She wasn't the type to sleep around. I'm such an idiot. She'd been calling me and leaving messages shortly after we moved home from the academy. I didn't return her calls. I was... I don't know what I was." I glanced at Kade. A muscle jumped in his jaw. "I fucked up. I didn't use a condom. I didn't follow what Dad taught us about safe sex." My stomach heaved, and I swallowed the bile.

Kade's eyebrows hovered at his hairline. "You never kept in contact with her?"

Cars six stories down crowded the busy Boston streets.

My gut twisted in several directions. "No. Look, Ruby was beautiful, fun, and she helped me through the dark days at the academy. But when we moved home, I wanted to put my life at the academy behind us. I wasn't ready for love. If you want to beat my head in, go right ahead. I deserve every ounce of punishment you want to give." Or at least one round of punishment. The second round would be more painful when I told my parents.

Kade sauntered up to me. "Brother, I'm not going to beat your head in. However, I can't say I'm not shocked. Regardless, we need to find this girl and find the truth. If she gave birth to a Maxwell, then she and the kid belong with us."

My head spun as I made my way back to the couch. I had to sit down before I collapsed.

Kade caught my arm. "We'll find her."

I laughed out of sheer panic. "What happens when we find her?" I would go to the ends of the earth to find this woman and my child. "I don't know the first thing about being a dad. Besides, it's clear in my mind that Ruby doesn't want anything to do with me. Otherwise, she would've contacted me again."

Kade drew me in for a hug. "Regardless, we're here to help you no matter what."

I hugged him back with all the strength I had. I almost bawled like a damn baby. "What about Mom and Dad? I can't imagine telling them."

Kade let go of me. "We will do it together, but not before we find Ruby. There's no sense in getting them all worked up if you're not the father." He pinned a look on Kody and Kelton. Both nodded.

Dillon sat, observing and pensive. I imagined he was thinking of his own family. He fought every day to keep his spirits up while continually searching for his sister. He had brothers, but he didn't talk much about them. "So, I take it I'm here because you want me to help find her," Dillon said.

Kade stalked over to the coffee table and took a swig of whiskey straight from the bottle.

"You do have a ton of connections," I said to Dillon as I walked on shaky legs back to my seat. "I've been thinking." My brain hurt from all the images, scenarios, and ways to find Ruby. "We might be able to start with her old man. Tasha told us he was busted for drugs. I'm not sure if he's still in jail, but maybe we can find out. If he is, then I can pay him a visit. He might know where she is."

"If the dude's in jail, then there's a public record of what went down." Kelton finally relaxed into the couch. "Well, maybe. If the feds were involved, then they could've sealed the records, depending on the drug bust. I'll look into that when I go into the office tomorrow."

I hadn't thought of that. Regardless, I was grateful that Kelton was working at a law firm while he studied to get his law degree.

"I just thought of something. I'll talk with Detective Rayburn." He and I had met when Kelton, Lizzie, Dillon, and I were at an illegal gambling game, and the cops had hauled us off to jail. Mark Rayburn was a fan of mine too. "He probably has easier access to get information on inmates than what you would find," I said to Kelton. "He also might be able to search his database for an address on Ruby." As soon as my excitement stirred, it was quickly squashed. Detective Rayburn was out of town at the moment. I'd spoken to him before my trip to the Berkshires, and he'd mentioned that he wouldn't be around for a couple of weeks. He had some assignment in New York.

"What's wrong?" Kade asked.

"It might be a while before I can get a hold of Mark. He's working on a case in New York." But I could at least call him.

"Dillon," Kelton said. "Lizzie told me one of your guys hacked into the BU computer system to find out more about her. Maybe he can hack into the government's computers. That might be faster than waiting on Mark or me to sift through records."

Dillon straightened. "The BU computers are one thing, but the government?" He shook his head. "That's asking for more trouble."

"Dude," I pleaded. "I'm desperate. Put yourself in my shoes. What if you knew you had a kid in this world? What would you do?" Dillon had a ton of connections outside of his guy who hacked into computers. Kelton was right. He might encounter red tape, and I might not get through to Mark.

Dillon grabbed the whiskey bottle. "I can't have my guys snooping. But I know someone who might be able to help. I'll pick you up on Saturday night," he said to me.

The room fell into an eerie silence. Kade stared into space. Kody continued to pick at the label on his beer bottle. Kelton focused on the muted TV. Dillon drank from the whiskey bottle. As for me, my brain spun with visions of a little boy running around who looked like me. My heart skipped a beat, then another. I had a feeling my heart wouldn't settle until I found Ruby.

CHAPTER 4

RUBY

Norma and I stood in a room in the basement of Firefly, waiting for Tommy. The strong odor of urine burned the hair in my nostrils. During the past week, Norma had recovered after I'd given her the NyQuil I'd stolen. It had taken her a couple of days, but thankfully, she'd gotten better.

"This is the craziest thing I've ever heard of." She watched me pace, pick at my nails, and twist strands of my long hair around my fingers. "I still can't believe that a few minutes from now, you're about to fight. When have you ever fought?" Her voice cracked.

"Never. But if I win, we'll have money to buy food." I hadn't even gotten into a spat or fight with any girls in school. Aside from my close friends, I'd always kept to myself, not sticking my nose where it didn't belong. Unlike the popular girls who'd wanted all the attention, the only attention I'd craved was from Kross or the audience at one of my ballet performances.

She grabbed my wrist. "Stop bouncing around. You're making me more nervous. You don't have to do this. We'll keep looking for jobs."

I stomped my foot like a two-year-old. Every fast food place I'd followed up with had given me the thumbs-down in the last week. "No one is hiring, or no one wants to hire me. I've got to get Raven back." I cried most nights at the thought of her with another family. I also cursed my mom for hooking up with one of my father's associates, who'd convinced her to step into my father's drug-dealing shoes. My mom had no skills other than being a stay-at-home mom. She'd tried to get a job as an office assistant, a fast-food worker, even a clerk at one of the big chain stores. I had given the job hunt a go too before I delivered Raven. But no one would consider a pregnant girl. So when my dad's associate approached her, my mom caved. I tried to convince her not to take the offer, but I couldn't blame her too much. We'd been desperate.

"Ruby, you could get hurt. I can't stomach that. All the money in the world isn't worth you risking yourself."

"I'm doing this for us, and for Raven. I'll never get her back if I can't show I'm responsible."

"Do you think fighting in a dump like this is responsible? This idea is as bad as the one I had to work for my pimp."

"We need to eat. I just don't know what else to do. I can't sit around the streets, begging for money. Like you said, we can put money away." Some days, I collected five dollars, but other days, I received nothing. I blinked away a tear. "I'll be fine," I lied. If I was going up against a girl twice my size, I didn't stand a chance. Then again, the way the adrenaline was coursing through my body, I might be able to wield a good punch or two, maybe even to the point where I could knock out my opponent. I blew out a breath. I could do this. I was a ballet dancer after all. Then I broke out in hysterics.

Norma cocked her head. "What's so funny?"

Ballet and fighting were vastly different. I didn't know a darn thing about bobbing or weaving, but Kross had always told me that ballet and boxing were very similar. "You dance to music. I dance around boxers. Both are about footwork," he'd said. *Argh! Kross Maxwell.* Since Raven was born, I couldn't help but be reminded of Kross. Every time she smiled, it was like Kross was smiling back at me.

My laughter turned into tears. I dropped down onto the dirt floor and hugged my knees to my chest.

Norma joined me, draping her arm around me. "Hey, you don't have to do this."

"It's not the fight. Well, it is sort of. Raven's daddy boxed. All week, I've been thinking of him, and how I used to watch him dance around boxers in the gym at school."

"Aw, honey. Why don't you try and find him? You know he might be the key to getting Raven back."

I shook my head vigorously. "Absolutely not. He can't ever know about her."

"He's her father," Norma said softly.

"I don't want him to see me like this. Besides, he didn't want to be bothered when I called him a thousand times. He left me like I was the scum of the earth. Besides, before I'm ready for her to meet her father, I need to have my life in order." I would die if Kross saw me now. My skin was pallid, as though I walked among the dead. I had dirty hair and nails, and I didn't feel pretty at all.

Tommy strutted in, looking as greasy as ever. "What's going on? You're not backing out, are you, Ruby?"

Norma and I jumped to our feet.

I wiped my eyes. "No." I tried to sound sure and strong. I couldn't keep feeling sorry for myself. I had to take control of my life, and if that meant physically fighting, then I would put everything I had into it.

"Good. Good," he said. "The crowd is off the hook tonight."

I could hear the voices in the distance.

"How much is the pot worth?" Norma asked.

Tommy swung his dark gaze between us.

Norma stuck her hands on her hips. "If you so much as—"

I took hold of her hand. "Tommy, I'm not doing this for three hundred dollars. I saw how that girl got her face bashed in last week. I also know you make fifteen thousand dollars on a fight."

He grinned, but it turned into a snarl. "Eavesdropping on me? Not cool."

"I want a thousand if I win." I would've said more, but I had to be realistic with a thug like Tommy.

He pursed his lips. "I like your feistiness. But I can't agree to that."

"Then I'm out of here." I wasn't sure what I was doing, but I recalled the conversation between Tommy and some man when I was hiding in the dumpster last week. The man had said, "Just make sure she shows. I'll be taking your nuts if she doesn't." I wasn't the *she* the man had referenced, but I had an inkling that if I walked out, Tommy would be without a fighter, which meant he would lose money.

Norma beamed from ear to ear as we headed for the door.

"Wait," Tommy said. "Eight hundred."

"Higher," Norma whispered in my ear.

"Nine hundred fifty," I countered, tossing a look over my shoulder.

Tommy's tone dropped. "You're not in any position to barter."

"You're not in any position for me to walk out." I wasn't sure if that were true.

He narrowed his dark eyes. "Nine hundred."

I exchanged a questioning look with Norma, and she nodded.

"Deal," I said.

"You got five minutes before show time." He stormed out.

"He must think you have a shot at winning." Norma darted her tongue over her lip ring. "Otherwise, I'm not sure he would've agreed to that much money."

"He agreed to my demand because his ass would be toast if I bailed. Besides, I have no shot. I'm fighting some big girl named Vickie."

"Do you know for sure?" Norma's hair was styled into a short bob, but she always tucked it behind her ears when she got nervous, just like she was doing now.

I'd assumed I was. Tommy had asked if I could take Vickie. "It doesn't matter, anyway. If I win, we'll get nine hundred dollars." Thinking about that amount of money sparked my adrenaline to new heights.

Norma helped me out of my coat. When the cold air hit me, goose bumps popped up along my bare arms. Then she smoothed a hand over my ragged T-shirt.

I shivered again. "I'm fighting. I'm not walking down a runway."

"So sue me. I'm nervous. Where's your hair tie?" She searched my jacket pockets and found a hair band. "Put your hair up. You don't want the girl to be pulling on it."

I twisted my oily hair up onto my head.

"Make sure you block your pretty face, and use anything you remember from watching Raven's daddy box."

"Did you have to bring him up?" In the time we had known each other, I hardly talked about Kross. Norma had caught me looking at his picture one night. So I told her he was Raven's daddy. But that was it. When she'd probed further, I shut her down by changing the subject. Regardless, maybe she was right. Maybe I could use a move or two that Kross had once done in the ring.

She pinched my cheeks. "Get loose."

I snorted. "Who are you? My coach?"

"I never told you this, but I was a long-distance runner in high school. Before every run, my coach would say, 'get loose.' I'm sure you stretched before you danced."

Of course, warm-ups were a routine before every ballet performance. But I was more skilled at ballet than boxing, and no amount of stretching would ease the tension in my body. Instead, I bounced on my feet, a move I had seen when I watched a boxing match with my dad. I'd even seen the move from Kross while he was waiting for the coach to start the fight.

The door opened. "It's time," Tommy said.

Norma rubbed her hands up and down my arms. "Kick some butt out there."

Before I got myself worked up or backed out of the deal, I marched out of the room and into a hallway. Norma hurried to my side and grabbed my shaky hand. She squeezed lightly. Tommy strutted on the other side of me. Within twenty feet, we stopped at a metal door.

"So, am I fighting that Vickie girl?" I asked.

"Nope," he said, ushering us in.

I didn't know whether to be relieved or even more frightened.

People were packed into the room like sardines. I waved off the thick cigar and cigarette smoke that floated in the air. Once I got my bearings, I zeroed in on the girl just inside the door. She was the same one Vickie had had a field day with. Her face was black and blue, but I didn't get the vibe that she was scared. If anything, she looked angry.

Tommy introduced us before heading into the ring. "Ruby, meet your opponent, Mel."

I didn't know if we were supposed to shake, but I extended my hand anyway. She glanced at it then turned her head as if I was beneath her.

Whatever. The less I knew of her, the easier it might be to smack her around the ring, especially if she cowered in a corner like she'd done against Vickie. The tightness in my stomach lessened. It might be an easy nine hundred dollars. It wasn't enough to get an apartment, but we could get a cheap hotel room for the night. Then Norma and I could shower, eat, and sleep in a bed for once.

Tommy held up his hands then pushed them down. "Quiet."

Within a second, the boisterous voices died.

"Hopefully, you've placed your bets. We have a newbie here tonight. I know how you like newbies. I think she'll give Mel a run for her money."

"If Mel doesn't fight tonight, this should be an easy win," someone said. "My bet is on the newbie."

"Asshole," Mel murmured next to me.

Suddenly, my pulse went haywire. Mel, the scared girl with blue streaks through her blond hair and bruises dotting her delicate face, was not so innocent. Then I remembered something. A man I'd been standing next to while watching Mel and Vickie had said, "Some shy girls have so much adrenaline and anger, they can beat the shit out of the larger opponents." I wasn't larger than Mel by any means. If anything, we were both the same height, and we both had small frames. But she had one advantage over me—anger. I wasn't nearly as enraged as she was at the moment. Besides, I was banking on keeping my cool. Maybe then I could fight strategically.

Norma's cold hand touched my arm. "You can do this."

I rolled my shoulders back. If I backed out, Tommy wouldn't be pleased. In fact, he might skin me alive if he had money on the line. Still, all the money in the world wouldn't stop my stomach from churning like a whirlpool.

"Go." Norma nudged me. "He's calling your name."

I zeroed in on the here and now to find that Mel was already in the ring beside Tommy, who had an evil look on his face. I shuffled through a group of old men. One patted me on the back. Another slapped me on the butt. I almost hauled off and kicked him but decided to reserve my energy for Mel.

"No rules," Tommy said once I was in the ring. "You fight until one of you gets knocked out. Shake."

We bumped fists as if we were seasoned fighters.

"I love this shit," Tommy mumbled as he walked away.

As soon as he left the ring, Mel came at me. Her fists were wild as though she was possessed. I shuffled, sidestepped, then ducked.

Whistles then shouts sang around the room. "Hit her already," yelled one man.

I danced around her. My footwork was sloppy. It had been a long time since I had even tried to practice any of my ballet moves. I nearly laughed. I was in an illegal underground fight with no clue about what I was supposed to do.

Mel was still swinging. I was still stumbling.

"Fight," Tommy said.

I threw a punch at air.

Mel laughed. "Pathetic."

I was trying to wrap my head around how much she'd changed since the previous week. *Screw that. Worry about your ass. Fight.*

She jabbed, her knuckles connecting with my cheekbone. Stars floated in front of my vision as I returned a punch to her nose. Pain shot up my arm. It hurt more to punch someone than to be hit. I went at her again but missed. She reared back, snarling. Whoa! This couldn't have been the same meek girl from the week before.

"What?" she asked as we both glided around each other. "Shocked I'm not the same girl you tried to get to fight last week? Well, thanks to you, I got off my ass. I won that fight."

Great, I'd helped her. Now she was going to beat my pathetic butt. *Weave, bob and dance,* I repeated. *I always tire my opponent out,* Kross had said.

"Come on, Ruby," Tommy shouted from somewhere close by. "I got money on you."

You have nine hundred dollars on the line. Nine hundred, my inner voice blared.

"Sucks that the tables are turned," Mel said. "Not so brave now, are you?"

The decibel level was deafening. Not to mention, the pain gripping my face was disorienting. *Stay focused on Mel. Don't waver. The moment you do, she'll knock you out.*

Her fists came at me. I ducked then punched. She bobbed her head to the left. I swung out with my right fist as I rammed my left into her stomach.

She bent over for a second then glared at me, nostrils flaring.

"See, I'm a fast learner. Unlike you." I had no business getting cocky, but the adrenaline was overpowering and energizing.

Growling, she lunged forward. She extended her right hand, and her fist crashed into my eye.

Pain exploded. Okay, maybe it hurt more to be hit. I shook my head as I winced and wobbled.

The crowd began to chant. "Hit her again, Mel, before she recovers."

As I blinked, her fist came around and rammed square into my jaw. I stumbled backward. Before I could center myself, she kicked me in the gut. The air left my lungs. My vision blurred as I held my stomach.

"Come on, Ruby," Norma yelled. "Win this fight."

"Nine hundred dollars," I muttered as I shook off the dizziness.

"You can always walk away," Mel said in a snarky tone.

I punched out, hitting her just above her left eye, drawing blood. I swung repeatedly, connecting with her jaw, her head, and her face. She returned jab after jab to my nose and anywhere on my face she could get to. The pain ricocheted as though I'd touched a live wire of electricity. Blood trickled down my upper lip. My right eye was cloudy, or maybe it was swollen. I tried to open it as I continued to exchange blows with Mel.

I stepped back to catch my breath and regroup. I used the sleeve of my T-shirt to clear the blood from my face. Mel rolled her neck one way then the other.

The voices in the room droned.

Then she dove at me. Before I had a chance to move, she plunged her fist into my stomach in the same spot she'd landed a kick earlier. I dropped to my knees, blowing out air. Pain or no pain, I had to win the nine hundred dollars. So, I planted two hands on the floor and pushed upright. My adrenaline burned through me at the sight of her bloody grin. I sneered, swore, and went at her, wailing my fists like a madwoman, hitting at nothing but air.

"Damn it, Ruby," a familiar voice shouted. "Put her lights out already." His voice was whiskey smooth—a voice that brought back memories of rolling green lawns, cozy bonfires, and dancing under the stars.

I whipped my head in all directions, searching every face in the crowd. I settled my gaze on Norma, who was wide-eyed. As I did, Mel's fist caught my temple. The room began to darken, and the voices dimmed. I crumpled to the dirt floor. Then blackness.

CHAPTER 5
KROSS

My mouth was permanently opened as I watched a waif of a girl run to Ruby's side and tap on her face. I wasn't sure I could move. I hadn't seen Ruby since the tenth grade, and I wasn't sure the girl in this dingy, disgusting dive was even her. Her auburn hair was darker than I remembered. She looked as though she hadn't eaten in months or years. Her features were drawn and hollow, and her clothes were ratty as if she'd lived in them for weeks.

"Is that your Ruby?" Dillon asked.

My Ruby was supposed to be in some posh ballet school in New York. "Pretty sure." *What the fuck was she doing in an underground fight?*

Dillon's friend Tommy spoke to the crowd. "Make sure you collect your winnings." Then he doted on Mel as she smiled, wiping her swollen face with her tank top.

The room began to clear. Some stragglers hung back, talking, cutting up, and laughing. I wasn't laughing. In fact, I'd been on edge for two days. It seemed everywhere I turned, I hit a wall. Mark Rayburn hadn't called me back. Kelton had struck out on all counts in trying to obtain information about a drug bust four years ago up in the Berkshires, and Dillon's contact, whom we'd spoken to only two hours ago, hadn't been any help. So we'd ended up in this dive. Dillon had wanted to chat with Tommy about money that Tommy owed him. I'd wanted to start visiting prisons to find Ruby's old man. I was glad I'd stuck with Dillon. Never in a million years would I have thought Ruby would be fighting. Maybe it was fate. Whatever the fuck it was, I wasn't complaining. It was time to get answers.

The blond girl at Ruby's side was petting Ruby's hair, much like one would do with a cat or dog.

Dillon slapped me on the back, jarring me from my zombie state. "Let's check things out."

We brushed past two men dressed in tailored suits. Both reminded me of high-powered businessmen on Wall Street. The one with a bulbous nose said, "I'll check with her pimp."

Dillon came to an abrupt halt, fisting his hands at his sides. The word "pimp" was vile in his book. He believed a pimp had lured his baby sister into a world where she didn't belong.

I wrapped a hand around his tense bicep. "Let it go, man." We weren't there to get into brawls or start trouble. I couldn't afford trouble. I was under a magnifying glass by Coach Jay and the media.

There had been an article in the Boston Herald recently about me taking a dive in my last fight. The sports columnist had torn me apart in his recent write-up. "How does a fighter go from a practically perfect record to giving away the fight? Kross Maxwell wasn't in it to win. I would suspect he was paid to throw the fight."

I growled. I'd never take money to lose in boxing or any game. Since then, Coach had counseled me to walk the straight line, especially when he found out that I'd ended up at the police station back in March with Dillon, Kelton, and Lizzie. Coach had overheard a conversation between Mark and me when Mark was working out at the gym. I wished Coach had dismissed the incident, but with Gail Freeman's potential contract hanging in the balance, he'd ridden my ass every day for the last two months. He was making me train as though I would never be good enough to win a fight again.

Dillon trudged up to Tommy, who was standing outside the taped ring, messing with his phone. The room had cleared of people, including Mel. She'd darted out of the place like lightning.

The blond girl was on her knees, still tapping on Ruby's face. "Wake up." Then she peered up at Tommy. "Do something or I'll have your ass on a cutting board." She bared her teeth at the man.

"She'll wake up, Norma," he said. Then his eyes went wide as he noticed Dillon.

"Why does the guy shit his pants every time he sees you?" I

43

couldn't figure out the relationship. Sure, Tommy owed Dillon money, but I got the feeling the tension went deeper.

"Later," Dillon said to me. He shook hands with Tommy as though they were meeting for the first time.

Tommy acknowledged me with a flick of his head. I'd met him once before when Dillon had tried to collect his money, only to find that Tommy couldn't pay him. Dillon had seemed too patient about the matter in my book, but his business was none of mine.

"I got your money," Tommy said to Dillon.

I squatted down opposite Norma, who had tears in her eyes. I pressed my fingers against Ruby's neck as I examined her face. Blood painted the area around her nostrils. Her eyes were beginning to swell, one more than the other. A cut on her eyebrow was bloody but didn't appear to need stitches. Aside from that, she was definitely the girl who'd rocked my world back in the tenth grade—the very same one with a dark birthmark high on her left cheek, buried in the sea of freckles smattered around her nose. Fuck, it gutted me to see her in this condition.

Her pulse beat against my fingers. "I'm sure she'll be fine. But to be safe, she should go to the hospital. She might have a concussion."

Norma was fixated on me as though she was seeing a ghost.

I waved my hand in front of her face. "Hello?"

"She'll be fine?" Norma's voice cracked.

Tommy chuckled. "They don't hit each other hard enough to kill."

Dillon glared at him and so did I. Underground fights could be lethal. It didn't matter how soft or hard a person punched. The right blow in the right spot could kill a fighter, as could one fall.

He returned a dirty look to Dillon. "What? You've been here enough to know they don't."

"Where did you find her?" I asked Tommy. There was no sense debating the safety of underground fights.

Tommy raised his hands shoulder height. "She found me. I don't pick girls off the street, anyway. They always find their way down here."

Dillon pointed to Ruby. "Is her name Ruby Lewis?"

"No," Norma blurted out. "She just used the name Ruby for the fight."

Tommy knitted his eyebrows.

I knew she was lying, but I would play along. The last thing I wanted to do was scare Norma or Ruby when she woke up. "Look," I said to Norma, who reminded me of a cute little pixie. "I'm searching for someone who looks just like Ruby." I pushed to my feet. "Tommy, you got some ice and a first-aid kit?"

"I'll be back." He headed into a room on the far side of the basement.

"Bring my money when you come back." Dillon raised his voice then turned to me. "Well, man? Is that Ruby?"

I swung my attention to Norma. "We're not here to hurt anyone. I want to help. I know your friend is Ruby Lewis."

She puffed out her cheeks as she grabbed Ruby's hand. "Then why did you ask?"

Tommy came back with a first-aid kit and a bowl of ice. I made quick work of getting the necessary bandages and antibiotic cream out. I took a gauze pad and dipped it in the small amount of water in the ice bowl. I was about to clean the blood off Ruby's face when her eyelids flew open. She zeroed in on me, horror flashing in her blue-green eyes. She scrambled away as though I had just come back from the dead. Maybe I had. Maybe I was dead to her. Or maybe she was disoriented.

Norma ran to Ruby, who tried to stand but wobbled. Ruby said something in the blonde's ear.

"Man, I thought you Maxwell brothers got all the girls, not scared them away," Dillon said low.

"Not the time, dude," I said as I went over to Ruby. "I'm sorry I startled you. I wasn't planning on everything going like this. I just want to clean up your cuts." If I started with "where is my kid," she would take off for sure.

She jumped to her feet. "Let's go, Norma."

"He wants to help," she said softly. "At least let him fix you up."

Ruby grabbed Norma's hand and tugged her to the stairs. Norma gave me a sorry look as she went willingly. Ruby was acting as if I was the devil on fire and had come to take her to Hell.

A pain stabbed my gut. I probably deserved whatever she wanted to throw my way, but she wasn't leaving until I got answers. Sure, I couldn't keep her there against her will, and I wouldn't. But I had to find a way to make sure she didn't leave.

She wants nothing to do with you, my subconscious niggled. Even if she wouldn't talk to me, Dillon had a way with women. Maybe she would at least let someone who she wasn't frightened of or pissed at tend to her wounds.

"Dillon, can you help?" I asked in an uneven tone. I was trying to be calm, but questions were on the tip of my tongue, aching to get out, aching to get answers. I was also desperately trying to keep my body from convulsing like a fish out of water.

Ruby waited for Norma at the base of the stairs.

Norma ran back and snagged the first-aid kit from me. "I'm sorry." Then she scurried to catch up with Ruby.

Dillon ran up to them. "Ruby, please. Let us clean your cuts, or let us take you to the hospital. You might have a concussion."

Tommy observed us as though he was watching an intriguing movie.

"I'm fine," Ruby said, but her face twisted as she glared at me.

I wasn't one for panic attacks, but all the signs were washing over me—racing heart, chest pains, sweat coating my body, and the room was swirling like a F2 tornado. *If you let her walk out, you might never find her again. Don't lose your chance.*

I stalked closer to Ruby, careful not to crowd her space. Apologizing to her might help. After all, that was my plan when I'd gone up to the Berkshires. "I'm sorry for not returning your calls." I stood three feet from her, itching to get closer and touch her.

"It's too late for apologies," Ruby said as she began her ascent up the stairs.

Fuck. I took in a deep breath, closed my eyes, and shook my head. "Star." I swallowed then tried again. If she wouldn't listen to my apology, she might listen to this. "S-Star light. Star bright." My deep tone carried throughout the deserted basement. "You're the first star I see tonight." I pictured us on the lawn at Greenridge Academy on a dark night, in the wet grass, music playing from my phone, the two of us dancing under the stars, or me watching her dance. "I wish I may. I wish I might. You're the wish I wish tonight."

I opened my eyes and found Dillon with his eyes as wide as basketballs, his jaw touching the floor. Tommy's expression matched Dillon's.

Yeah, I was fucked up. But the nursery rhyme, or my variation of it, had always made her jump into my arms and plant kisses all over my face. Not that I was ready for her to do that. Hell, I didn't deserve her in my arms. But I hoped the sentiment still worked enough to at least keep her from leaving.

Norma hadn't moved from the bottom step, except she now had her hand over her mouth. Ruby stood beside her, tears streaming down her face.

I shuffled over to her. My fucking heart was beating out of my chest. I shoved my hands into my jeans pockets so she wouldn't see them shaking even though I was relieved she hadn't left.

She held up her trembling hand. "Please don't come any closer."

I honored her request. "Ruby, can we go somewhere and talk?" My subconscious was telling me to break the ice. Or better yet, maybe if we got to know one another again, she might open up to me. I quickly erased that thought. We needed time to get to know one another, and at the moment, my heart and soul didn't have time to wait.

She ran her gaze over me, her one eye swollen shut. "I can't." Pain laced her tone, but whether it was emotional or physical, I couldn't tell.

Norma nudged her in the arm.

"At least let us clean your cuts," I said.

Even with her drawn features and bruised face, Ruby was still pretty. Beneath the dirt and blood was skin of silk. I remembered how I would drag my fingertips over her nose, her cheeks, and down her neck, feeling her softness. I reached for her, dying to touch her, help her, and protect her.

She shuffled backward.

"I'm not going to hurt you." I had no idea what had prompted her to fight in this dive, but I wanted to help her, especially if fighting was her gig. I knew sanctioned places that were far better, with laws and rules governing fighters to keep them safe.

She coughed. Then she took off up the stairs, holding her stomach.

"Ruby, please. I just want to talk," I said loudly. "I know about the baby."

Norma gasped.

Ruby zeroed in on me from above. "You don't know shit." Then in a flash, she was gone.

I clenched my teeth. "Norma, tell me the truth."

Sadness swam in her brown eyes. "It's not my story to tell."

I growled, wanting so fucking desperately to get Norma to at least tell me something. "Please. I can help." I couldn't force Norma to tell me, and deep down, I wanted to hear whatever the story was from Ruby. "I train and work at Crandall's Gym on Newbury Street. Tell

Ruby I'm there most days. If not, ask for Jay. He'll know how to get a hold of me."

"I'll relay the message," Norma said. Then she bolted out the door.

I fisted my hands, looking for something to hit.

Dillon came up beside me. "She'll come to you."

"Yeah? How do you know that for sure?"

"Your declaration of love slammed her in the heart. Otherwise, she would've been long gone. You got to her. I promise you."

"He's right," Tommy said. "That star shit was something else. I think I even had tears in my eyes."

"Fuck you," I said. "It's not love." I didn't care how mushy or less manly I appeared. I would do anything to get answers. Sure, I might have gotten to her some. After all, tears had been flowing down her face. But she'd also gotten to me. I wanted to know her story. I wanted to help. Maybe it was out of guilt, or maybe it was because my heart beat a little faster at the sight of her.

"You keep telling yourself that," Dillon ribbed.

"I have a feeling she'll be back," Tommy said. "She's hungry for money."

"Do you know where she lives?" I asked.

"My guess?" Tommy rubbed a hand over his unshaven jaw. "Her and her friend sleep on the streets."

It was Dillon's turn to growl. I muttered a curse. Her physical appearance, and that of Norma's, screamed homeless or at least unhealthy. That made the hairs on the back of my neck stand at attention. If we had a child, then that meant my child was living on the streets. I shouldn't have let her leave.

"When is your next fight?" The word "fuck" was on repeat in my head.

"Two weeks," Tommy said. "But that fight doesn't include Ruby."

I took the stairs two at a time. Maybe I could still plead with her, grovel, anything to get her to talk. *Get a grip, man. Get a fucking grip.* Fuck no. I wasn't about to let our child live on the streets.

I tore through the dingy hallway, up another set of stairs, then out into the crisp, cold night. I scanned the narrow expanse of the dark alley. Nothing. I ran until I reached the street. Again, I came up empty.

"Motherfucker," I screamed at the top of my lungs.

"Kross," Dillon called before he jogged up to me.

I turned with my hands on my head. Tommy was at Dillon's side. I stalked up to Tommy and grabbed his collared shirt. "If she shows up here again, I want you to call me."

He pushed me. "Chill."

"I'm serious. I'll kick your ass from here to California if I find out she's hanging around here and you haven't called." Then again, she would probably stay as far away from this place as possible now that she'd seen me.

He snarled. "Both of you are fucked up."

Dillon stepped in between us as I was about to lunge. "I know you don't want me on your ass. But you also don't want Kross either. Now get me my money."

Tommy marched back down the alley without another word.

"We'll find her," Dillon said, turning back to me. "She couldn't have gone far. Let's check the area. If we come up empty, then I know some places the homeless hang out."

The word "homeless" sent a knife-like pain to my heart.

CHAPTER 6
RUBY

The streets of Boston were bustling with businessmen and women who hurried in all directions, probably late for a lunch meeting. They were vastly different from the types of people who roamed the streets at night. I sat cross-legged on a busy sidewalk corner in front of a coffee shop. My cup was at my side as it normally was during the day when I wasn't dumpster diving for food. A sharply dressed lady dropped a few coins into my till, and they dinged against the other coins.

"Thank you." I glanced up at the woman, who was already hoofing it down the street.

A siren wailed in the distance. More people hurried by me. I touched my eye, which was healing. Four days had passed since I had gotten my face pummeled by a timid girl who'd turned into a demon. It had also been four days since Kross Maxwell shocked me, angered me, and made me cry.

Argh! Those damn blue eyes of his had always caused me to say and do things without thinking. I had almost thrown myself at him. I couldn't breathe when I saw how good he looked—tall, toned, and muscular. He smelled wonderful too, like sugar and spice. When he recited his lyrics to *Star Light, Star Bright*, the tears blasted out before I could stop them. He'd said our nursery rhyme with such conviction that I almost believed he had feelings for me. But my tears quickly dried when he asked about the baby. All the anger I harbored for him rushed back quicker than a runaway train. I'd almost jumped off the stairs and cold-cocked him. Particularly, since he had been responsible for my nine-hundred-dollar loss.

I whipped out an old photo of Raven before she'd gone into foster care. Seeing her always helped to calm me. I smoothed my finger over her picture. Her black hair was pulled up in a ponytail, her blues eyes were framed by the longest lashes, and she had her hands on her hips, posing as if she was modeling a new outfit. A tear spilled down my cheek. I was a terrible mother. I shouldn't have been stealing with her at my side. Maybe Norma was right. Maybe I should talk to Kross and tell him everything, dump my problems on him so he could take care of Raven and me. Maybe he was my ticket to getting Raven back.

The jangle of change caused me to look up. A young girl, who looked to be about ten years old, smiled at me. Then she removed her yellow scarf and handed it to me. "This will keep you warm."

More tears streamed down my face. "You keep it, sweetie. It's cold out here."

Her mom ran up, bundled in her own winter gear. "Jenny?"

"She looks cold, Mommy."

The lady nodded at me with sad green eyes. "Please, take the scarf. She doesn't like seeing homeless people." Then she pulled out her wallet and gave me two ten-dollar bills. "This is for a warm meal."

Tears continued to spill as I took the money. The change in my cup added up to maybe three dollars, and Norma and I needed to eat. Since the night of the fight, we'd only found stale bread as our sustenance. "Thank you."

Jenny wrapped the scarf around me. Then her mom grabbed her hand. The little girl waved as they merged into pedestrian traffic.

I tightened the soft fabric around me. It smelled of baby powder, reminding me of Raven. More tears dropped. I stuffed away her photo before I became a blubbering frozen mess on the street.

Out of nowhere, Norma bounded up. She'd ducked into a diner a block away to apply for a waitressing position. She sat down then felt my scarf. "That was nice of the little girl to give this to you. So, any luck?" She peeked into the cup. "Mmm. Not much. Hey, why are you crying? Have you been staring at Raven's picture again? Or thinking about her hot daddy?" She buttoned her oversized men's coat that we'd found while raiding a donation bin.

I ignored her questions. "Did they let you fill out an application?"

"Yeah. But they don't have any openings." Norma wiped her nose with the back of her gloved hand. "Have you thought anymore about going to see Kross?"

"No." It would have been so easy to depend on Kross, and so wonderful to have him in my life again. The thought of being a family with him and Raven was fantastic. But I couldn't depend on him or anyone else. I had to show my daughter I could be a good mother. Most of all, I was in no physical condition to see Kross. No way. No how. Not ever.

"Ruby." Norma's tone dropped like it normally did when she didn't agree with me. "He can help you. You didn't see the despair written all over his face the other night. The man was begging me to tell him something."

I didn't need to see his face. Norma and I had heard Kross swear at the top of his lungs as we'd run from Firefly. While his pain tugged at my heartstrings, two things waged a war inside me. His apology was weak at best. I got the feeling he'd said he was sorry for not returning my calls because he wanted to know about the baby. Second, I couldn't figure out how he knew about Raven, and I was worried that he might try to get custody of her.

"Again, I'm not ready. Please tell me you won't go over to that gym you said he worked at and rat me out." Or maybe Norma was the one who had found Kross and told him about Raven and where I would be. As quickly as that thought entered my head, I let it go. We were like sisters, and we trusted one another.

"I'm not a tattler. But I can't promise you I won't go over to that gym and check things out." She giggled then waggled her eyebrows.

I snarled. "Don't you dare." Knowing Kross, he would give her his puppy dog eyes or his sad face like he used to do to me when he wanted to know what was bothering me.

"I was kidding. I promise."

I jumped up. "Let's go." My butt was frozen from sitting on the cold concrete. I had twenty dollars in my pocket. Any hot meal would thaw me out and get rid of my hunger pangs.

"We should hang for another hour. We only have a couple of dollars in the cup."

I pulled out the wadded-up ten-dollar bills.

She scowled. "You didn't pickpocket some dude, did you?"

I was good at stealing, but it wasn't something I was proud of, and I only stole when we were desperate. "That little girl's mom gave it to me."

She plastered on a hungry smile. "Where to?"

We started walking. "Tommy's place."

"Are you crazy?" she asked. "That place is a dive. Unless you have something else up your sleeve."

"Hear me out. No one is going to hire us. But Tommy owns Firefly. Maybe he'll give us a shot at a waitressing or let us work in the kitchen." I knew my way around a kitchen. My mom had taught me to cook when I was twelve. Actually, I loved to bake. But I would clean the bathrooms if it meant a steady job and money in my pocket.

"Fine." Norma eyed me. "As long as you don't fight."

"Yeah, well, I wouldn't mind another shot at Mel." Even with all the pain that came from fighting, I did get a high out of the adrenaline rush. Not that I would sign up today, but a part of me still hungered for the big money.

She punched me lightly on the arm. "I'll kill you myself if you fight again."

I dipped my chin inside my new scarf as we walked the five blocks toward Firefly.

"So, aren't you afraid that Kross will show up at Firefly?" Norma asked.

I shrugged. In the back of my mind, I always knew that one day Kross and I would run into each other. I just wanted that time to be on my terms when I was ready. "We need a job." I didn't know if Tommy would hire us, particularly since I had lost the fight and caused trouble the first night I met him. Still, I had to try. "If Kross does show up, then I'll deal."

"You said Kross had brothers. Triplets, huh?" Norma asked.

"Seriously? We're trying to survive, and you're thinking of men?" After I had bolted out of Firefly as if my life depended on it, Norma and I had found a secluded spot in an abandoned warehouse not far from Tommy's place. I had spent the night in her arms, crying and telling her all about Kross and his brothers. I couldn't blame her too much for asking about the triplets. After all, Kross times three would make any woman do crazy things to get their attention. I'd witnessed it firsthand at the academy when the girls would giggle and squeal every time the triplets were together in the halls. A couple of those same girls had snarled at me when they found out I was dating Kross, although most of them had doted on Kelton. He'd been the one brother who hadn't seemed to brood or sneer at someone if they looked at him the wrong way.

Fast forward four years, and wow. I couldn't shake the image of Kross. I hadn't had a date, sex, or someone to hold me since him. I wasn't sure I even knew how to kiss anymore.

Norma hooked her arm with mine as we crossed over streets and fought pedestrian traffic. "We're human, Ruby. I'm sure you have sexual urges. Sometimes, I miss being a lady of the night. I had some badass men who were great in bed."

With Raven and my pathetic life, sex was the last thing on my mind. But I had pleasured myself a time or two. "I'll kill you if you start selling yourself."

The large Firefly sign came into view, jutting out from the two-story brick building. As we approached, a patron walked out of the main entrance, bringing with him the smell of grease and a reminder of the fat, juicy hamburger Tommy had given me the night I'd met him. "Let's eat before we talk to Tommy."

The inside was somewhat dark, and a handful of people were scattered between the bar that stood directly in front of us and a table near the window. A stand-up sign said to seat yourself. Norma and I wound around the bar and headed to the back of the restaurant. We slid into a booth near what appeared to be a small stage carved into an alcove. Norma plucked a menu from behind the table's jukebox. I knew I wanted another hamburger.

A round-faced waitress came over. She scrutinized Norma and me as she pulled a pencil from the bun on her head. "What'll you have?"

"First, I want a hamburger with fries," I said. "Then I'd like to put in an employment application."

Her perfectly made-up face twisted, and a crease formed between her light-brown eyebrows. Then she relaxed and smiled. "We don't get much business in here, and the owner is a prick."

I raised an eyebrow. "I know." Norma and I busted out laughing.

"Ah." She snapped her gum. "You were in the fight last Saturday." She twirled her forefinger around my healing eye. "I hate watching ladies get their faces ruined."

"Is Tommy here?" I asked.

She glanced at the bald, bearded bartender then scooted in the booth and sat next to Norma. "Look, you don't want anything to do with Tommy." She kept her voice low. "And you shouldn't be fighting."

"I don't want to fight." I laced my fingers together on the table. "I told you I want to waitress."

She cocked her head. A strand of light-brown hair fell from her bun. "No offense, but you two are in no shape to apply for a job. You both look like you live on the streets. When was the last time you showered?" Pity rolled off of her.

Normally, I would have smarted off, but I couldn't argue when it came to our hygiene. Norma and I had to sneak into the YMCA on occasion to shower. Otherwise, bathroom gas stations were places where we could at least brush our teeth.

"Lady," Norma said, "we want to eat. If you don't want us to work here, just say so."

"My name is Alex. I'm trying to help you." Her tone was flat. "I had a sister who lived on the streets. Unfortunately, she didn't survive. So before you get all snotty with me—"

"We're sorry." I glared daggers at Norma. "Look, we realize our hygiene isn't spectacular, but we're trying to remedy that. You see, once we have some money, we'll be able to buy some decent clothes. I'm Ruby, by the way."

Everything about Alex seemed genuine—her smile, the fact that she was giving us the time of day, and the motherly look in her brown eyes. I would have guessed her to be in her late twenties, and something told me she didn't want to be in this place.

"We just need a break." I wanted to spill my guts about how dire my need was for a job and a roof over my head so I could get my daughter back. But I barely knew her.

"Alex," a deep voice from the bar said.

"Be right there," she called. Then she looked at us and rolled her eyes. "This place doesn't see much action, but Tommy has booked a band for the first time in a long time. So we'll need the help on Saturday for sure. We also had a waitress leave, but Tommy's not going to hire you until you clean up." She climbed out of the booth, dipped her hand inside the pocket of her apron, and placed a key on the table. "My apartment is next door, above the bakery. Apartment three. Go shower. I have clothes in my closet that should fit both of you. I also have food in the fridge. Take your time then come see me."

"Alex, why are you helping?" I asked. She'd said she had a sister who'd lived on the streets. Still, Norma and I could rob her of everything she had.

"Life is precious," she said with a frown before she strode over to the bar.

Norma and I stared at each other for a mere second before we hurried out of there. The thought of a long hot shower, new clothes, and food had me rushing up two flights of stairs to apartment three.

After we closed the door, I laughed out loud. The place was bare except for a dilapidated couch, a rickety coffee table made out of boxes and plywood, and a wicker basket full of wine bottle corks that sat next to the couch. "Not much to steal if we wanted to."

"We wouldn't do that." Norma stuck her head in the fridge. "Right?"

Alex was giving us a break. I wasn't about to ruin the opportunity to get squeaky clean and sated. As Norma rummaged around for food, I went in search of the bathroom.

After two hours of showering, eating, and raiding Alex's closet, I felt like a human again. My hair had never been silkier, my skin was clean and smooth, and the shampoo I'd just used made my hair smell like coconuts. Not to mention, I was wearing new clothes. I borrowed a pair of jeans, boots, and a pullover sweater with sleeves that fell to my fingertips. The clothes were looser on me than on Norma. She'd found jeans, a pair of Chucks, and a tight-fitting cotton shirt that accentuated her large breasts. Her short blond hair was shinier than I'd ever seen it. We went as far as applying a little foundation. For me, the makeup was more to cover up my bruises. We found a plastic bag in the kitchen and stuffed our dirty clothes in it before we made our way back to Firefly.

The restaurant had more people in it now, at least around the bar. I wasn't surprised, considering it was approaching happy hour. I glanced around for Alex but didn't see her. We claimed the same booth in which we'd sat earlier.

My stomach cramped. "I need to use the restroom." The ham I'd eaten wasn't agreeing with me. I rushed down a long hallway, following the sign to the restrooms, and flew into the ladies' room. When I was done, I headed back to Norma. I was just taking a left out of the restroom when Tommy's voice reverberated from a room down the hall to my right.

"You will do as I say," Tommy yelled.

"I'm not working for this jerk," Alex retorted.

I only hesitated for a second. As I did, my stomach gurgled. I crept closer to the office door, which was slightly ajar, and smacked into Alex as she hurried out.

Her eyebrows went up. "Ruby?"

Tommy loomed behind Alex. "The girl from the fight?" He whistled as he shoved Alex out of the way. His dark eyes were dancing. "Are you here to fight again?"

"Not a chance." Then again, it depended on the money. I shook off the thought. The social worker would definitely question me if I showed up to visit Raven with bruises and cuts all over my face. More importantly, I couldn't scare my daughter.

Norma came up behind me. "What's going on?"

Tommy smirked as he laid eyes on Norma. "What have you two done with yourselves? Did you find a sugar daddy? Or did Dillon and that dude, Kross, find you the other night and take you in? Dillon is like that. He finds girls and gives them a warm bed. Fucker is always on my ass."

"If you didn't try to screw Dillon out of money or stab him in the back with the cops, he might not want to chop off your head," Alex spat.

"Shut the fuck up." Tommy's face turned red. "And stop drooling over the asshole." He sounded jealous.

Alex threw him the finger.

Tommy ignored her and turned to us. "What are you ladies doing here?"

"They need a job," Alex said. "Waitressing."

Tommy waved his hand. "Come in, ladies."

With Alex and Tommy arguing, it was probably best that Norma and I came back later. "It seems you're in the middle of something," I said.

"We were finished." Tommy walked deeper into his office.

I followed with Norma and Alex on my heels.

Behind the door, a man lounged on a leather couch. He was dressed in an expensive business suit and had one leg crossed over the other. His large stature overpowered the piece of furniture he sat on, and the dim light from a table lamp enhanced his fat nose. The way he smirked, with one side of his mouth upturned as he scrutinized me from head to toe, reminded me of the men who stalked the street corners where the hookers worked.

"Norma and Ruby, I would like you to meet a business partner of mine, Trent." Tommy raked his gaze over me. "You're prettier than I remembered, and your face is healing nicely." He sat on the edge of his desk.

"I told you once before that I'd kick you in the balls if you didn't stick your tongue back in your mouth." It didn't matter if I wanted a job or not. I wasn't about to be treated like a piece of meat.

Norma elbowed me.

"What should I do?" Tommy asked rhetorically. "I'm supposed to alert your boyfriend, Kross, if you show up here."

I clenched my fists at my sides. "No!"

"Tommy," Alex chimed in. "Hire them. We have that band this weekend. You've been looking to hire another waitress, anyway." Alex kept glancing at Trent then Tommy, biting her lower lip.

Tommy scratched his neck. "I can't." Then he turned his attention to Trent. "What about you, man? You got an opening?"

"No!" Alex shouted.

Norma and I exchanged a what-the-hell-was-that-all-about look.

Tommy rubbed a hand down his nose and over his mouth. "Alex, leave us. You have customers to wait on."

Alex didn't move. She and Tommy glowered at one another as though they were speaking telepathically.

"If it's experience you want, Norma's held jobs waitressing," I said. "As for me, I'm a quick learner, but I could work in the kitchen. I'm a good cook."

"It's not your experience," Tommy said with an evil laugh. "I guess you don't know Dillon Hart, the ponytail dude with your boyfriend."

I barely remembered him. I'd been too riveted on Kross and his beautiful rendition of our nursery rhyme.

"He'll fuck me up. Well, it's not just Dillon, but his crazy brothers. And Kross is a beast. Have you seen him fight?" Tommy asked his business partner. "You should put money on the guy."

Trent raised an eyebrow as he sat quietly.

Alex snapped her fingers at Tommy. "Focus."

"I can hire Ruby," Trent piped in as he looked at me and drooled.

My spidey sense was warning me to stay away from Trent. "Is it because of Kross you won't hire me?" I asked Tommy. "If it is, you have nothing to worry about." I had no idea what I was saying. I would have even said the sky was purple to get a job. "You don't strike me as the type of guy who scares easily."

"Until you know the Hart family, don't judge me," Tommy snapped. "You weren't the one threatened by Kross either."

I couldn't catch a break. For four long years, I hadn't heard a peep out of Kross. Now, I couldn't get a job because of the man unless I considered whatever Trent's job offer was.

"Come on," Norma said. "We don't need this shit."

Normally, I would have walked away. But if I wanted to get my life back on track, I couldn't give up. "Please, Tommy. We need this job," I said sweetly.

"We beg all day long," Norma bit out. "We don't need to beg this asshole or anyone else." She snarled at me.

"As much as I agree with you," Alex said to Norma, "I really could use the help on Saturday." She glared at Tommy. "Seriously, you're not going to hire them because of Dillon and Kross? You're not that much of a pansy ass."

Tommy growled. "Watch your tongue." The room fell silent for a second as Tommy scrubbed a hand over his jaw. "If I hire you, I'd have to alert your boyfriend."

I shrugged. If it meant I would have a decent job, then I would suck up whatever consequences came my way.

He tapped a finger on his lips. "Okay. I'll hire both of you on one condition."

I rolled back my shoulders. "I'm listening."

Tommy pressed the heels of his hands on his desk. "If Kross comes in here with his fists flying at me because of you, you're fired."

"I can't control him or what he does. He's not going to kick your ass because of me, anyway." I wasn't sure about that. Kross might've been sweet when he was reciting a nursery rhyme, but the way his muscles had tensed the other night meant that he'd been holding his emotions in check.

"Then you have nothing to worry about," Tommy said.

I looked at Norma for approval even though I was taking the job no matter what. She blinked, albeit reluctantly.

"Fine," I said, jutting my chin out. I would face Kross if it meant I could work there.

"If things don't work out here, then come talk to me," Trent said.

In your dreams.

"I'm glad that's settled," Tommy said. "Alex will show you the ropes. Now, Trent and I have business to discuss."

We headed to the door.

"One more thing," Tommy said.

I held my breath. There was always some last detail that was left out of the deal.

"Where are you two living?" Tommy swung his gaze between Norma and me. "I can't have you living on the streets with no means of keeping up your hygiene."

There went that opportunity.

"They're staying with me," Alex said.

Norma and I gaped at her. I wasn't about to question her reasons for being super nice, but I couldn't help but wonder why. Then again, the streets were harsh. The nights were harsher, and food was scarce. Tommy was giving us an opportunity. Alex was giving us shelter. Those two things equaled survival, and that alone erased any curiosity I had about Alex's intentions. For the moment, I would do the best job possible and start rehearsing what I was going to say to Kross.

CHAPTER 7
KROSS

A car sat up on cement blocks, askew and devoid of tires on the somewhat deserted Boston street. As I wheeled by, I noticed the driver's door looked as if someone had rammed into it with a tanker. I'd spent one long and tortuous week searching homeless camps and shelters for Ruby. The past few nights, I'd roamed the streets alone. I hadn't been able to sleep, so I'd ventured out into places Dillon had told me about. He'd offered to tag along, but he was meeting with a real estate investor about a potential investment property for a home for runaway girls. A place I wished he already had. Then we could've offered a room to Ruby and her friend, Norma. Aside from all that, I checked in with Jay's receptionist to see if I'd gotten any calls from Norma or Ruby.

"No date with Penelope?" Kody asked from the passenger seat.

"Nope." Since I'd seen Ruby and learned that I could be a father, I couldn't focus on anything. Penelope had been the furthest thing from my mind. "I'm calling it quits with her." I had never planned to get serious with her in the first place.

I shot Kody a side glance. "So, Ms. Sharp, huh?" Kody had taken Ms. Sharp from Greenridge Academy on a dinner date last week.

"Dude, she's fucking hot. She wore this pencil skirt that reached her knees, and when she sat down, it rode up a little, exposing the sexiest thighs I've ever seen."

"Dare I ask if you explored more than her legs?" As brothers, we did share some details of our dates, but we kept the most intimate ones private.

"Let's just say she's a sweet lady."

Flames flickered from a garbage can as we rolled by a group of homeless men trying to keep themselves warm. The neighborhood grew darker the farther down the street we got. A sinking feeling took root in my stomach. Every night, I envisioned Ruby and our child sleeping out in the cold temperatures that dropped into the twenties at night.

Broken windows poked holes in the dilapidated brick buildings along both sides of the street. Steam swirled from a manhole as I made a U-turn at the end of the road.

"We should've brought a handgun," Kody said as he scanned the streets.

"We're looking for a homeless girl, not a thug." Still, he may have been right about the shadiness of the area.

"Do you want to get out and walk a bit?" Kody asked.

"Nah, I only saw that group around the fire. It doesn't look like anyone else is out here. Besides, it's Saturday. I want to check with Tommy at Firefly." I hadn't heard from Tommy since I'd almost used him as a punching bag.

"You know, Bro, don't you think Ruby would've found you by now if there was a kid? It's been four years."

"I've been thinking the same thing. But there are so many different scenarios. Maybe she had a miscarriage." That was one possibility that stuck the brightest in my head.

"Well, when you do actually talk to her, don't tear her head off. You'll only scare her away. Remember what Dad always says: 'Until you know their story, you shouldn't judge or freak out.'"

I harrumphed. Easier said than done when I could be a father.

After ten minutes of navigating the streets, I parked alongside a curb outside of Firefly. Kody and I hopped out of my truck and crossed the street, blending in with a group of guys making their way into the place.

An earthy scent reached my nose as I stepped up on the curb. Rain was forecasted for that night—a cold rain that could turn into ice, sleet, or even snow. I shivered at the idea that Ruby would be somewhere on the streets in bad weather. My shoulder brushed someone as I trudged into Firefly.

"Watch out," the stranger said rather tersely.

I honed in on the man, who was a few inches shorter than me. When our eyes locked, I growled. It was the businessman I remembered from the fight last week, the one with the bulbous nose, talking of pimps. The hair on the back of my neck rose. Kody slid his hand in between the man and me. The man's phone rang as he gawked at me with disgust and anger in his bloodshot eyes. If the fucker wanted to go a round or two with me, I'd be game. It was too bad Dillon wasn't there to get in on the fun.

The man's phone continued to buzz.

"Come on, Kross," Kody said. "Take it down a notch."

The phone stopped ringing at the same time the man lost his fucked-up expression. "Kross? Kross Maxwell?" He held out his greasy paw.

"Who's asking?" My voice was hard.

A couple came out of the club, forcing us to move out of the way.

He withdrew his hand. "I'm Trent Baker, a business partner of Tommy's. He's told me a lot about your boxing abilities. I wouldn't mind discussing an opportunity with you for a potential fight."

I wracked my brain, trying to figure out why his name sounded familiar. The man was dressed in an expensive tailored suit, complete with a handkerchief sticking out of his breast pocket. Rich Businessman Trent Baker and Thug Tommy didn't match as business partners in my book. Then again, maybe Trent was mafia. The mafia entered into deals and partnerships with all kinds of people.

Dillon had mentioned Tommy was into all kinds of illegal stuff, from the underground fights to theft. Apparently, Tommy stole high-end cars for some dude who sold them on the black market for more than the cars were worth. Maybe Trent was the guy. Regardless of cars, I associated Trent with pimps, and that alone made my blood boil.

"I don't deal with strangers. If you're interested in setting up a match, then talk to my coach at Crandall's Gym." Jay wouldn't go for his proposition. Jay was all about legal fights and keeping his business legitimate.

Trent whipped out a business card from his suit pocket. "If you change your mind, then give me a shout." He handed me his card then strode off.

I briefly glanced at the card that read Trent Baker, Owner of Baker Shipping. Now I knew why his name was familiar. I'd read about Baker Shipping in the Herald when Penelope's father's shipping company was up for sale. Apparently, Trent's company wanted to buy out Penelope's old man. Not only that, Trent Baker had his hands in other businesses like car dealerships.

Kody snatched the card from my hand and read it before he said, "Scum."

I agreed, but he was a scum who was richer than Donald Trump. I pocketed the card as we entered Firefly. Maybe I would have my buddy, Detective Rayburn, check out the man. I wasn't into ratting on people, but Trent must be up to something bad.

People filled every table, chair, barstool, and corner in Firefly. Hard rock music pumped out of poor-quality speakers as the voices tried to talk above it. A round-faced waitress zipped around, plucking empty glasses off tables and serving drinks in the process. I was just about to step up to the bar when Kody tapped me on the arm.

"Hey, man." He pointed to our right. "Isn't that Penelope?"

I wasn't sure I heard him. Penelope Harris came from a prestigious family. She would have never hung out in a dive bar. She was the type of girl who was pampered with spas, cars, a credit card with a thirty-thousand-dollar limit, and her daddy's company jet at her disposal. She recently tried to get me to join her and her friends on a weekend getaway to Costa Rica. My old man certainly had money, but we didn't flaunt it like her family did. Then again, Penelope and I had values that didn't jive. I didn't care about material things. She did. I was all about family. She was all about herself. The only connection we had was in the bedroom.

When I turned in her direction, her green eyes bugged out. We weren't committed to each other. We weren't in love, or at least I wasn't with her.

She hopped out of her chair, said something to the girls she was with, then bounced over. "Kross? I'm so glad you came." Her blond hair was piled on top of her head in some type of funky style.

I cocked my head to one side. "Come again?" I searched my brain for something I might've missed. I hadn't seen her in two weeks. I hadn't even called her, which wasn't unusual with my boxing schedule.

"I told Kelton where I'd be. He told you. My friends and I are here to see Wyatt play tonight."

I raised an eyebrow. I hadn't talked to Kelton since yesterday morning. "No, he didn't. You and your friends shouldn't be here." Her scantily dressed rich friends were being ogled by a table of men with beards and leather vests that sported the name of a motorcycle club on the back.

She reared back. "Why? Are you doing something behind my back?"

Fuck. I didn't have time for her, but I also wasn't a complete jerk. "What I mean is this place isn't exactly your style."

She rubbed her breasts against my arm as she grabbed my hand. "It's so nice to hear you're worried about me."

Kody tapped me on the arm then subtly flicked his head at the bar. "Is that her?"

I glanced in the direction of the bearded bartender. When I did, I about lost my breath. Standing on the other side of the bar was Ruby. A pendant light above her head shone down. Gone were the bruises, the swollen eyes, the ashen skin, and the greasy hair. I was looking at the girl I'd met back in the tenth grade. Her skin glowed. Her auburn hair was pulled into a side ponytail, and I swore she was the angel I remembered. She smiled at the bartender as though she was reacting to a compliment. Hell, she was beautiful.

"Who are you looking at?" Penelope asked.

My past. A girl who could be the mother of my child. A woman who was certainly a mystery. Tommy had thought she was homeless, yet she was working there. That meant he'd known her all along, and the fucker hadn't called me like he was supposed to.

I ground my teeth, the fury burning through my veins. I was going to kill him.

"Kross, I'm talking to you," Penelope whined.

"Bro, are you in there?" Kody asked. "That's her, isn't it?"

I was about to answer him when Ruby's eyes met mine, erasing my rage for the moment. Instead, my heart sputtered because she smiled as if she was happy to see me. Then, in an instant, her lips turned downward, fear claiming her beautiful face. She scoured the room every which way as though she was searching for an escape route.

Not a chance in hell was she getting away from me tonight. I would lock us both in the bathroom until I got answers. I leaned into Kody. "Can you keep an eye on Penelope and her friends?" As much as I wanted answers, I also wanted to make sure the women were safe. Those biker dudes were chatting with Penelope's friends.

"Don't worry," Kody said. "I'll take care of them."

"Kross," Penelope said.

Her voice faded as I pushed through the crowd. The closer I got to Ruby, the more my pulse sped up. For an entire week, I hadn't been able to sleep. I'd hardly eaten. I'd fucked up so bad during training that Jay threw up his hands and stalked off. I'd even knocked out poor Liam during a sparring session.

A large man blocked me. We danced around each other before he moved one way. Then I had a clear view of Ruby's blue-green eyes, which were wide as saucers. Those same eyes held me prisoner where I stood. She blinked once then scanned the room again for a way out.

Fuck. I wasn't a bully. I wasn't going to hurt her. I couldn't imagine why she would be frightened, unless Tommy had something to do with her state of fear. I clenched a fist. He and I would have a chat as soon as I talked with Ruby.

CHAPTER 8
RUBY

I blew out breath after breath, feverishly wanting to hide or run. My heart leapt into my throat, thinking of how I should react or what I should say to him. The past few days had been busy, so I hadn't rehearsed what I would say to Kross if I even ran into him. Honestly, I'd tried to push him out of my mind. I needed to focus on the ins and outs of waitressing.

I tracked his movements from the other end of the bar until he disappeared into the crowd. When he came back into view, my brain shut down. Actually, it shut down the moment I met his gaze from the other side of the bar.

As he started toward me again, a big-breasted blond girl, dressed in a silk top and shiny jewelry that screamed money, hooked her arm through his. I couldn't hear what she was saying over the band, but thank God. She'd given me at least a minute to catch my breath.

I couldn't say I was surprised to see Kross. After all, Tommy had said he would let Kross know that I was working there. I'd been so busy with learning the ropes of waitressing that I hadn't had time to check with Tommy. I didn't want to know anyway. The less I knew, the fewer nerves I would have. Yeah, like that worked. My nerves were singing a tune to a drummer's beat in a metal band. In fact, I'd been jittery for the last two days, constantly dropping what I was doing to check each customer that entered.

"Something wrong?" the bartender, Pete, asked.

"No. Just nervous about serving so many people." It wasn't exactly a lie. I'd only been waitressing for three days. My skills were improving, although two customers would have argued that I was a screw-up. But serving drinks was the last thing on my mind at the moment. I scanned the room and found Alex waiting on tables. I kept searching until my gaze landed on Norma. She was also busy. I needed her advice, but I knew what she would say. "Talk to Kross." The problem was that this wasn't a good time. The club was hopping. Not only that, but I had to figure out what I would say. The truth came to mind. I certainly had to atone for the many questions Kross would have. I also had several questions for him. In all, I was terrified. What if he fought me for custody of Raven, especially after he found out the life I'd led up until this point? I'd also been fooling myself if I believed that the three of us would become an instant family. My muscles tightened as I thought of how I'd repeatedly called him. He hadn't even texted back to say hi or to let me know he wasn't interested. Instead, the man had ignored me as though we'd never had sex or even dated.

Pete's warm hand touched mine. "Ruby."

"I need to use the bathroom." I had to collect myself, get my hands to stop shaking, my heart to stop fluttering, and my stomach to stop churning.

"Drinks first." He set down the last drink for my order. "Can't keep your customers waiting. Boss won't like it."

I sucked in air as I snagged a lime wedge. As I squeezed a bit of its juice into a gin and tonic, I peeked in Kross's direction. He had his back to me, shaking his head at the blond woman who was pouting.

I breathed a sigh of relief until he cupped the girl's face in an adoring gesture. She smiled. A pang of jealousy took root inside me. I had no reason to get all weird about some girl, who was probably his girlfriend. After all, I was trying to avoid the man. Still, I would have given anything to have him touch me like that.

"Get your ass in gear," Pete ordered. "If the boss finds you standing around, he'll give you and me the third degree."

Pete had been nice to me when I'd spilled drinks. The last thing I wanted to do was get him into trouble or have Tommy breathing down my neck, especially not with Kross in the house.

I picked up my tray, turned, and *Boom. Crash. Splash.* The drinks smashed in between Kross and me. Bottles fell to the floor. The couple closest to me cussed as they checked their shoes, which took the brunt of my clumsiness. Suddenly, the room began to disappear. My stomach pitched and rolled. Alcohol soaked into my blouse. Not caring if I had a wet T-shirt vibe going on, I stared into the deepest blue eyes. They reminded me of Raven. *Keep it together, girl.* I wasn't sure I could. Kross's spicy scent tickled my nostrils, and those damn blue eyes nailed me to the bar. Butterflies scattered in my stomach.

"I'm s-sorry," I managed to say.

"Just like when we first met," Kross said. "Only you dropped your books and keys."

Wow. He remembers.

Pete's voice resounded from somewhere behind me. Other voices hummed nearby, and the music played, albeit softly, or maybe not at all. Maybe I was hearing the ballet music I'd danced to as Kross watched me practice.

One side of Kross's mouth quirked up, displaying the lone dimple in his right cheek. "You look amazing." His whiskey-smooth voice belied the hard look on his face. The rippling planes of his muscles strained against the tight long-sleeve shirt he was wearing.

My tongue was glued to the roof of my mouth as my body heated in ways I'd never felt, or at least didn't remember. I had the sudden urge to launch myself at him, hug him, hit him, kiss him, and tell him how much I saw him when I looked at Raven. A lone tear slipped out. I longed to be part of a family. I wanted Raven to know her daddy. I wanted to know her daddy. I wanted so much, but I didn't deserve anything, not until I could prove I was a good mother. I quietly inhaled, praying my heart would stop trying to pound out of my chest.

"I'm sorry about this," he said, bending down.

I licked the dryness from my lips and slowly squatted, never taking my eyes off him. When he placed an empty bottle on the tray, his hand brushed mine. My body reacted before my brain, and I started wiping beads of alcohol off his stark blue T-shirt. My fingers stopped over his heart. I glanced at my hand to make sure I wasn't shaking as fast as his heart was beating. Then as though someone snuffed out the fire inside of me, my body went cold. He was trying to use his Maxwell charm on me. He was trying to get me to cave. He knew I had a weak side when it came to him, particularly if he started to recite *Star Light, Star Bright*.

Run now. No, tell him what he wants to know. Then get back to your job. Oh, shit. My job. As the voices in my head argued, I couldn't move. In fact, my cheeks burned. I couldn't even withdraw my hand from his hard chest. It had been way too long since I touched a man. But Kross wasn't any man. Kross was the father of my child. He was my first love, the boy who made my palms sweat. The boy I gave my virginity to. Even now, four years later, I wanted to sit under the oak trees at Greenridge Academy and talk about nothing as he played with my hair. I was suddenly lost in the past, in his spicy scent, in the heat of his body, and the desperate longing in his midnight-blue eyes.

From far away, a gruff voice tried to cut through the bubble I had created around Kross and me.

"Ruby. Ruby." Irritation colored Tommy's tone as he said my name close to my left ear.

Kross dragged the backs of his knuckles over my cheek, the one with the beauty mark. He'd done that same gesture many times when we'd been together. I leaned into him, not wanting this moment to end. *You're supposed to be mad at him.* I silently screamed at my inner voice to shut up.

"Ruby." Tommy said my name again before he tapped on my shoulder.

My dreamy bubble burst. The music grew louder, and voices became clearer, especially Tommy's.

I briefly closed my eyes before I jumped to my feet. I peered up at Tommy's scowled face. Then I looked back at Kross, who was now on his feet with a similar sneer, but it was directed at Tommy, not me. I got a sinking feeling that Tommy hadn't called Kross.

Tommy had his hands on his denim-clad hips as he eyed me then Kross. "I see you two have now talked. Good. Now clean this mess up. Oh, and those drinks are coming out of your paycheck." Then he stormed off.

I pinched my eyebrows together. Tommy didn't yell, and Kross didn't punch him. But the line between Kross's eyebrows was unyielding as he watched Tommy head back down the hall. Not a good sign.

"Ruby," Pete called.

When I turned, I was met with a towel that Pete had thrown at me.

"Clean up. Then get moving." Pete pointed a fat finger to another round of drinks he'd whipped up while I was skipping down memory lane.

I hurried and picked up my mess. Surprisingly, the glasses weren't broken. On my way to the bar, Kross stormed down the hallway with his hands fisted. I'd seen him in a similar fury when we were at the academy just before he had gotten into a fight with a boy who thought he owned the school.

No. No. No. I practically threw the lemon wedges, glasses, and cherries at Pete. I was not about to get fired because of Kross. I flew down the hall in hopes of stopping the imminent brawl.

"Ruby," Pete yelled. "Get back here."

Not a chance. I had to save my job. But as I skidded to a stop, I saw that Kross was in Tommy's face, and Tommy had his back plastered to the paneled wall outside his office.

"You were supposed to call me if Ruby showed up." Kross's voice thundered down the long hallway. "Do you know what I've been through in the last week?"

"Fuck off, man. I don't owe you squat. So get the hell out of here. This is my business, and you're trespassing." Tommy literally spat in his face.

I didn't have time to stop Kross's fist from connecting with Tommy's jaw. Even if I could have, I wasn't strong enough to intervene. Tommy's head flew to the right.

Kross positioned himself to hit Tommy again.

"Stop," I shouted.

Kross wiped the spit from his eye as he stalked up to me. "I've been searching every fucking place in this city, looking for you." His voice was so deep, a chill zinged down my spine. "Every minute of the day and night, I roamed the streets, looking for you and our child. All this time, you've been here under this asshole's nose." He turned to Tommy, who was rubbing his jaw. "We're not through yet."

"Yes, you are." My tone was firmer than the bunched muscles on his arms. "The fight is between you and me. But right now, I have to work. So if you want answers, get out of here until I finish my shift." That was if I had a job. Tommy was a businessman that didn't break deals, or at least I assumed he didn't. I would beg and plead and do whatever it took to keep this job. This was my one shot at a better life. Granted, it wasn't the greatest job, but it sure beat begging for change, eating out of dumpsters, and sleeping in dark alleys.

"Problems, Bro?" Either Kelton or Kody strutted up as though scuffles were an everyday occurrence with the Maxwells. Oh, wait. They were. The triplets had been hellions at the academy, always in trouble with a teacher for mouthing off or acting out. Still, after not being around them all these years, it was hard for me to tell the difference between Kelton and Kody. Not to mention, when Kross and I had dated, I hadn't exactly hung out with his brothers, although Kelton had teased me a time or two.

Tommy did a double take. "Dillon didn't tell me there were two of you."

"Three," Kross's brother said in a light tone. He pointed to Kross. "But he's the one you don't want to fuck with." He wasn't as broad in the chest as Kross, and his hair was shaggier.

"Kody," Kross said, his eyes fixated on me. "Can you make sure Penelope and her friends are okay. I'll be just a minute."

"Nice to see you, Ruby." Kody sauntered off, leaving me alone with two angry men.

Kross glared at me as though I was the one who had never returned his calls. "You and I are talking before I leave here."

"Oh, now you want to talk? Years go by, and out of the blue, I'm supposed to drop what I'm doing to talk to you? Yeah, think again. I have a job to do, and you're interfering."

"No, you don't," Tommy said. "We had a deal. You're fired." He held his bruised jaw.

Like hell I was. "As I said, I'm finishing my shift." I glowered at Tommy then Kross. "We have nothing to discuss."

Kross folded his large arms over his chest. "I'm not leaving, darling."

"I'm not your darling. You lost the right to call me that when you all but ran like Freddy Krueger was chasing you."

Tommy disappeared into his office.

Kross pushed up the sleeves of his shirt, exposing the head of a snake on his right forearm. He looked ready to rumble.

I laughed. "Is that move supposed to scare me?" The man I knew wouldn't hit me. He was frustrated, but I wasn't about to let him bully me into talking when he wanted me to.

"I said I was sorry for not returning your calls." His voice was softer.

"Kross." The blonde wiggled her curvy hips up to him. "What's going on?"

I had a sudden urge to tell the girl to take a hike. But once again, she was the perfect distraction.

"I'll give you time." The hardness in his tone returned. "But don't get any ideas of running because we're talking tonight, even if I have to get my cop friend to put out an APB on you." He grasped the blonde's hand and stalked out.

My mouth fell open. I wanted to scream, shout, and tell him to fuck off. Instead, I stormed into Tommy's cluttered office. I needed to save my job first, then I could deal with Kross.

"You're definitely fired. I don't want cops sniffing around this joint. Who the hell is Kross to you, anyway?" Tommy plopped down onto his couch. "He keeps asking about a baby. Care to elaborate?"

"Are you firing me or trying to be my shrink? I mean, why do you care?"

He moved his jaw from side to side. "The fucker can hit."

"First, you started it by spitting in his face. Second, you don't strike me as a whiner. You run a business. You set up illegal fights. You deal with bad men." Maybe my last statement was a shot in the dark, but his business partner, Trent, was bad in my book. "Why are you afraid of Kross? Or is it that friend of his?"

"That dude"—he pointed to the door—"is wired to kill. If I were you, I'd tell him about his baby. Well, if there is one."

"You can't fire me," I said as though I owned the club. "Look, I promise Kross won't be a problem anymore. Besides, you need the help out there." Alex had been right about the band drawing in a crowd.

"A deal is a deal." He rested his head against the couch. "I'll have a check for your wages cut when I run payroll next week. I would highly suggest you get your sweet little ass out of here and tend to the open wounds that boy has."

I stomped my foot. "You're not firing me." Tears burst out. "Please, Tommy. I need this job. I don't want to sleep on the streets anymore." I wasn't certain if Alex would keep letting Norma and me stay with her if we didn't have a way to pay her.

Tommy appraised me, a habit that was getting extremely old. "Tell you what. I just lost my fighter for next Saturday. You fight, you get to keep waitressing."

I didn't want to fight. I wanted a job that didn't give me bruises or cuts or cost me my life. *That could happen waitressing. You could slip on a spilled drink and crack your head open.* But the odds of that happening were higher if I fought.

I joined Tommy on the couch. As soon as my body sank into the soft leather, I wanted to close my eyes and take a nap. "Why do you set up fights with women? Why not men?"

He shrugged a shoulder. "Guys like to see women fight, and I make more money. Look, Ruby, you're good. You have great footwork. You could make a lot of money. I could make a lot of money. Who knows? I've had some girls who become so good, they go into legal professional boxing." His voice held compassion.

I'd never thought about fighting professionally. I could make money that way too. The professional arena would also be safer. I would have to toss around that idea a little bit more. "I always wanted to do ballet."

"Ah," he said. "See. If you train, you could be really good. Maybe you can get Kross to teach you a few moves before next Saturday."

I flew off the couch. "No way." I would be a ball of slush with him, and he reminded me too much of Raven.

He leaned forward, his elbows on his knees, and rubbed his jaw. "Suit yourself. That's my deal. Fight and keep your job or leave."

Illegal fighting wouldn't get Raven back, but waitressing would. I picked at a nail. "You know, one minute you're sweet like you care, and the next minute, you're a dick."

He grinned. "That's what women tell me."

"How much can I win?"

He unfolded his bulk and sauntered over to his desk. "Two thousand dollars."

I flew off the couch, my jaw locked open. "For real?"

"You win, you get the money. No lies."

I'd never seen Tommy in a calm and serious mood. He was either acting like a jerk or yelling at someone. His demeanor told me he wasn't lying. "Who am I fighting?"

Tommy arched an eyebrow. "Does it really matter?"

Two thousand could be a deposit on an apartment plus first month's rent. "I'm in." Norma wasn't going to be happy.

CHAPTER 9
KROSS

I gripped the edge of the bar so fucking tightly, my fingers were about to meld into the tacky wooden bar. For two long, agonizing hours, I sat with rigid posture and a scowl on my face, my gaze skating everywhere and nowhere. Blue-collar folks mixed with college preppies as they listened to the band. Penelope hung with her friends even though I sensed she wanted to sit by my side with her hands all over me.

I was a bomb waiting to explode as I tracked Ruby. She zipped around tables, smiled at men, laughed freely, and seemed to be having the time of her life. Meanwhile, my insides were burning. Tommy had the fucking nerve not to call me. Even worse, he had the balls to spit in my face. He and I weren't even close to settling our shit.

Kody ambled over from Penelope's table. Thank God for my brother. He'd kept Penelope away from me. "Penelope keeps asking questions. At least talk to her. Or get some fresh air. It looks like you could use some."

Not bad advice on the fresh air part. The club was suffocating. But I wasn't letting Ruby out of my sight. As far as Penelope was concerned, I did owe her an explanation, but not until I calmed my nerves.

"Seriously, Bro"—Kody wedged his way in between me and the dude sitting beside me—"stop looking at Ruby like a stalker. That bartender is onto you. He keeps eyeing you like he's about to kick your ass out of here."

"Let him try." I drilled my gaze into Ruby as she filled her tray with drinks. Norma stood beside her and whispered in her ear. Ruby threw her head back and laughed.

My face reddened. How could she be so casual and flippant while a powerful storm brewed inside me. *Maybe because what you believe to be true isn't. Maybe there isn't a child.* Whether that was true or not, just knowing the story would relieve some of my pent-up tension.

The bartender banged a hand on the bar in front of me. "Mister, I don't know what your intentions are, but if you keep staring at the girls like you want to rape them, I'm calling the cops."

Steam came out of my nose.

"Kross, go outside and get some air." Kody glared at the bartender. He wasn't one to throw fists unless he was being attacked, but lately, he'd been working out a lot in the gym when he wasn't performing or writing songs.

The cold November air would quell the rage in me. The bartender didn't deserve my wrath. He was only protecting the waitresses.

A light drizzle fell from the sky. I strode down the block and around the corner into the alley. A can tumbled. Two cats meowed. I had to calm my fucking nerves before I talked with Ruby. Hell, I had to get myself under control for my upcoming match, which Jay was still working out the date and details for. Or maybe I could use my anger to beat Reggie. The problem with that idea was that I got sloppy when my brain was clouded. I paced down the alley and back three times before Kody found me.

"Bro, the band is done with their set, so I'm going to walk Penelope and her friends to their car. Also, I talked to Ruby. She still has an hour before she's done with her shift. She said she knows you and her need to talk. So, relax."

My shoulders slumped. I couldn't say I was relieved. I wouldn't be until I got answers, but it was good to know she acknowledged that we needed to talk. Regardless, I wanted to position myself back on my barstool just in case she got any ideas to slip out on me.

I walked Kody back to the entrance, where Penelope waited with her friends. I needed to apologize to her. I took hold of her hand. "Can we talk for a minute, privately?"

She nodded as I guided her to a quiet spot near the corner of the building.

"I'm sorry. I didn't mean to be an ass in there. I've got a lot of shit going on." I didn't know if this was the right time to tell her I didn't want to see her anymore, but I couldn't lead her on. "Look, you're a beautiful girl."

She searched my face. "But?"

"I can't date you anymore. You want a steady relationship. I'm not that guy. I'll still train you, but nothing more." She'd been one of my clients, which was how I'd met her in the first place. I couldn't drop her as a client. Jay would have my hide. Besides, she needed to keep up her self-defense classes, especially if she was planning to frequent dives like Firefly.

"Does it have something to do with that redhead waitress?" Her eyelashes, which were thick with mascara, fluttered as though she was holding back tears.

"It does, and it doesn't." It was time for the truth. "I'd been thinking about calling it off with you before tonight."

She stuck out her chin. "So have you been dating her too?"

The drizzle started to turn into a steady rain.

"No."

"Let's go," one of Penelope's friends called.

"I can't change your mind?" she asked. "Don't answer that." Her bottom lip trembled before she lifted up on her toes and kissed me on the cheek. "You have my number if you change your mind." Then she hurried back to her friends.

I followed, but at a slower pace. I hated to hurt her feelings, although if I knew Penelope, she wasn't the type to give up.

"I'll be back," Kody said before he escorted Penelope and her friends down the street.

I slipped into the club and commandeered the same barstool. The band was packing up, and people were saying good-bye to each other.

The bartender glared at me as he wiped a glass. I raised an eyebrow then scanned the room again. Norma and the other waitress were collecting empty glasses from tables as Bob Seger's Night Moves blared from overhead speakers. But no Ruby. I bounced my knee, trying not to blow a gasket.

"What's your problem?" I asked the bartender.

He shuffled over. "My problem, man, is you. The waitresses don't need men like you drooling at them."

I bit my tongue. *No trouble. Jay will have your balls on a skewer.* I itched to erase the disgusted look off the bartender's face, though.

Norma glided up. "He isn't any trouble, Pete. I know him."

He nodded lazily at Norma as he continued to pierce me with daggers.

She tucked a strand of her short blond hair behind her ear. "Ruby ducked into the bathroom."

I liked Norma. The first night I met her, I'd gotten the sense that she was trying to tell me something without coming out and saying it. Whatever was going on with Ruby, it wasn't Norma's responsibility to tell me.

"You look a lot better tonight than you did when I first met you." I scanned her pretty features, wanting to know more of her and Ruby's story. "What changed?" Gone were the dirt and grime under her fingernails. Her hair was shiny and clean, and her skin glowed like Ruby's.

"Norma, a customer needs you." Pete flicked his chin to a man sitting at a table near the wall, who had his hand raised.

She licked her lip ring. "Got to run."

I kept an eye on my watch as the secondhand ticked by. One minute turned into two, then five, then ten. A bathroom stint didn't take that long unless Ruby was sick. My gut was telling me she wasn't in the bathroom. Maybe she was in Tommy's office, trying to save her job. He'd fired her when we were in the hall, although she'd said she would finish her shift. Then again, she had walked out on me before. *And you left her behind without even blinking an eye.* Oh, how I loved my subconscious. Anger pushed through the guilt poking at my stomach.

As I hopped off the barstool, Pete picked up the phone on the wall. He was probably alerting Tommy. Fuck if I cared. I had some unfinished business with the fucker, anyway. First, I wanted to make sure Ruby was okay. I headed in the direction of the restroom. I'd barely made it to the hallway when heavy footsteps thudded behind me.

"Where do you think you're going?" Pete asked.

I whirled around. "Are you serious? Last I checked, this was a public place. I have every right to take a piss. Unless of course you want me to relieve myself right at your feet."

Pete stood two inches shorter than me, but he was built to fight with muscular arms and a chest that would no doubt have power behind a punch. "Leave now. Or else the cops will escort you out."

I glanced past him. "I don't see any cops."

He snarled. "They'll be here in five."

I laughed. "They won't arrest me for wanting to take a piss." I pivoted on my heel. My gut told me not to push this dude, but Ruby came first.

A large hand wrapped around my arm and spun me around. "I told you to leave. You've been making the girls very uncomfortable all night."

I ground my teeth and fisted my hands. "Get your hand off me."

Stars dotted my vision as I jerked away, or at least tried to. The fucker had a strong grip around my arm. I was trying desperately to keep myself out of trouble. *Go outside and wait for her or find another way into the restroom.*

But when Pete dug his nails into me, breaking skin, all sense of doing the right thing vanished. With my free hand, I threw the first punch. He let go of me. Then, like a linebacker, he tucked his chin to his chest and came at me. Before I could react, my body was pinned up against a wall. A crowd formed. One guy from the band tried to pull Pete off of me. But Pete was in his zone. He grabbed my head as I reared back for a punch. My face met his knee. Once. Twice. Three times. The adrenaline flowing through me was fucking high, making the pain weak at best. Blood oozed out of my nose, slipping into my mouth. When the iron taste exploded on my tongue, I shrugged out of his hold then threw a fist toward his face. He ducked.

"Seriously?" I asked in a deep voice. "You want to fight me?"

We circled around each other as if we were in a boxing ring. Actually, the crowd around us formed a ring of sorts.

Pete smirked, showing crooked teeth. "I've been dying to bash your head in all night. I hate when men drool at the waitresses."

I couldn't argue with his last statement. Kody had even said I could pass as a stalker. The thought of apologizing flitted through my mind. But I wanted to fight. I wanted to feel my knuckles connect with muscles and bones. I wanted to hear the "oof" or the grunting sounds coming from my opponent and witness the blood flying in all directions. Yeah, I was a little out there, but that was the thrill of boxing.

"Hit him, Pete," a male voice said. "Like you used to do when you boxed."

S.B. ALEXANDER

I waved him on. "Yeah, Pete. Hit me."

His eyes became slits. His nostrils flared, and he lunged at me. We tangled with each other, punching with fists and elbows. Blood, spit, grunts, and heavy breathing ensued. The voices around us were barely noticeable. I pushed him away. When I did, he spun around, and before I could flinch, his booted foot hit the side of my head. I stumbled backward. The dude didn't box. He fought dirty. Then again, we weren't in a sanctioned event.

I squeezed my eyes shut as I bent over, pain gripping my ear. Before I could get my bearings, a hand was secured tightly around my neck.

"Stop!" a female screamed. I couldn't make out if the voice belonged to Ruby above the ringing in my ears.

I scanned the faces as best I could while Pete anchored my neck in place. My lungs burned for air. I opened my mouth. Nothing. I took in air through my nose and choked. I had to give him props for his dirty move. Then again, Mixed Martial Arts fighters used roundhouse kicks.

A pair of hands landed on Pete's shoulders. I blinked several times and found Tommy lurking behind him. "Pete." Tommy's voice was hard. "Let go. This dude will kill you."

Pete laughed through gritted teeth. "Does it look like he'll kill me?"

With my airway cut off, I had no way to retaliate.

"All right, break it up," a baritone voice said.

"Cops are here," Tommy announced.

"It's about fucking time." Pete dropped his hand. "Hey, Roy."

I bent over again, taking in breath after breath as my lungs jumpstarted. The people around us parted then scattered. I searched the room for Ruby, but no luck.

Norma ran to my side. "Are you okay?"

"Where's Ruby?" I sounded like a guy who'd been smoking all his life.

"I lied to you. I'm sorry. She took a break. She went down to the diner to get a coffee." Regret shone in her brown eyes. "I thought she'd be back by now."

My pulse sped up as I straightened. "She took off because of me, didn't she?"

"Give her some space. You can't expect her to throw herself at you. Seriously, where have you been for four years? Why didn't you call her when she called you repeatedly? After a while, a girl gets the hint that the boy doesn't want anything to do with her."

Kody came in with a wild-eyed expression on his face. "What happened?" His hair was soaked.

"Where have you been?" I asked, not that I was thinking of my brother when I was getting my head bashed in.

"It's pouring out, so the girls and I ducked into an all-night diner a block from here until the rain let up. But when I saw the blue lights speeding down the street, I bolted."

"Did you see Ruby in there?" Norma asked.

"No," Kody said.

Pete and Tommy were talking to Roy.

I rubbed my ear. I shouldn't have let my anger get in the way. I should've walked out the moment Pete told me to. I couldn't get arrested. Jay would have a coronary.

Roy headed our way. "Sir," Roy said to me, "it's time to call it a night." It was hard to discern any features of cops with all the gear they wore, although Roy sported a mustache and had fine lines fanning out from his hazel eyes.

I darted my gaze to Pete and Tommy, who were watching me while the other cop guided people to the door. Pete subtly flicked me the middle finger as he combed his beard.

I narrowed my eyes and took one step toward Pete. The fucker was itching for another fight. "If you want to fight, meet me at Crandall's Gym," I said loudly.

Roy tossed a quick glance over his shoulder.

"Come on, Bro," Kody said. "Another day."

"I'm not leaving yet."

Roy grabbed my arm. "Yes, you are."

"Look, I want to say something to my friend. Then I'll leave." I switched my gaze between his hand on my arm and Norma.

She shook her head and mouthed, "just go."

"One minute. Please," I said nicely to the officer.

Roy nodded. "Make it fast."

I snagged a used napkin from Norma's tray and wrote down my cell number. "Have Ruby call me when she's ready to talk." I had to take a step back and clear my head. I couldn't keep stalking her or fighting for no reason. I had my boxing career to think about. Plus, Norma's little speech had some truth to it. The more I forced Ruby to talk, the more I pushed her away.

She smiled sadly as she pocketed the napkin.

Roy escorted Kody and me out of the building. "The owner doesn't want you in his club anymore. If you do show yourself, he'll press charges."

I wasn't about to argue. I would deal with Tommy and Pete another day. For the moment, I had to work out another angle to break the ice with Ruby.

CHAPTER 10

RUBY

A loud shriek penetrated through my subconscious. Then claws were digging into my hand. I sat up to find a black-and-white cat on me. The beginning of daylight spilled in through the shattered windows of the abandoned warehouse. Then as the world around me crystallized, I shot to my feet. The cat screeched as it jumped off. I checked my trusty Timex. Norma! I'd told her I was going to get a coffee at the diner, but that was at one a.m. It was now five thirty in the morning. She was probably worried out of her mind. Not to mention, I had promised Kross that we would talk.

I ran out of the warehouse, hopped four steps, then took off down the alley. I'd had every intention of sitting in a booth at the diner until Norma got off work. But when I had seen Kody in there with Kross's girlfriend, I kept walking, enjoying the night, the light rain, and the feeling of space. However, when the rain had gotten heavier, I'd turned into an alley to seek shelter for a brief moment. But the rain had kept pouring down. I could've sucked it up and faced the rain. I had many times before when sleeping on the streets. But I'd wanted a quiet moment away from the loud music and the pressure of Kross's stare. I was also tired from being on my feet all night. Still, I envisioned Norma calling the cops.

The cat was perched on top of a burnt car that sat up on blocks on the main street. The wind picked up, and with it, a scent of fish, no doubt from the Boston Harbor in the distance. I bundled my wool coat, secured the yellow scarf the ten-year-old girl had given me, and started for Alex's place. I doubted Kross was waiting around Firefly since it was closed. I owed him a visit. Maybe he would be at his gym later that morning. The cat snuck up on me, meowing. Poor thing was probably hungry.

"I am too, buddy. If you follow me, I'll buy you a bowl of milk."

My mouth watered just thinking about the bakery below Alex's apartment. They had the most amazing glazed donuts. I rummaged around in my pockets and pulled out a wad of dollar bills. I sniffed the money as though it was a delicacy. At least I could buy myself breakfast this morning, thanks to the club customers who had tipped me. I couldn't remember the last time I had this much money on me. I could, however, recall all the money my mom had had. Other than selling drugs, she'd also been responsible for collecting the drug money and flubbing the books for the head boss of the drug ring. The man who was my dad's best friend. The man who was responsible for sucking my mother into the underworld of drugs. The same man who was in jail with my parents.

The cat snuck down another alley. He probably detected a rat or a mouse. Better for me since I was mildly allergic to cats.

I began to jog. As my feet pounded the pavement, the events of the previous night ran with me. Customers had screamed for their drinks. The loud music blared in my ears, causing my head to hurt. Tommy kept checking on me, although I suspect he was making sure Kross wasn't drumming up trouble. Most of all, I swore I could feel Kross's piercing gaze burning through my back. All of that contributed to me spilling drinks on customers, not to mention, the pile of drinks I'd dropped when I crashed into Kross. He was everywhere. Even when he stepped outside, he was still with me, maybe because Kody stood watch for him. I tried to avoid Kody, but I had to serve a table close to him. He was insistent on talking. He kept asking if I would talk to Kross. Finally, after his last plea, I said I would. At least that had been my goal until I remembered how angry I was at Kross for the past and for threatening me with the cops and the APB.

When I reached the bakery, I debated whether to get breakfast or wake up Norma and Alex, although I doubted Norma would be sleeping. She never slept through the night when we were on the streets. She'd always been afraid of someone attacking us or stealing from us.

My decision was made for me when I saw the sign that read "open at six a.m." I had five minutes, which was plenty of time to grovel to Norma then get a box of donuts. I climbed the stairs two at a time until I reached apartment three. I didn't have a key. Usually, we accompanied Alex back after our shifts. I turned the knob, but the door was locked. I knocked softly. I didn't want to wake up the neighbors.

After a minute, I pounded harder. "Norma," I said loudly. "It's me."

Footsteps clobbered up the stairs behind me, followed by voices. Familiar voices. Kross's voice. Norma's voice. *What the hell?*

"You know, Tommy's friend Trent gives me the creeps," Norma said. "What if he got a hold of Ruby?"

"That dude gives me the same vibe," Kross added. "Let's check the apartment. If she's not there, then we'll call the cops."

They sounded chummy as though they had bonded over coffee. I would strangle Norma if she said anything about Raven to Kross.

When they rounded the banister, Kross's eyes went wide while Norma jumped at me, throwing her arms around my neck. "Where have you been? I was worried sick, searching everywhere for you."

"What's he doing here?" I asked as calmly as I could. "What have you told him?" I didn't want to bring out my claws, but I had to know what I was walking into.

She let go of me, her pretty face twisted. Yeah, she was ready to chop off my head. On the other hand, Kross's soft gaze was anything but angry. His mouth twitched with a quick smile, and my belly fluttered.

"I got him out of bed and asked him for help in finding you." Her tone was motherly. "You didn't answer me. Where have you been?"

"It's a long story. I'll tell you later. Right now, I'd like to take a shower," I said in a snippy tone. Again, I didn't mean to be all bitchy. I was beginning to worry that if she went to Kross for help in finding me, she might have broken down and told him about Raven. If she hadn't, then she might if I continued to push Kross away.

"Don't get any ideas about disappearing again. You two need to talk," she said firmly as she unlocked the apartment door.

The need to stomp my foot was strong, a habit I'd always had when I didn't get my way or didn't want to do something.

Norma crossed the tiny living room to the bedroom. "I'm going to use the bathroom."

I trudged into the apartment with Kross on my heels. "Don't wake up Alex."

"Alex left with some dude last night. She said she would see us at work later," Norma said loudly from the bathroom.

I was afraid to turn around and look into Kross's eyes. No doubt I would cave and kiss him or something. Not that there was anything wrong with kissing him. But would he want to kiss me back? His cologne lingered around me, making my cheeks heat up. So I made a beeline into the bathroom. "I can't be alone with him," I whispered.

Norma splashed water on her face. "You've got to talk to the man."

"I don't know where to begin. I'm afraid of what could happen. This isn't the time, either. I have a job. I'm making money. I need to get Raven back first."

She snagged a towel off the sink and patted her face. "Life doesn't work that way. He's in your life for a reason. That reason is to help you."

I chewed a nail. "What if he judges me? What if he doesn't like me?"

"Start at the beginning. Tell him the story. Tell him how mad you still are. Tell him all those things you told me. You did nothing wrong. Life always gets complicated, and Ruby, you've had one fucked-up life. Make things right now. He could be your savior." Sorrow flooded her brown eyes.

I couldn't argue. I had many things to atone for. More than anything, Raven came first. "I want to be my own savior. I want to prove to myself that I can make it on my own. I'm tired of relying on people to take care of me. My mother did a good job of that, but look where it got her and me." As much as a knight in shining armor sounded like my ticket to a better future, I had to fix my own depressing plight. If I didn't, I wouldn't be my own person. I wanted that feeling of confidence back.

"I know, sweetie. But Kross is the father, right? He deserves the truth. At the very least, start a dialogue. Reconnect. Then take it one step at a time. Okay?"

I nodded. One step did sound like something I could do rather than detailing the last four years in one sitting. The nausea building inside me didn't agree. Or maybe I was just hungry. "If he threatens me again, I'm done."

"Fair enough. Now, come on. I'll be in the bakery while you two talk." She grabbed my hand. "You'll do fine."

I wasn't so sure of that.

Before I could calm my trembling hands, she pulled me into the living room. Kross was leaning against the window that overlooked the street below.

Norma released my hand. "Come get me when you two are done."

"You can stay," I blurted out as my pulse quickened. I felt the need to go back an hour to the empty silence of the warehouse, listening to the cat complain. Even turning back time three weeks when Norma and I had been living on the streets seemed like a better option. Sure, being homeless wasn't easy, but at the moment, it sure seemed easier than what I was facing now.

When the door clicked shut, I flinched. A heavy silence stretched between Kross and me as I held onto the arm of the couch. We were two people who had known each other well, who had explored each other's bodies, learning how sex should go, telling each other things about likes, dislikes, and what we dreamed about, and we couldn't even speak. He was probably waiting for me to say something. After all, he'd asked me about a baby, and while I knew deep, deep down that he deserved to know about Raven, I was at a loss for words. I was also frightened out of my freaking mind with what-ifs. What if he fought for custody of Raven? He could take her away from me completely, especially when he learned that I'd been homeless and could very well be again if Alex kicked me out. Not only that, but my brain couldn't function with his intimidating stature in the tiny apartment. All six feet of him exuded sexiness—his unshaven jaw, messy hair, ripped jeans, and muscles I knew rippled underneath his clothes.

I needed space and air.

"I'm here to listen," he said. "I'm not going to force you to give me answers. If you're not ready to talk, then I'm okay with that."

My fingers dug into the plaid fabric of the couch as I lowered my gaze. "So you're not going to put out an APB on me?"

"I deserved that. I'm sorry." His attitude had certainly changed overnight. "Do you hate me that much?"

I jerked my head up then scrunched my nose. As much as I didn't want to be in this apartment with him, I could never hate him. In my mind, that would mean I would hate my daughter, who was a mini Kross. The only feature Raven had of mine was her small nose. She even had one lone dimple in her right cheek like her daddy. A tear snuck out suddenly. I quickly dashed it away.

"Kross, can we go for a walk? I promise I won't do a disappearing act. You can even hold my hand." I smiled. The feel of his skin on mine would be nice. On second thought, it wouldn't. I would want more, and I couldn't have more. I wasn't as beautiful as his girlfriend, and I certainly didn't have the emotional backbone to deal with my feelings.

I diverted my gaze to the shag carpet.

In three strides, he was standing in front of me. He touched my chin then gently guided it up. "You're still shy. I've always loved that about you."

I wanted to say, "Careful, you might not love everything I have to say."

"I'd rather be in a quiet place," he said. "The streets are too loud. Why don't we go to my apartment?"

I inched back, shaking my head like a wet dog. "No. I'd feel more comfortable outside." I wanted to go back to the abandoned warehouse where I'd slept earlier. No one would be there. But if I took him there, he would judge me. *Make him feel what you feel. Show him your life. If he judges, then you'll know where you stand.* "Actually, I know a quiet place." If we were about to talk, I had to be on my turf.

CHAPTER 11
KROSS

The same burnt car I'd seen the other night appeared stark against the graffiti-strewn walls of the desolate buildings lining both sides of the street. In the distance, the Boston Harbor loomed with its dark water, rippling with the light wind.

After we'd informed Norma of what we were doing, we walked in silence. Many times during our trek, I'd wanted to take Ruby up on her offer to hold her hand. Not that I was afraid she would run from me, but I wanted to squeeze her hand, let her know I was there for her and that I wasn't the scared sixteen-year-old boy who had run with his tail between his legs. But I chickened out, afraid of the contact of her skin on mine and what it would do to me.

"Why here?" I asked when we arrived at an abandoned warehouse.

"My turf."

A black-and-white cat darted across the road and into the building closest to the harbor.

"Are we at war?" I kept my tone playful, but in reality, I wasn't kidding. From my standpoint, she didn't want anything to do with me, and I wanted answers that she wasn't giving up. *If you hadn't been a dick, threatening her with the cops and stalking her like a freak, she might've talked to you last night.*

Lifting her delicate shoulders, she gave me a half smile. "Maybe.

Look, you want to talk, and I feel comfortable in places like this." She followed the path of the cat.

I silently cursed for many reasons. The idea that she was comfortable in neighborhoods like the one we were in sent a dagger straight through my chest. But what kept driving that sharp blade clear through to my back was the fact that her life had not turned out as she'd dreamed. She'd been a skilled and beautiful ballerina. She'd lit up every time she talked about her dream of performing for the New York City Ballet one day.

A blast of fish odor, motor oil, and a strong scent of urine burned the hair in my nostrils as I walked into the warehouse. *Good God.* I choked.

My phone buzzed as Ruby headed toward a room that was carved into the far corner.

"What?" I said sharply into the phone as my voice bounced off the cement walls, echoing several times.

"Bro, calm down. I just wanted to make sure you were all right," Kelton said. "Lizzie got worried when you bolted out the door. It's way too early in the morning for you to be up. What's going on? Is it Ruby?"

I hung my head. "Sorry I bit your head off. I'm with Ruby, but she won't talk to me." I tried to lower my voice, but the emptiness of the building wasn't my friend. I shrugged. If Ruby was listening, I couldn't do anything about it unless I left the building. But I didn't want to. I wasn't hiding anything from her. If she was going to trust me or even open up to me, then she should know how I feel. Sure, I should be telling her instead of Kelton, but at the moment, I needed my brother's advice. "I'm not sure how much more I can take."

"You should talk to Dad," he said. "Or Kade."

I barked out a laugh. "My brother Kelton is now giving sound advice. This is one for the books. Harvard suits you. Or I should say Lizzie suits you." Kelton's way of dealing with shit was pulling on his hair or punching his fists through walls. The latter wasn't such a bad idea, but I couldn't risk breaking or fracturing my hand like he had done not that long ago, not with my boxing career on the line.

"I'm not an expert, but give her space. When she's ready, she'll talk to you."

I almost laughed again. He was the second or third person to give me that advice. "You didn't let Lizzie be. Besides, we're Maxwells. We don't walk away, especially from family." I was getting ahead of myself. I still didn't know if I was a father. Nevertheless, I would do anything and everything to help Ruby and Norma get off the streets. Norma had confirmed that they'd been homeless until that waitress, Alex, had taken them in.

Man, Dillon was rubbing off on me. After hanging out with him and listening to his business plan for a homeless shelter for girls in need, I couldn't help but admire the dude. I'd told him I wanted to help him in any way I could, although I'd never imagined I would be in a real-life situation with a homeless girl, especially one that had a small home in my heart.

"You never stopped caring for her, did you?" Kelton asked.

"Seeing her after all these years, I don't know. She's beautiful, Bro." Even battered and bruised, the sight of her had given me goose bumps. "She still makes my stomach do crazy things." When she had crashed into me with those drinks, my body had heated and my heartbeat had pounded all over the place. It was as though I'd bumped into her for the first time all over again. Her skin was soft beneath my touch. Her blue-green eyes flashed with a look that told me she wanted me as much as I wanted her. It was then I had wanted to show her how much of a man I'd become—a man who was dedicated, responsible, protective, caring, and had a heart.

Kelton chuckled. "The stomach thing is the first to go before you drop to your knees and worship her. Good to hear that my brother may be falling for a girl. Later, dude."

I chuckled. Ruby and I had millions of miles separating our lives with problems stacked so high in between us, I wasn't sure we would ever meet in the middle.

Pocketing my phone, I crossed the vast expanse of the trash-ridden floor to the room I'd seen Ruby duck into. Broken windows helped to infuse the building with a light scent of salt air from the harbor, which masked the acrid scent that was attached to my nostrils.

"Is this where you live?" Ruby's voice filtered out of the room.

I poked in my head to find her talking to the black-and-white cat that was perched on a sink. Ruby was petting him, then she sneezed.

I stopped in the doorway. "Bless you."

The room appeared to have been a lunchroom. In addition to the sink, a picnic table and a dented fridge were scattered about.

She dragged her hands down her jeans. "I'm allergic."

"I remember." The academy had a stray cat or two, and she'd always petted the creatures even though her allergies got the best of her.

Her gaze met mine. "You think I'm beautiful?"

"Eavesdropping?" I smirked, but inside, I was jumping up and down for joy. "Yes."

"Even when you found me fighting?"

The cat hopped down, brushed against my leg, then slinked away.

"Honestly, yes."

She looked away, biting her lower lip ever so gently. *Fuck.* My body came alive. One minute, she could be spunky, then the next, she was shy. That combination made my blood heat in ways I hadn't felt since I'd been with her. Since we were sixteen, dancing under the stars, cuddling under a blanket on cold nights near the Greenridge Academy football field while I played with her hair or kissed her body anywhere she would let me.

Calm the fuck down, dude. Shit, no girls I'd been with since Ruby made me feel the high I was experiencing at the moment. "So, I'm on your turf. Do we duke it out now?" I teased. I wanted to be that lower lip so fucking bad, I had to conjure up images of punching my opponent in a ring. Kelton had told me he always recited a mantra of sports or some shit when his dick wasn't cooperating. I'd laughed at him. Now I was laughing at myself.

She puffed out her chest. "I might be able to kick your butt in the ring."

I turned one side of my mouth upward. "Is that so? Maybe we should head down to the gym. I'd love to get you in the ring." I'd love to do more than box, but that wouldn't happen. Not now, anyway. Fuck if I wasn't a pervert at the moment. I wanted answers, yet all I was doing was thinking about the physical and not in an emotional, professional, or friendly manner.

She dropped her gaze. "I'm fighting again on Saturday. I might take you up on that offer."

"What?" I pinched my eyebrows. "You can't." My tone was hard. I didn't want to watch her get her butt kicked again. She'd been all over the place with her punches while her opponent had been determined to knock Ruby's lights out. Not only that, people died in illegal underground fighting. On the boxing circuit, I heard all kinds of stories about those who hadn't made it out alive. "You'll get hurt." The only good move she'd exhibited was her footwork. But that wouldn't get her far since she didn't know how to anticipate her opponent's next move. "Also, you shouldn't be working for Tommy. The dude is into some bad shit. If you need money—"

Her rosy cheeks darkened. "Don't." A snarl cut through her pretty face. "Don't you dare. I can take care of myself. You think you can ride in on your high horse and save me? Well, news flash. You can't. And another news flash. You were the one who got me into trouble with Tommy."

I raised my hands. "I'm sorry about that. I'll talk to him."

"No. Stay out of it."

"Look, I'm offering my help."

"No, you're not. You're bossing me around, something I recall you and your brothers doing a lot of with kids at the academy." She huffed then sank back against the sink, holding herself. "Why didn't you return my calls?"

I stretched my neck. "Why did you tell me you weren't pregnant if you were?"

Her gaze was steadfast, piercing as she popped off the sink. "If you only tracked me down to find out if I was pregnant, then get out of my life." She blew past me, bumping her shoulder into my bicep.

I caught her wrist. "Wait."

"For what? You don't want to know how I'm doing. You haven't even asked me. You want one thing, and I'm sorry. I can't give it to you. If you're looking for a baby, then you'll be looking for a ghost."

My pulse kicked into high gear. "Are you saying we don't have a child?" Over the last two weeks, I had grown accustomed to the idea that I could be a dad.

She closed her eyes, her delicate nostrils flaring.

I used that brief moment to wrap my arms around her. Then I tensed every muscle in my body, waiting for the onslaught of whatever she was about to dish out, whether emotionally or physically.

But she didn't fight. She didn't run. She didn't even protest. She wrapped her arms around my waist. She sniffled as she buried her head into my chest as though she was trying to get inside of me. I rested my chin on her head, inhaling a faint aroma of strawberries. Her scent took me back four years when being with her made me smile, made me temporarily forget death, my sister, my mom's problems, and everything else our family had been through.

"Please, Ruby. Talk to me. I've been a crazed man for two weeks. I don't know which way is up anymore. I can't box. I can't sleep. I can't do anything. I've got to know if I'm a father."

She jerked out of my hold. Emotion after emotion shuddered across her face with fury taking the lead. "Again, you're not going to ask me how I've been?" Her voice rose, almost blaring as a tear slipped down her face. "You left me, Kross. You went back to your life. Not once did you return my calls. Not once did you even write a letter. If you didn't want anything to do with me, then why didn't you man up? All that bravado you and your brothers exuded, and you couldn't even tell a girl you didn't want to see her anymore?" She shook her head in either disgust or pity. It didn't matter which because she was so fucking right. "I thought we were friends, and friends don't just leave without even a good-bye." She pursed her chapped lips together. "So many calls. So many nights I didn't sleep. I cried for months. Everything changed after I told you I loved you. Was I just a piece of meat? The time we spent together, didn't it mean something?"

I'd been nowhere near falling in love with any girl. "You know how fucking scared I was when you said you missed your period? Don't you remember what I was going through with my family? My mom? I couldn't get serious with anyone."

"You could've at least told me we were done. Instead, you drove away, not even looking back."

"Damn it." My voice shook. "You lied to me."

Her expression hardened. "I never lied to you. You never gave me a chance to tell you what I needed to tell you."

I opened my arms. "Well, I'm standing here now."

"Now is not good enough. You can't fix me. You can't change the last four years. The high and mighty Maxwell brothers. You boys thought your shit didn't stink. You and your brothers got any girl you wanted. But *you* zeroed in on me. Did I have a sign on my forehead that said, 'I'm a sucker. Pick me.'" She growled. "Well guess what? You can't waltz into my life and think I'm going to drop everything for you or tell you what you want to know. I suffered. Now you can." She stuck out her chin. "When you're ready to have a conversation about us and not a baby, then you know where to find me." With her head held high, she crossed the large warehouse floor, her footsteps thumping as fast as my pulse.

I pounded my fist against a cement column. *Fuck. Fuck. Fuck.* I'd told her I was sorry. I wasn't sure what else to do.

The echo of her footsteps began to fade.

"Ruby! I don't want to fix you." I said it so fucking loud that my voice sounded like a sonic boom. "I was serious when I told my brother Kelton on the phone earlier that you were beautiful. After all these years, the sight of you still gets me hot." Dirty, clean, pale, glowing, curvy, or rail thin, her presence did something to me. I chalked up the fluttering feeling to the beauty in her eyes, the spots of freckles that dotted her cheeks, and a smile that could knock me to the ground in one second.

Her retreating form stopped near the door.

I sighed heavily as I ran to her. "That's the truth." I prayed she heard the conviction in my voice. I knew she didn't know Kross, the man. She only knew Kross, the boy, the sixteen-year-old who hadn't seen past his own problems to open up to a girl. Sure, we'd talked about my family, but I'd never gone into detail about how I felt when my sister died or how I'd felt when my mom had entered into a mental health facility. I never could bring myself to say 'I love you,' not when I was confused and wasn't sure. Even so, Ruby held a place in my heart. She'd been my shining star amid the darkness in my life.

She turned to face me, her expression tempered, although her bottom lip quivered every now and then.

"I'm the one who needs to be fixed." I pointed to my chest. "I'm the one who's the jerk. I'm sorry for not calling you back. When I was up at the academy a few weeks ago, I went to look for you to apologize for being a royal dick." I closed the distance between us until four inches separated us. "I can't change the past. I know I don't deserve your attention, but I would like to start somewhere. I want to get to know *you* again." It was the truth, and not just because I needed answers about a kid.

She locked her fingers together. "Why? What's changed?"

"The butterflies for one." I grinned. "They're crazier than when I first met you at the academy." Another truth.

She glanced away. "Don't do that."

I placed my forefinger under her chin. "Do what?"

She slowly peered up at me. "Flash me that dimple of yours."

I frowned teasingly, my heart swelling with happiness that I still affected her.

"I'm homeless, Kross. I'm not beautiful like you think I am or like your girlfriend. I've only been sleeping at Alex's place for three days.

I'm not sure how much longer that will last. So don't you dare feel sorry for me or offer me a place. I'm just laying out my cards. If you want to get to know me again, then you need to know empty, abandoned buildings are my home. Dark alleys are comforting to me. I walk miles around the city. I eat out of dumpsters. I beg for change. All that is part of my daily routine."

A knife-like pain twisted several ways inside my chest. I hated that her life hadn't turned out as she'd planned. "Then I'll sleep in this warehouse with you. I'll roam the streets with you." I was so fucking serious. I couldn't change who Ruby was, but I could show her how serious I was about rekindling our relationship.

Her mouth fell open briefly. "I'm not sure I believe you." She studied me with caution.

"Okay, then pick a spot, and we'll sleep there tonight. On one condition, though."

"Ha, I knew it. What is it with deals? First Tommy and now you."

I clenched my jaw. "Is he making you fight?"

"I'm fighting because I want to. So what's your angle?"

It was my turn to study her and the trepidation glued to her face. It might have been too much to ask her to spend the afternoon with me. I had to take baby steps or else I would lose any chance of getting answers or building a friendship—two things I needed and wanted. More importantly, I had to give her some space. Hell, I had to give myself time to regroup. I'd been sick to my stomach during the last two weeks. I also had to trust that if there was a child, he was safe. Ruby didn't strike me as a person who would be an irresponsible mother.

"I'd like for you to come down to the gym this week so I can show you some boxing moves. If you insist on fighting, then let me teach you a move or two."

She pressed a finger to her lip. "Okay, but I'm there to learn, not for you to give me the third degree about my past." She steeled her shoulders.

Another step in the right direction. "Do we shake on it?" *Or maybe kiss on it.*

She edged back. "No touching."

"Earlier, you had your arms around me," I said playfully.

She gave me one of her shy looks that turned me on. *Fuck me.* She was making it hard for me to be a gentleman.

CHAPTER 12
RUBY

Norma and I were on our way to Crandall's Gym. I'd filled her in on my conversation with Kross. I'd asked her to accompany me because I didn't want to go alone. It wasn't that I was afraid of Kross. I was more afraid that I would run the moment I walked through the gym doors. For the last three days, I'd been a nervous wreck, dropping drinks, biting my nails, tossing and turning at night. I'd replayed the conversation with Kross over and over again. I couldn't get past his admission of how beautiful I was or how he still got butterflies when he was around me. Yet I had to guard my heart. I couldn't let his charm, his blue eyes, or anything about him woo me into a spell that would lead to hurt and heartache. Until I knew what would happen when he learned about Raven, I wasn't risking her heart, particularly if he got cold feet and ran again. Or worse, took Raven from me.

"I can't stay long. I picked up a shift tonight," Norma said in a tone cold enough to match the weather.

"You're still mad because I'm fighting on Saturday." It was more of a statement than a question. I promised her I wouldn't fight—desperate times and all that. "I'm sorry I broke my promise, but we could use two thousand dollars." If I didn't fight, I could also lose my waitressing job.

She pulled her knitted hat down over her ears. "You're not going to win, Ruby. You have no idea what the hell you're doing. That girl you fought last time knocked you out. I can't handle that."

We drew to a stop in front of a pawnshop across the street from Crandall's Gym.

"I was scared out of my mind when you didn't wake up. Frankly, Kross shouldn't let you do this."

I mashed my lips together so hard it hurt. "First, I'm here to learn a few moves from a guy who boxes for a living," I said as nicely as I could. She was worried. I got that. I didn't want to fuel her fire. The more she got upset, the more I got upset, and I needed my head clear so I could put all my energy into winning the fight on Saturday. "Second, you've said yourself that women shouldn't let men boss them around. You hated when your pimp told you what to do."

"Kross isn't a pimp," she yelled above the brisk wind.

I tugged on my scarf. "He doesn't own me. This is my life." As screwed up as it was, I had to make my own decisions. For too long, my mom had made all the decisions while I took care of Raven. It was time for me to take control. Whether I made good or bad decisions, they were mine to own up to. While fighting might not have been the best decision, it was an opportunity to make money. "You're supposed to be my friend."

"I am your friend. Friends tell each other when they don't agree with something. Damn it, Ruby. Think. Think about Raven. Not only could you get hurt badly, but Tommy's fights are illegal. Do you want to do jail time like your parents?"

Screw trying to keep my anger at bay. I narrowed my eyes into slits so small, I could barely see her. "I am thinking about my daughter. I am trying everything I can to get a steady job so I can find a place to live." Norma was right, which was why I was so darn angry at myself more than I was at her. "I'm fighting. End of story." I had to go through with the fight. I'd committed to it. Tommy said I could be good. More importantly, if I won, then I wouldn't lose my job, which meant we could get an apartment, and in turn, I could get Raven back. Alex's hospitality would only go so far.

"If you fight, I'll tell Kross about Raven."

My jaw came unhinged. "Why are you so insistent on Kross knowing about Raven? Why? Tell me now." We'd only been friends for two months, and I didn't know everything about Norma. I knew she ran away from home. I knew she'd been a hooker. She rarely talked about her family. When I'd asked her why she ran away, she'd said her parents were too strict.

A teardrop slid down her wind-burned cheek as she moved to lean against the pawnshop. Then she bent over to hold her stomach.

"What's going on?" I asked gently. Norma hardly got emotional. She was the strong one in our friendship.

She straightened, sweeping her blond bangs to the side. Tears rushed out. "I ran away from home at fifteen because I was pregnant. I didn't want anyone to know. I didn't want my parents to look at me and be disappointed." She sucked in her lip ring. "I lost the baby, Ruby. I was running from some creep who was chasing me one night. I turned down a dark street, and I didn't see the stairs. I fell head first. Next thing I knew, I was bleeding." She sobbed, crouching down until her butt met the pavement. "To this day, I haven't told my parents."

My chest tightened. "I'm sorry. I know the feeling." Tears burned behind my eyelids, not only for Norma's pain, but for mine.

"What do you mean?"

I grabbed hold of her hands. "I was pregnant with twins. Raven had a sister. But she didn't make it. Riley was stillborn from a genetic defect, according to the doctors."

She reached out and hugged me, practically tackling me to the ground. "If I hadn't run away from home, if only I'd been brave enough to tell my parents, then the baby would still be alive." She sobbed in my ear, drowning out the sounds of a passing car.

I focused on the closed sign in the window of the pawnshop and rubbed her back, much like my mom had done after the doctor took Riley away. "I'm here for you." The pain of losing a baby, whether from a miscarriage or stillbirth, hurt. But when compounded with the *what-ifs*, it made healing an uphill battle. Sometimes, I thought God had punished me for not trying harder to find Kross and tell him I was pregnant. "I go through all the scenarios of what would've happened if Kross would've returned my calls, or if he would've been with me when Raven was born. I'm not sure my life would've turned out differently."

Her sobs became sniffles. I eased back and wiped away a tear from her face.

"I love that you're worried about Raven. I am too. But she's with a good family." I'd met them briefly on my last supervised visit two weeks before. The couple had smiled and waved at me. Sure, outward appearances could be deceiving, but Raven had seemed happy, talking about the dolls her foster mom had bought her, and the books they'd read to her before bed. Tears stung. I wanted to be the one reading to my daughter. *Damn it.* I squeezed my eyes shut, collecting my emotions. I couldn't go into the gym with red eyes and a splotchy face. Kross would probably think Tommy had done something to hurt me, then Tommy and Kross would scuffle. Then Tommy would fire me for sure. "You're right. I shouldn't fight. But Tommy thinks I'm good. Maybe Kross can help me get better. Maybe I can make fighting a career."

She scrunched her red nose. "Do you like getting hit?"

"I like the adrenaline rush." I would rather dance, but that door had closed a long time ago. Ballet dancers usually peaked somewhere in their mid-twenties, and those were the ones who had been practicing consistently since they were kids. If I couldn't be a dancer, I would love to maybe teach ballet someday.

"Ruby, I regret what I did. I don't want you—"

"Nothing is going to happen to me. Except some cuts and bruises."

"If something did, then Raven would be without a mom, and Kross wouldn't know his daughter."

I cocked my head and grinned. "I'm sure you'll be the first one to tell him." I had no doubt that Norma wouldn't hesitate to introduce Kross to Raven.

She gave me a tentative smile and a heavy sigh. "I'm sorry for getting all emotional. I've kept that secret to myself all these years."

"I'm glad you told me. But maybe it's time your parents knew."

She shook her head vigorously. "No effing way. I don't want to see the pity on their faces or take the chance they don't want to see me. They probably hate me."

I lifted my eyebrows. If that was how she felt, then I wanted to tell her not to be so insistent on telling me to inform Kross about Raven. Instead, I said, "I bet they would love to see you. Maybe it's time to put the past to rest."

She wiped her hand underneath her nose. "Tell you what. You come clean with Kross, then I'll reach out to my parents."

I looked at her for a long moment. "I'm late. I should get inside." I dashed across the quiet street.

"You're avoiding me," she said, following closely on my heels.

I opened the door to the gym and smacked right into a Kross look-a-like. He wasn't Kross because he didn't have the large muscular arms.

Sure, he was buff with a gray Harvard T-shirt stretched across his toned chest, but he didn't have a snake inked on his forearm like his brother.

His blue gaze sized me up as he moved out of the way to let me enter. "Ruby, right?"

Okay, so he wasn't Kody either since Kody and I had met at Firefly, and he would've remembered me.

The man in front of me sported a cocky grin as he eyed Norma, who glided in and stood beside me. "I'm Kelton. Do you remember me?"

I wanted to laugh hysterically. Their unabashed attitudes and their arrogance at the academy were hard to forget. Girls had followed them around school, trying to get their attention. They had made a name for themselves, not only because of their good looks, but they'd been in the principal's office on a daily basis for acting out in class, telling a teacher off, or getting into fights.

"Norma, this is Kelton Maxwell. The other triplet." I punctuated the last three words in a snooty tone. Kelton and I didn't get along back then. He'd sat behind me in two of my classes and tried to play with my hair every chance he had. But when he'd outright sniffed my hair, I'd whirled around in my seat and slapped him. He'd laughed. I'd gotten detention.

"You still hate me. It's been four years, Ruby." His grin screamed arrogance. "I see you still have long hair."

I clenched my fists.

"Hi," Norma said.

Kelton laughed. I walked away.

"Nice to see you again, Ruby," he said to my back.

"He's a bit pompous," Norma said at my side. "But really hot."

A potent smell of sweat and man penetrated my nostrils as we stood at the empty check-in desk. Grunts, shouts, and clangs sounded. Men and women worked out on weights, rowing machines, and treadmills. I squinted at the bright lights as nostalgia swept me from the room.

Spotlights had shone down as I danced to music of Tchaikovsky, practicing for my role in the Sleeping Beauty performance.

"Cut the music," Ms. March shouted, her voice echoing throughout the auditorium.

I stopped. "Am I doing something wrong?" She'd been riding me for two solid months about my form, my attitude, and my smile.

"Head up and shoulders back," Ms. March said.

I wanted to tell her I was exhausted, but that would only fuel her ire. Then she would have made me practice another two hours. I understood her strict teaching. If I looked good in front of an auditorium of people, then so did she. Above everything, I didn't want to disappoint myself. I had to be perfect. The artistic director of Joffrey Ballet School in New York would be present for my performance.

"Can we take a break?" I had desperately needed some water.

An elbow pushed into my side, startling me back to the present. "Kross is over there." Norma's voice registered as Ms. March's waned. Norma tipped her chin to the left.

Kross was sparring with a young brown-haired boy, who looked to be in high school. I watched in quiet fascination at the lithe way Kross danced around his opponent. I was mentally taking notes for my bout on Saturday.

"Look at him move," Norma said in awe, or maybe she was drooling.

I couldn't blame her. Kross's body was covered in a sheen of sweat, highlighting the way his muscles rippled every time he jabbed. He was so much bigger now than when we were in school. *Hey, idiot, he's a man now. A very large and sexy man.* Actually, he was more like a sexy beast. My stomach fluttered as I licked my lips. "Maybe I should go." I couldn't take boxing lessons from him. I could, however, take kissing lessons or something more.

"You afraid you might give in to him?" Norma's voice held giddiness.

I would have loved to have given him every inch of me. "Not a chance."

She giggled. "Liar."

I bit my lip as I willed the tornado in my stomach to calm the heck down.

A short, bald man who had his back to us threw up his hands. "God damn it, Kross. Get your fucking act together. Hit Liam like you mean it. Reggie is going to pummel you into oblivion."

Kross stretched his neck one way then the other. Liam bounced on his feet before throwing a punch. His gloved fist landed square in Kross's jaw.

"Your footwork is lacking, Kross," a guy with a ponytail next to the coach said.

Kross growled before he lunged at Liam. One fist hit Liam's nose. The next one hit his mouth. Liam raised his forearms as Kross let loose a series of jabs and hooks.

"That's it. Keep that footwork going," the coach said with pride in his voice.

"Liam, fight back," I shouted. As soon as the words left me, I slapped a hand over my mouth. I should have been rooting for Kross, but I always liked to root for the underdog.

Kross whipped his head in my direction. When he did, Liam landed a left hook into Kross's face. Kross stumbled backward into the ropes. Ponytail guy and the coach shot fiery glares at me. All the sounds in the gym died. I scanned the room and found that all eyes were on me. Suddenly, I wanted to crawl into a dark hole.

"Isn't that the ponytail guy who was with Kross at your fight? Dillon, right?" Norma asked with way too much excitement in her voice. "Alex likes him. Maybe he's the one she's been spending time with. I'm not one to step into a girl's territory, but for him, I might have to."

"I'm leaving."

"No, you're not." Norma blocked me with her body. "Two thousand dollars."

I briefly closed my eyes. *Money. Lots of money. You can do this.* At the moment, I hated my subconscious and Norma.

"One minute, you don't want me to fight. The next, you're encouraging me. Is it because you're foaming at the mouth for Dillon?"

"In all honesty," she said, "no. Sure, he's hot, but if you're in that ring with Kross, then you have a chance to win."

Kross held his jaw as he glanced my way with a blank expression. Dillon, on the other hand, swaggered over with a gym bag in his hand. His brown gaze appraised Norma and me. "I didn't think you would show." His voice was husky. "I'm Dillon Hart. I was at your fight with Kross. We never officially met, though."

"Why does Tommy hate you?" Nerves sometimes caused me to stick my foot in my mouth or babble.

"Ruby," Norma said. "Sorry. My friend says weird shit when she gets nervous."

"It's still true. Tommy is also afraid of you," I said.

Dillon chuckled. "We have a long history."

It had to be quite a history. Then again, it really wasn't any of my business.

Dillon handed me the gym bag. "Kross would like you to change into workout gear while he finishes up."

I stood dumbfounded as I fixated on the gym bag.

"It's okay. It's just clothes," Dillon said. "You'll have more flexibility in the workout gear than your jeans."

Norma grabbed the bag. "Thanks."

Oh my God. No one had bought me anything in years, not since Raven was born. The money my mom had made had gone to purchase diapers, formula, and clothes for Raven.

"Locker room is behind the boxing ring," Dillon said.

Norma dragged me with her as we headed in that direction. As we passed the boxing ring, Kross grinned at me, his lone dimple popping out. I blew out a breath. I couldn't get in the ring with him. The minute he touched me was the minute I would cave. That wouldn't be so bad, would it? Or I could look at this another way. *I get to take out my anger on him.* Suddenly, I couldn't wait to get in that ring.

CHAPTER 13
KROSS

Kade, Dillon, and I were huddled outside the ring. I was waiting on Ruby to emerge from the ladies' locker room. Kade had been working out with Kelton earlier and wanted to meet Ruby. My sparring partner, Liam, had cut out early to study for an exam he had the next day at the academy. Jay had retreated to his office to finalize a date and time for my upcoming fight with Reggie Stockman. But my fight, which was my vie to impress Gail Freeman, wasn't in the forefront of my mind even though it should have been. For the last year, Jay and I had worked tirelessly, entering every fight we could so I could get exposure. But the last two promoters weren't interested. They'd said I wasn't ready, and that I still had much to learn before I faced the champions on the circuit. Hence, Jay was down my throat constantly. I didn't blame him. I wanted a boxing contract as badly as he did. He'd worked just as hard and lost sleep at night, trying to get me ready.

But Ruby was on my mind twenty-four, seven. How could I build trust with her? Would she show? Would we argue again? Would she open up to me? So between Jay's yelling and my mind wandering, my footwork sucked. My jabs were weak at best, and Liam was in a better position than me to fight Reggie Stockman.

Kade snapped his fingers. "Bro, are you with us?"

I tore my gaze away from the locker room door, blowing out a breath. "Maybe you should meet her another time." I was afraid Kade might scare her. Sometimes, he could be quite imposing to a stranger.

Kade wiped his face with the towel he was holding then threw on a T-shirt. "I'll say 'hi' then leave."

"And you?" I asked Dillon.

"I'm curious if she'll change into the clothes you bought her. When I gave her the bag, I got the impression she thought there was a bomb in the bag."

"A little dramatic, don't you think?" Even though his comment didn't surprise me, I had to try. Ruby had said she didn't want a hand-out. If she was sticking to her guns and fighting at Tommy's trashy dive, then I wanted her to be able to move freely. It was easier to throw a punch or a kick without the weight of heavy boots or tight jeans. At least in my mind, wearing street clothes to fight was like trying to swim in wet clothes. The fabric just got heavier with each stroke.

"In all seriousness," Dillon said, "I wanted to tell you one of my rooms at the house just opened up. I'd like to offer it to Ruby and her friend if you're okay with that. It will be months before the building I bought is transformed into a place for runaways."

Man, Dillon had to be an angel in disguise. At first sight, he came off as a scary dude. He normally kept the scruff off his face, his hair was tied back into a ponytail, his body was tatted up, and he had piercings in his nose and ears, as well as a new one in his lip.

"Thanks, dude. I'll ask, but I highly doubt it." Ruby wanted to be her own person. "She's staying with that waitress Alex at Firefly."

Dillon winced when I said Alex's name. Kade and I exchanged a confused look. The words "care to elaborate on Alex" started to fall from my lips when a door creaked open, drawing my attention away from Dillon.

Ruby glided out of the locker room with Norma holding her arm. Ruby's auburn hair was tied up in a ponytail, and she was wearing the clothes I'd bought for her. I grinned like an ass. I had to thank Lizzie for knocking the clothes size out of the park. I'd enlisted her help, giving her a description of Ruby, which was similar to Lizzie, except Ruby was shorter than she was.

Clothes sizes aside, I drank in every curve on Ruby. Each one was accentuated in the tight-fitting sports bra and yoga pants that hugged her body. I shut down a growl that clamored in my throat. Her breasts were bigger than I remembered.

I couldn't wait to get her in the ring. If she was still as nimble as she'd been in high school, I was in for a treat. Back at the academy, I couldn't take my eyes off her when she'd practiced ballet. She'd moved to the music with grace and beauty. *But nimrod, you're not here to salivate like a guy who can't keep his dick in his pants.* I tensed every muscle in my body. I was in for a tough hour. Control would be the key as I trained her.

Hot air brushed over my ear as Dillon spoke. "Close your mouth, dude. It's rude to drool like a starved man."

I *was* a starved man. Starved for her touch, her kiss, or whatever she would give me, especially the truth of what had happened to her in the last four years. I waved her over. Norma stopped her and whispered something to her. Ruby shied away from Norma, biting her lip.

Motherfucker. Blood rushed to my dick.

"Don't forget to ask her about my place," Dillon said. "You should also talk her out of the fight. That shit is dangerous."

"Bro." Kade blocked my view of Ruby. "Are you listening to Dillon?"

"I got it. Place. Fight. Dangerous." I scrubbed a palm over my mouth. "I'll do my best, but I can guarantee you she won't listen to me." *She has no reason to trust me. She thinks I boss her around as it is.*

Dillon slapped me on the back. "I'm sure you will." Then he leaned into Kade and whispered, "Your brother has it bad for her. He recited some Star Light shit to her the first night he found her. He could've gotten me to drop my pants after that romantic spiel. Maybe I should get in the ring with her, Kross. You're not in any shape to train her."

"Get out of here." My tone sounded a little lethal. "No one is touching her except me."

Kade grinned. "I believe Dillon is right. You're smitten."

"Call the love police," I bit out. "Now, do you want to meet her before I kick everyone out of here?" The gym was thinning out, and I would be locking the doors soon. I'd planned our meeting time so that Ruby and I could be alone.

"Remember what we talked about," Kade said. "Make her feel comfortable. Let her open up to you. Don't go all commando on her, or you'll never get answers."

The girls slowly sashayed over. Norma's mouth moved the entire time, and my stomach knotted the entire time.

"Did you decide if you're going to invite her to Thanksgiving dinner at our house?" Kade asked.

I'd thought long and hard about it. Mom and Dad would have questions: How did we meet? What did Ruby do? Was she in college? Where did she live? All those questions that parents usually asked. I wasn't sure they were ready to learn that Ruby had been homeless. I also wasn't ready to put Ruby or myself in an awkward situation. "I don't think she's ready. Nor are Mom and Dad."

Kade opened his mouth but quickly shut it when Ruby and Norma joined us. Norma waved at Dillon as if she was trying to get him to notice her. I wanted to check on Dillon's expression, but as Kade had said, I was smitten with the beauty next to me. Her light-blue sports bra brought out more of the blue in her blue-green eyes. Kelton had said Lizzie's eyes changed with the color of her clothes, and it drove him wild. I was learning from Kelton that we had several matching tastes when it came to women.

"Ruby and Norma, this is my older brother, Kade," I said.

Ruby flashed one of her ball-tightening smiles. My dick jerked inside my cup.

"Nice to finally meet you," Kade said. "Treat him with kid gloves in the ring, or else I'll have to live with his bruised ego."

Ruby kept her smile, and my dick kept growing. I was glad my cup was in place, although the fucker was beginning to pinch the side of my groin as I held back a groan.

"Hi, I'm Norma." She tucked a short strand of her blond hair behind her ear.

Kade smiled at her.

"All right, let's get to work." I grabbed the ropes as I eyed Ruby.

We either work or make out. One of the first times we'd made out had been in the academy's gym. I almost laughed out loud at the parallelism from the setting to the uneasiness between us. I wasn't an amateur when it came to a woman's body, but Ruby wasn't any woman. She was one who was breaking down my walls, igniting emotions that I'd kept dormant and hidden.

She blew out a breath then said good-bye to Norma. I did the same with Dillon and Kade.

After they left, Ruby and I didn't move until the sound of someone dropping a weight shattered the trance we were both in. My gaze darted to the weight area. Detective Rayburn was lifting. He'd returned from his assignment two days ago, but I didn't need his help anymore now that I'd found Ruby.

I pulled apart the ropes. "After you."

She hopped in the ring like an expert boxer. I followed, my limbs a tad unsteady.

"Why don't you get your muscles loose?" *I'll just stand here and drool.*

She gnawed her bottom lip.

"Okay, ground rules." She couldn't keep acting all shy or else I really would have her splayed out on the floor of the ring.

Penelope's voice filled the sparse gym. "I'm sorry I'm late." She giggled as she staggered toward us from the reception desk.

A chill slid down my spine because she was drunk or high on something. Detective Rayburn lowered the weight bar and whipped his blond head around.

"I thought you said you didn't have a girlfriend." Disappointment or jealousy or both rode Ruby's tone.

"She's only a client. I teach self-defense." But Penelope's appointment wasn't until tomorrow.

Mark ran to her side. "Whoa! Penelope. Are you okay?" He knew Penelope since he spotted for her whenever they were in the gym at the same time.

She waved him off. "Fine. Fine." She giggled again as she smoothed a hand down her miniskirt and kicked off her high heels. "Kross, you're supposed to teach me self-defense tonight."

"She's drunk," Ruby said.

She was on something. That was for sure.

"Stretch. I'll be back." My voice came out rougher than I'd intended.

As soon as I jumped out of the ring, Penelope threw her arms around me before I could get my feet on the floor. "I missed you," she cooed as she mashed her breasts into me.

What the fuck? I gently grabbed her arms and removed them from me. "Our appointment is tomorrow, and you're wasted." I didn't smell alcohol on her. "What are you on?" Her eyes appeared to be dilated. I hadn't known her to do drugs, but then again, I didn't know every detail about her.

She let go of me and wobbled.

"Easy," Mark said as he steadied her, his hazel eyes going wide.

Penelope peered up at Ruby with droopy eyelids. "Is that the drabby girl from Fireants? Raby, is it?" She snorted. "I heard him talk about you. Ooh, I feel dizzy."

"You heard who?" Ruby asked from above me.

"He..." She licked her lips. "The big guy." Her gaze drifted back to me.

She was probably talking about my interaction with Ruby at Firefly last week since Penelope had been there when I'd threatened Ruby.

Penelope swatted at air as she tilted her head back. "Kross, what's Raby have that I don't have?"

"It's Ruby," Ruby said with a sneer.

"I think she's tripping on something strong," Mark said. "I can take her home."

"Are you sure?" I hated to dump my problems on Mark.

A heavily accented voice drew our attention toward the entrance. "She owes me money." A thin older man with dark skin stood at the check-in desk.

Penelope hiccupped then swatted at air again. "Oh, yeah. Cabby. Oooh, that rhymes with Raby."

"I'll pay the cabby," I said.

"No, I got the cab." Mark hooked Penelope's arm through his as they made their way toward the check-in desk. "I jogged over here earlier, so I don't have my truck."

"Let me jot down her address." I trailed behind them. After I gave Mark Penelope's address, I ushered them to the door.

Before Penelope walked out, she gave me a chaste kiss on the lips. "We had fun." She swayed.

"We did," I said as I steadied her. "I'll see you tomorrow for training."

Mark gently took hold of her arm. "Let's go."

Once they were gone, I locked the door. I was thinking about what in the world Penelope could have been on when I banked left toward the ring. When I did, I wobbled to a stop, losing the air in my lungs.

Ruby was stretching in one of her ballet poses, standing on one foot with the other leg lifted toward the ceiling, holding the back of her thigh. After a long second or two, she lowered her leg then her entire body to the mat in one of those splits that gymnasts did. Another second passed. She bent over her leg, extending her arms out toward her foot. Man, those moves got the blood pumping through my veins.

Slowly pushing upright, she set her gaze on me. "What's wrong?" Immediately, she wrapped her arms around her midsection as though I had caught her naked. "You told me to stretch."

I shook my head. Naked. Stretches. That bare skin around her midriff only helped spur the fantasies going through my head. It was my fault she was dressed in that tight, revealing outfit. Women dressed like that all the time in a gym. But Ruby wasn't every woman. "Nothing. I was just thinking about Penelope." *Big, fat lie.* "I haven't known her to wig out on drugs."

She shrugged. "People do it all the time. I see a lot of homeless people who are junkies."

Reality roared back, quick and cold. I padded across the gym floor and hopped in the ring.

"What big guy do you think she was talking about?" Ruby asked.

"She was probably remembering when you and I were arguing in the hall at Firefly. Afterward, I called it quits with her. Let's forget about Penelope. So where were we?"

"You were about to go over ground rules," she said, letting go of her stomach.

Fuck ground rules. Whatever happened tonight happened, and I wasn't going to stress over anything else, including my dick, which wasn't cooperating. "Footwork. Let's start there. Keep moving around your opponent. The goal is to tire her out as you deliver each blow. The minute you stop is the minute she takes control and the minute you get knocked out. Like you did."

"That was your fault," she said in a not-so-nice tone. "You distracted me."

"No. You let your guard down," I said dryly.

"Because of you. You should practice what you preach. You let your guard down earlier when I was rooting for Liam."

I couldn't argue with her on that. "Why did you?" I was more curious than hurt.

"I don't know. He was the underdog, and maybe part of me wanted to get back at you."

"Fair enough. Now that we're even, let's talk about blocking." Fisting my hands, I raised them in front of my face so I was looking at my forearms. "Do as I do."

She did, and I gently grabbed her left wrist. "Hold this one in place to keep your face protected while you punch with your right.

The opposite works if you punch with your left hand." I stepped back. "Now throw a punch." She'd been wild when she fought at Tommy's before. I wanted her to be more controlled. "While you're punching, you're moving, and you're watching your opponent. She goes right, you go left, always keeping yourself protected. If she comes at you on the left, use your forearm to block her. Try a few moves on me."

She grinned as though she'd been waiting forever to hit me. I smirked but shouldn't have.

She threw a right hook that hit my jaw. "Not so tough, are you?" She puffed out her chest, sucking in her lip.

She could hit. I would give her that. "Again," I said in a serious tone before I tackled her to the mat. Her moves were turning me on. Just the way she danced on the balls of her feet was sexy.

For the next thirty minutes, Ruby used me as her punching bag. I blocked as she jabbed. I coached as she jabbed again. I couldn't say I was excited about her fighting, but at least now she had a few moves in her boxing bag of tricks.

"Okay." She wiped the sweat from her forehead with the back of her hand. "I think I got a couple of good moves." She sounded excited. "Thank you." She sank her teeth into her bottom lip.

My dick jerked. "Ruby, bite your lip again, and I will kiss you." For the last half hour, I had done my best to be the consummate professional. But I was hanging by a thread. *Fuck patience. Go on. Get what you want, and take what's yours.* That was always my motto. Certainly, acting like a gentleman was first and foremost, just as Kade and my old man had taught us boys. Hence, the warning my dad had ingrained in us: *Let a lady know your intentions.*

Ruby's tongue snaked out. "You're still impatient."

I moved until a paper-thin space separated us. "I'm not playing, Ruby." My voice was husky.

"Then kiss me. Unless you're afraid." Her shyness vanished as though she had flipped a switch to her sassy alter ego.

One side of my mouth twitched. I grasped her arms gently around her biceps then leaned in. My gaze riveted to hers. She tensed as though I was squeezing out all the feistiness in her. She was nowhere near ready for me to kiss her. Hell, she wouldn't even look at me, and suddenly, my gut formed a big knot. I was the asshole who'd left her. She didn't want anything to do with me.

"I don't want you fighting on Saturday," I exclaimed as I took in a quiet breath, trying to calm my erratic pulse.

She jerked out of my hands. "I told you not to boss me around."

"Underground fighting can be dangerous. And what if the cops raid the joint? You could go to jail."

She casually lifted a shoulder. "So? Not the first time."

I locked my jaw. "What?" Surprises were popping up everywhere. "You've been in jail?"

"How do you think I get food? You think I can walk into a restaurant and get served for free? I can't eat out of dumpsters every night." A chord of sarcasm threaded through her voice. "I'm not Penelope. She strikes me as a girl who would get what she wanted even if she was homeless."

"Stop comparing yourself to Penelope," I said in a firm tone. "You're beautiful on the inside and outside." Silence ticked for a beat. I softened my voice. "What happened to you, Ruby?"

She scanned the room just as she'd done at Firefly when she saw me from across the bar, no doubt searching for a way out of the gym. Then her eyes closed as her chest rose. When she opened her eyes and set her sights on me, peace replaced the frustration she'd had a moment ago as though whatever internal battle she'd had going on had been resolved. "If you want answers, then pick me up next Thursday. I'd like to show you something near my old house."

"In the Berkshires? But that's Thanksgiving. Why don't you join my family and me?" I would prep my family not to grill her. Maybe by hanging with us, she would see I wasn't that scared boy anymore. She would see that family meant everything to me. "We can also talk quietly before dinner down by the lake behind my house."

She let out a nervous laugh. "No way."

"Then show me before then or on Friday."

"I can't. I have to work at Firefly up until Wednesday, and the weekends are always packed. It's okay. Look, thank you for tonight. I've got to run. I promised Norma I wouldn't be long." She climbed out of the ring.

I could beg, but she wouldn't listen. "Remember to block," I said instead. "Anticipate her moves, and keep your opponent guessing."

She sashayed to the locker room.

What the fuck had just happened? *Your manly ego got in the way, moron.*

"Ruby," I called.

She tossed a blank look over her shoulder.

"Wear those clothes. It will be easier for you to move around. Oh, and I'll be there on Saturday night."

She tilted her head. "Norma said you were banned from Firefly."

"So?" No amount of cops, Tommy, or even the dipshit bartender, Pete, would keep me from watching over Ruby.

CHAPTER 14

RUBY

I waited at the entrance to Boston Public Garden on Arlington Street for my social worker, Ms. Waters, who'd been assigned to my case. My supervised visits with Raven were at the garden. Apparently, Raven's foster family lived nearby, and they had been taking her to see the ducks and swans every Saturday. So, Ms. Waters recommended we meet there. I didn't mind at all. I had a great time seeing the excitement on Raven's face when she saw a swan or a duck or any wildlife. More importantly, I enjoyed holding Raven's hand as we walked the grounds, feeling at peace, feeling protected from the outside world, and just being a mom... even if it were for only an hour or two.

People ventured in through the gates to my left. An elderly couple lingered for a moment, talking about the George Washington Statue behind me. Then the old man readied his phone camera before he snapped a picture.

"Ruby," Ms. Waters called from my right.

"Mommy." Raven's sweet voice penetrated through me, sending an ocean of warmth to my heart. Sixteen days since I'd last seen my daughter, and I swore time had moved in slow motion. I crouched down as she ran to me, throwing her tiny arms around my neck.

"I've missed you, baby girl." Tears shot out without warning as I inhaled her powdery scent, hugging her as if she was my last breath.

She let go of me and gave me a quizzical expression. "When are you taking me home?"

I tugged her pink knitted hat down over her ears. Then I smoothed my hands over her long black hair that spilled around her shoulders. "Soon." I swallowed the mountain in my throat, praying that soon meant next week.

I knew better. I gave Ms. Waters a cursory glance as she loomed over us. She was in her mid-forties and wore black-rimmed glasses that hid the lines around her brown eyes. Her light-brown hair was pulled back into a bun, exposing more lines on her forehead. She'd counseled me that my case could stretch out for six months or more, depending on my living situation. She was a nice woman. She was honest, direct, and seemed to want the best for Raven.

Ms. Waters's red-painted lips spread into a pitiful smile. "Let's walk. Raven, would you like to see the ducks?"

Raven's blue eyes went wide as her lone dimple emerged. "Swans, too?"

A pain clamped down on my chest. When I looked at Raven, I saw Kross. I had since she was born, although anger had always come with my visions of him. But not at that moment. All I could think about was the three of us becoming a family. I didn't know the odds of that. I wanted to believe that Kross and I could work out our differences, and that I could get past my anger.

I had almost given into him when he came close to kissing me the other night. At the last minute, I'd gone from confident to coward, but not because I didn't want his lips on mine. It was more out of fear that if I kissed him, I would want forever. I wasn't certain forever with him was possible. When I'd tensed in his arms, sadness and hurt washed over him. He'd covered up his emotions quickly by getting all bossy on me. I believed deep, deep down in the recesses of my soul that he cared for me. I believed he was trying to right a wrong even before he knew about a supposed child. That alone meant I had a place in his heart, at least to me.

With Raven's hand in mine, we strolled into the garden. Ms. Waters lingered behind. Tourists stopped to admire the George Washington Statue and take pictures.

Raven glanced up at me with the darkest blue eyes. "Mommy, will you take my picture?"

"Let's go see what the ducks are up to." I didn't have the heart to tell her I didn't own a camera or a cell phone with one, for that matter.

"Oooh, there's a swan boat." She took off running, which wasn't surprising since she loved the swan boats.

"Wait for me." I hurried my pace, catching her at the water's edge of the garden's lagoon. "How about we go on a swan ride?"

"Yay!" She tugged my hand, urging me to hurry.

We ran back to Ms. Waters, who was lingering near the George Washington Statue.

"We're going on a swan ride," Raven gushed.

Ms. Waters angled her head. "We are?"

"Would you like to join us? I've got money." I didn't know if money was a concern or if she didn't like boats.

"Tell me more." Ms. Water's voice hitched.

"I'm waitressing at Firefly restaurant and bar. I'm also staying with one of the waitresses. I know I have to get my own place, but it's a start."

"Is that how you got the new shoes?" she asked.

"Mommy, let's go," Raven whined.

I squatted down. "Just a minute. Okay?"

She wrapped her arms around my leg as I straightened to my full height, holding her to me. "The shoes are part of my waitressing uniform." I was lying, but I wasn't ready to dive into the subject of Kross yet.

"That's great, Ruby," Ms. Waters said. "I'll make note of that in your file. You know, I'll have to confirm your employment."

"Of course." I made a mental note to prepare Pete. He was the one who answered the phone behind the bar. I should probably fill Tommy in too. I shivered. If I told Tommy about Raven, then he would hold that knowledge over my head and use it to goad me into another slimy deal.

"Mommy." Raven's voice sliced through my fear.

"Yes, baby girl. We're going."

"Ruby," Ms. Waters said. "Is everything all right? You look a little pale."

"Fine." I couldn't trust Tommy to keep a secret. If I pissed him off, then he would somehow screw me, not literally, but he could blab to Dillon or Kross, although Kross wasn't allowed at Firefly. *Stupid thought. Kross will be at the fight tonight.*

I wouldn't ruin my time with Raven. "Let's go for that swan ride."

Take out your frustrations on the girl you're fighting tonight. My stomach knotted. Tommy would tell Ms. Waters I was fighting illegally. No, he wouldn't. He couldn't. If he did, then he would only be ratting on himself. Then another scary thought surfaced. Kross had brought up the possibility of the cops raiding Firefly. There was a real chance of that occurring since the fights were illegal. If that were to happen, then I could land in jail and kiss my chances of getting Raven back goodbye. If I didn't fight, then I would lose my waitressing job.

Raven let go of my leg and began tugging on my hand, pulling me toward the swan rides.

I sighed heavily and painted on a happy face. At least, I hoped my smile reached my eyes. "Are you going with us?" I asked Ms. Waters. She had to keep a close eye on us, but it wasn't as if I could flee with Raven. The boat left from the dock where we were standing and returned to the same spot. I wouldn't dare try anything, anyway.

"It is a nice day," she said. "The sun feels good. Sure."

Raven talked the whole time between the ticket booth and getting on the boat. She told me about the new doll her foster mom had given her, and about her new friend, Matty. As I listened, I couldn't help but feel happy and sad at the same time. I was so thankful she had a warm bed to sleep in and food in her belly. Yet the pain of her not being with me clenched my entire body as though I was pinned under a pile of cement rubble. *Drop the illegal fighting and focus on waitressing.*

The boat pulled away from the dock, carrying a handful of people in addition to the three of us. Raven sat in between Ms. Waters and me. As we glided down the lagoon, Raven went completely quiet, taking in her surroundings. I draped an arm over her, and she snuggled into me. My tears were on the verge of falling. I wanted to stay like this forever.

But forever was only fifteen minutes. So I closed my eyes, letting the light breeze wash over me. That sense of peace I had felt earlier waned as turmoil seeped into every pore. My hives bloomed with the memory of Norma's words. "Kross could be your ticket to getting Raven back." I rubbed a hand along Raven's arm.

"Ruby," Ms. Waters said. "Have you heard from your mother?"

My eyes flew open, and I checked on Raven. Thank God she'd fallen asleep. Any mention of Nana got her all excited. "No."

I knitted my eyebrows. Ms. Waters knew I didn't have a cell phone, but then I had an idea. I could use Tommy's club phone to call the correctional facility in Framingham. I would love to hear my mom's voice. The last time we had spoken was just before she'd gotten arrested. Sure, I was furious with her for her decision to sell drugs. But she was my mom. She'd done what she thought she had to do to survive. I wasn't any better than she was. I stole to survive. I could've gotten a job despite my mom's advice for me to bond with Raven. Women had babies and worked all the time.

"Ms. Waters, you said my case could take a long time. Is there anything that could speed it up?" Like a miracle.

"As I said, we'll have to show a judge that you're working, that you can provide for Raven, and that you have a roof over your head. Based on your new job, you're moving in that direction." The wind picked up, and she buttoned the top of her coat.

I kissed the top of my daughter's head. "What about Raven's father?"

"What about him? Your records indicate that you don't know who the father is."

I pursed my lips. I had to know what impact Kross would have on my case. Good or bad, I had to be prepared. "If I did, what would that mean?"

The boat began to head back to the dock.

Ms. Waters had a contemplative look on her face. "There's no mention of a father on Raven's birth certificate. So if he does come forward, then he would have to prove he was the father through a paternity test, which involves a lawyer on his part. Then the lawyer would have to petition the family court for a genetic marker test. In essence, the judge would need to approve the order to have a DNA test done on both Raven and the father. That could take weeks. However, that process could go quicker than your case."

My chest expanded, but then fear squeezed it shut. If Kross filed for sole custody, then I could lose Raven. At least now, I could see her two or three times a month. *He's her father. She's ten times better off with family.* She would love the lake that Kross had mentioned was near his house. Raven was a fish in water. Mom and I had taken her to the YMCA on occasion not long before Mom got arrested.

The boat docked. I lifted Raven in my arms and carried her. She stirred slightly but didn't wake. Ms. Waters and I walked back to the main entrance in silence. My heart started beating like a drumroll. I didn't want to let go of Raven. After our last visit, I had hidden for a solid day, crying.

We were almost to the George Washington Statue when a lady who looked an awful lot like Alex jogged through the gate. She wore running shoes, a sweatshirt, and yoga pants. Her brown hair was pulled back into a high ponytail.

I did a double take. "Alex?"

She stopped. "Ruby?"

"You jog?" I shouldn't be surprised. Alex was in great shape. Now I knew how she'd gotten her toned legs.

"I love running through the gardens," she said.

Ms. Waters cleared her throat.

"Oh, sorry." I made the introductions and explained to Ms. Waters that Alex was the lady I was living with.

"So, you have a kid?" Alex asked.

I nodded. We hadn't talked much about our lives. If Norma, Alex, and I were there together, we practically crashed the instant after our long shifts. Besides, Alex was staying at some guy's place.

Ms. Waters's phone rang. "I've got to take this. I'll meet you outside the gate," she said to me. "Don't be long. I need to get Raven back to her foster family."

Raven stirred awake.

"Hey, there," I said as I set her on her feet then grabbed her hand.

She rubbed her eye.

Alex bent down. "Hi. I'm Alex. You're adorable."

Raven leaned into my leg.

"She's tired," I said. "We should go"

Alex stood. "It was nice to meet you, Raven." Then she glanced at me. "I'll see you back at the apartment." Then she jogged off.

I'd thought about asking her not to say anything to anyone about Raven. But since Ms. Waters would check up on my employment, I had to at least tell Pete. Alex didn't know Kross, so I didn't have to worry that she would tell him.

We found Ms. Waters just outside the gate. My heart began to pound. This was the part where I got all emotional. It killed me to say good-bye to Raven.

Ms. Waters ended her call. "Alex seems like a nice lady," she said as she pulled out her car keys.

We walked in silence to her car, which was parked not that far from the gate. She pressed the key fob. Two beeps sounded from the tan car.

Raven began to cry. "I don't want to leave you, Mommy."

"I know, baby girl." I quickly buckled Raven into her car seat before I lost it. Once she was strapped in, I gave her a long kiss on her forehead. "I love you bigger than the universe."

Tears streamed down her face. Then I couldn't hold my own tears in anymore. "I'll see you soon."

She held out her arms. "Bigger than the universe."

I kissed her one last time then ducked out of the car, dashing away tears.

"So about Raven's father," Ms. Waters said. "If you know who he is, he could play a key role in your case."

My ears perked up as well as my pulse. "How so?"

"The family court system wants children to be with family first. As well they should. Raven should be with her mom and her dad, or at least an aunt or grandparent. But something tells me you're not ready to come clean." Her gaze swept over me like a metal detector. She was a smart lady. I imagined that in her line of work, she came across all types of people and personalities. That meant she could probably read people better than a psychic.

"I'm not ready." I wasn't going to lie, but I wasn't about to give her names either, not until I spoke to Kross.

"If you're worried about losing Raven because the father comes forward, you shouldn't. Again, the family court system values the relationship between mom and child."

"But it's not like I have a home or money."

"You said you were working. The next step is an apartment. But if the father is stable with a good job and home, then why not consider the possibility of Raven living with her daddy? Think about it. Our next visit is in two weeks. You have my cell phone number, and now that I know where you're working, I can contact you there if I need to. Think about what I said." She climbed into her car.

Waving, I edged back. I had a lot to think about.

CHAPTER 15
RUBY

I tore into Firefly through the backdoor then ran up the stairs. Loud voices filled the hall from down below. Tommy was probably seething that I was late for the fight. I wasn't scheduled to waitress, but I had to fight or I wouldn't have a waitressing job.

After I'd parted with Raven and Ms. Waters, I'd done some soul-searching and roamed the streets too far in the wrong direction. However, I considered my time productive. My original plan was to take baby steps with Kross. I'd planned to show him Riley's grave near my old home in the Berkshires and start at the beginning. But if a paternity test proving that Kross was Raven's daddy was a quicker route to getting her out of foster care, then I had to put aside my own selfishness and do what was best for Raven, no matter the consequences.

I slipped past Tommy's office.

"I don't know where the fuck she is," he yelled.

I cringed. I was certain he was talking about me. Before I got my ass handed to me, I had to show my face to Norma. She knew I normally liked some alone time after I visited with Raven, but today, I'd been gone too long.

I stuck my head into the bar area. Pete's eyes went wide, then he crooked his finger. I shook my head, but he waved me over more firmly this time. His features transformed into those of one scary dude. His lips mashed into a thin line, a deep crease between his eyebrows traveled up to the crest of his baldhead, and his eyes formed into slits, his nostrils pulsating. I'd never seen him mad, but Norma had. Apparently, Pete had almost laid Kross out on a stretcher. That was hard for me to believe since Kross was more muscular than Pete.

I ventured over to the bar, mostly out of respect for Pete since he had given me so many pointers on serving drinks and addressing upset customers.

"First, glad to see you're in one piece. Everything okay?" The angry look on his face belied the sweetness in his tone.

"I had to take care of something. It went longer than I expected. And as you know, I don't have a cell phone. So I couldn't exactly call."

"Tommy is furious. You're thirty minutes late for the fight."

I hung my head. He reminded me of my dad when I'd gotten into trouble. Dad wouldn't yell. He would say in a firm but calm tone how disappointed he was in me. I shouldn't care what Pete thought, but I did. He was a big teddy bear. He kept an eye out for Alex, Norma, and me. More importantly, he kept us shielded from Tommy's mood swings most of the time, at least while we were working.

He flicked his head toward the hallway. "Well, you better get in his office."

I swallowed hard. "Am I still fighting?" Given that I was late, I wasn't sure. I would prefer to put all my effort into becoming the best damn waitress in Boston. By doing that, I could show Ms. Waters I was responsible and prove to myself I could stand on my own. But I had a deal with Tommy first. Nausea began to churn.

Someone tapped me on the shoulder. If it were Tommy, Pete wouldn't have a warm smile on his face.

Norma cleared her throat. I turned to find my best friend with a scowl on her face.

"Before you yell or tell me how worried you were, I'm sorry. You know how I get after—" My voice dried up when I spotted Tommy. He and I locked gazes.

I had bigger problems than Norma. Tommy's dark features grew darker with every step he took in my direction. He paused in the doorway between the hall and the main part of the club. "Get your ass downstairs right the fuck now."

Well, crap. I was still fighting.

"Don't fight," Norma whispered.

A war battled inside me. If I didn't fight, then I would be out on the streets again. I wouldn't have food in my belly. Above all else, my case to get Raven back would take even longer. "I made a deal." One last fight. One last deal.

I pushed off the bar as I remembered a conversation I'd overheard between Tommy and Trent that very first night I'd hidden in the dumpster.

"The fight should yield us close to fifteen thousand dollars," Tommy had said.

"Just make sure she shows. I'll be taking your nuts if she doesn't," Trent had added.

Granted, that conversation hadn't been about me then, but somehow I got the eerie feeling that it was tonight. Sweat beaded on my body. If Tommy's nuts were on the line because I was late, then he would hold me responsible. I just wasn't sure how.

"We can find another job," Norma said at my back.

Time was our enemy and so was the storm brewing in Tommy's dark eyes. I weighed my options. I could either run or take my licks until Tommy decided for me. When I was within his reach, he grasped my arm hard.

It was time to fight.

⚜

THICK CLOUDS of cigar and cigarette smoke billowed out of the boisterous room as Norma and I approached.

"You can still back out," Norma said. She'd been telling me that nonstop during the two minutes Tommy had given me to change into my workout gear.

"Chill." I blew out a breath as I entered the room. In my mind, I couldn't run. I'd made a deal, one that would allow me to at least keep waitressing whether I won or lost the fight.

"Holy Moly. You're fighting Sasquatch," Norma all but screeched.

Vickie, the very large girl I had told to fuck off the first night I'd found Firefly was cracking her knuckles and bouncing on her feet. Her body gleamed with sweat. She regarded me with a bone-chilling smile as though she was ready to beat my head into the dirty floor.

Suddenly, I berated myself for not spending more than thirty minutes training with Kross. "She's not seven feet. She's six."

"You can't fight her." Norma's voice hitched. "She's going to seriously damage your body parts."

Vickie had the advantage. Her sports bra was stretched tight over her well-toned chest. Her biceps reminded me of Kross's, big and cut. Her short shorts revealed thick thighs. But her muscles weren't what had me shaking where I stood. Her hands were big. One punch, and my entire face would be bruised. Then Ms. Waters might think it wasn't safe for my own daughter to be around me. Heck, I didn't want Raven to see me all black and blue. I was also beginning to think Tommy had gotten me all excited about winning two thousand dollars when he knew I didn't stand a chance. A psychopathic laugh broke out in my head at something Tommy had said. "You have potential and great footwork." Those two attributes did nothing to quell my nerves.

"Kross gave me some good pointers," I said to Norma as I looked for Kross in the crowd.

Norma chewed on a long nail. "If you're looking for Kross, he's banned. Remember?"

"He said he'd be here."

"He's not walking through the door upstairs. Pete will kill him this time."

I'd gotten in through the alley door, which had been wide open earlier.

Tommy circled the police-taped ring, extending his arms. "Sorry that we had a snag."

Whistles and shouts erupted from the throng of men gathered around the ring. The room was packed, but not as much as it had been the last two times I'd been there.

"Are you ready, Vickie?" one man shouted. "I got a lot of money on you, sweet thing."

Vickie cracked her neck and pumped her fists. "Kill," she shouted, bouncing her way into the ring like a prizefighter.

I swallowed thickly as Norma held onto my arm for dear life.

Tommy glared at me. I guessed that was my cue to get my ass in the ring.

Norma hugged me tightly. "Be careful."

A guy wolf-whistled as I pushed men out of my way and stepped into the ring. I wasn't anxious to fight, but I was anxious to get this night over with.

"You two know the rules," Tommy said.

"Wait," a smooth and tingly baritone voice shouted.

"Fuck," Tommy muttered.

Kross appeared from behind a group of men, cutting a visceral path through the spectators. Power and confidence oozed off of him.

"Hey, isn't that Kross Maxwell?" someone asked.

He pushed toward me with a sense of purpose, his long, thick, denim-clad legs closing the distance between us.

Butterflies took flight in my stomach when I saw how his muscles bunched along his arms. I swore that snake tattoo on his forearm slithered. Or maybe it was the light-headed feeling that settled within me.

"Yeah, they call him rattlesnake in the ring," a guy added.

I had no idea why. But at the moment, the why didn't matter. What mattered was that Tommy was ready to throw down, which was surprising, considering he was afraid of Kross, although he was more afraid of Dillon, who was behind Kross. Suddenly, Tommy unclenched his fist.

"Let's fight," I said to Tommy. It was better to get this party started before a huge brawl broke out and before Tommy fired me. I'd promised him Kross wouldn't be any trouble.

"Hold up." Kross ducked under the yellow tape like an expert fighter.

Okay, I was getting fired.

"You know Kross Maxwell?" Vickie asked me with awe in her voice.

Maybe if I said yes, she wouldn't kill me.

"You're banned from this establishment." Tommy's tone was all businesslike as he addressed Kross.

Out of the corner of my eye, I spotted Tommy's business partner, Trent Baker. He was with a pudgy man, dressed in a tailored business suit, standing out like a sore thumb among the men who were dressed casually in jeans. With his arms crossed, Trent pointed at either me or the ring then said something to his friend.

"I need a minute to confer with my fighter," Kross said.

Holy cow! I'd thought he would try to stop me. I smiled.

Dillon stared Tommy down until Tommy lifted his hands. "No trouble."

Kross got super close to me, just as he had the other night when I thought he was going to kiss me. "Walk away. Leave with me. You don't stand a chance with that girl."

The light-headed feeling vanished as anger seeped into my veins. My pulse jumped a notch.

The room buzzed with chatter.

"Way to motivate your fighter. I made a deal. I'm sticking to it."

"Ruby." He lowered his head, piercing me with a look that would have knocked me out from lust if I weren't hurt and angry that he was still trying to be bossy.

"No," I said. "I get she's big. I get I probably don't stand a chance. But I'm not running like a scared animal." My voice was several octaves lower than the restless drone in the room, so I didn't think anyone could hear us. Then again, I didn't care. "I'll tire her out. I'm winning this fight." Okay, maybe my bravado was a little too strong. But if I let the fact that I didn't have a chance consume me, then I definitely wouldn't win. I needed to win.

He latched onto my arms with his strong hands. "God damn it. You should've let me train you more the other night."

Even though I agreed with him, I realized another hour or two of training wouldn't have made me an expert fighter.

"Are you going to kiss her or let her fight?" a spectator asked.

I cocked an eyebrow. If he so much as touched my lips with his, I might have had to use a boxing move or two on him. I didn't need him to replace my confidence with a dreamy state of mind.

"Just stay close and give me pointers while I'm fighting," I said. Maybe that would make him feel better. Hell, it would make me feel better.

He lowered his gaze to my lips. "If I see you faltering, I'm stopping the fight."

"This isn't your boxing world with rules."

His gaze shot up to mine. "I know that. I'm also aware of how people in underground fights get their heads torn off. Remember, block, keep your face shielded, punch hard, often, and fast. And keep your footwork going. Do. Not. Stop."

"Maxwell, get the fuck out of her way," Tommy said.

"Go." I pushed him, or I at least tried to push him.

He gave me a cocky grin before he stepped out to stand close by, next to Norma.

"If Maxwell is in her court, my money is on that girl," someone said.

The men began waving money in the air as though they were

swaying to some melodic music. Vickie, on the other hand, was flaring her nostrils and fisting her hands, ready and anxious to beat my lights out.

Tommy held out his arms between Vickie and me. "Only one rule, ladies. You fight until one of you gets knocked out." He gave Vickie a nod then me before he ducked out.

The buzz of the crowd energized me as Vickie and I met in the middle then bumped fists. Once we stepped back, we both bounced on the balls of our feet. *Footwork,* I had to keep telling myself. Punch hard, often, and fast. I could do this. I might have been five foot four, but I could also be the Tasmanian Devil if my life depended on it.

She lunged, throwing the first punch directly into my mouth. Pain ricocheted up through my nose. My eyes watered. She came at me again. This time, she jammed her Sasquatch paw into my gut.

On reflex, I bent over, air gushing from my lungs as though someone had popped a balloon.

"Ruby, hit back," Kross instructed.

As hard as it was to straighten, I swallowed the pain. I charged her with my fists flying. She darted to the right, and I hit air.

"You're too wild," Kross said. "Block with one hand, punch with the other."

"Let's face it," Vickie said. "You're going down."

I snarled as I lunged. This time, I kicked, my foot landing in her gut.

An "oof" then a groan dropped from her lips as she held her stomach.

"Again, Ruby," Kross said.

Vickie swung her gaze to Kross. In that split second, I punched, my fist connecting with her side. She bent over, giving me easy access to her face. I jabbed hard, once, twice, three times in quick succession. Blood sprayed from her nose. *Don't stop now. You don't want her to recover.* I landed another blow to her mouth. She narrowed her dark-brown eyes at me as she spit out blood.

"Hit her again," some men bellowed.

Adrenaline pumped through my veins at warp speed. My pulse pounded in my ears. If pain existed anywhere on my body, I couldn't feel it. All I knew was I had to keep hitting her, wearing her down. Otherwise, she would probably beat me until I couldn't open my eyes.

She groaned. I rammed my elbow into her temple. She staggered.

"Again," Kross shouted.

"Come on, Ruby," Norma shouted. "She's tiring."

Only one way to win—knock her out. I came around with my other elbow and caught the left side of her jaw. When her head swung right, I immediately followed with a swift and hard punch directly to her nose. She shook her head like a dog shaking off water. Then she brought a hand up to her face, wiped the blood, then smiled as though she was enjoying herself. I felt as if I'd just swallowed a handful of rocks. This woman wasn't going down.

I retreated to catch my breath. As soon as I did, Vickie launched her large body at me like a diver in the Olympics. I wanted to laugh because she made the same move she had when I'd told her to fuck off that first night. I danced to my left. She stumbled before righting herself. She came at me, throwing a fist to my gut.

Air left my lungs as I shuffled backward.

"Stay upright," Kross said.

I blew out a breath. But before I could orient myself, she landed a blow to my ear. The pain brought tears to my eyes along with a blinding anger. Screw control. I went wild, attacking her with all the energy I had left in me. She blocked her face as I delivered punch after punch to her gut and anywhere else on her body. My breathing was all over the place, but I wasn't stopping.

Vickie shuffled two steps back, giving me the opportunity to gain control of myself. But I couldn't lose the momentum. If the audience was hooting and hollering, I barely heard them, especially with the ringing in my left ear. Then for some reason, my ballet training came to mind. I did a pique turn. Normally, in ballet, I would step onto a full point. Instead, I lifted my right leg as high as my limber body would allow me. Then with all the power in my leg, I kicked out, my foot connecting with the side of Vickie's head.

She listed to one side then another, her eyes going wide as gravity took control. She fell. Her head hit the hard dirt-covered floor with a resounding crack followed by a whoosh.

The room fell silent.

Vickie didn't move. I squeezed my eyes shut as dizziness crept in. I began to sway to one side when strong hands caught me.

"I'm here," Kross whispered in my ear as he cocooned me in his arms.

At that moment, pain began to take over my body.

Whispers hummed in the distance.

A hand touched my back. "Ruby, you did great," Norma said.

I didn't feel so great.

"Is Vickie dead?" someone asked.

Horror settled in my veins as I pushed off Kross. "Dead?" I sucked in all the smoky, dank air I could. When my lungs expanded, bile rose to settle in my throat. Oh, God. If I killed her, I was certainly going to jail. My life was over. I would never see my daughter again.

A crowd formed around Vickie.

"Norma, hold onto Ruby," Kross said as he pushed the men out of the way.

The spectators moved but not far. The men I could see standing over Vickie wore concerned expressions.

Please let her be okay. I couldn't be charged with murder. "I'm so going to jail."

"Shh," Norma said. "Don't get ahead of yourself."

Kross lowered to his knees near Vickie's head. Dillon was tapping on Vickie's face, and Tommy was on his haunches, sweat dripping down his temple.

Kross opened one of Vickie's eyelids, then the other. He moved his fingers down to her neck. He checked her as though he was a skilled doctor or trained in CPR. "She's got a pulse." His shoulders slumped as he sat back on his heels.

A huge exhale zipped around the room as though a large gust of wind had blown through the dingy basement. I hung my head, cele-brating with everyone.

"That creepy Trent is looking at us," Norma whispered in my ear.

Wincing in pain, I searched the crowd. Trent was standing at the opposite end of the ring behind Vickie, leering in my direction.

"Again, yuk." Norma shuddered. "He reminds me of my pimp."

I broke eye contact with the man and went over to Vickie. Her chest rose softly. Mine didn't. I took in another humungous breath. Fighting was definitely off my list of career options. Legal or not, I didn't want to worry that I would hurt someone, or worse, kill some-one. Not to mention, the pain. My entire body felt as if I'd been run over by a tractor-trailer, not once but ten times.

Kross popped to his feet then pulled me to him so fast, I grunted. I wanted to tell him not to hug me so tightly, but I would endure any amount of pain to be in his arms. He smelled like heaven and felt like home. I wanted to be home. I wanted to be with him. Suddenly, I wanted to bawl like a baby and tell him about Raven. I wanted, no, *needed* him to rescue me from a life that had gotten out of control. A life that had taken the wrong path. But I couldn't feel sorry for myself. I'd made my choices. As my mom had always said, "Your decisions in life will make you who you are." Those were her words as she was carted off in handcuffs.

Easing back, Kross placed his large palms on my face. Panic shone in his dark-blue eyes as he rubbed his thumbs over my cheeks.

"I'm good, Kross." I was more than good as tingles spread through my entire body.

"You're not fighting in this dump again." His voice was soft but firm.

He wasn't getting an argument out of me. I had fulfilled my obligation to Tommy, and I could keep my waitressing job.

Tommy's voice broke through the fluffy cloud I was on. "She's awake."

Vickie moaned.

Kross turned his attention to Vickie. "Hey, slugger."

Her eyelashes fluttered at Kross. "Maxwell? Am I dreaming? I can't believe you're here."

"In the flesh," he drawled in that whiskey smooth voice of his.

Her smile grew wider. The girl had a major crush on Kross.

"All right. The fight is over," Tommy announced. "The winner is Ruby."

The men huddled into small groups as they exchanged fistfuls of bills.

With all the fear that was spiking my adrenaline, I didn't exactly feel elated.

"You won," Vickie said as she sat up. "By the way, what kind of move was that? You looked like you were about to do some kind of ballet dance."

"Are you sure you're okay?" I asked her.

"I'm alive," she said.

The word alive was the catalyst to replace my fear with joy. *Oh my God.* I glanced at Kross. "I won two thousand dollars." I threw my arms around him. "Thank you."

"I didn't do anything. You're the one with that fancy ballet move." He let out a hearty laugh. I loved that sound from him.

"I can't believe it," Norma said. "We have money."

The amount wasn't enough to live off of since rent in Boston was so high. Still, it was money to deposit into an account.

Tommy sauntered up to me. "My office in ten minutes." His tone was even. "Norma, get your butt back to work."

"I should go," Norma said. "My break was over fifteen minutes ago. I'll meet you upstairs."

The roomed emptied out with the exception of Kross, Dillon, and Vickie.

"We should get you to a doctor," Dillon said to Vickie.

"Vickie, I'm sorry," I said.

"No worries. That's what happens in fights." Then she shifted her crush-filled eyes to Kross. "I'm such a fan."

Kross flashed her a dimpled grin. "Would you like to come to my next match? It's invitation only, but I have a few tickets left."

Her whole face lit up as though she'd just walked into her favorite candy store. A small jealous pang hit me from Kross inviting her to his match. I wanted one of those tickets. I would love to see Kross in action. I almost asked him for one then decided not to. If he wanted me there, then he would invite me.

"I've got to go." My money was waiting for me, and I had to find some Advil then see if Pete needed a hand.

"About Thanksgiving," Kross said. "I'll take you up to the Berkshires like you wanted me to."

I didn't want to take him away from his family. "Um, maybe another day."

Hurt washed over him before he quickly banked it.

"Are you free Wednesday? I don't have to work until seven." I didn't know if Ms. Waters would agree to let me see Raven on short notice. She might if I came clean about Kross.

"I am in the afternoon," he said.

"Then I'll meet you outside the gym at noon." The faster Kross met Raven, the faster we could get the paternity paperwork started.

※

THIRTY MINUTES LATER, I was walking into Tommy's office. After I'd left Kross, I changed back into my jeans then went in search of pain medication. Pete had a bottle of Advil behind the bar.

Trent and Tommy were lounging on the couch, talking until I sat down in a chair across from them.

Tommy glanced at his watch. "I said ten minutes."

"I'm here. I want my money."

Trent laughed. It was a sound that grated on me. In fact, the hairs on the back of my neck rose.

"You see, Ruby"—Tommy's voice stiffened those hairs on my neck —"you were late for the fight. Which meant I lost money. Lots of it."

I clenched my fists in my lap. "How did you lose money? Your customers got a fight."

"That room downstairs is always packed from corner to corner on fight night," Tommy said. "When you didn't show, people took their money and left."

His first sentence was correct. I'd noticed it wasn't as crowded tonight. "I won. Therefore, you owe me money." I knew nothing about how he made money, and frankly, I didn't want to know.

Trent plucked a folder from a pile of disorganized papers on the coffee table, which was cluttered with empty beer bottles and an ashtray overflowing with cigarette butts.

My nails dug into my palms.

"Tommy isn't lying to you," Trent said. "Our entry fee is one hundred dollars per head. We had a packed house of two hundred. After thirty minutes, half of them got restless. So, we had to return their entrance fee. When it was all said and done, we lost ten grand in entry fees."

"Bull," I blurted out. I was savvy to the knowledge that numbers could be calculated any way to suit someone's needs. My mom's boss had done that a time or two.

They both let out a chuckle that made me feel degraded.

Assholes. Stars clouded my vision. "I won fair and square. That's my money," I nearly shouted, pressing my hands into the arms of the chair.

"It's no longer your money." Tommy's voice dropped, mean and deadly. "You lost it all when you decided to stroll in late. We run a business on our time, not yours."

The need to kill him skipped through my mind. "Then pay me half." A thousand dollars was still a lot of money. Besides, I deserved it.

"Ruby." Trent's tone was nice and calm. "You're no longer dealing with Tommy. The ten grand that was lost tonight is mine. I'm a businessman that doesn't like to be screwed out of all that cash. You now work for me. You *will* pay me back."

I jumped out of my chair. "Fuck you. I owe you nothing."

"Do you want to keep your waitressing job?" Tommy asked.

"Seriously? You're using the waitressing position to threaten me again?" The need to kill him grew brighter than a full moon on a clear, dark night.

"A Ms. Waters called me today." Tommy's tone was smug.

Visions of holding a loaded gun to Tommy's head completely vanished. If he knew that piece of information, then he also knew about Raven, although Alex could've told him about Raven. My mouth fell open as the office spun. I grasped the arms of the chair.

Trent pushed to his feet, holding that folder in his hand as though it held secrets, my secrets. "Do we have your attention?" He climbed over a box and reached into the fridge near Tommy's desk. He snagged a beer and twisted the cap.

A pregnant pause filled the room, my fear rising as though I was on a sinking ship.

Tommy rested his elbows on his knees. Trent took a long pull from the bottle.

"So, talk," I said as a dull pain throbbed in my chest from the morbid anticipation of what they had in mind.

Trent set down the beer bottle on the desk, the folder still clutched in his other hand. "I have a client I want you to entertain."

I sucked in a sharp breath. "No fucking way." I shook my head violently as I darted for the door. "I'm out of here." I wasn't about to jump from illegal fighting to illegal "entertaining," whatever he meant by that. I wasn't stupid, though. He meant sex for hire. That type of work wasn't in my vocabulary. Norma had prostituted herself. I understood why. But I wasn't Norma. I stole to survive, and I would continue to do so before I entertained anyone by using my body.

"What about your daughter?" Trent asked as though he knew he'd won the battle.

Blood rushed out of me. I flared my nostrils as I gripped the doorknob. "What about her?"

"If you don't do as I say, then I'll make sure your case to get your daughter back falls on the bottom of a judge's docket for months or longer."

I spun around. "You can't do that." No way he had a judge in the palm of his hand. Then again, my mom's boss had had relationships with people in high places.

Trent removed a piece of paper from the folder and extended it to me. "See for yourself. I can also inform social services of your illegal fighting."

My heart crashed against my bruised ribs, heightening the pain. I shuffled over and took the paper with a trembling hand. The heading read, "Ruby and Raven Lewis, case file number 5218." The words on the paper blurred. "You're bluffing." *He isn't bluffing. He has a copy of my file, which means he knows someone in the family court system.*

Ms. Waters's name came to mind. No. I refused to believe he knew her or manipulated her. She'd seemed sympathetic to my situation and didn't strike me as someone who would take a bribe. She had given me pointers on the legal procedures to prove Kross was the father. "How did you get this?"

Trent's fat nose widened as he smirked. "I'm a highly respected businessman with a judge on speed dial. Do you want to call my bluff?"

If I hadn't been in a sinking ship before, I was now. I could go to Ms. Waters and ask her if Trent could do something like this. But then she would know I was illegally fighting, which would show I wasn't a responsible mother, and further slow the process. I couldn't go to the cops. I had nothing to prove that Trent was threatening me with a judge. I didn't even know who the judge was.

It was more important than ever to tell Kross about Raven. I had to speed up the process of getting her out of foster care, especially if a paternity test was a faster route. Not only that, Trent didn't know Kross was the father. So Trent couldn't screw with Kross's case.

In the meantime, I would do anything to get my daughter back.

"What do you want me to do?" I asked.

CHAPTER 16
KROSS

I sat in the locker room at the gym, lacing up my boots. With the exception of Kody and me, the locker room was empty. Jay was closing up at noon for the Thanksgiving holiday, which was when I was due to meet Ruby. My stomach was in a ball of knots, tightly wound and ready to snap open. Since I'd seen her fight, my body, my mind, and my soul hadn't been the same.

Her beauty had done things to me in high school, like give me flutters and butterflies and sweaty palms. Those same feelings were back, only at a heightened state. I'd thought watching her dance ballet was a sight to see. How wrong I was. I was in awe as I watched her dance in the ring, driving her fists into Vickie over and over again. Pride had risen in me as Ruby had continued to fight despite the pain she endured from Vickie's fists. I knew how bad it hurt to get a fist to my gut. I knew how hard it was to fight through the pain. In that moment, in that fucking disgusting basement, I'd wanted to claim her as mine. I'd wanted to shout from the rooftops that she was my girl.

"What are you and Ruby doing this afternoon?" Kody asked as he stood at the locker across from me, buckling his belt. He'd been sparring with me since Liam was home with his family for Thanksgiving week. Jay had me on a workout regimen so I wouldn't lose momentum before my fight with Reggie Stockman.

"Not sure. At first, she'd wanted me to take her home to the Berkshires. But when I told her I would take her, she'd said another day. So I'm not sure what we're doing today." I didn't care if we ended up at that warehouse she'd taken me to or if we roamed the streets. As long as we were together, we were building that highway of trust between us.

Kody combed his hair. "So she hasn't mentioned a kid?"

"You sound like Kelton." Even though he'd advised me to give Ruby space, he'd been grilling me every chance he had. "No." I believed she was close to opening up, which was why she'd asked me to take her to the Berkshires. Although if we weren't going up there, I wondered if she had changed her mind.

"Is she joining us for Thanksgiving?"

I stuffed my gym bag in my locker. "No." I'd asked her, and she'd said no. I wasn't pushing her, mainly because I wasn't ready to be bombarded with questions and grilled at the dinner table. "Look, I've got to meet with Jay before I leave. I'll meet you guys at home later this afternoon."

We were all gathering at my parents' house. We had a Thanksgiving tradition in which we gathered down by the lake around a small camp-fire and told each other what we were thankful for. Before I'd learned that I could be a father, my Thanksgiving speech was dedicated to family and how thankful I was for all of them. While I still was grateful for them, I was now thankful that fate had brought Ruby and me together.

I prodded through the gym and into Jay's office. I hoped our conversation was swift. Ruby would be there in less than ten minutes.

Jay glanced up from the TV. He was going through tapes of Reggie Stockman. I'd seen them about a hundred times. Reggie was consid-ered a slugger, his style similar to that of the famous George Foreman. Sluggers had raw power and often went in to attack their opponent with one hard punch. Whereas a fighter like Reggie lacked mobility, an out-fighter like me was quick on his feet, making a slugger work for his punches, and in turn, he tired easily. I wasn't getting cocky. I knew all too well how a slugger's punch packed some severe heat. The fighter I'd met in the ring a few weeks ago had knocked me the fuck out. I still had work to do, but seeing Ruby fight had given me some of my mojo back. I had been concentrating more, and my punches were spot-on.

"You see what he does," Jay said without taking his eyes off the tape.

"Yeah, he has that wide left hook that comes out of nowhere."

"He's a quick motherfucker for a slugger." Jay paused the tape then sat back. "Your fight is set for one week from this Saturday. We have standing room only, and this is an interview fight. Not a match that will go on your record."

"You didn't call me in for something I already knew. What is it?"

"A buddy of mine saw you at an illegal underground fight on Saturday. Is that true?"

Fuck me. I'd been trying to keep a low profile. I couldn't afford Jay's wrath. I couldn't throw away my career. Yet I'd needed to be there to support Ruby. I'd had to be there in case she'd gotten severely hurt or if the cops raided the joint. The chance always existed that cops would bust into an underground event of some kind. I knew all too well from the underground gambling game I'd been part of with Kelton, Lizzie, and Dillon that anything could go wrong. So, Dillon and I had made a plan just in case. He'd been at Firefly enough to know that a tunnel existed in one of the rooms in the basement. Luckily, we didn't have to go through with our plan, although I hadn't figured in that a friend of Jay's would be at the fight.

"Yes." No sense in lying. "I was there helping a friend."

He pinched his hooknose. "Tommy Delano is a gnat's ass away from getting caught by the law for his illegal fights and anything else he's into."

I angled my head. "You know him?"

He cocked an eyebrow. "I know every underground fighting circuit in this city. If I catch you or get wind that you're at one again, we're through. You can find another coach." His voice escalated. "I've worked too hard with you to fuck all this up. I don't give a shit who you were helping. Am I clear?"

I raked a hand through my hair. "Crystal." I might have just lied to him because if Ruby continued to fight, then I would continue to be there with her.

"We train again on Monday. Have a nice holiday." He turned back to the TV.

I lifted a foot to get the fuck out of there before he called off the fight. This was my third warning. I'd received one for the predicament I'd gotten into with the cops at the mafia gambling game. The second had been for not having my head in the ring, which had led to me losing a fight. Now, the underground fight. Boxing was everything to me, but so were family and friends. "Jay."

He paused with his finger on the remote.

"If you must know..." I hardly shared my personal business with Jay. He did, however, know that friends and family were important to me. "I was at Firefly to help someone who is dear to my heart." Truth. "She could be my future."

"Boxing is your future." He rubbed a hand over his bald head. "Or are you telling me it isn't."

"It is. Look, I knew the risks of showing up at Firefly. I know Tommy is scum. But you know me. I don't let friends get hurt. Ruby, one of the girls who was fighting, didn't know how to fight. I couldn't let anything happen to her."

"Admirable. But how many times are you going to stick your neck out for someone before it fucks with your career? For months now, your head hasn't been straight. You're putting yourself into sticky situations that could mess up your career. I'm not trying to be a dick. What I'm saying is when you're in that ring"—he pointed to the door—"make sure you're all in, head, heart, and soul. At the match, I want to see Kross, the great fighter that you've become. The one that knocks out his opponents. The man who people revere. The rattlesnake."

I chuckled at the public's nickname for me. A sportscaster had mentioned that I was like a rattlesnake. When I went in for the kill, one side of my mouth turned up, alerting my prey that I was about to attack. Then before they knew what had hit them, they were out cold. I'd tried to be aware of my tells, but when I was zoned into punching someone's lights out, it was hard to change my habits.

"Yes, sir."

Jay returned to watching the tape. I made my way out. I would dump all my energy and effort into impressing Gail. I would also show Reggie I was still the better fighter. He and I had met in our first amateur fight four years ago. I'd come out the victor, and he was pissed. I wouldn't doubt that he itched to even the score. I also wouldn't doubt that he had sharpened his skills. Just from watching the tape, I saw that he was a better fighter. So was I. My brothers had been talking shit about Reggie and me fighting again, Kody especially. Reggie had been part of Greg Sullivan's posse in high school that had helped put Kody in the hospital. Even after four years, Kody wanted to see Stockman bleed.

It was three minutes past noon, the sun was shining, and I had a long weekend to spend with family and hopefully Ruby. I glanced up and down the street. No sign of Ruby. She didn't have a cell phone so I couldn't call her. A man in his late forties was locking up the pawnshop across the street. He waved then tucked his hands in his pockets and began walking. Then the gym door clicked open.

"Ruby called. She wants you to meet her at Boston Public Garden, the Arlington entrance," Jay said.

After twenty minutes through stops and turns, I parked my truck then hotfooted it the two blocks to the Public Gardens. My heart picked up a beat every time my foot pounded the pavement. Images of Ruby in my arms after she'd fought made my stomach tingle. She had fit perfectly in my arms, and the bare skin on her back had melted into my hands. Her cheeks had been silky beneath my thumbs. I had the urge to feel more of her. Hell, I had almost shoved my tongue through her supple lips that night. I couldn't ruin whatever we had building between us. She was coming around, and I wanted her to make the first move. That way, I would know without a morsel of a doubt that she wanted me.

Ruby paced in front of the George Washington Statue that stood amid the backdrop of the city. The park was quiet except for a swan floating down the lagoon. My pulse—not so quiet. Ruby continued to carve a path in the pavement until she spotted me.

When I saw her eyes, I was immediately drawn into a sea of blue-green, sparkling water surrounding some faraway deserted island. My pulse ticked higher.

She gave me a rueful smile that contradicted the pensiveness in her eyes. "Sorry I couldn't meet you at the gym."

Abruptly, my euphoria changed to caution. "Is everything okay?"

Her chested heaved as she cupped her hands together. She nodded, tears pooling. "For so long, I'd been so freaking mad at you. Then when I saw you at the fight that first time, I panicked. I never wanted you to see me as a homeless person. We had something back in the tenth grade. Didn't we?"

Whoa! A knot formed in my stomach at her desperation. "What's this about? Did someone hurt you?" She didn't have any visible signs of bruises. Then Tommy came to mind. I would kill him if he'd done anything to her.

"No. Please answer the question." Anguish weaved through her words.

I grabbed her hands, which were cold and clammy. "I was in a different place than you back in high school."

"And now?"

"I've told you how I feel when I'm around you."

She dropped her gaze to her feet. "I need to hear it again."

Even though that knot in my stomach grew tighter, I grinned because she was wearing the new Nikes I'd bought her. "Hey." With a finger under her chin, I guided her to look at me. "The more I'm around you, the stronger my feelings get. But why do you sound so desperate to hear how I feel?" Visions of high school surfaced. She'd been insistent, asking me how I felt about her then. Only now, I didn't want to run, even though I didn't like when someone backed me into a corner and demanded an answer. "We're not sixteen anymore. I'm not running if that's what you think. I was serious when I said I wanted to rekindle what we had."

"No matter what?" She searched my face in earnest.

I glanced past her to the lagoon. I didn't scare easily, but she was doing a good job of making my pulse soar, and not because I loved the way her auburn hair blew in the light breeze, or how her long lashes fluttered when she shied away, or how her pouty lips called my name.

"I thought so," she said, hurt washing over her features as she walked to the gated entrance.

I followed her. "Ruby, wait."

Just past Ruby, a woman walked through the gate, holding a little girl's hand. Before I could get another word out of my mouth, the little girl ran up to Ruby. The child had jet-black hair pulled into two ponytails with pink bows, and the bluest fucking eyes I'd ever seen. I faltered where I stood. Then I shook my head, closed my eyes, blinked several times before I set my gaze on the little girl again.

She jumped into Ruby's arms. "Mommy." She planted her tiny hands on Ruby's face. "I missed you."

The world around me spun. The sky darkened. My heart leapt out of my chest. *Mommy?*

A hand landed on my arm. "You must be Kross Maxwell," the woman said.

I wasn't sure who I was, or who the woman was standing beside me. I couldn't take my eyes off the little girl. My hands began to shake as I stood stock-still, my mind and limbs frozen. I would have sworn my heart stopped.

Ruby set the girl down, grasped her hand, and walked up to me. "Raven, I would like you to meet a friend of mine. His name is Kross."

She waved and beamed with a smile, revealing a lone dimple just like the one I had and on the same right side. I was a tough, powerful man. I punched men out for a living, hardly cried, knew what death felt like, and knew what heartache felt like. But at that moment when Raven smiled, I was reduced to nothing. Tears burned, hot and fierce, before they spilled out like a rushing waterfall.

Raven walked up to me. Automatically, I squatted down as though she had some magical abilities over me.

"Why are you crying?" Her sweet voice slid over me, creating a surge of goose bumps. "You know, the swans and ducks always make me smile. Do you want to go with me to see them?"

I glanced up at Ruby. Tears slid down her face. I couldn't tell if she was happy or sad at the moment. Then I set my sights on Raven. "Can I talk to your mom first?" I was ninety-nine percent sure she was my daughter. But I wanted to hear it from Ruby.

The lady next to me cleared her throat. "Hi. I'm Ms. Waters. I'm Ruby's social worker."

I pushed to my feet on shaky legs as several emotions plowed through me like a bulldozer on steroids—happiness, sadness, anger, fear, joy, and confusion. My brain was too foggy to figure out which one took control of my body.

Ms. Waters pushed her glasses up higher on her nose.

I blew out a long breath. "Social worker?" I pinched my eyebrows together. Questions piled up on the tip of my tongue.

Ms. Waters glared at Ruby. "You didn't tell him?" Irritation scraped her tone.

Ruby shook her head as fear swam in her eyes. "I haven't. I didn't have time."

She'd had all the fucking time in the world.

Raven hugged Ruby's leg. "Mommy, can we go down to the water?"

Ruby patted Raven's head. "Just a second, baby."

"We talked about this on the phone," Ms. Waters said. Then she addressed me. "I'm sorry. If I knew she hadn't told you, then I would've said no to this meeting."

"Does it matter?" I asked.

"Absolutely. It's clear that you're more than surprised. I wanted you to have time to process the news before you met Raven. That way, the time spent today would be getting to know her, not asking why, what, when, and any other questions you have mulling in your head." She angled her dark head at Ruby. "I specifically told you to make sure you had a conversation with him prior to today."

"Can you give Kross and me a minute?" Ruby asked Ms. Waters.

Ms. Waters held out her hand to Raven as she scowled at Ruby. "Let's go find the ducks."

Raven beamed from ear to ear, and my heart followed. I had to shake off the nerves, confusion, and every other fucking emotion that gripped me by the throat and squeezed so fucking hard that I could barely breathe. As Raven and Ms. Waters left, I walked around the George Washington Statue.

When I came around to the front of the iconic piece, Ruby was standing there, wiping tears away. "Kross, I'm sorry."

"Is she my daughter?" My voice broke. I knew the answer. I was the father. Raven was the spitting image of my mother. Not only that, she looked like me, Kody, and Kelton. *Fuck me.* I drove a hand through my hair and pulled. "Well?" I wanted her to say it. I wanted her to start talking and telling me why she'd told me she wasn't pregnant when she was.

Ruby's lips trembled. "When I told you I wasn't pregnant, that was the truth that I believed. I thought I'd gotten my period. I spotted for two days, but it wasn't a normal period. I chalked it up to stress and ballet practice and getting ready for my performance." She dashed away more tears. "Then the next month came, and no period. My body started changing. And..." She inhaled all the cool air she could. "You are the father."

"Why didn't you tell me?" As soon as the words left my mouth, another word came to mind. *Schmuck.* I'd never returned her frantic calls. I'd completely ignored her.

She narrowed her watery eyes. "Seriously? If you would've picked up your phone or answered my damn calls—"

"I get that part. But four years, Ruby. What happened in that time that you couldn't track me down?"

She pointed to the lagoon. Raven and Ms. Waters were watching the ducks that were gliding down the water. "A baby. Being a new mom. Dealing with my father in jail. Then my mom got busted for selling drugs like my dad. Anger at you. Fear if I did tell you, then you wouldn't want anything to do with me. Fear you would take Raven away from me. Each time I got the courage to find you, something happened."

"Why now? It's been clear you don't want anything to do with me."

"It's not like that." Her voice softened. "I've been confused and selfish and angry and scared. But every time I look at Raven, I see you. Every time she smiles, I see you. My heart breaks each time. Then you show up in my life. Those feelings I had for you in high school just sat dormant until I opened my eyes that day after my first fight. My heart flipped out. When you told me you still get butterflies around me, I feel the same around you. I'm not a bad mother. I'm not a monster. I want Raven to know her daddy. I just had to get over my anger toward you. I don't want her living in foster care. I screwed up when I got caught stealing food for us. Now she's paying for it. If you want to take her away from me and fight for sole custody, I wouldn't blame you." She bowed her head as she covered her face with her hands and started crying.

I brought my hands up to my mouth, dragging them down my chin as I looked up at the clouds rolling in, much like the rolling in my stomach. I wanted to go to Ruby and tell her that... I didn't know what I wanted to tell her. My thoughts were a fucking jumbled mess. I needed space. I needed to get out of there. I had to think. Granted, I had been processing the idea that I had a kid on this planet. But the realization of the truth, seeing Raven, trying to figure out what my next move would be, was all too much for my brain.

"You introduced me as your friend. Why not tell her I'm her father?" That information should come from Ruby since Raven didn't know me at all.

"Honestly, I'm protecting her feelings until we can work this out. Don't get me wrong. You are the father. But if you get cold feet, I don't want her hurt."

I couldn't argue with that. I wasn't running, though. Then again, I wasn't sure what I would do.

"Kross." My name carried on the strong breeze from Raven's lips.

I parked my state of mind for the moment and absorbed the little girl running toward me.

Rather than jumping into my arms like she'd done with Ruby, she stopped and pointed to the water. "There's a swan over there."

A shard of hurt gripped my chest that she didn't run into my arms as she did with Ruby. I craved to hold her and give her a big bear hug. "Hi." I crouched down. "Do you like swans?"

Her mesmerizing blue eyes glimmered as her little dimple emerged, showing baby white teeth. Fireworks went off inside me. This little girl was part of me. I'd helped to create her.

Holy Fuck!

"And ducks, birds, lizards, dogs, and cats, and bumble bees."

Kelton would be stoked when he learned Raven had a thing for lizards. "Bumble bees?" I pushed a stray bang out of her eyes.

"Yep. Mommy says they sting. I just like their colors."

A warmth blanketed me. My brothers were going to fall in love with Raven. *Oh, shit.* My parents were too. *Oh, shit.* I had to break the news to my parents.

"We need to go," Ms. Waters said.

Raven ran into Ruby's arms. "Mommy, I don't want to leave you," she cried.

My heart fucking broke as I pushed to my feet. Ruby was right. Raven needed to be with family. She needed to be with me.

"I know, baby." Ruby's voice broke. "I promise I'll see you soon."

"Kross," Ms. Waters said. "I know this is a lot to process. When and if you're ready, call me." She handed me a business card. "We can talk about the next steps to get Raven out of foster care. You'll need a lawyer. Then we'll need to prove that you're the father."

I pocketed the card. "Thank you." I joined Ruby and Raven. "I have to go. It was nice meeting you, Raven."

"You're leaving?" Ruby asked.

I wanted to stay and get to know Raven. I wanted to run around with her, watch the ducks, show her some lizards, and even play dolls with her.

"Sorry. The family is expecting me back in Ashford." For a miniscule second, I thought about inviting Ruby. I couldn't. I needed to be alone and wrap my head around how my life was about to change. Then I had to break the news to my family.

CHAPTER 17
KROSS

The driveway at my parents' house was teeming with cars. The entire family was there, including Lacey and Lizzie. On occasion, we had family from out of town visit us for Thanksgiving. Not this year. According to Mom, my aunts and uncles had other things going on.

I parked behind Lacey's Mustang, cut the engine, and held onto the steering wheel. I banged my head against my knuckles, once, twice, three times. *Fuck.* I had a daughter. The most beautiful little girl I'd ever seen. I had no idea how to break the news to my parents. I mustered all the courage I could as I climbed out of my truck. My parents were understanding individuals. They had big hearts. Yet all I could envision was how disappointed my old man would be, and that would gut me. He'd always counseled us boys to be practical and prepare for anything. He'd told us as growing teenagers to always wear protection when having sex and to always treat people with respect. I'd missed the mark on being prepared when Ruby and I had first had sex. It was the only fucking time I hadn't worn a condom.

I plodded up the stairs to the back deck and found a sticky note on the sliding glass door. *Down by the lake. Waiting on you.*

I trudged along the path around the garage, my heartbeat on a course to shoot out of my chest. Tall trees swayed and rustled around the rippling water of the lake. The sun cast its late afternoon rays down before it disappeared for the night. In the forefront of the calming scenery, my family sat around a campfire. Their voices, laughter, and the strum of Kody's guitar trickled on the wind.

I stilled on the grassy incline. I couldn't break up their happy evening. I couldn't stand to erase the smile from my mom's face or to even look at her. As soon as I did, I would see Raven, her thick black hair, her sparkling blue eyes, and a smile that knocked me backward. For sure, I would lose my shit as though my mom had taken my bottle away from me when I was a baby. Not to mention, the news of Raven might be too upsetting for her mental health. She'd been doing so well lately.

I had a daughter.

A sharp voice in my head bit out the words, *man up*. Famous advice from either Kade or my old man. How could I man up to anything when I didn't even know how to be a father? I started to backtrack as nausea toyed with my stomach, spinning, churning, and waiting for the right moment to expel the contents of what I'd done.

Everyone was enjoying Kody's ballad as he picked at his guitar, crooning, "You're the Only One For Me."

As I took another step backward, Lacey spotted me and waved. "Kross is here."

The blood rushed everywhere but my heart. I gulped in small breaths then let them out slowly. Orange and deep blues streaked across the sky, providing plenty of light to see the panic on my face. I feigned a smile as I put one foot in front of the other. That swirling in my stomach increased like the raging whitewater rapids we'd rafted on as kids.

I had a daughter, an out-of-this-world beautiful creature that was part of me.

Fuck.

I forced my facial muscles to relax, shoved my hands in my jeans pockets, and tacked on a smile as I walked up to the group. Kelton and Kade, who'd been lounging with their girls in their arms, sat upright as though they were ready to catch me. Kody eyed me warily.

"You're late." Dad pushed his honey-colored hair off his forehead.

"Martin." My mom squeezed his thigh. "We didn't have a set time." Her long black hair framed her face as she gave me one of her award-winning smiles that always warmed my heart.

I diverted my gaze to the fire that danced, crackled, and spit embers up, the wind taking them away. I wished the wind would take away the myriad of emotions that was lodged in my throat, stomach, head, and heart.

Concern slashed my mom's delicate features. "Is something wrong, honey?"

Images of Raven bombarded me. I had a daughter. I couldn't get those four words to go away. Maybe, the more I said them, the more I would believe them. *Fuck.* She was real. Paternity test or not, that little girl, who was worming her way into my heart, was a Maxwell. I knew in my soul that she was mine.

"Bro," Kade said on my left. "You look like—"

"You've seen a ghost," Lacey finished for him, her green eyes swimming with worry.

"He's been like that for two weeks," Lizzie added, tucking strands of her dark hair behind her ear.

I made a mental note to apologize to Lizzie. I lived with her, Kelton, and Kade, and I'd been curt with her on two occasions. Kelton had said she was worried about me. I'd learned from him that Lizzie wasn't good with secrets. So I'd asked Kelton to keep a lid on the situation with Ruby and the notion that I could be a father, at least until I knew for sure.

"Son." Dad kissed my mom's head. "What's wrong?" His tone dropped into psychiatrist mode, warm and inviting.

As long as he stayed in his doctor mode, I might be able to get through this. I lowered myself to the flannel blanket at my feet then sat on my haunches.

"Honey," Mom said.

I briefly closed my eyes, cleared the lump in my throat, and glanced out at the lake. "I believe I'm a daddy."

My mother, Lizzie, and Lacey gasped, drawing my attention back to the group, mainly my old man. Wrinkles creased his forehead, his copper gaze tracking from one side of my face to the other.

My gut curdled like sour milk. His mouth hung open. I wrapped an arm around my stomach, willing the nausea to go away.

Lizzie and Lacey had the same open-mouthed expression as Mom and Dad, while my brothers had blank expressions.

Silence hung thickly over the campfire as I took in slow and steady breaths. Saying it out loud lifted a five-ton weight off me. But I still had ten more tons to go. I had no idea how to be a father or even where to begin when it came to getting Raven out of foster care. When I did, would she accept me? Where would we live? I had many, many other life-changing decisions to make.

"Start from the beginning," Dad said quietly and calmly as he hugged my mom to his chest.

Again, I cleared my throat. "It started four years ago back at the academy," I began as though I was telling a normal campfire story. I let out a whisper of a nervous laugh. It might not have been a scary story to them, but it was to me. "I met a girl named Ruby Lewis. We dated, and we had unprotected sex." Heat stung my face at saying the word "sex" in front of Mom. She didn't react. Instead, she listened intently.

Horror blanched Dad's face. "Are you telling us that the child is four years old?"

I wasn't sure if Raven was four yet, although she had to be close.

I zoned in on the fire, watching it flicker, casting shadows outward, as I contemplated how to tell my father I was an ass to Ruby. "Treat people with respect," he'd always said to us boys. Not returning Ruby's frantic messages wasn't anything but rude and low.

"Is it a boy or a girl?" Lizzie piped in with too much giddiness in her voice as though she wanted to find Raven and hug her. That didn't surprise me. Lizzie was dying to have kids.

"Let him talk," Dad barked out in a deep voice.

The fire became my friend as I continued. "At first, Ruby thought she was pregnant. Then a couple of days later, she came to me and said it was a false alarm because she'd been spotting. After that, I moved back to Ashford. She tried to call me." Rubbing my jaw, I tilted my face toward the sky. A darker blue overtook the orange hue as twilight set in. Soon the stars would be out. *Stars. Ruby.* Stars always made me think of Ruby. *Fuck.* "But I ignored her calls." I righted my head. "She never once said in her messages that she'd left me that she was pregnant."

"I don't understand how she thought she wasn't pregnant when she was," Kelton said.

My chest tightened as Mom wiped away a tear.

"Sometimes women spot that first month," Lizzie said. "My mom did when she was pregnant with me."

"Why don't you kids head up to the house and get the lasagna in the oven," Dad said, inclining his head toward Kade.

The five of them scrambled to their feet. Lizzie and Lacey bolted for the house, whispering to each other. Each of my brothers patted me on the shoulder as they walked by.

"I'd like Kelton to stay," I said. "I'm going to need a lawyer." Not that Kelton was one, but with his part-time job at the law firm, he would be able to help.

My dad nodded then pushed to his feet before helping Mom to hers.

Immediately, she came over. I stood before she threw her arms around me. No sooner than she did, a grunt thundered from me as though someone had split open my chest. Then I was sobbing in my mom's arms.

She rubbed my neck. "We're here for you, honey. You're not in this alone." She sniffled.

"I disappointed you and Dad."

"Shhh," she whispered.

A hand landed on my back. "Kross," Dad said, his voice breaking apart like my heart.

I let go of Mom as the tears flowed. She held my hand, soft to hard, mom to son.

Dad blinked a couple of times as confusion, hurt, and disappointment played across the hard planes of his face like a slideshow. "Why are we just finding out about this? Where have the child and the mother been for four years?"

Kelton shoved his hands in his jeans pockets as he sidled up next to the three of us, standing close to the fire. He nodded at me as though he was my lawyer, giving me permission to speak.

Telling my parents about Raven was hard. Telling them about Ruby and her situation only made my insides queasier. I wasn't sure why. "Ruby is homeless. Well, technically, not anymore. She's living with a friend."

Mom squeezed my hand, and that one gesture said, "I'm here for you" made me shed more tears.

Dad sighed heavily.

"And the child?" Mom asked.

I grabbed fistfuls of my hair with both hands. The trees' branches rustled together. Embers spat up again from the fire.

Kelton clamped a hand on my shoulder. "Breathe."

I was trying to, but I couldn't get enough air in to slow my pulse. "Raven lives with a foster family."

"Raven. It's a little girl?" Mom pressed dainty fingers to her lips, her blue eyes swimming with love, excitement, and joy. I wasn't too surprised at her reaction. After my sister died, my parents had tried for another child. My mom had desperately wanted another little girl.

Dad scratched his unshaven jaw. "Homeless, foster family, what else?"

"According to Ruby's social worker, I need to get a lawyer and take a paternity test to prove I'm the father so that I can get her out of foster care."

Dad pressed his lips into a thin line. "Do you know for sure that you're the father?"

I briefly glanced at Kelton. Not that I was looking for his approval. It was just a habit we had as brothers when we were in a pickle with our parents. My brother didn't exactly speak for me, but his presence was enough to give me the courage to face my dad. "I believe Ruby. Plus, Raven's the spitting image of Mom. She has jet-black hair, dark-blue eyes, and like me, she has one dimple."

Tears ran down Mom's rosy cheeks.

A light chuckled escaped me as I eyed Kelton. "She's beautiful. She loves ducks, swans, even lizards."

One side of my brother's mouth tweaked upward. "Seriously?"

Silence mingled with the snap and crackle of the fire.

Mom grasped Dad's hand. "Martin, we have a granddaughter."

My dad's rigid posture softened as he brought a hand up to Mom's cheek. "One step at a time, sweetheart."

"Dad's right," I said. "I need to get that paternity test done."

"I'll speak with Mr. Davenport on Monday," Kelton said. "Since Raven is a ward of the state, we'll need to petition the family court."

"Can I get a paternity test done next week?" I asked.

"I can't answer that. We'll do our best to push things through," Kelton said.

"Ruby's social worker told me to call her with any questions," I added. "So I'll reach out to her on Monday." I also wanted to ask her if I could spend some time alone with Raven.

Dad scrubbed a hand down his face. "Kross, I'm not going to lie. I'm extremely disappointed. But I can't change what happened. The only thing your mom and I can do is support you."

I hated myself for disappointing my father. But my pulse slowed for the first time in two weeks. At least, for the moment.

"Honey," Mom said. "Do you love Ruby?"

Kelton let out a chuckle. "Kade said he's smitten with Ruby."

To say I was in love with Ruby... I wasn't sure. I had a growing desire to run my fingers through her auburn hair and kiss her lights out. Maybe then I would know for sure.

"Mom, back in high school, when Ruby told me she loved me, I wasn't in the same place. Now, I don't know. She's beautiful. She's tough. Yet shy. She stirs things in me I've never felt with another woman. I haven't even kissed her yet." *Fuck, I'm dying to, though.*

"That sounds familiar." Dad smiled at Mom. Then he gave me a pointed look. "Boxing may not be the job to support a family."

Boom. Reality begins.

I chewed the inside of my cheek. "I'll do whatever it takes." I would work five jobs if I had to, although if I signed with Gail Freeman, I could have my future set. In the meantime, I had money saved from my previous bouts, and Jay paid me well to train clients. I could find a small apartment for Ruby and Raven.

A cold hard wind blew.

"Let's put out the fire and get some dinner," Dad said.

Kelton grabbed a small pail of sand that we always had ready when we built a campfire.

Dad pulled me in for a hug. "I love you, son. I know you'll be the best damn father."

Doubt niggled in the back of my psyche. I didn't even know where to begin to be a father or how to gain the patience to be one.

"When can we meet Ruby and Raven?" Mom asked.

As we broke apart, Dad and I exchanged a not-so-surprised look. We both knew Mom wanted to spoil Raven.

"Sweetheart," Dad said. "Let's make sure Kross is the father."

Great idea. I didn't want Mom getting attached if Raven wouldn't be in our lives.

"Then Ruby," Mom said. "Invite her to dinner tomorrow."

I'd left Ruby with my cold attitude. She probably thought I didn't want anything to do with her or Raven. I had to make sure she knew that wasn't the case. "I'm not sure she's ready." But maybe now that I'd met Raven and the truth was out on the table, Ruby would reconsider meeting my parents.

CHAPTER 18
RUBY

The yellowed, weathered colonial home stuck out like the bad stepchild among the other houses on the street. The black shutters were chipped at the corners. Overgrown bushes hid the quaint wooden porch where I used to sit on warm, balmy summer days. My mom had even sat with me, crocheting as we rocked in the handmade chairs my dad had made, talking about school, boys, ballet, and the future. So many dreams had shattered in one night as the world came to a screeching halt with one knock, one piece of paper, and a team of detectives. They'd stormed in with a warrant, tearing our memories from drawers, walls, and closets, while my mom and I watched in abject horror.

I'd wanted to believe my father was innocent and hadn't done anything to jeopardize our lives. But it was hard when pictures and surveillance had told the whole story. At first, anger and shame at what my father had done became a staple inside me. But as my own life had taken a turn for the worse, I began to realize that my dad had gone to great lengths to provide for his family when he'd lost his office job because of downsizing. It was ironic how my own life mirrored his. I wasn't selling drugs, but I would do just about anything to get Raven out of foster care, including make a deal with Trent. I didn't know the specifics yet. He'd said he would be in touch. But I filed away Trent and his deal when I boarded the bus. I wanted a reprieve from my life in the city.

The For Sale sign leaned, touching the tips of the weeds and dying grass.

"Ruby?" A male voice called my name, pulling me from shattered memories.

Nick Mendoza, who'd once been my friend, sauntered through the bushes that separated our properties, pushing his blond wavy hair from his light-brown eyes.

"Nick, is that you?" The boy I'd hung out with late at night on my porch was no longer a boy, but a good-looking man. Up close, he was even prettier. He had clear, smooth skin, an angular jaw, bright-white teeth, and nice lips. "What happened to your pimples?"

He rumbled out a hearty laugh. "I see you still know how to win a guy over. I also see you've turned into a knockout."

I dropped my gaze to the dead grass. "Hardly." If he'd seen me a month ago, he wouldn't have complimented me.

He chuckled lightly. "Still shy, too."

My mom had sold the house not long after my dad was carted off to jail. "Do you know why the house is vacant?"

"After you moved, the house was sold to a young couple, who got foreclosed on about six months ago. According to my mom, the market sucks. So, my sister, Tasha, gave that Kross Maxwell dude my number. He called me a few weeks back. I'm sorry, but I told him that you'd been pregnant. Did he ever find you?"

I bobbed my head. "Yeah. The neighborhood hasn't changed much." Today was one day I didn't want to think about Kross.

I'd been stupid not to listen to Ms. Waters. I should've told him way before yesterday. I should've prepared him. Every time I had thought about telling him, I'd gotten cold feet. In truth, I wanted him to see Raven first. I believed in the cliché that seeing is believing. That way, he couldn't have exactly denied the resemblance. I was probably scum to him. "He needs time," both Norma and Ms. Waters had said. Maybe so, but hurt still wormed its way into my chest.

Nick dangled his car keys in his hand. "What brings you up here anyway?"

A gravesite. Solace. Fresh country air. Memory lane.

An engine rumbled, drawing our attention to the quiet street.

"I should get going, anyway. I just wanted to see the old house." I'd taken the bus up here that morning, and I had a return ticket for later in the afternoon.

A silver truck slowed, turned toward us before stopping at the edge of the driveway. The windows were tinted, or maybe the overcast day prevented us from seeing in.

Nick whistled. "Sweet ride. A friend of yours?"

I didn't have any friends who drove shiny trucks. Inch by inch, the window rolled down, revealing the one person whose presence always coaxed a slew of tingles and butterflies from me. A waft of his spicy cologne drifted out, causing a blazing heat to trail up and pinch my cheeks.

Kross plastered on a knowing smirk as though I had a sign on my forehead that read, "Kross Maxwell gets me hot and bothered."

The word "asshat" sat on the tip of my tongue. I would've said it out loud if it weren't for the way his blue gaze undressed me, making my brain shut down.

Nick shuffled over to Kross and stuck out his hand. "I'm Nick."

"Kross Maxwell."

Nick closed his fist as he touched his mouth. "No way. I guess you found Ruby."

Kross flicked his head to one side. "I guess I did."

"Nice seeing you again, Ruby," Nick said. "I've got to run." He dashed off the same way he'd come.

"Get in," Kross said in his bossy tone.

"Pfft. If you came all this way to be possessive, then go home."

His eyes softened like quicksand and so did his voice. "I came all this way to finish our conversation from yesterday."

I smiled slowly, tucking my cold hands into the pockets of my wool coat. "How did you know I was here, anyway?"

"I didn't exactly. I caught Norma before she left for the bus station. She said you were headed up to the Berkshires. This was my first stop."

Norma was one reason I was taking a trip down memory lane. We'd had a deal. I would come clean with Kross about Raven, and she would make an effort to visit her parents after seven years. She decided that Thanksgiving would be a good time to catch them at home. I didn't want to hang around the city alone, so I decided to visit Riley's grave. Nevertheless, I hadn't figured that Kross would search for me on Thanksgiving. After all, he'd wanted to spend the day with his family.

"Although, she thought you might've made a stop to see your mom," Kross said. "If you haven't, I can take you."

My plan had been to visit my mother until I'd spoken to her yesterday. She'd asked me to come on another day since she had a bad case of the flu. She didn't want me to get sick. So, we had talked. It had been good to tell her that Kross had found me, and that I'd told him about Raven. She'd been pleased and said, "He'll be good for Raven." After seeing how he had interacted with Raven even for those few minutes, I agreed with my mom.

I fidgeted under his gaze. "What about your family and Thanksgiving?"

"You are my family," he said easily.

My eyebrows flew into my hairline. I'd been praying all night that Kross would accept Raven. It was hard to miss how affected he'd been when he laid eyes on her. I had never pegged Kross for a crier or a man with deep emotions. The Kross I knew was strong and rough around the edges. The deep heartfelt emotions he'd displayed with Raven blew me away.

I sank my teeth into my bottom lip. *I* was his family. Could've fooled me by the way he'd abruptly left yesterday. "Raven is your family. Not me. We're not playing house because we have a child." In no way was I living with someone who didn't have feelings for me.

He groaned, shifted the truck into park, and stormed out like a man possessed. His jaw flexed as he stalked up to me, reached out as though he wanted to touch me, then lowered his hands. He puffed out air as fury swirled like a storm at sea in those blue eyes. He paced back one step, glared at me, then drove a hand through his unkempt hair.

Kross had always been on edge when he was at the academy. Back then, I figured his impatience stemmed from his family troubles. His brothers had similar traits as they had acted out in class. Then again, we'd been teenagers with raging hormones and mood swings.

I scanned the neighborhood out of habit. After the cops had raided our home that night, the neighbors had all but shunned us or looked at us as though my mom and I were criminals.

Kross leaned against his truck, all six feet of imposing muscle, sizing me up. Again, I fidgeted under his scrutiny. I always had with him. He emitted a dark and dangerous aura that seemed to seep into my pores, weakening my knees.

He crossed one ankle over the other. The storm that brewed in his gaze calmed. "Since Raven is our daughter, that makes you family in my book."

I stuck out my chin. "Kross, just because we have a daughter doesn't mean you have to take care of me. Actually, I don't want you to be my superman." In part, it was the truth. I had to get on my own two feet and build something for myself.

Pushing off his truck, he walked up to me. Then he gently grasped my elbows before pressing his forehead to mine. He inhaled as though he was trying to suck my energy into him. "What if I want to be your superman?"

I gave him a half smile. "It's sweet." So sweet my heart was breaking. I'd traveled one bad road after another. The only good in my life was Raven. She was my shining star. I wanted my daughter to see her mom succeed, not because a man swept me off my feet, but because I worked my ass off to better myself and showed her to do the same as she grew older. My mom had made the mistake of allowing a man to take care of her, and she did have regrets. I wasn't saying that a man couldn't sweep me off my feet for love. I just didn't want anyone to feel obligated to take care of me because of a child.

I touched Kross's warm cheek. "You need to focus on taking care of Raven. We both do. We both need to show her that we love her."

"Even though we both get butterflies around each other. That doesn't mean anything to you?"

"Ruby Lewis," A squeaky voice said my name from somewhere to my left.

Kross tensed as he let go of me. "Tasha."

"Nick said you were out here with Kross." She bounced up with her ponytail swinging high on her head. "Hi, Kross. How's Kody?"

I raised an eyebrow at him.

"Tasha was the one to tell me you'd been pregnant."

Figured. Tasha had always been a gossip girl like her mother.

Her chin dipped to her chest before she looked at me. "I see you two found each other. Anyway, my mom is basting the turkey. She wants to know if you would like to come in and stay for dinner."

"Thanks for the offer," Kross said. "But Ruby and I have plans."

Tasha wrapped her long bangs behind her ear. "So, is your brother seeing anyone?"

"He is. Sorry, but we're late." Kross bounded around the truck to the passenger door. "Come on, Ruby."

I waved at Tasha. "Nice to see you. Say hi to your mom." Awkwardness came to mind when I thought of how dinner would have gone with the Mendoza family. Too many questions that I wouldn't have been prepared to answer, especially the one that Mrs. Mendoza would no doubt have asked. "How's your mom?" I shouldn't have cared about gossip since I didn't live there anymore. I wasn't moving back, but my mom had friends there. If she ever decided to return, I didn't want to taint her relationships with her friends.

I hopped in, and Kross clicked the door shut before he flew around the truck then into the driver's seat. He threw the truck in gear and sped down the road, leaving Tasha on the curb with her mouth open.

I giggled when he slowed at a stop sign.

"She kept drooling for Kody that day we were up here," Kross said on a sigh. "Are you hungry?"

"Starving." *For more than food.*

"The other day you said you wanted to show me something in the Berkshires. How about after we eat, you show me?"

I was here to visit Riley's grave, and if he was going to be part of my life, then he needed to know everything, regardless of how that would affect our relationship.

I nodded as I listened to a raspy singer belt out a song that gave me goose bumps. Or maybe the goose bumps were because Kross was offering me his hand, palm up, on the console. I hesitated for a split second, afraid that the moment we locked hands was the moment I would fall deeper for him. That alone scared me more than living on the streets.

CHAPTER 19

KROSS

I rolled into a cemetery while Ruby gnawed on her fingers. Over lunch, we'd talked mainly about Raven. Ruby had chatted excitedly about how smart our daughter was. The minute Ruby's pretty blue-green eyes had filled with tears, I'd changed the subject to something totally random. Sure, I wanted to learn as much as I could about my little girl and the years I'd missed, but I'd gotten choked up a couple of times as well.

The clouds grew darker as I shifted the truck into park. The forecast called for snow. My mom didn't want me on the road today. I'd explained that I owed Ruby an apology, and I wanted to spend time with her, although I would love to spend time with Raven, too. That wouldn't happen until I could sort out the paternity test.

"So you want to show me a gravesite?" A morbid chill ran through me as Karen's small coffin flashed before me. The last time I was anywhere near a cemetery was at Karen's funeral.

Headstones of all shapes and sizes dotted the landscape out the truck's window. Flowers gave color to the etched weatherworn gray stones, while the dying leaves kicked up around them. A snowflake fell, then another, slowly covering the windshield.

Ruby climbed out without so much as a word. Her fingers had to be raw from expending all that nervous energy she'd consumed from the restaurant to here. When she'd told me she wanted to show me something, I sifted through my brain but came up empty. I'd gotten the sense she wanted to take me back in time and show me some of the things we'd done when we had dated. The oak tree we'd carved our initials in at the academy came to mind.

I jumped out then jogged up to her as she headed for the white clapboard church off to the right, her auburn hair swaying behind her. A faint outline of the mountains in the distance painted a backdrop against the cloudy sky. More snow drifted to the ground as my boots sank into the damp earth. Dodging headstones, I couldn't shake the memory of my sister's funeral or the days before when my mom found Karen's body. Mom had screamed for hours until my old man gave her a sedative. My muscles coiled as I tried to erase my memories. Surrounded by death, I wasn't sure I could.

Ruby finally stopped at a short gravestone that stood about two feet in height. The name on the gravestone read Riley Lewis. When I settled next to her, she reached out and grabbed my hand.

I jerked away. My mom had done the same thing in front of Karen's coffin at the gravesite. One of her small hands had grabbed mine, and the other had grabbed Kody. She would've gathered all of us if Kade hadn't been consoling Kelton. He'd been an emotional basket case at the funeral, more so than any of us.

"Please. I want you to understand how emotionally drained I was to even contact you after Raven was born. You need the whole story. Riley is Raven's twin."

A freaky sound escaped me as though someone had taken a sledgehammer and swung it across my back, knocking the wind straight from my lungs. Death. Again. And not just family, but someone I'd created.

Holy motherfucker.

"Join me," Ruby whispered, squeezing my hand and jarring me from my numb state.

I lowered to my knees because I had to. Otherwise, I would've fallen flat on my ass. The wetness sank into my jeans as I sat on my heels. "Twin?"

"She was stillborn. Doctor said it was a genetic defect." Her tone was melancholy.

I had no words. I didn't even know how I should feel. This girl had rendered me speechless so many times since I'd found her in that underground fight. Today wasn't any different. In my book, Ruby's life was something Hollywood would probably put on the big screen. She'd gotten pregnant at sixteen. I'd left her without a word. Her mom and dad were in prison for drugs. Ruby lived on the streets and fought in illegal fights. She'd been in jail, lost Raven to social services, and lost a baby. Recounting all that, I blinked to ward off the dizzy feeling. I was beginning to realize how my parents felt over the loss of a child.

Ruby's hands landed on my cheeks as she knelt facing me. "Are you in there, Kross?"

I blinked again. Her pretty face helped to calm me for the moment.

She dipped into her back pocket and removed an envelope. Then she pulled out pictures. She flipped through them then held up one. "My mom took this before the nurses carried away Riley." She handed me the photo. "Riley is on the right with the nurse in blue. My mom is holding Raven on the left."

Riley had a head full of black hair just like Raven. I clenched my jaw. I should've been there. I should've returned Ruby's calls. My breathing grew shallow.

Ruby's cold wet hands were on my face again. "I'm so, so sorry, Kross. I should've found you. My mom wanted me to, but I told her you didn't want anything to do with me. Then my dad got arrested, and things got crazy."

I curled my fingers around her small wrists. Guilt, anger, heart-break, and devastation competed for a spot within me. But as my dad had said, we couldn't change the past. I wanted to so fucking bad, though.

"Say something," Ruby pleaded.

I glanced at the picture of my girls. *Get your shit together. Be the man who your father believes you to be. Be the father that Raven needs.*

Big fat snowflakes were falling at a rapid rate. I wasn't sure I could speak. The memories of my past, my sister, and this new news of Riley were more than suffocating.

Ruby's face scrunched. "Kross?"

"I wished I would've been there for you," I said as calmly as I could, hoping the irritation that I harbored at myself didn't come through. I wobbled as I pushed to my feet.

She jumped up and caught my arm. "Are you okay?"

Hell, no. "The snow is getting heavier."

She stuck her hands on her hips. "Talk to me, Kross. You wanted to know my story. You wanted answers. So now you have them. All of them." Her bottom lip overlapped the top, trembling slightly.

Fuck. "I'm just mad at myself," I said in a flat tone. "We should get on the road." I started for my truck.

I needed to get my head around Ruby, my daughters, my fucking life. My heavy boots pressed into the earth. With each step, I swore the dead were reaching out of the ground and pulling me down. I glanced at the picture of my girls, tiny and precious, and my heart broke into a million fucking pieces. I shoved down my emotions or else I wouldn't be able to drive. I reached the truck and opened the passenger door for Ruby, but she wasn't there. I pivoted on my heel and froze. She stood in the distance like a statue, almost blending in with the scenery if not for her auburn hair contrasting with the gray and white colors around us. I shivered at the way her gaze bore into me as though she was trying to get into my mind and will me to come back to her. I didn't trust myself. I didn't trust that I wouldn't break her if I touched her. If I kissed her, I was afraid I wouldn't stop until I sucked out all her oxygen so I could breathe.

I closed my eyes. The snowflakes hit my face, the coldness a welcome relief to the inferno inside me. I relished the quietness even if just for a second. As more snow covered my face, I thought about my mom. She'd always told us boys that snow was an angel's blanket. How ironic that I was among the dead in a cemetery with snow falling. Maybe angels were present. Maybe they were watching over us. I hoped so.

Heaving a sigh, I pocketed the picture then stomped back to Ruby who hadn't moved. I peered down to find remorse and sorrow swimming in her eyes. "I'm sorry again for not returning your calls. I'm sorry I wasn't there to help you through Riley and Raven. I'm sorry I've been acting cold and weird. I'm just so angry with myself."

"I'm at fault, too." Tears pooled in her bright eyes. "You don't need to apologize for being cold and weird. It's a lot to take in."

As I raked my gaze over this beautiful woman, I said, deep and firm, "I am your superman whether you want me to be or not."

She smiled, her gaze moving slowly down to my lips.

My pulse jumped. Then her fingers came up to my mouth. I wanted nothing more than to have her lips on mine instead of those cold, soft fingers. She rubbed my bottom lip then the top as she licked her own.

Banishing any gentleman's qualities, I hoisted her in my arms. Her legs went around my back, and her hands dove into my hair before her mouth crashed to mine, greedy, hungry, and wild. Electricity fused us together, sizzling hot as I opened for her on a strangled groan. My body burst into flames, my dick growing as hard as the gravestones.

Her tongue slowly slithered in, exploring lazily as though she was savoring the kiss. Hell, I was. Although I was on edge, wanting to take control, to devour her, to bury myself in her. *Not yet.* I wanted her to take the lead. If she did, then that meant she was ready. Not to mention, I was enjoying the feel of her nails scraping my scalp, the way she was tasting every part of my mouth, and the sexy purrs she spewed as she kissed me.

She took a breath, and a snowflake dropped on her nose. I carried her to the truck.

The snow was piling up, and my dick was straining against my zipper. She bounced in my arms as she held onto me with her head on my shoulder. God, if she didn't feel like she belonged in my arms.

"Why didn't you kiss me back?" she asked as I set her in the passenger seat. "Is it because of Penelope?"

"Hell, no. If I kissed you back, you would've been naked on the snow-covered ground."

She blushed. My dick jumped.

I closed her door, circled the truck to the driver's side then hopped in.

My phone rang. I plucked it from my jacket. "Hey, what's up?" I turned the ignition then blasted the heater.

"You good?" Kade asked. "Mom's worried."

"Ruby and I are fine. The snow is getting heavy, though. I'll check in with you later."

Ruby waved her hands in front of the vents. "I didn't realize how cold I was until I got in."

Her face held that flushed look, while I was burning up from all the emotions flickering through me, especially the way she'd felt against me, soft and perfect.

She blew into her hands. "Kross, I'd rather not go back to Boston tonight."

I whipped my head around to look at her. Not that I didn't want to spend the night with her up against me, tangled around me, kissing me, touching me. Sure, she'd kissed me. *But is she ready for the next step? Am I ready for the next step?*

"I haven't slept in a soft, comfortable bed in ages. Alex's couch is not a bed." She sank her teeth into her bottom lip. "I have money for a hotel." She averted her gaze.

That shy look of hers was enough to drive me insane.

Her seatbelt wasn't on yet. So I tugged her to me as far as the console would allow. It was my turn to attack her sweet lips, to get lost in her. One hand went into her hair, and the other underneath her chin. I brushed my lips over hers. Her eyelids fluttered. Slowly, I slid my tongue into her mouth. Then I got lost in the sugary taste left over from the apple pie she'd had for dessert combined with the sweet taste that was just Ruby—the girl who was the mother of my child, the girl who was cracking open every part of my heart, the girl that still gave me that feeling of riding the tallest, scariest rollercoaster.

The cemetery vanished as she met each stroke of my tongue. I cupped the back of her head then pulled her closer to me as I continued to suck on her tongue, nibble on her lips, and breathe in her essence. When I broke the kiss to settle on her ear, she shivered then whimpered.

"I don't think the hotel is a good idea," I whispered huskily. "I wouldn't be able to keep my hands off you."

Her hand settled on my dick. "So? I want you, Kross, even if it's just for you to hold me." Her tone was seductive as she squeezed my erection.

I had to hold back until I found a hotel because I wanted a bed underneath us, and nothing else.

CHAPTER 20
RUBY

I wiped the steam from the mirror in the hotel bathroom then dipped into my backpack and found my brush. As I untangled my wet hair, I sifted through the last few hours, and a host of emotions flitted through me. But one shined brighter than the sorrow, hurt, sadness, and despair that had consumed me in the cemetery— hope. Hope that Kross and I could build a relationship. Hope that we could live as a family and watch Raven grow up. Hope that he had the same feelings for me as I did for him. I wasn't naïve enough to believe that he loved me. I did, however, believe he cared for me. I prayed it wasn't just because of Raven, but because he wanted *me*.

A warm tingle started in my chest and worked its way down to my toes as I replayed Kross's kiss. Electrical sparks ignited parts of me I hadn't felt ever, not even when we were teenagers exploring each other or kissing for the first time. I'd been so consumed with him that I found myself playing with his huge, solid erection. My heart did a wild tap dance at that thought. I swallowed the dryness in my throat. I was equal parts excited and scared out of my mind. It was as though I was teetering on the edge of life's cliff, hanging on by the tips of my fingers, and at any moment, I would fall so hard and fast. In the end, Kross and I would be together or he would walk away again.

"Through fear comes strength" was my mom's favorite saying. I'd had my share of fear, and I was stronger for everything I'd been through. But when it came to my heart, I wasn't sure I could test her wisdom.

Kross knocked on the door. "Ruby, are you coming out?"

I giggled softly. We'd found a hotel not far from the cemetery. I'd offered to pay, but Kross wouldn't let me, which was fine. Payment for a hotel wasn't a reason to argue. I'd taken my time in the pristine tiled shower, sampling the soaps and shampoo, washing my hair twice, making sure my nails were clean, and brushing my teeth. I'd purchased a razor, toothbrush, and toothpaste in the hotel store, so I was able to shave my legs and other spots.

"Almost done."

Pulling the brush through my hair, I smiled at myself. The dark circles underneath my eyes that I'd had for so long were fading. Norma had even noticed how much healthier I looked. She did as well. We'd both gained some needed weight. As I set the brush down on the sink, I wondered if she had been able to see her parents. I couldn't exactly call her since we didn't own cell phones. I frowned. Not only did I want to find out how she was doing, I wanted to tell her about Kross, our kiss, and ask her for advice on sex.

My pulse accelerated as I slipped on my underwear then Kross's T-shirt that he'd given me to sleep in. I giggled again. I wouldn't be able to sleep, not with Kross beside me in that king-size bed. I checked my stomach to ensure I wasn't covered in hives, which often occurred when I was nervous. I braved a quick look in the mirror. Red colored my neck and the upper part of my chest. I checked my arms and stomach. All clear. I inhaled and exhaled, splashed water on my face, then patted it dry with a towel.

After another calming breath, I smoothed down the T-shirt, which fell to my knees, then opened the door. A wave of cool air swooped in as I went out. The TV was on, but muted. Outside the window, the snow came down in big flakes. On the bed, Kross sat bare-chested with his back to the headboard, his denim-encased legs kicked out to cross at the ankles. He wiggled his bare feet, absorbed in something on his phone. Lazily, I continued to assess the man I wanted to spend my life with. Yellow briefs peeked out of his unbuttoned jeans. His rippled abs had a couple of drops of water that lingered from the shower he'd taken before me. The man was downright gorgeous with his freakishly toned chest, six-pack abs, and biceps that flexed and relaxed every time he typed on his phone. The urge to feel all that hardness beneath my fingers was enough to cover me in goose bumps.

When he lifted his gaze, my knees went weak, my stomach tumbled, and a fuzzy, tingly sensation throbbed between my legs. Even though I'd pleasured myself in the past, my arousal was different, stronger this time.

He tracked me from head to toe in a slow, languid path as though he was snapping picture after picture. I thought about locking myself in the bathroom because I wasn't sure I would survive if he had his way with me. I would want more, more, more. "*So*" was all my subconscious said. *But will he want more with me?* And not just sex. A life. A family. Those two things were a tall order.

He patted the spot next to him on the down comforter. "Come here."

I moved on his command, the sweetness in his voice seemingly the trigger to get me to put one foot in front of the other as I crossed the carpeted floor to the bed.

He gave me one of his dimpled grins. Yep, I wouldn't survive the night. I wouldn't survive the next five minutes. I climbed up on the bed, adjusted my T-shirt, and crossed my legs underneath me as I faced him. Then I toyed with the hem of the T-shirt, not sure what else to do or say.

"Breathe, Ruby." His voice was hypnotic and packed with raw male strength intertwined with pure silk. "We're just two adults watching TV."

I giggled through the nerves. I either had a frightened look, or my damn neck was splotchy again.

He set his phone on the nightstand. "Do you want to watch a movie?"

No. "Sure."

He flipped through channels as the last of daylight spilled in through the window. I should probably turn around to see what movies he was searching for. Maybe the distraction would quell my racing heart. But I had one problem. I couldn't take my eyes off him. Anticipation sparked through my veins, giving me a full cup of courage to trace the writing on his left arm just above the crease of his elbow. In cursive, the tattoo read, *blood comes first*, and behind the writing were five hearts. When I dragged a finger over the words, a string of goose bumps popped out on his arm.

"Family," he said as sure as it was snowing outside, "always comes first."

It was then I knew without a shadow of a doubt that Raven would be loved and taken care of as though she was his princess. My heart tripped as I also realized that the feelings I had for Kross just multiplied. "And the hearts?"

"My sister, Karen, loved them. Each heart represents a sibling. One for her, Kade, Kelton, Kody and myself."

If I hadn't believed him about family, I certainly did now. Tears stung the backs of my eyelids. I wanted to be part of his family. I blinked once then twice to dry the tears. This wasn't a night to cry or feel sorry for myself, or worse, have Kross pity me. It was a night to relax, to sink my head into a plush pillow, to feel the softness of the sheets against my body, and just maybe sleep in Kross's arms, or better yet, do more than sleep.

"So a snake, huh?" I asked. Raven would like that. She loved lizards and worms and frogs, anything related to nature.

"Rattlesnake. Some reporter dubbed me with the name after one of my fights."

I remembered someone at my fight shouting out "rattlesnake" at Kross.

"Every boxer has a tell. Mine is that I curl my lip on one side before I go in for the kill. Since then, it's stuck."

"Does the snake bite?" I asked playfully.

"Only if you want him to," he returned with a menacing grin.

I chewed my lip. "As long as he's not poisonous."

"His venom is filled with sugar and all kinds of pleasure."

A heady rush of bravery washed over me. Before I could grasp what I was doing, I was straddling him.

He grinned all kinds of sexy as his hands disappeared under my T-shirt. Immediately, my skin pebbled in goose bumps. Then he dragged his fingers lightly over my thighs, the feeling soothing, yet keeping me alert. He watched me as though he were waiting for permission to continue. So I wiggled against him.

He sucked in a sharp breath as he pulled me closer. I closed my eyes, disbelieving I was alone in a hotel room, in a huge comfy bed, sitting on Kross Maxwell. The throbbing between my legs intensified, even more so when I adjusted myself on his rock-hard erection.

"Fuck," he barely got out. "Too many clothes."

I swallowed thickly at the feral look in his eyes.

He grabbed the edges of my T-shirt. As though he was program-ming me, I lifted my arms. In less than a second, the T-shirt was gone. I shivered, not only from the cool air that instantly hardened my nipples, but from how that predatory look in Kross's dark-blue eyes intensified as his gaze raked over me.

I looked beyond him to the buttoned gray fabric headboard as though the piece of furniture had the answers as to what I should do next.

He caught my chin between his thumb and forefinger. "Hey, look at me."

My gaze returned to his.

"I love when you're shy. To me, it makes you that much sexier. But I sense more than shyness. I see some fear in those pretty eyes."

"I..." I was afraid to tell him I hadn't had sex with anyone since him. He might think I was pathetic. I had experience in childbearing, living on the streets, sleeping in dark alleys and abandoned ware-houses, eating out of dumpsters, stealing, jail, begging for change, and fighting. But sex? No freaking experience. My only memory was how uncomfortable sex had been my first time with him at sixteen. *You had his child. The man will understand.* "I... um. I haven't had sex since you." I held my breath.

He cupped my face in his humungous hands. "Hey, you shouldn't be afraid of that."

I knitted my eyebrows. "What if I'm no good?"

"There's no right or wrong way. It's all about you and me and what makes us feel good. What will make me feel good is you, and pleasing you." His tone was gentle.

I leaned in and kissed him. After that heart-warming response, I didn't care if we did or didn't have sex. I just wanted to kiss him and have him hold me. The only problem was when our tongues touched, sparks went off, and the throbbing between my legs was back.

I nibbled on his lower lip. "Make love to me?"

He growled, low and husky. Before my brain could catch up with his next move, I was on my back, and Kross was hovering over me, kissing his way down my body until he reached my breasts. When he teased one nipple to a painful peak, I squirmed and squealed at the same time.

He chuckled. "Too much."

"More."

He let out a soft laugh as his mouth closed around my nipple, bit lightly, then moved on to the other one. I wiggled again, moaning and whimpering until he lifted his head and climbed off me.

"Don't move," he said as he removed a condom from his wallet. Then he shucked his jeans and his briefs.

When he was completely naked, I sat upright with my mouth open. The man was every girl's wet dream. His muscles were cut in all the right places, and while that made my mouth water, his huge erection was a different story. He was long, hard, and thick. Instantly, my throat dried to the point I had no saliva in my mouth. My mind scrambled to understand how he would fit inside me. I was a petite girl. One who hadn't had sex in four years. That tidbit alone drove me to wince. The first time was painful, and in essence, this would be my first time again.

He crawled on the bed. "No need to be nervous," he said through a satisfied smirk. "I'll go as slow as you need me to."

"You weren't that big in high school." I slapped a hand over my mouth. Damn nerves. Damn foot in my mouth. My friend, Nick, had always teased me about how I came out with the craziest things at the craziest times.

Laughter rumbled from Kross's chest as he settled next to me. "Thank you for the compliment." He lay on his side as he propped his head in his hand. "I didn't have a chance to ask you. How are you feeling after the fight? Vickie punched you hard in the gut."

I stifled a laugh. The man was naked, oozing sex, and he wanted to talk about my injuries. My stomach had been sore, but the pain was fading. I stretched out to face him. "I'm fine. Sorry to ruin the mood."

"You didn't." He grasped my hand then guided it to his very hard erection.

As soon as my small fingers wrapped around his shaft, he groaned, a sound that made my body tingle. So I squeezed. He groaned again. Feeling quite brave and loving that I was eliciting those thigh-squeezing sounds from him, I dragged my hand up then down his shaft. The feel of velvet came to mind as I got into a rhythm. With my bottom lip between my teeth, I peeked at him out of the corner of my eye. My breath caught at the pure hunger beneath his hooded eyelids.

He buried his hand in my hair then pushed his tongue into my mouth. I grabbed his toned butt then pressed my hips to his, but it wasn't enough. I was about to guide him into me until I realized he needed to put the condom on, and I was still wearing underwear. As though he knew what I was thinking, he moved down so he was kneeling in between my legs. When he slipped his fingers inside my panties, I cursed the fabric that separated me from ecstasy. He watched me as though he was waiting for me to protest. *Hell, no.* My trepidation had faded. More than anything, I wanted him.

CHAPTER 21
KROSS

I sat on my knees in between her legs, holding all the wildness inside me. I started to remove the only piece of clothing separating me from having my way with the mother of my child. The woman I wanted to make love to. The woman I wanted to show that she meant something to me, and not because of Raven. Ruby was more beautiful than I remembered. Her stomach was toned, even after giving birth to twins, although a couple of stretch marks marred the area just below her navel. Her auburn hair sprayed out around her, her skin felt satiny, and her breasts were perfectly round. As she lay there with her chest rising and falling, her gaze riveted on me, I couldn't help but think how much of a moron I'd been to her. *That's in the past. Focus, asshole. Show her the man you are now.*

Her eyes glistened as she shimmied her hips right out of her panties. If she was frightened before, she wasn't showing any signs as she softened in my hands. Then a maniacal laugh broke out in my head because suddenly I was the one who had a tiny bit of apprehension. When she'd admitted that she hadn't had sex with another man since me, I nearly pumped a fist in the air. *But could I please her? Would she enjoy it?*

"Kross, are you okay?" She sat up, pressing her hands into the mattress behind her.

"Sorry, baby. I guess I'm the one who's scared."

As if my admission was what she needed to totally let go of her anxiety, her legs parted slightly. "Why?"

I rubbed a finger lightly over her clit. She fell back, releasing an audible whoosh of air. I did it again, only a little harder.

She squirmed, lifting her hips and clutching the blankets. She whimpered loudly, and my balls tightened. I drove one finger inside her.

"More," she breathed.

Sweat broke out on my entire body. I slid down the bed then lowered my head and captured her clit in my mouth. I slowly swirled my tongue around it as my gaze crawled up her body.

Her eyes were heavy, but watchful, and her voice was breathy. "Don't stop."

I fell into a rhythm, licking, lightly pulling, and sucking. She hummed low. I stopped briefly. "Baby, grab your nipples."

Without breaking the soft sounds, she touched her breasts before her fingers pinched her nipples. I resumed my assault as I watched her roll her nipples between her fingers. A pleasurable pain slashed across her face. Beautiful.

Then I pushed two fingers inside her, and I thought I would lose my mind at how fucking wet she was. She rocked her hips up. I kissed the inside of her leg as I pumped her with my fingers. She thrashed around, her mewling sounds growing louder. I fought the urge to grab my cock and jerk off, but as tight as she was, I had to feel her around me.

I moved my lips from her leg to her clit and sucked, flicking my tongue as I thrust my fingers inside her. She screamed my name, her back arching, her body shuddering.

While she rode out her orgasm, I kissed and licked my way up her stomach to her breasts, my cock grazing her body along the way. She shot up, her cheeks a deep red, her hair wildly messy, with a satisfied look in her eyes. I grinned, knowing I was the only one to take her to that place of euphoria.

I crawled up further and nipped at her chin. "Hi," I said.

She attacked my mouth, my jaw, and back to my mouth as she lifted her hips. "I need more."

I reached over and snatched the condom. Then I sat on my knees as I tore open the packet. Before I could whip that baby on, Ruby took it from me with a seductive smile. "I want to put it on."

As long as her hands were on me, I wasn't about to question her reason.

Instead of rolling the condom on, she planted a hand on my chest. "Lie down."

Stretching out my legs, I leaned back on my elbows as she sat on her knees. I wasn't missing this. Then she curled her small fingers around my shaft and lifted her gaze to me before her tongue slithered out to lick the tip of my cock.

Holy fuck! When we were sixteen, we'd fooled around, but she'd never gone down on me.

"Baby, I would love your mouth around me, but I'm not going to last one fucking second if you keep doing that."

She gave me a proud look then licked the tip again.

My muscles constricted and coiled, my breathing shallow. "That snake is ready to bite," I said through clenched teeth.

She giggled as she closed her mouth around my cock and sucked. For a moment, I gave in, relishing the way her tongue swirled around before she sucked as hard as she could. A sheet of white blinded me. All I could think about was how tight she would feel when I was inside her.

"Ruby," I barely said as she held me prisoner between her lips.

She stopped, eyeing me.

"Condom." I held out a hand. "Now."

Handing me the condom, she pouted through a smile, seemingly thrilled that she was affecting me. The woman who hadn't had sex since me was letting herself explore and feel, and that was sexy in itself.

I rolled on the condom, wasting no time in adjusting us so I was on top. I considered having her on top, but since this was her first time in four years, I needed to be in control until I knew she was feeling pleasure and not pain.

I kept my gaze on her as I pushed in slowly. She gnawed on her lip.

"Spread your legs a little more." When she did, I inched in further then pulled out then back in, but her whole body was still too tense. "Talk to me, baby."

"It's a little painful."

"Do you trust me?"

She nodded

"Then play with yourself."

"Huh?"

"It will help you relax." That was true, but it would also drive me insane.

Her cheeks turned a dark shade of pink as she slipped her hand in between us then down to her clit. She started to rub herself as I began to move. She was extremely tight. I had to squeeze my ass cheeks so hard so I wouldn't lose it. I stopped, took in a breath, and let her get into a rhythm. Within a second, she parted her legs wider, opened her mouth, and spewed those soft noises that drove me fucking wild.

In one motion, I thrust all the way in and stilled, making sure she was okay, although I wasn't. A drop of sweat dripped from me, hitting her forehead. A tiny crease formed in between her eyebrows for a second before her features relaxed. I pressed my hands farther into the mattress as I pumped in then out, her walls gripping me in a sweet and painful way. I groaned.

She abandoned her clit then locked her legs around me. When she did, I drove in harder, faster, flying, soaring, approaching that one place that sparked pulsating waves of ecstasy.

Ruby met each thrust until her nails dug into my back. Then she screamed my name. As though her release was the final piece to our puzzle, I crashed my lips to hers with one final thrust. Then I was freefalling as wave after wave of pure bliss blinded me. I sucked on her tongue as my body continued to shudder with release. If I thought I was done, I wasn't. Ruby tugged on my hair, her teeth grazing my jaw. I rolled us over, our bodies sliding together, sweaty, slick, and smooth. I grabbed her ass, anchoring her to me. Then I pushed into her one last time, my cock throbbing inside her, my chest heaving.

She planted her hands on my chest, her hair falling to graze it before she sat up. Sweat slid down in between her breasts. Her cheeks were flushed, her lips swollen, and her nipples were still hard. Man, she looked beautiful.

"Hi," I said, panting. "Are you okay?"

Her eyebrows pinched together. "You didn't seem scared. What were you afraid of?"

I rubbed my hands up her thighs. "Not being able to please you."

"You made me feel things I've never felt before. How come we didn't know all those moves in high school?" She squeezed, clamping down on my cock.

I briefly closed my eyes, absorbing the arousal flowing through my veins. I couldn't tell if she knew what she was doing to me or not. It didn't matter. She was so much sexier with the innocence in her eyes.

"Well?" She dragged her nails down my chest.

A laugh rumbled out. "Says the girl who hadn't had sex since then," I teased as I lifted her off me. I had to take a breather. I didn't want to wear her out too fast since it was only eight p.m., and we had all night. "Be right back." I went into the bathroom to dispose of the condom and quickly cleaned up. When I rounded the corner, Ruby had my phone in her hand, pursing her lips.

"Did I get a text?" I'd texted Penelope a couple of days ago, and I was waiting on a reply. I'd also texted Kade while Ruby had been taking a shower to let him know I wouldn't be home until tomorrow.

"From Penelope." Her face twisted. "Are you still seeing her?"

The bed dipped as I snuggled up against her naked body, taking my phone from her. "Again, no. She missed her training appointment. I wanted to make sure she was okay after her drug-induced state. I also wanted to find out why she was babbling about you and some guy."

The text read, *I'm out of town. Chat when I get back.*

"You said she was referring to you."

"I'm almost positive she was, but I just have to make sure." I wanted to be cautious. Firefly wasn't exactly the safest place to work. I kissed her softly and tentatively, not only because I was dying to, but with the unease in her voice, I didn't want her to worry. "Thank you."

"For what?"

I trailed a finger over her eyebrow. "You." Sex had never been that amazing.

Her eyes watered.

"I didn't mean to make you cry. Talk to me."

"We have a child, and I know that I'll see you because of Raven. But—"

"Hey, what we did tonight wasn't a one-time thing. I want more with you." I couldn't let her think it was just sex. I wasn't sure what would happen tomorrow, but I was sure I wanted her with me tomorrow.

"I do too, but I'm scared. I have to be my own person. I want to get my diploma, a good job, and a nice place to live so I can provide a good home for Raven. I don't want to be my mom, who relied on my dad for everything until he went to jail. Then I relied on her to take care of Raven and me. I have to show Raven that I'm a hard worker, a good person, and a good mom."

"Why can't you do all that with me?"

Laughing, she rolled her eyes. "Because you're bossy and possessive."

I couldn't help but smirk. "I'm protective. Let's just take one day at a time. We have a lot to do with lawyers and paternity tests. For now, we'll hang out when we can." I wanted to keep things casual and not scare her or suffocate her with what I wanted, and that was I didn't want her working at Firefly. Tommy was into some bad shit, and whether she kept fighting or not, it wasn't *if* the cops raided the joint. It was *when*. I also didn't want her staying with Alex and Norma. Not that they were bad ladies, but my selfish side wanted her with me, regardless of whether Raven was my daughter or not.

CHAPTER 22

KROSS

Books and toys were scattered around the floor and tables in the small daycare room Jay had for our gym members. I collected the LEGOs and placed them in a plastic container. Raven was scheduled to arrive within the hour along with Ms. Waters and a medical technician for the court. During the last week, I'd met with Mr. Davenport at his law firm about the paternity test. I'd learned it wasn't as easy as someone swabbing my mouth. Because Raven was in foster care, Mr. Davenport had to petition the family court for a genetic marker test. Once a judge approved the order, then a DNA test could be completed on Raven and me. To my surprise, Mr. Davenport had gotten a judge to sign the order yesterday. Kelton had counseled me that the court system didn't work fast, but when it came to children, the courts moved quicker. They wanted to see children reunited with their parents or family members as soon as possible. That was the same message Ms. Waters had given me when I'd spoken to her earlier in the week.

Voices from a group of workers filtered into the daycare room. "Put it down there," someone shouted.

Jay had hired a company to move equipment around so they could relocate the boxing ring into the center of the gym in preparation for tomorrow night's fight. I'd given Jay all I had in training. He'd seen a vast difference in me. I was sharper, edgier, and back to my old self. I was ready to take on Reggie on Saturday night, and I had to thank Ruby for that. Since our amazing night up in the Berkshires, we'd been inseparable. She often spent nights at my apartment, and in between our intimate web of being tangled together, we talked about the past, the future, her parents, my family, school, and Raven, although I sensed some unease in her. I chalked it up to me, and her thinking that I would leave her again. I had to give her time.

When we weren't together, she dominated my thoughts—how she lightly snored, how she snuggled against me the entire night, how her strawberry scent drove me fucking crazy, and how I loved waking up to her beautiful face.

I was deeply immersed in all things LEGOs when a loud noise in the gym broke my concentration. Snapping on the lid to the LEGOs container, I glanced up. Ruby stood in the doorway with a ghostly look on her face.

I pushed upright faster than a cat who had just spotted a mouse. "What happened? What's wrong? I thought you had to work. Did Tommy do something to you? I'll kill the fucker."

She smiled, but it never reached her eyes. "Chill. I do have to work in an hour, and Tommy didn't do anything. I told you I could handle him. Stop being all freaked and bossy."

"Stop looking like you've seen a ghost. You're pale." I snatched her hand. "Besides, you like when I'm bossy."

"Only when we're alone."

Visions of being naked with her, her playing with her nipples, my mouth on her, and her mouth on me flickered slowly through my head, pausing on the sexy positions that made my libido kick into gear. I kissed her ear. "I want to dance naked with you under the stars."

She tensed.

Not the reaction I was going for. "What's wrong, baby?"

"I wanted to see you and Raven."

"I'm right here. But what's really going on?" I wasn't complaining. Far from it. I wanted her by my side as much as possible. I also understood a mother's need to see her child. Maybe she didn't trust me with Raven. Maybe she didn't trust me period. I couldn't blame her. No matter how many times I assured her that I wasn't running, words were just words. Nevertheless, she had to work in an hour, and Firefly was at least an hour on foot since she didn't own a car.

"I'm tired," she said on a sigh.

Something wasn't right with her. "Baby, tell Tommy you quit. Kade wants you to work for him at Rumors anyway." Kade had offered her a job earlier in the week. Ruby told him she would think about it. I believed she was overwhelmed by all the attention she'd been getting from my brothers and Lizzie. Anytime Ruby had been at my apartment, Kade, Kelton, and Lizzie had fired questions at her about Raven. She'd been a trooper, answering them all.

"I can't. Norma isn't back yet, and Pete needs me."

I ground my back teeth together. Pete, the asshole bartender. I wasn't going there. Ruby wanted space to become her own person, but she was driving me nuts with her staunch attitude on working at Firefly. I'd asked her if Tommy had approached her about fighting again. She'd said no.

"Ruby, I'm trying really hard to help here. I can't if you don't tell me what's going on. I sense something more than you wanting to see me and Raven." Whenever she talked about Raven, she always had a huge smile on her face. Not at the moment, though.

Her delicate throat moved. "Kross, we've had a great week together." Her lips quivered.

Anger morphed into panic as my blood gelled. "We did have a great week. With many more to come." God, I hoped so. My heart couldn't take it if she decided she didn't want to see me anymore. I was beginning to understand why Kelton had built a wall around his heart for years. Mine hurt just thinking that Ruby and I wouldn't be together. *Yeah, dickwad. Now you know how she felt when you moved back to Ashford.*

"Sorry. I don't know how to say this without freaking you out." Her tone caused my pulse to pound in my ears. She puffed out her chest. "I love you," she said as her face went completely white.

Angling my head, I drew in my eyebrows. Probably not the look I should have been displaying. I should have been grinning and kissing her. I just couldn't get past the oddness of her timing, and at the gym of all places. Not that we had to be in the throes of sex or anything. The desperation in her voice confused me and scared the fuck out of me. It sounded as if she was saying good-bye.

"Kross, I need your help," a voice behind Ruby said.

I diverted my attention to the man with the hard hat. "Be right there."

He flicked his head then lingered behind Ruby.

Since we were on the topic of love, I was tempted to share my feelings. But the hard hat man was hovering. "I'll be right back." I kissed her on the forehead. "Don't go anywhere."

She grabbed my hand. "I'm also sorry."

I could feel my forehead creasing harder than before. "For?"

"Kross," the hard hat man said again. "We're on the clock."

I swallowed hard. Jay had needed to run some errands, so I was in charge. I just hoped he would return quickly. I didn't want to be interrupted while Raven was there, especially during the paternity test. "Let me answer this guy's question. Then we can talk." I kissed her on the lips. "Okay?"

She nodded as fear blanched her face, making her whiter than when she'd walked in. Fear was certainly squeezing my limbs into a tight knot. I didn't want to leave her, but Jay would have my hide if he returned and the ring wasn't moved.

I walked over to the hard hat man. "Make it quick," I barked.

"I need more rope clamps," he said nicely as though my bite didn't bother him in the least. "Apparently, some were missing to begin with. I also need rope spacers. Three shit the bed when we were taking the ring down."

I would have told him not to worry about it, but rope clamps were essential for the boxers' safety so they didn't fly out of the ring onto the floor, or worse, into the crowd.

"I'll check the storage room. Jay usually keeps extra clamps." I shot a look over my shoulder at Ruby before I reluctantly crossed the gym floor to a small entryway that held two closets. One housed boxing and gym equipment. The other closet stored cleaning supplies. I ducked into the equipment closet, flicked on the light, and searched the shelves for clamps. As I did, my mind tumbled, trying to figure out why Ruby was so frightened.

Because the last time she told you she loved you... "Shut the fuck up," I said out loud. It wasn't the thought of me running that had her scared. Something else was going on if she had trekked from Firefly to the gym with only an hour to spare before work—something besides her wanting to tell me she loved me.

I spotted the box of clamps, grabbed them, then dug into a plastic bin and plucked a handful of rope spacers. I jogged back to the hard hat man, who was standing beside the half-assembled ring in the middle of the gym. "If you need anything else, let me know." Without waiting for him to acknowledge me, I hurried back to Ruby. On my way, Ms. Waters walked in with Raven and a skinny dude in his thirties with a canvas bag strapped across his body.

"Hi, Raven." My voice carried over the muddled sounds of tools in motion. I wanted to wait until after the paternity results came back to tell Raven that I was her father. I wanted to be one hundred percent sure. Then it dawned on me. Maybe Ruby was worried about the paternity test. Maybe I wasn't the father. Nah, I was. Looking at Raven as I stood there, I could see she was a Maxwell without a doubt. Besides, Ruby wouldn't lie about something as big as Raven's father.

Raven waved her tiny hand as Ms. Waters removed her knitted hat. I glanced back at the daycare room, expecting that Ruby would have emerged when I'd said Raven's name. Nothing.

While the threesome made their way over, I poked my head in the daycare room. Ruby was gone. *What the fuck?* I glanced around the gym. No sign of her. Maybe she went to the restroom. I was about to check when Raven ran into the room.

"Hi, Kross." Raven's dimple popped out as she beamed up at me. "Ms. Waters told me we're going to play for a little while."

"We are." I waved my hand around. "What do you want to do first? We have dolls, LEGOs, I can read a book to you."

She stuck her finger in her mouth. "LEGOs."

Ms. Waters walked in with the skinny dude on her tail.

"Raven." Ms. Waters pushed up her glasses. "Before we play, let's allow Mr. Matson to do his job like we talked about."

Her striking blue eyes were wide. "With the Q-tip?"

"Yeah," I said. "It doesn't hurt. It probably tickles."

"I'm ticklish," she said so seriously.

"So am I," I added. "We'll giggle together." I crouched down then unzipped her coat. "Let's get comfortable."

She shrugged out of her coat. "Do you like my new shirt?" She stuck her hands on her hips and twirled around like a ballerina, showing off her white cotton shirt that had tiny purple flowers on it.

"It's pretty." My stomach did some weird flips at how freaking adorable she was and at the thought that she was even my child.

With her ponytail swinging, she dropped down on the mat next to the bookcases, where we stored containers of toys and books.

Before I sat down, I glanced out through the window then the doorway, hoping Ruby would return. All I saw were the workers. I joined Raven, crossing my legs underneath me, although I wasn't as limber as she and her mom were.

Mr. Matson readied his test, removing a long Q-tip from a package. "This won't take but a second."

Ms. Waters made herself comfortable in the only adult chair in the room. She watched as though she was taking mental notes on the interaction between Raven and me.

As we waited for Mr. Matson, I dumped out the LEGOs I'd collected earlier. As Raven began sifting through them, my phone vibrated. I pulled it out of my back pocket. The text from Kelton read, *Kade and I will be there in five minutes.*

I'd forgotten all about my brothers joining me. They were salivating to meet Raven. My parents were as well. But we didn't want to overwhelm Raven too quickly, at least not until the paternity results were back. Plus, Ms. Waters recommended that we keep the introductions to a couple of family members for the time being.

"Ms. Waters, you're still okay with my brothers joining us today?"

She nodded. "It's fine. It's also uncanny the resemblance between you two." She gestured at me and Raven with a painted pink nail.

I grinned while I set my gaze on Raven. She was engrossed in building something with the LEGOs. I'd seriously thought she would go for the dolls. I couldn't wait for my brothers to meet her. My heart was firing on all cylinders just knowing she could be my daughter. Scratch that, she *was* my daughter. If that DNA test came back with results saying I wasn't her father, I would flip out. Then I would have a serious chat with Kody and Kelton. Because this little girl was a Maxwell.

"I'm ready." Mr. Matson proceeded to swab my mouth first. When it was Raven's turn, he said, "Open wide."

She did as he instructed. After he was done, she giggled. "That didn't tickle."

"Easy peasy," I said. Then we dove into playing with LEGOs.

"There's a rush on the order," Mr. Matson said as he packed up. "Results should be ready within the week."

"Thanks." I snapped a LEGO together, silently thanking Mr. Davenport as well for helping me to get the ball rolling.

Kade and Kelton ambled in as Mr. Matson took his leave. Kelton was carrying a box covered in a black cloth. I smirked, knowing what was underneath.

Kade and Kelton eyed Raven. With her legs stretched out, she was absorbed in everything LEGOs.

"The daddy thing suits you, Bro," Kade said low, not taking his eyes off of Raven.

Kelton's mouth dropped open as he too fixated on Raven.

Ms. Waters came over to them. "Hi, gentlemen. I'm Ms. Waters."

Raven looked up. I couldn't tell if she was staring at Kade or Kelton, but in one second, she crawled the six inches over to me and sat in my lap. I would have sworn that my heart burst open.

She pointed at Kelton. "How come he looks like you?"

"Those are my brothers. The one that looks like me is a triplet."

Kade had tears in his eyes, while Kelton still had his mouth open.

Raven touched my face. "What's a triplet?"

"Triplet means three. And three of us look exactly alike."

"He doesn't." She pointed at Kade, who was blinking as though he was either trying to dry his tears or keep himself from breaking down. I knew the feeling all too well.

"Kody isn't here," I said, wanting to tell her everything about our family.

After Kade and Kelton managed to snap back to reality, they acknowledged Ms. Waters as they found a spot on the floor with Raven and me. With our large physiques, Kade, Kelton, and I seemed so out of place in this small room. Yet we were so at home and at ease hanging out on the floor with a kid, surrounded by toys. Weird.

"What's in your hand?" Raven asked Kelton.

His blue eyes flashed with excitement. "I heard you like lizards."

Her head of thick black hair bobbed up and down as she curled a small arm around my neck. I was a goner. She had me hook, line, and sinker.

Kelton removed the cloth. Inside a Plexiglass container with holes on top was his iguana.

Raven hopped onto Kelton's lap in a flash. "What's his name?" She studied the reptile with fascination.

"Harry," Kelton said.

"Again?" Kade and I asked in unison.

"Family joke?" Ms. Waters asked as she sat near us on a small child's chair.

I laughed. "Every pet lizard Kelton had, he named him Harry."

Raven tapped on the box. "Can you take him out of the box?"

"Maybe another time," I said. With my luck, Harry would take off, much like the lizards Kelton had owned when we were kids. My mom or my sister would scream when Harry surprised them. I couldn't risk Harry surprising someone during the bout tomorrow night. I glanced up at the door again, wondering where Ruby was. She must've left the gym. Otherwise, she wouldn't have missed Raven for the world.

Kelton answered Raven's questions about Harry while Kade and I watched the amazing interaction between my brother and my daughter. I'd never pegged Kelton for a daddy. He'd always been the lady's man. He was going to be a great father whenever he and Lizzie had kids.

When Harry moved, Raven giggled as she jumped onto Kade's lap. As though he was a natural with kids, his arms went around her, and tears surfaced in his eyes again. "He's not getting out of that box," he said as he tucked a stray hair behind Raven's ear.

"Will you protect me if he does?" she asked.

"Always," Kade responded.

Yeah, Kade would make an awesome dad one day as well.

A lull of silence grew among us as Kade, Kelton, and I exchanged grins.

Then Ms. Waters fired her own questions. "Kross, where do you live? Where do your parents live? Have you thought about finding a place to settle down?"

I'd talked to my parents about the boathouse my old man had converted into a man cave for us boys when we'd first moved to Ashford. Currently, Kody was staying in the man cave. He'd offered to move back into his old bedroom in the main house, at least until I found a place closer to Boston.

"My parents have a separate place behind their house that they've offered until I can make other arrangements." Lizzie would have loved for Raven to live with us at the brownstone in Boston, and I would have loved that setup too. But according to Mr. Davenport, the judge wanted to see a family home environment, not one with roommates and parties. Not that we had parties.

Ms. Waters opened her mouth to speak when Penelope glided in with her gym bag on her shoulder. "Why is the gym closed?"

I guessed she had completely overlooked the sign on the main entrance that said we were closed.

Her green gaze narrowed in on Raven sitting in Kelton's lap. "Kelton, you have a daughter?"

"No." Kelton set the lizard down on the other side of his leg and grabbed some LEGOs. His tone was even, quiet, and not the cocky Kelton tone he normally used around Penelope. He wasn't fond of her. He'd always thought Penelope was after the limelight I received for boxing and nothing else.

I pushed to my feet at her startled expression. "Can I talk to you outside?"

Once we were out in the gym area far away from the daycare room, I came unleashed. "Where have you been? Obviously, you're okay. What happened to you?"

"Is the little girl yours? Because she doesn't look like Kade."

"She's mine."

Her eyebrows snapped up. "Since when?"

"It doesn't matter." I gripped her elbows. "Focus, please."

"I'm fine. I was just drunk that night."

I wasn't about to argue that I hadn't smelled alcohol on her. I had to stick with my own advice and get to the heart of the matter. "That night, you were babbling about a guy and Ruby."

Her smooth forehead wrinkled. "Ruby? Guy?"

I huffed out air. "Pen, I don't have time to play games." Granted, it had been over two weeks since she'd been high as a kite. "Ruby is the girl with auburn hair who works at Firefly."

"Oh, that girl. Yeah, well. I overheard Trent, you know that guy who made my dad's life hell when he tried to take his company. Anyway, Trent was at Firefly that night I was there listening to the band. I'd gone to the restroom before you even showed up, and there was an office not far from the restrooms. I couldn't help but over-hear him telling someone he had a client that was interested in Ruby."

I let go of Penelope and fisted my hands at my sides as I tempered my anger. Twice now, Ruby had fought. Maybe Trent had a client who wanted Ruby to fight again. But all I could think about was Trent talking about pimps.

"Did you hear anything else?"

"No." She checked her phone. "I just remembered. The gym is closed for your fight."

"Yeah. I've got to get back." I wasn't sure what to make of Trent and his client, or how Ruby played into that conversation. If it had anything to do with pimps...

My nostrils flared at the image of the short, squat businessman who'd stood out at Ruby's fight against Vickie. He'd been dressed as though he was in a courtroom—tailored suit, silk tie, and crisp white shirt. Maybe Vickie worked for him. After Raven left, I would give Vickie a call. She'd given me her number after the fight with Ruby. "Glad to see you're okay." Then I headed to the daycare room.

"Kross, wait," Penelope said.

I turned. The men were wrapping the ropes with the cushioned covers.

She swung her hips toward me. "I just remembered one other thing. I did overhear Trent asking if Ruby had a pimp. Are you dating a prostitute?"

My anger had been building since Penelope mentioned Trent. Now, my face had to be redder than blood.

"Kross," Ms. Waters called.

Motherfucker!

Penelope's phone rang. She answered as she took off. Good thing. I had the urge to scream at her. I would have bet she'd seen Ms. Waters behind me and wanted to throw me under the bus. *Penelope doesn't know that Ms. Waters is a social worker.* True, but the rich girl had a knack for fucking things up. *Breathe, man.*

I relaxed my shoulders as I faced Ms. Waters, cussing under my breath and praying she hadn't heard Penelope. She'd heard. Penelope's voice carried in the gym, even above the noise of the workers.

I couldn't make out what was going through Ms. Waters's mind because her expression was completely blank. In her line of work, I guessed she'd seen and heard all kinds of things.

Ms. Waters touched the corner of her glasses. "Prostitute? Is Ruby selling her body?"

"Absolutely not." She worked as a waitress and fought in underground fights.

However, she had physically transformed from dirty and grungy to clean and normal overnight. Not to mention, she worked for that scumbag, Tommy. Who knew what else he was into other than stealing cars and holding illegal fights? Plus, Trent had been at Firefly each time I'd been there. He had dropped the word "pimp" into a conversation he'd had with a friend the night I'd first found Ruby. *Stop doubting. Ruby is not selling her body.* Maybe not, but she had been uneasy all week, and she had been acting odd earlier. No. I refused to believe Ruby would sell her body.

"Then why does your expression say you're not sure?" Ms. Waters asked. "Is there something you want to share?"

"Firefly isn't the best place to waitress, but Ruby works hard there. I can assure you that she isn't selling her body." Absolutely not. When we'd had sex the first time in the hotel, she had been shy and nervous. That alone gave me proof she wasn't selling her body.

Ms. Waters pressed her lips together. "I'll determine that. It's time for Raven and me to go."

No amount of pleading or begging would have erased the disappointment slashed across her face. Man, things had just gone south. I had to get my ass over to Firefly and convince Ruby to take Kade's job offer.

CHAPTER 23
RUBY

Chomping on a fingernail, I was alone as I paced around a penthouse in some building in downtown Boston. The one-bedroom suite overlooked the city skyline and screamed expensive with leather furnishings, stainless steel appliances, artwork that probably came from a museum, and fresh flowers in every room. The sweet fragrance of orchids tickled my nose as I drifted past the dresser in the bedroom. I hugged myself as I took in the panoramic view. The lights from buildings near and far twinkled around me. I wished I was stargazing rather than standing there with my heart sputtering, thinking how stupid I'd been to get myself into this predicament or to show up at the gym to tell Kross I loved him. He knew something was awry. Regardless, he had to know how I felt about him before I gave myself to a complete stranger. My decision and actions tonight were strictly to protect us and keep the wheels moving so we could get Raven back. Hopefully, in the end, the three of us could be a family.

"Who are you kidding?" I asked out loud as I tossed a look over my shoulder at the skimpy black dress that was laid out on the bed with black pumps beneath it. "Kross won't want you if he finds out what you've done."

Making my way to the bed, I huffed then laughed, sounding like a maniac. I'd torn out of the gym in a heap of tears. I couldn't face Kross any longer. I was afraid if I spilled my guts to him, then Trent would make things much worse for my case. So, for the last two hours, I'd been trying to figure a way out of my mess. I sat on the edge of the bed, and a shiver crawled down my spine as I thought of Trent's final words before I'd gone to see Kross. "If you do anything to screw this up, not only will I make sure your case is buried, but I'll send pictures of you fighting to your social worker with a note that you're a bad mother."

A sob burst out of me. I was a bad mother. I'd let my daughter be taken from me. I'd let myself be lured into fighting. I'd all but begged Tommy for a job. *No sense in pitying yourself. It isn't going to get you out of the task at hand.*

I glanced at the clock on the nightstand. I had under an hour to get ready. Trent's instructions were specific—be dressed by the time his client arrived. I had no idea who his client was. I'd asked, but Trent had said that I didn't need to know.

I ran a hand over the silky dress on my left that reminded me of a piece of lingerie. It was short with a scooped neck and spaghetti straps. Another sob erupted. I balled up the garment then threw it at the window. I wasn't changing into that.

Buck up!

With tears stinging my eyes, I studied the phone as though it was my lifeline. Maybe it was. Maybe Norma could help talk me out of this mess. I pulled her parents' number out of my pocket. Pete had given me Norma's number after she had called the bar last weekend to let us know that she wouldn't be back in town for a while. Since then, I'd spoken to her on two occasions from the bar phone. I'd kept the conversation light because Pete had been lurking nearby, but all I'd wanted to do was tell her about Trent. I'd planned to tell her the night I'd made the deal with him, but she'd been excited about me coming clean with Kross and had been babbling about making arrangements to visit her parents. I hadn't wanted to depress her. Honestly, I'd thought of backing out of the deal at the time, but if Trent could convince a judge to bury my paperwork, then he could do the same for Kross and his paternity test.

I dialed her number. The line rang once.

"Hello." Norma's voice was light and relaxed. A pang of envy gripped me for the briefest of seconds. I was more than happy for her, but I longed for the day when I could be with family and not have a care in the world.

"Norma," I said.

"Ruby? I was about to call you at Firefly. I'm taking the train in tomorrow for Kross's fight."

"Really?" I tried to infuse happiness into my voice.

"Why do you sound like you've been crying? What's going on? What did Tommy do to you?"

I sniffled. "It's not Tommy." Well, it kind of was. "I need some advice."

"Did something happen between you and Kross?"

I laughed through another sniffle. "Please don't judge me or hate me, but I'm working for Trent."

"No!" she shouted as though she knew what I was doing.

We'd both agreed he was the scum of the earth, but we'd never discussed what we thought he did.

"Don't do it, Ruby." She didn't sound mad, but remorseful.

I bounced my knee. "You don't even know what I'm doing."

"Oh, yes I do."

I rubbed a hand on my leg. "How do you know?"

She lowered her voice. "Remember when we met Trent in Tommy's office, and Tommy asked Trent if he had an opening for us? Then Alex shouted no. I asked her flat out that night after you fought Vickie if he was a pimp. Her face went white. Then she confirmed he was and that she worked for him. So, Ruby, don't let some asshole take away your dignity. I've been there, and I regret what I've done."

I couldn't help but think that Alex owed Trent too.

"Why didn't you tell me?" It wasn't as though her knowledge of Trent would have changed the situation since she'd learned all this after I made the deal with Trent. It wouldn't even change my current decision to stay or leave. I was curious, though.

"I promised Alex I wouldn't tell anyone. She was scared and ashamed. Besides, you were fighting and not on Trent's radar."

"Did he confront you?" I asked.

"No. Every time he looked my way, I gave him the finger. I promised you I wouldn't sell my body. I meant that."

I promised I wouldn't fight. Look at me now. Silence filled the line as bile crept up my throat. "Trent says I owe him ten thousand dollars."

She choked. "For what? Diamonds?" A little sarcasm filtered through her tone.

"Because I was late for the fight. He and Tommy lost money. I know even if they did lose money, I should tell them to fuck off. I did until Trent threatened me with Raven. He knows a judge that could bury my case. He told me before I came to the hotel that he would send pictures of me fighting to Ms. Waters with a note that I was a bad mother if I backed out of the deal. I can't screw this up with Raven. Even if Kross gets custody of her sooner than me, the court could ban me from seeing her because of what I've done." *Or Kross could fight for full custody without visitation rights if he finds out I'm prostituting myself.*

"Ruby, where are you?"

A tear dropped. "A penthouse in some apartment building called The Lexington."

"Don't do this," Norma said softly. "Please. Think of Raven."

"I'm doing this for Raven, to get her back."

"Losing your dignity isn't the way. Take it from me, you'll regret this." She sounded as desperate as I felt.

Nausea churned in my stomach.

"I'm sure you haven't told Kross," she said. "But think about what will happen when he finds out what you're doing? Do you want him to look at you differently? You two have had a great week rekindling things. Don't mess that up, either." She was good at laying the guilt trip on thick. It was actually the truth, which I'd needed to hear.

"I miss you." I flinched at the sound of the key in the door then the click of the handle. "I've got to go."

"Ruby, wait," she pleaded. "Leave. Get out of there."

"It's too late." I hung up the phone. Then with all the courage I could muster, I swallowed my nerves before walking out of the bedroom.

My jaw hit the floor. Trent Baker was standing at a table near the door.

"You're the client?" I couldn't look past his bulbous nose that stuck out like a deformed appendage.

"Disappointed?" he asked flatly.

Trent wasn't ugly. With the exception of his large nose, he was in good shape for a man I would have guessed was in his late thirties. What made him disgusting was the evil in his brown eyes.

"I'm not doing this," I said with a rigid posture.

He locked the door. "I thought you would say that." He dipped his hand inside his suit jacket and pulled out his phone. After a few swipes of the screen, he handed me his phone. "I think this will change your mind."

Not taking my eyes off him, I took the phone. "I don't need to see pictures of me fighting."

He bowed his head. "They're not of you."

Slowly, I lowered my gaze to the screen. When I did, my eyes bugged out of my head. Raven was playing in a park with a little girl I'd never seen before. I suspected the little girl was the one Raven had spoken about the other day.

"Go to the next picture," he said smugly.

With a trembling finger, I flipped to the next picture. Raven was standing at the edge of what appeared to be the lagoon at the Boston Public Garden. I sucked on my tongue, trying to get some saliva to coat my throat. *Keep it together, girl. You're stronger than you realize.* I had no strength to play his despicable game. *If you give yourself to him tonight, then he'll keep holding something over your head. You'll become his slave like Alex.* She was working at Firefly and for Trent. *How long has she been his slave?*

"So you have pictures of my daughter," I said in a small voice.

"I'm sure you don't want anything to happen to her." Again, his voice was smug.

My vision clouded. "You wouldn't dare." The words were strangled. I would've never pegged Trent Baker, scumbag extraordinaire, as the type to harm a child. Then again, I was dealing with a criminal.

One thick brow lifted. "Try me."

The asshole knew he had me under his thumb. The game had changed. We weren't talking about paying off judges, but about Raven's life. Ninety percent of me knew he wouldn't harm her. He was using her to get to me. That was all. But I couldn't risk that ten percent. Even if I called the cops, it was his word against mine. Then again, if he had a judge in his back pocket, I wouldn't be surprised if he had the head of the police department as well.

"Why are you so hell-bent on me?" Much prettier and sexier women existed out there. Maybe he got off on desperate women.

"You owe me money, and you're beautiful." His voice was even, and he'd lost the self-satisfied expression. In fact, his brown eyes had glazed over. "Get dressed. I want to see those sexy legs."

I clutched his phone so tightly that my muscles began to twitch as I glowered at the man, then past him to the door, the only door out of the penthouse.

He gave me a wry smile. "Usually when I tell a woman she's sexy, it breaks the ice."

The only thing I was breaking was his skull. I needed to regroup. More like, I needed to breathe in clean air rather than the acrid smell of him. I hauled his phone at him, narrowly missing his nose. Instead, his eye took the brunt of the impact.

His face darkened.

I stormed toward the door, the same one he was blocking.

"You want to leave? You want to test my power with the judge or maybe a cop?" He picked up his phone, sifted through it, then handed me the phone again.

Judge Carroll's name was on the screen along with his mobile number.

"Maybe I should call him now," Trent said, snatching the phone from me.

I crossed my arms over my chest. "Go ahead." I shouldn't have been cocky. Custody of Raven was in his hands.

He shrugged. "If you don't want your daughter back, then okay." He dialed the number.

I did want my daughter back more than anything, but I couldn't sleep with Trent. I would never forgive myself. Norma was right. I would lose my dignity. I would never be able to face Kross again. "Put him on speaker." Nausea crept up to settle in my throat.

After two rings, a male voice answered. "Trent, what can I do for you?"

"Sorry to bother you, Al. Remember that child custody case we were talking about?"

"Sure. Lewis right?" the judge asked.

All the blood drained out of me. I shouldn't have been surprised, but reality sank in.

I yanked the phone out of his hand before hauling the piece of technology against the wall. Then I stalked into the bedroom, slammed the door, and slid down to sit on the floor with my knees to my chest. I took several breaths as I scrambled to think of my next move. I wasn't changing into that dress or doing anything with him. That man wasn't touching my body. *You don't exactly have a way out. You're on the fortieth floor. The only way to freedom is the door you came in.*

My gaze darted to the large vase of flowers on the dresser. If I threw that at his head, it would give me a second or two to escape. *Then what? He has men watching Raven's foster family. He'll go after Raven. Not if I get to her first.*

I pushed to my feet. In five strides, I had my hands on the vase. *As soon as you walk out with a large vase of flowers, and you're not dressed, he'll stop you before you have a chance to throw it at him. Make him believe you're doing what you were told.*

Reluctantly, I shed my clothes then piled them in a heap on top of my coat, which was in a plush chair by the window. When I bent down to pick up the lingerie, I caught my reflection in the window. I stood in my bra and panties with fear carved into my pale features. I closed my eyes, taking a deep breath as the voices in my head argued with one another. *Don't do this. I have to go through with the deal. No, you don't. Yes, I do. He wasn't lying about the judge.* I covered my ears and silently screamed, *shut up!*

Inhaling the fragrant flowers, I opened my eyes then pulled out my pictures from my coat pocket. Looking at Raven's pictures always calmed me. I found the one of her modeling her new outfit. I smiled as I ran a thumb over the picture. "I love you, baby girl." I picked through the rest, stopping on the one of Kross lounging on the lawn under an oak tree at the academy. God, he was handsome as he grinned at me with his sparkling blue eyes.

"I love you, too," I murmured. "I'm doing this for us. I hope you can forgive me."

A knock sounded. "Ruby, hurry up," Trent said in a taut tone.

"I'm almost ready," I fired back.

I pocketed the pictures. When I did, my hand landed on my knife. Instantly, a new plan emerged. I quickly changed into the skimpy black dress that revealed way too much of my cleavage and legs. I slid my feet into the six-inch heels, fluffed up my hair, pinched my cheeks, and steeled my shoulders. I checked myself in the full-length mirror in the bathroom, turning from front to side. My legs appeared long, my calf muscles accentuated, and my thighs toned. *Wow! Where did those legs come from?* As I admired my small waist and larger-than-life breasts, I would have sworn that the person I was looking at wasn't me. I was pretty. I pulled my hair forward to drape over my breasts. A giddy feeling coursed through me then quickly vanished. I wasn't here to look pretty. *Yeah, but you'll certainly blind him. He won't know what hit him.*

On my way out, I grabbed my pocketknife. It was small but could be effective. As I wobbled to the door in those shoes, I wished myself luck. I would either fall at Trent's feet because of my clumsy gait, or if I had the stamina, I would dig one of my heels into his groin.

With a killer smile on my face, I clutched the knife behind my back and walked out.

Trent's head came up from where he sat on the couch before his body shot upright. "Holy shit!" His dark gaze swept over me as though he was painting slime on my body. "Turn around."

"I'd like a drink," I said, distracting him for a moment so he wouldn't see the knife. I darted my gaze to the door, which was no longer blocked by his big body, then back again.

He cocked his head. "You want to try for the door again? Or maybe we can call Judge Carroll again."

I wanted to inflict pain on Trent before I did anything else. "I asked for a drink."

He nodded a couple of times. "Sure. Sure." He scurried from the living room into the kitchen.

I crossed the room carefully until I was standing at the island that separated the kitchen from the living room. With the granite countertop as my shield, I placed my hands in front of me then unleashed the blade.

Trent made quick work of getting the glasses, ice, and a bottle of vodka. He set the ingredients down on the bar as his gaze got stuck on my cleavage.

"Drink," I said again.

He blinked before pouring vodka into both glasses. Then he slid one glass across the counter. I didn't drink alcohol. I'd tried beer once after I stopped breastfeeding Raven. I didn't like the taste, and I'd never tried any hard liquor. Tonight, I needed more than a picture of Raven to calm my nerves. I probably needed that entire bottle of vodka if I was going to stab him.

He raised his glass. "Cheers."

I grabbed my glass and brought it to my lips. "Fuck you." Those were the only words that came to mind.

He narrowed his eyes as he sipped. "You didn't believe that I knew a judge?"

I'd wanted to believe he'd been bluffing. I down the vodka in one shot then winced. A stream of fire slid down my throat, and as it did, I choked.

Trent rounded the island. "Are you okay?" Gone was the roughness in his voice. In its place was a caring quality that gave me the impression he could be a nice guy instead of a jerk.

I continued to choke, hunching over slightly. Nice man or not, when his hands landed on my arms, I plunged the knife into his thigh.

"You bitch," he shouted in that gruff, slimy undertone that was stronger than before.

I ran for the door. When my feet hit the tiled foyer, my right foot twisted. I listed to one side, the wall catching me.

"Get back here," he bit out as heavy footsteps thudded.

I wobbled two feet to the door. I had my hand on the doorknob when someone pounded on it from the other side. I turned the knob just as Trent's hand landed in my hair.

I screamed, turned, and punched him in the nose. He didn't flinch or remove his hand. All he did was grunt while blood slid down his upper lip.

Someone banged on the door again. "Ruby!"

"Kross!" I shouted.

"Open this door," Kross barked.

Trent pulled hard on my hair.

I managed to twist around, the pain in my scalp burning, feeling as though Trent was ripping out my hair. I kneed him in the groin. His face reddened as he let go of me.

I opened the door and practically knocked over Kross.

He grasped my hips. "What the fuck is going on?" His neck corded as he examined me. Then he gently pushed past me into the suite.

My heart thumped as I followed him. "Let's go. We don't need any trouble." I almost laughed at myself for saying that. If I didn't want trouble, then I shouldn't have shown up there or agreed to Trent's demands, or stabbed him.

"A little late for that." Kross's fists were balled at his side as he stepped deeper into the room.

Trent had retreated to the kitchen, where he was pouring himself another vodka. He eyed Kross then me, appearing as though he didn't have a care in the world, almost as if he'd been expecting Kross to show up. "What you did, Ruby, will cost you more than money now."

"Touch Raven, and I will kill you." My voice was even.

Kross's eyes became pinpoints as he regarded me. "What are you talking about? What's going on?"

"I messed up." I hugged myself, feeling naked beneath his scrutiny.

"Your girl owes me ten Gs," Trent said in a nasal tone. "But now that you're here, Maxwell, I have a better plan to get my money back." He downed the vodka.

Kross jerked his head at me, his carotid artery pulsing at what had to be two hundred beats per minute. "How in the world do you owe him that much money?" Contempt coated his words.

"Don't judge me," I snapped.

Fire flickered in his eyes. "What happened in the last week for you to fall prey to this fucker?"

My own pulse increased astronomically. "It's called survival."

"I've been trying to help you since I found you. Instead, you ask him." Kross stabbed a finger at Trent, anguish flitting across his face.

Holding back tears, I pushed down all my emotions for the moment. This wasn't the place to cry, scream, apologize, or anything else. "It's not like that."

"Then tell me what's it's like. Tell me that the girl I love isn't here to sleep with this fuckwad. Tell me that the girl I love didn't make a deal that involves our daughter."

The room spun for so many reasons. I knew I should have pleaded my case. I knew we shouldn't have been discussing any of this in front of Trent. Except I couldn't help but ask, "You love me?"

Trent clapped, severing the fireworks that were shooting off in my chest. "Wonderful," he mocked. "I want my money, and Kross, you're the one to deliver."

Kross set his attention on Trent who held a napkin to his nose. "I'm not fighting for you," he said as though Trent had approached him already.

"You don't need to fight for me. But you do need to lose that fight of yours tomorrow night."

"Or what?" Every facial muscle on Kross looked ready to burst open.

I held my breath, knowing what was coming.

"Do you ever want to see your daughter again?" Trent asked.

Kross leapt across the room then grabbed the collar of Trent's shirt. "You so much as touch her, you're a dead man."

I ran to Kross. "Stop. Trent has pictures of Raven. He's been following her. He threatened to bury my paperwork with a judge." I didn't want Kross to agree to Trent's deal, but I also didn't want him to cause more trouble for us.

"Listen to your girl," Trent said. "I can make it so you'll never get custody of her."

Kross shoved him. "Bullshit. No one has that much power over a judge."

Trent's back hit the fridge. "Do you want to test that theory? I can call Judge Carroll again. Right, Ruby?"

"Kross, he's telling the truth about the judge. He called him in front of me."

"I'll pay you the ten Gs," Kross said.

Trent barked out an evil laugh. "No. The deal changed when Ruby stabbed me and you stormed in here. You know I can file charges against Ruby."

I didn't have the energy to protest. If he did press charges, then that would add to my growing list of ways I'd screwed up my chances of getting my daughter out of foster care. More importantly, the cops could arrest me for prostitution since I was there to have sex with Trent. Then I would definitely lose custody.

The silence grew to a deafening height as Kross considered Trent then me. We could explain our predicament to Ms. Waters. Then she would know that I was illegally fighting, prostituting my body to pay back a debt, and that I stabbed Trent. Aside from that, she followed the laws of the system. She would never believe that someone could pay off a judge.

"So what's it going to be, Maxwell?" Trent's voice severed the brick wall of tension.

I couldn't let Kross throw away his career. The entire time we'd dated in high school, he'd talked about boxing, and how he would be the one to beat someday. I just didn't know what else I could do. Trent didn't want me anymore. Trent didn't want the ten thousand dollars. If he was planning to bet on Kross losing, then he stood to make more money.

"Don't do it, Kross." I grabbed his hand, then I glanced at Trent. "I'll do whatever you want me to do to work off that money."

Before Trent could respond, Kross blurted out, "You got yourself a deal."

"You can't do that," I protested.

Trent smirked. "Glad to see you came to your senses."

"Go get your clothes," Kross demanded rather roughly.

I obeyed since I couldn't do anything else. Once Kross and I were alone, then maybe we could come up with another plan that wouldn't cause him to lose his fight. One that would help us get Raven back at the same time.

I piled my clothes in my arms then hurried out. The faster we got out of there, the less of a chance that Kross would beat the lights out of Trent. We couldn't afford more trouble.

"Remember what's at stake," Trent said loudly as Kross and I walked out.

I swore I would find a way to get back at Trent.

CHAPTER 24

KROSS

I wore a hole in my bedroom rug as Ruby sat ramrod straight on my bed, gnawing on her fingers. Kade, Kelton, and Lizzie weren't home, which was good for the time being. Otherwise, I might have lashed out at them. I didn't want to subject them to the rage flowing through me.

It was all I could do not to bite Ruby's head off during the distance from Trent's place to mine. To a large extent, I was furious more with Trent than her. I'd been wracking my brain on how to handle the situation, but I kept coming up empty except for killing him. If I ran the situation by Kelton, I could already hear his response: "You have no evidence. Threats won't get a cop to call you back, and hearsay doesn't hold up in court."

Man, how did my life change so fucking drastically within the span of a month? I shouldn't have been blown away at the sight of Ruby standing in nothing but a scrap of lingerie in Trent Baker's penthouse. The woman had surprised me and brought me to my knees time and time again since I'd found her. But I was appalled that she could have even entertained the idea of giving herself to a sleazebag like Trent, even more so since she'd told me she loved me.

I'd been on my way to Firefly to see Ruby when Norma called.

"Get over to the Lexington ASAP. Ruby is in trouble," Norma had said. "That Trent Baker guy is involved. She's in a penthouse in that apartment building."

I knew something had been off with Ruby. She'd acted weird and had been whiter than a ghost when she was at the gym earlier that day.

I had tried to probe Norma for more details, but my cell reception had dropped. Like a wild man, I'd sped through the streets of Boston in a daze. I couldn't get past the doorman fast enough until I'd threatened him with his life. Then when I'd heard Ruby scream, I wanted to kill. I still did, but not her. *Save your frustration for the ring.* The way I was feeling, Reggie Stockman would be a dead man if I let loose the rage inside me. Maybe it was best if I threw the fight.

"Kross, stop," Ruby blurted out.

"Stop what? The hurt I feel because you didn't come to me for help?"

She lifted her chin. "Why? So you could look at me differently? Or stop me? Then what would've happened? You would've killed Trent and anyone that got in your way. Then you would mess up your chance to fight. You said yourself you couldn't get into trouble with your coach. And what about Raven? If you landed in jail, then you wouldn't have a shot at getting custody of her."

Squatting down in front of her, I placed my hands on her bare knees. She was still wearing that skimpy dress. As soon as my palms touched her soft skin, something in me snapped. It was as if the contact with her switched off my anger. "I don't see you any differently. If I did, I would've walked away the minute I saw you fighting at Firefly that first night. But after everything you've told me, I'm still here. I love you, Ruby Lewis. Even if Raven wasn't my daughter, my feelings for you would be the same, flaws and all." I did love her. I couldn't deny it any longer. When I was away from her, she was all I thought about. When I was with her, I couldn't get enough of her. The sad part of my declaration was that I had probably always loved her but had never had the balls to admit it to myself.

She gave me a weak smile, and my heart sputtered. I'd expected a happier reaction than that.

"Kross, you can't throw that fight. I can't let you do that. I can work for him. This is my mess. I'll do whatever he wants until I can pay him back."

I stiffened. "You're not working for that man, not in this lifetime. Don't even start with telling me I'm bossy because no matter how you slice it, Trent will have you under his thumb for the rest of your life. There will always be something or some deal that locks you to him."

She threw up her hands. "Then what are we supposed to do? I'm worried about Raven. What if he harms her?"

I rubbed along her thighs. "I lose the bout tomorrow night." For fuck's sake, I had to. According to Ruby, Trent was telling the truth about the judge. That didn't really surprise me, given the mess that Kade had been through with Lacey's mob family and how they'd had the Boston Police Department in the palm of their hands. "Trent isn't going to do anything stupid." The man might have been into stealing cars and preying on women to get them to sell their bodies, but I didn't get the impression he would harm a child.

"What about your career?"

I would still have a career in boxing, of that much, I was certain. It just might not be with Gail Freeman or even Jay. "Ruby, you and Raven are my life. Blood comes first. Again, I love you."

She launched herself at me, throwing her arms around my neck.

Finally, my heart opened wide.

"I thought I would never hear those words from you," she said. "As I tell Raven all the time, I love you bigger than the universe."

Laughing, I fell backward, taking her with me. "Bigger than the universe?" I guessed it wasn't any weirder than Kade telling Lacey that he loved the crap out of her.

She sat up, straddling me, beaming from ear to ear. "Yeah. Raven loves when I tell her that."

I drank her in, from her million-watt smile to the velvety feel of her thighs to her breasts that were falling out of that skimpy dress. At that moment, my dick jumped, or tried to. She was sitting on it, and that thought alone made more blood rush south.

Then the light went out in her eyes. "Do you think losing will end things with Trent?"

I lifted up to rest on my elbows. "It will. Because if he doesn't back off, then I'll do whatever it takes to make sure he goes down." I wasn't certain how yet. I had to get through the fight first. Then I could figure out a plan.

Ruby brought her finger to her mouth. "You're not mad at me."

Deep down, I knew her actions were driven because of Raven. I knew she'd fought for money, for food, and for a place to live. Besides,

S.B. ALEXANDER

I couldn't exactly be mad when I was giving into Trent's demands, too. "No."

She abandoned her finger then latched onto the waistband of my jeans. She gave me one of her shy looks, holding her bottom lip hostage. I was ready to rip off her dress and throw her on the bed. But I did want to talk with Kade and seek his advice before I got too tired. Then again, I probably wouldn't sleep, not with everything on my mind. Kade was working, anyway. He wouldn't be home until three in the morning when Rumors closed.

Ruby swept the backs of her knuckles against my bare skin just inside the band of my briefs. I sucked in air as my dick jerked. Not taking her eyes off me, she unbuckled my belt. I dragged a hand along the inside of her creamy thigh until my fingers found the edge of her panties. Then I slid my fingers in and found her soaking wet.

Fuck. My body ached for more than her feather-light touch or hungry gaze. I craved to have my mouth on her, everywhere, to be inside her as she screamed and moaned. I teased her clit, eliciting the purr I'd wanted desperately to hear. She wriggled back and forth over my erection, spewing little noises as her eyelids drooped. Then she splayed her hands on my chest as she lowered her body, moving her hips slowly and seductively. The prong of my belt buckle dinged against the metal housing as she continued to build friction between us.

I rolled us over and ripped every piece of clothing off her until she was naked. I scrambled to my feet, lifted her onto the bed, then shed my clothes as fast as I could. I fished for a condom in my nightstand as I swept my gaze over her. Her nipples were hard, skin flushed, legs open and ready. I wasn't going to last a second, not when her velvet skin slid along me and moved with me. The thought of how she would feel, tight and wet, was enough to make me lose it before the condom covered my cock. I tightened every muscle in me as I tore open the wrapper. The sound was muddled over the pulse pounding in my ears. Once the condom was on, I lowered to her until my hands were on either side of her head and my cock was at her entrance. I ran a hand over her hair as we locked gazes.

"Give me all of you," she whispered. "Fast and hard."

I could fill that order and then some. If she felt anything like she had in the hotel room in the Berkshires, then restraint wasn't in my vocabulary. I brushed my lips over hers. "I love you." I searched her face, keeping my entire body taut.

"Show me," she said.

With my pulse racing, I thrust hard and fast into her sweet warmth.

She gasped and bucked then scrapped her nails along my ass. Any sense of control was history, completely forgotten as I rocked and pumped.

Ruby's breasts bounced. I tried like hell to suck on her nipple, but the way she was gripping me, I couldn't break the friction. Instead, I crashed my mouth to hers. Automatically, her tongue snaked out. I sucked and nibbled before I plunged my tongue inside her, exploring the taste of her.

She moaned. I growled.

She rocked. I rolled.

Our sweat-sheened bodies moved in unison, our tongues competing, her hands flying into my hair. We were dancing, flying, and soaring. With each moan and groan, we danced faster, flew higher and harder, the heat searing us together.

She tugged on my hair, arching into me, whimpering.

I lifted my head, sweat dripping from me and onto her.

"Kross, I want to be on top."

Without breaking us apart, I rolled us over. She splayed her hands on my chest, a pleasurable pain lancing her flushed cheeks. She squirmed herself into position before she got into the rhythm. My stomach flipped in all the right ways as I watched the ecstasy burn her beautiful face. Her hair stuck to her forehead, while sweat trickled down in between her breasts.

I sat up and covered my mouth over one of her nipples as I played with the other. When I lightly bit, she shoved me down. Her breathing grew labored as she picked up her pace. Her eyelids were heavy, and her mouth was slightly open.

Grabbing her butt, I met her pace as I pumped. I was so close yet so far. This wasn't just sex. This was two people making love, feeling every sensation, every heartbeat, every pulse. I had never believed Kade when he told me that sex was different when you loved someone. He'd said it was more intense and the feelings were out of this world.

Fuck, yeah they were. With Ruby, I swore my heart was about to have its own orgasm.

A soft, gorgeous sound came out of her before she said, "I love you, Kross." Then she stilled, her walls hugging me tightly.

In a flash, I flipped us as she continued to ride her orgasm. I thrust once then a second time as the rush of the room and Ruby disappeared, replaced by a blinding white light. Tremors controlled my body as I gritted my teeth. Then I let out a guttural growl.

Her hands tangled in my hair as my body quieted and my vision cleared.

"Exquisite." I peppered kisses all over her damp face, tasting salt and sugar.

She traced her fingers over my tat. "Will me, you, and Raven be a family?" Her tone was on the verge of sadness.

We loved each other, so I didn't see why we wouldn't. But Ruby had said she wanted independence, to be her own person and get her diploma. "Why wouldn't we be?"

"When Ms. Waters finds out that I've been fighting, she'll tell the court that I'm not fit to be a mother."

Shit. Ms. Waters.

She gripped my dick like a vise. "Why do you look like I hit a nerve?"

Man, with a feeling like that, I wanted nothing more than to go a second and even a third round, but she was giving me the evil eye to answer her. "Let's take a shower, and I'll fill you in."

Once the shower was beating down on us, I lathered soap over her very mouthwatering breasts. "Penelope was at the gym when Ms. Waters was there today. Penelope asked me if you were a prostitute."

She reared back.

"Before you get upset, I explained that you weren't."

"Did she believe you?"

"Honestly, I don't know." I wasn't about to lie. "But we should go talk to her first thing in the morning. She needs to know the truth. It will help our case if we're honest. We can also check on Raven."

Ruby shook her head. "Telling her the truth will only harm my case. She'll never recommend that I get custody of Raven."

I cupped one side of her face. "Baby, Ms. Waters can help protect Raven."

She rested her head on my chest and sighed.

"We'll get through this," I whispered. If it took every ounce of energy I had, I would fight to the death for her and Raven.

CHAPTER 25
RUBY

The next morning, Kross and I sat in a busy coffee shop in a suburb of Boston. The constant drone of the coffee machine, the voices, and the chairs scraping against the floor competed with the pounding in my ears. Every time the door opened, my head shot up along with my pulse.

Kross slid his hands across the table and latched onto mine. "Ms. Waters will say yes."

I wished I had his confidence. Visits with Raven were supervised. I didn't think Ms. Waters would spend the entire day with us. I also would have bet my life she wouldn't allow Kross and me to take Raven unsupervised.

"But first, I have to come clean," I said. That was the scary part. I didn't want to lose Raven. Yet I knew in the long run, Kross was right. Ms. Waters did need to know the truth, not only to help my case, but also to help protect Raven.

"So, you fought for money. You didn't go to jail. You still worked legally as a waitress." He traced circles on the backs of my fingers.

The soothing sensation did nothing to erase the nausea in my stomach. Even the coffee aroma that I loved smelled putrid. But in the midst of my internal turmoil, his words were soothing. I would die for Raven.

The door opened, and Ms. Waters breezed in. I waved a shaky

hand. She padded around two tables, removing her gloves. When she reached us, her dark gaze regarded me then Kross.

Ever the gentleman, Kross rose and pulled out her chair.

Ms. Waters angled her head as though surprised. "Thank you." She lowered herself into the chair, then Kross returned to his. "What's so urgent that it couldn't wait until Monday?" she asked matter-of-factly.

I hated that we had to bug her on a Saturday. I also hated that time was of the essence since Kross was fighting tonight. "We'd like Raven to spend the day with us." I held my breath.

She swung her creased forehead from me to Kross then back to me. "Why today? Why the last-minute desperation?"

I knew she would sense that something wasn't right. Kross and I went through every objection Ms. Waters might have. We didn't want to lie. We also didn't want to alarm her since we didn't know for sure if Trent would harm Raven. He'd never said he would, although the underlying threat was out there. Our plan was for Kross to bring Raven and me to his house in Ashford, where I would stay with his parents until his fight was over.

"My parents have been dying to meet Raven," Kross said. "We'd like to take her out to their house in Ashford for the day."

At first, Kross had been reluctant for his parents to meet Raven until the paternity test came back. But now that Kross wanted me in his life, it didn't matter. Raven would be with us regardless of any paternity test.

"You could've asked me this on Monday. Again, what's the urgency? Does this have anything to do with what I overheard at the gym about Ruby being a prostitute?" She said the last word in a low voice.

I heaved a sigh. Here went nothing. "I told you that I had a job waitressing at Firefly. That's true. What I haven't told you was I'd been in two street fights for money. However, in no way have I made money selling my body." The coffee shop wasn't exactly the best place to talk about me, although judging from the noise level, people were engaged in their own conversations around us.

Her jaw dropped as her eyes narrowed. "Okay. I'm a little shocked at the fighting, but I still feel you're not telling me something. What am I missing?"

She wasn't about to allow Raven to spend the day with us unless we told her the real reason. Even then, she would say no. Or hell no, especially if she suspected that Raven's life was in danger. With my luck, she probably thought Kross and I would run with Raven. That idea wasn't far-fetched in my mind. Several times since yesterday, I had considered snatching Raven from her foster family and leaving the state.

A phone shrilled. Kross glanced at his on the table. Ms. Waters dug in her purse for hers. As she pulled it out, the ringtone grew louder.

"Hello," she answered. "When? How?" The fright in her voice matched the fear on her face. "Did you call the police? I see. Yes. I'll be there as soon as I can." She lowered her phone, inhaled all the coffee-laden air, then blew it out as her eyes darted between Kross and me several times. "Does the urgency of your request have anything to do with the fact that Raven is missing?"

"Fuck," Kross muttered.

I opened my mouth, but nothing came out. The noise in the shop dulled. The room and the people in it shuddered in and out of my vision. I blinked and blinked and blinked until Ms. Waters's cold, soft hand landed on mine.

"Ruby." Her voice was far away.

Kross flew out of his chair and rounded the table to my side. "Baby, breathe." His lips were on my ear, warm and soothing. "We need to go."

"I want you two to come with me. I'm meeting Mr. and Mrs. Santos, Raven's foster family, at their home. They've already called the police."

"Give me the address," Kross said in a harsh tone. "I'll meet you there."

I rose like a zombie, every limb locked, while Ms. Waters jotted the address on a napkin. When I was on two feet, I faltered into Kross.

He grabbed the napkin from Ms. Waters with one hand and wrapped the other around my waist. The minute his hand was on my hip, something in me snapped. I bolted out of the coffee shop, pushing people out of the way. Once outside, I hunched over and lost the contents of my stomach.

A little boy passed by with his dad. "She's sick, Daddy. We should help her."

I wiped my mouth as I dropped down onto the curb next to a parking meter. No amount of help would erase the bile, acid, panic, and fury, as well as the need to kill the person who took Raven. Trent

Baker's threats were on repeat in my head. Maybe he didn't take Raven. Maybe something else had happened.

"She'll be okay," Kross said behind me before his hand was on my back. "Ruby, we need to go." His voice had an edge to it.

"Go straight to the address I gave you," Ms. Waters said in a tone that permitted no argument.

I got the feeling that she thought we were responsible. She would be right. I was the one at fault. I was the one who had put Raven's life in jeopardy. I deserved the worst punishment.

Kross helped me up then ushered me to his truck across the street. Once we were both strapped in, I busted out crying. "This is all my fault."

Kross wheeled out of the parking space before he took my hand. "Don't go there. You were doing your best to survive and get Raven back."

I appreciated his words, but it didn't help take away the panic or fear. "Do you think Trent took her?"

"One hundred percent. Once we're done with Ms. Waters and the foster family, we're going hunting."

CHAPTER 26
KROSS

R uby and I were a block from Firefly. After hours of confessing to Ms. Waters and answering the cops' questions, I was a bomb waiting to explode. The Santos's home was more than suffocating with Mrs. Santos crying, Ms. Waters scolding Ruby for putting Raven in harm's way, and the cops interrogating us as if we were the ones who had kidnapped Raven. We answered all their questions and explained what we knew, and we told them that we suspected Trent Baker.

Waiting for the light to turn green, my mind jetted through ways to kill Trent. The fucker had had the nerve to kidnap Raven in broad daylight at the Boston Public Garden. Okay, I was getting ahead of myself. Maybe someone else had taken Raven. It just seemed coincidental given Trent's threats.

According to Mrs. Santos, she'd gotten a phone call while she and Raven were at the Boston Public Garden, waiting to get on the swan boat ride. She turned away for a split second. When she hung up the phone, Raven was gone. She didn't see anyone in line that stood out to her, but she said Raven had waved to someone. Before she could see who that person was or ask Raven who she had been waving to, Mrs. Santos's phone had rung.

The light changed. I gunned the gas. Ruby jerked forward then back as she snacked on her fingers. On the drive from the coffee shop to the Santos's, Ruby had been a complete mess, crying and saying how she was at fault for Raven going missing. But since we left the Santos's house, she had been super quiet.

With one hand on the wheel, I reached over and plucked her hand from her mouth. "We'll find Raven." I couldn't have said if I believed my own words. But I had to. I had to hang onto the notion that my little girl would be okay.

Ruby tucked her hands in between her legs. "The cops said she could be lost in the gardens. What if she wandered into the water?"

"Hey, didn't you tell me she knows how to swim?" The thought of her going into the water had crossed my mind since Raven loved the ducks and swans. But with tourists and the swan boats traveling the lagoon, I was confident someone would've seen her in the water. "The cops are searching the entire area in and around the Boston Public Garden. We'll head over there after we confront Tommy." We would've gone there first, but my gut was telling me that Trent took Raven. Since the cops were on their way to question him, I wanted to question Tommy. He might be able to shed some light on the situation. Besides, I doubted that Trent would answer the cops' questions truthfully.

I wheeled into a spot across from Firefly. The neighborhood seemed eerily quiet for midafternoon. Then again, except for the bakery and diner, most of the other buildings around Firefly were empty, with For Rent or For Sale signs on them.

I hopped out of the truck with my adrenaline in overdrive. The steam coming out of my nose, the fire burning in my chest, and the need to strangle someone drove me into Firefly.

"Wait, Kross," Ruby shouted as she hurried to my side. "Don't knock Tommy out until we get answers."

I wanted to kiss her for that last statement. I was expecting her to say, "Don't do it. Your career is important, blah, blah, blah."

Blood comes first.

"I want a piece of Tommy before you." Her small hands were balled into fists.

That's my girl. Her mood had instantly changed after she'd confessed to Ms. Waters about her illegal fighting, the money she owed Trent, and Trent's threats to bury her case with a judge he knew. Needless to say, Ms. Waters wasn't too happy with Ruby or me.

"There will be consequences for your actions," she'd said, wagging a finger at Ruby. "Major consequences. I want both of you to stay put. We're not through."

As soon as she had left the room, Ruby and I snuck out of the house. We would both deal with the aftermath of the consequences once we had Raven in our arms.

"Baby, do all the damage you want. Just save some for me." That was, if Tommy was even inside. Or maybe we would get lucky and find Trent inside, or even Raven.

Nah, Trent wouldn't have been that stupid. But a father could hope.

Firefly was like a dungeon—dim lighting, musty odor, sticky floor, and cold atmosphere. Pete's head swiveled around like a scene from a horror movie. Okay, I was exaggerating a little.

"You're not welcome here," he snapped, pressing his meaty hands into the bar as though he was ready to vault over it. I was ready for him to do just that. Instead, he watched us as we wound around the bar and tables that were inhabited by a handful of people.

"I work here, and I need Kross with me," Ruby spat out in a voice that sounded as though a man occupied her body.

Pete cocked his head as he regarded Ruby. I couldn't quite grasp if I was turned on or freaked out by her sudden transformation. The woman I loved was deathly determined to chop off heads, and for that, I was more turned on.

Pete took long strides until he was blocking the hall entrance. "Where do you think you're going?" He crossed large arms over his chest.

"Let us through, Pete." Ruby's voice was saturated with sugar and all female this time. "We're not here to cause trouble. We just need to speak to Tommy."

Pete glared at me. "He's not here."

I almost threw him the finger, but fighting with the asshole would only delay our mission, and time was of the essence. I had four hours until my fight and less than thirty minutes to get my ass to the gym for my pre-fight warm-up and strategy meeting with Jay.

"I'm allowed back," Ruby said, using her sweet tone again.

Pete frowned. "Not anymore. Tommy wanted me to tell you you're fired."

Out of nowhere, Ruby throat-punched Pete. His face darkened to a deep red as he choked, holding his neck.

That dire need to kiss her coursed through me.

"My child's life is on the line. So go fuck yourself." Ruby ducked under his arm and ran down to Tommy's office. I hesitated for a split second to make sure he didn't get any crazy notions to hurt her.

His eyes bulged out of his bald head. "I didn't know. Still, you got ten minutes before I call the cops." His voice was strangled as though someone was squeezing the life out of him.

He could call in the cavalry. I wasn't leaving until I got answers. I rushed into the office.

"I don't know where Trent is." Tommy leaned back in his desk chair as though he didn't have a care in the world, while Ruby loomed in front of his desk, ready to pounce.

"Liar," I said as I stormed in, kicking the piles of boxes out of my way until I was standing next to him. "You tell us where he is"—I plucked him out of his chair, grabbed his ostrich-like throat, and clamped down on it—"or else there's a hospital room with your name on it waiting for you."

Ruby darted around to Tommy's other side.

Tommy shifted his dark gaze between Ruby and me.

"Tell us where Trent is," Ruby commanded in that low voice that I was beginning to find sexy.

He opened his mouth, so I eased up on the stronghold. He gulped down air.

"Tommy, we're talking about a little girl, my little girl," Ruby said. "If she gets hurt, you could go to jail for kidnapping."

His eyes became as big as basketballs.

I removed my hand. "Talk."

"Maybe I should call Kross's friend, Dillon. Oh, what did you tell me one time about Dillon." Ruby pressed her forefinger to her mouth. "Yeah. 'He'll fuck me up. Well, it's not just Dillon, but his crazy brothers.' That's what you told me. Not that Kross can't put you in the hospital."

Fear slashed Tommy's ugly features at Ruby's threat.

I couldn't help but smirk at Ruby. "Good one." I'd forgotten that Tommy shit his pants every time he saw Dillon.

"You need to talk to Alex." Tommy raised his hands. "Honestly, I don't get involved with Trent except for the fights here."

Ruby and I backed up as Tommy held onto his cluttered desk.

"Do you know anything about Trent kidnapping my little girl?" Ruby asked.

"I haven't spoken to Trent in two days," Tommy said. The serious expression on his face led me to believe he was telling the truth.

Splotchy red marks dotted Ruby's face and neck. "Were you lying when you and Trent told me that you lost ten thousand dollars because I was late for the fight?"

I noticed when she got nervous, her fair, creamy skin showed the signs.

Tommy scratched his dark head. "No. When you didn't show that night, Trent and I were furious. But he stood to lose more than me. He's a greedy bastard. He said you would pay us back no matter if you won or lost."

Greedy or not, ten thousand dollars was nothing to a man like Trent, who was richer than Donald Trump. Maybe Trent lured Ruby into his deal to have sex with her. Part of me believed that was one of the reasons. I did agree with Tommy, though. Trent gave me the vibe of being quite greedy. What didn't register in my brain, though, was kidnapping someone for the measly money. *People do things all the time that don't make sense. Greed and power are usually at the crux of people's actions.* Again, I shouldn't have been questioning any of this since Lacey's grandfather had kidnapped her until her old man could produce a book that was a map to buried money. Not only that, Trent stood to make more than the ten Gs if I threw my fight.

Ruby let out an exasperated breath.

"Look," Tommy said, "I'm into petty shit, but not kidnapping. No fucking way." His tone was serious and firm. "Trent, aside from his greed, he's got one big fucking ego. His actions are driven by power. He'll stomp on you until you're nothing, and he gets what he wants."

I believed him. Penelope's old man, Mr. Harris, had been through the wringer when Trent tried to buy his company. I wasn't certain of all the details, but Mr. Harris's company went bankrupt because of Trent Baker.

"What's he making you do?" Tommy asked.

Ruby raised an eyebrow. "You don't know? You're his business partner."

Tommy pressed his lips into a thin line. "Again, I haven't talked to him."

"He wants me to throw my fight tonight." I had come in there with the intent to beat answers out of Tommy. But his meaningful tone and expression led me to believe he wanted to help.

"So he can get his ten Gs and then some," Tommy said.

"I know Alex works for Trent, but why would she know where Trent was?" Ruby asked.

That revelation was news to me. I was beginning to wonder if all waitresses at Firefly worked for Trent.

Tommy sucked on his cheek. "Mm. If you knew she worked for Trent, then I thought you would know the rest of the story. Alex is in charge of all his girls. She's responsible for getting them outfitted, giving them pointers, the whole nine yards before they meet with clients."

My jaw hit the floor.

On the other hand, Ruby didn't seem too surprised.

"Why does she work here?" I asked. I was missing something. If she worked for Trent, he had to be paying her a decent wage or better money than she was making waitressing at Firefly. Maybe Trent was so power-hungry that he wouldn't pay Alex enough to support herself. Or maybe he was holding something over her head like he was with Ruby.

"Or live in that dump above the bakery?" Ruby asked.

"I can't answer that. What I do know is Alex hasn't shown up for work in two days. I've tried her cell phone. All I get is her voicemail. You live with her," Tommy said to Ruby. "Don't you know where she is?"

Ruby released a frustrated sigh. "I've been staying at Kross's a lot."

"I'll need her cell number," I said.

Ruby started for the door. "I'm going to check her apartment."

"Ruby," Tommy called. "You may not believe this, but I am sorry. I was serious when I told you that you would be good at fighting." Sincerity weaved through his tone.

She gave Tommy a cursory glance before she rushed out.

I bobbed my head. "Cell number."

He wrote it down on scrap paper.

I snatched the crumbled paper. "I'm not sure you helped us, but thanks for apologizing to her." Then I ran out, down the hall, past Pete, who had a satisfied grin on his face, out the main entrance, and right into the hands of Detective Rayburn, who was holding Ruby's arm as she hung her head.

I stopped cold, confusion clouding my brain for a brief second until

I remembered Pete's threat with the cops, hence the satisfaction written all over his ugly mug. "Mark, what are you doing here?" Detective Mark Rayburn wasn't a beat-cop. He didn't respond to disturbance calls.

Mark was decked out in his normal plain-clothes uniform of jeans and a shirt. His gun was strapped to his holster, which peeked out from underneath his leather jacket. "I heard your name on the radio. I figured I would respond. What's going on?"

Ruby flicked her disheveled head toward the bakery with a pained expression on her face.

"I never formally introduced you to my girl, Ruby," I said as I nodded at her.

Mark released her. "I remember her from the gym that night."

She sprinted down to the bakery then vanished into the entry beside the store.

Mark motioned to chase her.

I blocked his way. "She's not going far."

"I know we're friends, dude, but I'm a cop first. So get out of my way."

I held up my hands. "Hear me out." I plastered on a pleading look, at least I hoped I did.

"You got one minute," he said.

As we walked to Alex's apartment, I filled him in on the entire situation, leaving nothing out.

"I'm sorry, man," Mark said as we climbed the stairs. "Let's see what's going on in the apartment. Then I'll make a few phone calls."

CHAPTER 27
RUBY

I was out of breath after climbing the steps two at a time, my lungs and thighs burning. I knew Alex worked for Trent, but as a madam? The hairs rose on the back of my neck. She'd lured Norma and me into her den. The pieces were falling together. Alex was quick to give us the key to her apartment. She had different styles and sizes of clothes in her closet. *She outfits the women.* Tommy's words skipped through me. She probably had called Trent after she'd given us the key to her apartment. That was why he'd been sitting in Tommy's office that day. He'd wanted to survey the next two pieces of meat.

What didn't make sense was the way Alex hadn't wanted Norma and me to work for Trent. Maybe that had all been an act on her part so Norma and I would believe her.

I banged on the door. "Alex. Alex, are you in there?" Norma had given me her key before I left for the Berkshires. Unfortunately, the key was in my bag at Kross's apartment.

I turned the doorknob. A click sounded, then I gently pushed. *Whoa!* My pulse raced as I entered. "Alex?"

The living room and kitchen were empty. I slinked into the bedroom. The bed was made, and the air smelled stale. If Alex had been there recently, the air would've been laced with her flowery perfume. I checked the bathroom. All her toiletries and makeup were gone. I ran into the bedroom and slid open the closet door. That too was empty.

I sat down on the bed. Norma and I had been played big time. Or at least, I had. I was the one who had fallen into Tommy's trap then Trent's. Norma had kept trying to convince me not to fight. I screamed, but it came out as more of a long, low growl.

I didn't hear Kross or Detective Rayburn come in.

Kross tugged me into his arms. "We'll find Raven."

His tone wasn't all that convincing. I knew he was trying to ease my nerves as much as he was trying to quell his own. He'd been redder than a tomato when Ms. Waters was reading me the riot act back at the Santos's house. I couldn't blame her. I expected her to have the cops handcuff me and throw me in jail. It was my fault Raven was missing, but I couldn't let my own self-pity get in the way of finding her.

I pushed Kross away. "Where? When? Before or after her kidnapper hurts her?" Oh God. The thought of anyone's hands on her sent a bolt of lightning through me. I launched several punches to his chest as I cried. I was such a mess. One minute, I wanted to kill someone. The next minute, I couldn't handle my baby being scared, lost, and hurt.

"Shhh," Kross whispered. He sucked me into his strong, strong arms while Detective Rayburn stuck his head into the bathroom.

Shuddering, I buried my nose into Kross's scented T-shirt and hugged him so tightly, I was afraid to let go. Afraid if I did, I would jump out of the window behind me. I would never forgive myself if Raven was harmed.

"Have a seat," Kross said, ushering me to the bed. "I'll try Alex's phone."

The bed creaked as I wiped the flood of tears from my face. All kinds of scenarios were filtering through my brain. Maybe Trent had kidnapped Alex. Maybe he was holding something over her head. Or maybe she'd taken off with Trent to avoid any trouble.

Raking a hand through his blond locks, Detective Rayburn settled against the closet door across from Kross and me, reading something on his phone.

Kross held his phone to his ear. "Alex."

I took the phone from him. "Alex?"

"It's her voice mail," Kross said.

"Alex, this is Ruby. I know you work for Trent. I don't know if you had anything to do with kidnapping my daughter, but I'm begging you to call me back. Pleading with you that you understand what I'm going through." I hiccupped. "You said your sister died on the streets. So you know what it feels like to have someone you love taken from you." Oh, God. I prayed Raven wasn't dead. "Please, please call me back." I handed the phone to Kross. "Can you tell her your number?"

He rattled it off then added, "Ruby and I will be at Crandall's Gym tonight. If you are involved in all this, then I highly suggest you cooperate. Kidnapping charges are severe. Oh, and tell your scumbag boss, Trent, that I'll do whatever it takes to make sure he's put away for a long time." Then he hung up.

"Okay," Detective Rayburn said. "I just got word that our team has done a complete sweep of the Boston Public Garden and questioned some folks. But they struck out. You said earlier that Mrs. Santos said Raven had been waving at someone. Maybe Raven knew that person. Kids tend to go willingly with people they know."

I slumped where I sat. Raven had only talked about a little girl she'd met. Then again, while she'd been in foster care, she could've met a lot of people, like Mr. and Mrs. Santos's friends.

"As far as I know," Kross said, "Trent hasn't met my little girl."

"But Alex has," I blurted out.

Kross knitted his eyebrows. "When?"

"My last visit with Raven at the Boston Public Garden." *Holy crap.* "She was jogging." Alex worked for Trent, and she'd met Raven, albeit briefly. Still, Raven had a great memory for faces and names.

Kross's phone rang. I bolted upright, taking his phone from him before he could answer. "Alex?"

"Um. No. This is Liam. I thought I dialed Kross Maxwell's number."

I frowned, handing the phone to Kross. Then I went over to Detective Rayburn. "Please tell me Raven will be okay." I needed some reassurance from him even though I knew he couldn't answer my question. No one could. But I had to have something positive to keep me from losing my mind.

He gave me a doleful look. "I'm sure you know I can't tell you that. But we are doing everything we can to find Raven." Then his phone buzzed. "I've got to take this." He stepped out into the living room.

I grabbed the back of my neck, massaging the knots of tension that were causing my head to pound.

"I know I'm late," Kross snapped at Liam. "Tell Jay I'll get there as soon as I can." When he hung up, he punched his fist through the wall.

Detective Rayburn ran in with his phone to his ear as he surveyed the situation. "Thanks, man. I've got to go." He lowered his arm. "What the fuck, Kross?"

"I can't fight tonight," Kross bit out. "I'll kill my opponent when I'm supposed to lose."

I went over to Kross then grabbed the hand covered in white flecks from the Sheetrock. His knuckles were red, but no sign of cuts or blood.

"You have to," Detective Rayburn said. "I just found out that we've questioned Trent Baker. His alibi pans out. He was in a board meeting with his company. So, the best thing you can do is stay on course. Go to the gym, get warmed up, try to calm down. In the meantime, let us do our job. We still have a few hours before the fight. Maybe we can put this to bed before then or before you throw the fight. Ruby, I'll need a description of Alex."

"Sure, but did they search Trent's penthouse or home or business-es?" I asked.

Silence dangled as Detective Rayburn scratched his head. "Not yet. Look, I don't want to get your hopes up. We've been watching Trent Baker for quite some time. All I can say is we're working on something with the Feds, and now coupled with a possible kidnapping, we might be able to convince a judge to give us a warrant before the fight to search his premises."

I stifled a laugh. "A judge, huh? Trent knows judges."

"We're well aware of that too," Detective Rayburn said. "Whatever we do with Trent Baker has to be done by the book so we don't miss our chance again. Now, that description of Alex."

I didn't know whether to be relieved or not. Nonetheless, I spewed the essential details of what Alex looked like.

Detective Rayburn took notes on his phone. Once we were done, he said, "I've got to get moving." He pinned a look on Kross. "Stick to throwing the fight. If I get wind or find anything out, I'll call you. Keep your phone handy."

Kross and I let out an audible sigh together. I couldn't sit around and wait. I had to do something. That something was finding Raven. I didn't need a warrant to search Trent's penthouse or anywhere else for that matter.

CHAPTER 28
KROSS

I straddled the bench in the men's locker room while Ruby bounced her knee. Since the gym was closed, no other men would be coming in to use the facility.

"I should go to Trent's penthouse. The doorman might let me in." Ruby gave me a sidelong glance. "I can at least rule out that place. It's going to take the cops forever to get a warrant."

After we parted ways with Detective Rayburn, Ruby and I doubled back to the Boston Public Garden. We'd wanted to do a search of the area ourselves. But we came up empty.

During that time, Jay had called me, screaming at me to get my ass to the gym. I didn't want to give Jay any reason to cancel the fight, although it took all my energy to ignore Ruby's pleas to swing by Trent's penthouse. I'd even called Kade and put him on speaker, hoping he could calm both Ruby and me down.

"You remember what I went through with Lacey and her kidnapping," Kade had said. "How I was ready to barge into the club and kill her grandfather and the men who took her. If I had, I could've fucked things up badly. As hard as I know it is for you, let the cops do their jobs. Stay away from the penthouse. You could contaminate the evidence, which would hurt the case against Trent. Besides, if you don't stick to the fight or come off as you're losing the fight, then you will make things worse for Raven. Trent will have someone at the fight making sure you're following through on the deal."

I scooted closer to Ruby. "You heard Kade. He speaks from experience."

"I know," she said in a defeated tone. "It's hard for me to wait, knowing Raven is probably scared out of her mind."

I held out hope that Detective Rayburn could and would find something before my fight, especially if Trent was being tailed by the Feds. They had to know his every move and every hidey-hole.

My phone sat ominously on the bench. Both Ruby and I willed Detective Rayburn to call us with some good news. "Take my phone in case Detective Rayburn calls."

Ruby plucked it from where it sat between us.

I tucked a clump of her hair behind her ear. "Baby, as difficult as this is, think about us as a family. Think about all the good times ahead of us." There was power behind positive thinking. I might have been a little out there on that notion, but my old man always counseled his patients with that motto.

"A family, huh?" She said it more as a statement than a question as though she was trying the concept on for size.

"Yes. A family," I said to reassure her. "My heart is yours, Ruby."

"Why?" She adjusted her body so she was straddling the bench with me. "You love me. But what triggered those feelings?"

Given what she'd been through in the last four years, including me dumping her like a bad virus, I couldn't blame her for asking.

We sat face-to-face, knees-to-knees, and hands-in-hands. "Because I love the way you lightly snore," I said. "I love the way you bite your fingers when you're thinking or nervous. I love that you can be shy and feisty. But more than anything, I love the butterfly feeling you give me every time I lay eyes on you. That hasn't changed after four years."

She averted her gaze as her teeth commandeered her bottom lip. Whether she shied away deliberately or not, the act still drove me to kiss her. When my lips touched hers, she purred like a satisfied cat after a good scratch session before our tongues tangled and danced.

The door squeaked open. Voices bounced off the lockers, echoing.

Ruby and I both froze before we pulled away from each other as though we'd been caught by our parents.

"She's in here," Liam said.

Liam and Norma emerged from around a bank of lockers.

Norma's big brown eyes got bigger as she ran to Ruby. "I'm so sorry. I just heard Kade telling Dillon about Raven. Oh my God."

Ruby hopped up and hugged Norma.

Liam's gaze ate up Norma as though he wanted to jump her bones. Hell, I wouldn't have blamed him. Her blond hair had grown out some, framing her face more, and the curves on her body were more pronounced, or maybe it was just the tight sweater hugging her big breasts. Aside from that, she was prettier than I remembered.

Pushing to my feet, I touched Ruby's arm. "I have to get ready. Why don't you and Norma head out to your seats."

She pulled away from Norma.

I planted a kiss on her lips. "I love you."

Norma gasped. "Seriously? Since when? You didn't tell me, Ruby." Norma's glossy lips split into a huge smile. "We have a lot to talk about, girl."

Norma would keep Ruby distracted, and for that, I breathed a little easier.

Ruby lifted up on her tiptoes. "As big as the universe?"

"As big as the fucking universe." And I did.

She quickly placed a chaste kiss on my lips then left with Norma.

"Time to tape your fingers, man," Liam said.

I dropped my ass onto the bench and buried my face in my hands. I was a second from collapsing. I'd never given up on anything in my life. I also had never felt so inept. "Reggie doesn't stand a chance tonight," I said more to myself than Liam. The pent-up anger inside me was enough to hurt Reggie badly. If I gave into it, I would ruin the deal with Trent.

"That's great, dude, because I overheard Gail talking with Jay. She's hoping you show her your moves."

Great! I didn't have the heart to tell Liam that I wouldn't beat Reggie even though I could. Then again, I shouldn't get cocky. Maybe Reggie would beat my ass fair and square without me having to throw the fight. Reggie had some key moves that could take me down in a second. In any case, I would at least go a couple of rounds before I threw the fight. That way, Gail would at least see some of my moves.

Liam stuck his hand in his jeans pocket and produced a roll of white tape. "Let's get started."

As he covered my fingers in tape, Dillon came in. As usual, Dillon sported his signature ponytail and a scruff-covered jaw. I hadn't had a chance to call him to fill him in on Raven's kidnapping.

"Is Ruby out there?" I asked him. I didn't think Norma would let Ruby take off. Still, I had to be sure. I didn't need to worry about her too while I was fighting.

"Don't worry, man," Dillon said. "Kade, Kody, and Kelton have her surrounded."

Thank God for my brothers.

Dillon sat down next to me and slapped my back. "Kade just told me. Sorry to hear about all this."

"Liam, can you give us a minute?" I asked.

Liam cocked his head. "Dude, you need to get ready."

I narrowed my eyes. "Two minutes."

He swung his gaze between Dillon and me then shook his head as he walked out.

Dillon waited until the door clicked shut to speak. "I just called Rafe. I asked him to swing by Baker's shipping company. He'll also check out his dealerships."

"Thanks," I said. "But don't get your men in a bind with the cops. Besides, that waitress Alex probably has a hand in Raven's disappearance."

Dillon's posture went rigid as his nose ring glinted off the lights from above. "What?"

I hit a nerve. "Talk," I demanded.

"I'm just surprised that she would have anything to do with kidnapping."

"Dude, she works for Trent. She wrangles the women of the night for him."

"I've known Alex for two years since she breezed into the city to find her baby sister. Like mine, hers left home because of an abusive father. She searched endlessly for her sister until she got a call from the cops one night. They found her sister dead in a dumpster in some alley. Someone had done a number on her. Since then, Alex has made it her mission to find out what happened. The cops followed leads, but then they dried up. It became a cold case. Then she got a lead about Tommy, who might be involved with her sister. Instead of confronting Tommy, she took a job there to play detective. She soon found out that Tommy is all about fights, and like my brother, he's a loan shark or steals a car here and there. Petty shit. I just assumed that she was still working at that dump because she held out hope." He rested his elbows on his knees.

"So, she's never spoken to you about Trent Baker?" This new information made me wonder if maybe Alex wasn't working for Trent.

"I haven't spoken to Alex in detail in a long time. When I'm at Firefly, I'm there because Tommy owes me something. I'm not there to hang out. And before you ask me if her and I dated, the answer is no. She's not my type. You know that."

In the time I'd known Dillon, I hadn't seen him with a woman, although I did know from conversations that he was into blondes, not brunettes.

Jay's voice filled the room. "Kross?" His short stature emerged. He had a scowl on his face. Then he glanced at his watch. "Why aren't you ready?"

Liam huffed out a breath as he came up behind Coach. "It's my fault," Liam said. "I had to get more tape." He wagged a roll of it between us.

I made a mental note to thank the kid.

"Good luck tonight." Dillon unfolded his bulk. "I'll be with your brothers." Then he left.

I needed more than luck. I needed Detective Rayburn to find Raven. But I had to concentrate on the fight. Otherwise, Reggie would knock me out with the first punch. I had to at least show some effort before I lost.

Liam quickly worked to finish taping my fingers while Coach gave me a list of pointers. "First, be careful of his hook. Second, footwork. Third, don't let him get near your face. Finally, in order to seal the deal with Gail, knock him the fuck out."

I laughed at his last statement. Like me, Coach didn't have any love for Reggie. We both respected his talent, but Reggie had been my first fight, and back then, Reggie was a cocky bastard. Coach hated players like that. I hated Reggie for my own personal reasons. That alone sent a pain of guilt through me because I had to throw the fight. Kody was salivating for me to hurt Reggie, but since he knew what was going on, he understood.

Not only that, I wanted my contract with Gail, more for financial reasons than for my own fucking ego. After tonight, I would be serving hamburgers at McDonalds or in jail for murdering Trent Baker if he was truly responsible for kidnapping Raven.

After I was dressed, primed, and ready for a fight I wanted to run from, I walked out of the locker room with so much trepidation that fear had to be written all over my face.

Voices droned from the crowd, which occupied the three sets of bleachers lining three sides of the ring. On the fourth side, chairs were set up for Gail and her team plus a handful of chairs for family and friends of Reggie and me. We were limited by fire code on how many people could occupy the gym. Therefore, the fight was invitation only. At first, Jay didn't want anyone at the fight except the essential people —referee, Gail, her entourage, and the EMS folks—but Gail wanted to see a fight complete with an audience. She'd said something about how the energy of the crowd affected the fighter's actions, whatever that meant. All I knew were two things. One, I was glad Jay nixed the idea of having any reporters at the fight. I'd been chastised for throwing my last fight when I hadn't, but tonight would be different. I didn't want or need the press. And two, I blocked out the noise and the people when I was in a ring.

Regardless, I'd invited my brothers, Ruby, Norma, Dillon, and that girl Ruby had fought, Vickie. I'd decided not to invite my parents, solely because I didn't want my mom seeing me get punched or bloody or any other gruesome act that might make her cringe.

I set my sights on Ruby. She was sandwiched in between Kade and Kody. She still looked pale. Kelton was sitting behind them with Norma and Vickie. Vickie flashed puppy dog eyes at me then pumped one of her muscled arms in the air as a silent gesture of encouragement for me to win this fight. Dillon sat in the end seat.

As I approached the ring, the referee began to spit out my stats. "Weighing in at two hundred and twenty pounds with a record of eight and one, let's give it up for Kross Maxwell."

Liam, who was walking alongside me, hit me on the arm. "Remember, no deer in the headlights tonight."

I harrumphed. When I'd first met Liam, he had the nerve to tell me how much I'd fucked up at my last fight. I'd almost popped him one, but I couldn't argue with the truth. Boy, was I in for another one of his tongue-lashings when I lost the fight.

The ref pointed behind me. "Fighting in the other corner, weighing in at two hundred and twenty-five pounds with a perfect record of ten and O, let's hear it for Reggie Stockman."

I quickly glanced over my shoulder at Reggie. We'd given him access to the women's locker room so he could dress. He hadn't changed much since the last time I'd seen him. His dark eyes had that "fuck you" look, his hair was cut in a military style, and he wore his usual superior smirk that made me clench my fists.

The crowd tittered more for him than me, which was odd considering the audience was made up of mostly gym members. Jay had extended the remaining invitations to the people who worked out at the gym. I searched the crowd for anyone who stood out or gave me an inkling that they worked for Trent Baker. I came up empty, although I spotted Penelope. She sat on the top row of the bleachers to my left. As the fleeting thought of her working for Trent skated through my mind, Ruby smiled at me, erasing thoughts of Trent for the moment.

I stopped and kissed her quickly then continued, passing a long pair of smooth, bare legs.

Liam whispered in my ear. "Gail is staring at you."

Shoving down all my problems, I planted on a smile as I passed the gorgeous woman. Man, her legs went on forever, disappearing underneath a classy red coatdress that was cinched at the waist by a belt. Her black hair was tied behind her head, revealing a long neck, angular face, dark slanted eyes, and red painted lips. She was the picture of a wealthy businesswoman.

She returned the gesture, showing bright-white teeth as she dipped her chin. When she did, the slight movement of her head made me do a double take at the main entrance behind her.

The noise dulled. I flicked a quick glance to Ruby then back to the fucker in the doorway. Trent Baker strutted in like a cocky son-of-a-bitch. I couldn't believe he had the nerve to show up there. Ruby screamed. The sound sliced through my psyche, propelling me into action. I leapt over Gail, or maybe she moved out of the way. People scrambled.

"Kross," Jay shouted.

He could fire me now or after I killed Trent Baker. I dove at him, landing my gloved fist into his bulbous nose. The impact didn't have the same effect as it would if I'd had bare knuckles. Before I could launch another blow, hands were pulling me away, while Kade was holding Ruby securely to him.

"You bastard," she screamed at Trent. "Where is my daughter?"

Trent held onto his jaw with a smug expression on his face.

I tried to jerk out of Kody's hands, but my brother was strong.

"You have the nerve to show up here?" I asked with venom gushing out of me.

Trent held up his hands as a small amount of blood oozed out of his nose. "I was invited."

I tossed a look over my shoulder at Jay. If he so much as let this bastard in here, then he and I were finished.

Jay pushed through the crowd. "I don't have time to hear what's going on. Kross, get your ass in the ring. Now," he said through clenched teeth.

"I want to know who let him in here." I wasn't getting in any ring until I knew. Even then, I wasn't sure I would fight.

Trent nodded his head at the ring.

I glanced over my shoulder. "Reggie did?" I shouldn't have been surprised. Reggie was friends with Kade's enemy, Greg Sullivan, who reminded me a lot of Trent, dirty and sleazy.

Trent held out his invitation. "No trouble. I'm here to protect my investment." He flashed Reggie a smile.

I couldn't tell if what he meant by his investment was Reggie or our deal.

Gail joined us. "Is there a problem?" Her voice was light but firm. "I don't have all night."

Jay pinned a glare on me. I knew I was ruining my shot at a boxing career, but I couldn't ruin his. He had connections in the industry and was well-liked and respected. He'd jumped through hoops to get an audience with Gail. Not only that, if Reggie was in cahoots with Trent, then this fight would be all the more interesting. I knew where to punch to make sure the blow would hurt without knocking him out.

"I'm cool," I lied.

"What?" Ruby all but shouted.

"Jay and Gail, one minute, please." I softened my expression the best I could.

"All right, everyone." Jay corralled the group around us. "Back to your seats."

I stepped closer to Trent with Kody close by me, ready to intervene. "Where is my daughter?"

He glanced around before he answered. "You stick to the deal." Then he casually sauntered off to find a seat next to Reggie's friends.

A primal instinct to beat the man until he couldn't breathe warred with the need to stick to the plan for Raven's sake. I briefly shut my eyes before I turned to face Ruby. I thought about having her call Detective Rayburn to tell him Trent was there, but he'd said the cops were keeping an eye on Trent.

She wriggled, trying to get out of Kade's hold. "Well, what did he say? Does he have Raven?"

"He isn't going to tell me." But the smug look he'd given me before striding off led me to believe he was responsible for Raven's disappearance.

Ruby stopped trying to get away from Kade as I ran into the ring.

CHAPTER 29
RUBY

I should have been marveling at the man I loved, whose ripped abs and bulging biceps were a huge turn-on. Yet I couldn't concentrate on anything except wondering where in the world my daughter was. She had to be scared out of her mind. I couldn't believe that Trent had the nerve to show up here. Maybe it was good that he was at the fight. That way, when the fight ended, I could tie him down until he told us the truth. I whipped out Kross's phone and held it in one of my hands as though it was my lifeline. Detective Rayburn had advised Kross to go through with the fight. I couldn't have said I disagreed. I was reminded of all those cop shows I'd watched, where the bad guys held someone for ransom, and the cops always recommended that the parents follow the kidnapper's orders. None of that made me feel any better, though.

Kade and Kody flanked me on each side as I bounced my knee faster than a car moving at a hundred miles per hour.

Kade gently placed his large hand on my knee. "Ruby, I know this is hard. I feel your frustration, pain, and every other emotion that is gripping the fuck out of you. But I promise you, Trent will get what's coming to him."

I peered up at Kade. Empathy and sympathy swam in his copper eyes. He'd been through something similar with his girlfriend, and for that, I felt connected to him. I covered my hand over his warm and strong one. He adjusted his so that he was holding mine.

I hoped his girlfriend would be okay with him holding my hand. I needed something to keep me from acting on my motherly instinct to hurt Trent Baker. "Please don't let go," I said to Kade.

He squeezed my hand. "I never let go of family."

I held back a burst of tears. The Maxwells were too real to be true.

Norma massaged my shoulders from behind me. "We all got you," she said.

I couldn't keep the tears at bay any longer, especially as Kody covered my other hand with his. As one, then two, then three tears found their way out and down my cheek, I focused on the fight. The noise level was low, at least for me. All I could hear was my heart pounding in my ears.

"Come on, Kross," Vickie shouted from behind me. "You can do better than that."

Reggie was punching Kross in a right, left, right sequence. Kross took a hit, ducked, then took another hit. When Reggie and Kross were locked together, the referee untangled them. Kross danced as he jabbed at Reggie. Reggie bobbed and weaved, taking a punch every now and then. For a boxing match, it seemed boring until Kross glanced at Trent. Then Pandora's box opened. One side of Kross's mouth turned upward.

"Rattlesnake," the crowd chanted.

No. No. No. He wasn't supposed to knock out Reggie.

Kross lunged at Reggie, punching him in the jaw, ribs, and stomach. Then in one smooth motion, Kross wielded an uppercut that sent Reggie backward. He fell with a thud.

I tried to jump out of my seat to protest, but as though Kade and Kody knew what Kross was doing, they both held me down.

"He needs to show he's at least fighting," Kade whispered with his hand glued to mine.

"Kross knows what he's doing," Kody said with surety on my right.

No matter how confident Kross's brothers were, I couldn't jump on their train. *Get up. Get up. Get up,* I silently repeated. The referee was counting. I stole a look at Trent. He had his arms crossed over his chest. His gaze was riveted on the fighters with that I-own-the-world look. Then I checked on Kross. A death beam shone from his eyes as he focused on Reggie, while the referee counted.

On each count, I swallowed the fear invading my body. When the referee reached six, Reggie stirred. As if in slow motion, he climbed to his feet, shaking his head. The ref scrutinized his eyes. "You okay?"

"Never better," Reggie snapped as he retreated to his corner where an old man gave him water.

I swung my attention back to Kross as my body deflated in the chair. He raised his gloved hands, his forearms in front of his face as he shifted from one foot to the other, raring to go at Reggie again.

I pinched my eyebrows at him, but he wasn't looking at me, or he refused to look at me. A rustling noise drew my attention away. I tossed a look over my shoulder. Dillon fidgeted in his seat as he nodded at me with a deadpan expression. On the other hand, Kelton was gnawing on a fingernail, his eyes glued to his brother in the ring. I reached over and touched his knee. I wasn't exactly sure why I did that. Maybe because he was the only one of the Maxwell brothers that seemed to be feeling what I was feeling, scared and nervous. Kross had mentioned that Raven took to Kelton instantly. Of course, that might have had something to do with Kelton bringing a lizard with him to meet Raven.

His blue eyes regarded me before he gave me a rueful grin. Suddenly, I wanted to hug him and tell him that everything would be okay, that he would be able to give Raven all the lizards he wanted. But I couldn't tell him that if I wasn't sure I would ever see her again. Kross believed we would be a family. Kade had a moral code of family, and he was at my side, comforting me. And Kody believed Kross knew what he was doing. Even though Kelton didn't give me the same vibe that Kody and Kade had, his emotional turmoil, or whatever he was struggling with, was enough to kick me in the ass and remind me that I wasn't alone. Family surrounded me. Kross, Raven, and I would be together, and for that, I had to roll back my shoulders, stick out my chin, buck up, and show Kross I could be strong.

The bell dinged at the same time the phone in my right hand vibrated. I flipped it over to find Mark Rayburn's name on the screen. I showed Kade before I excused myself to find a quiet spot near the main entrance.

"Detective Rayburn, Trent is here at the gym."

"I know. We have a tail on him. Look, tell Kross not to throw the fight. I'll be there in two minutes."

"Do you have evidence?"

"Just tell him, Ruby." The phone went dead.

I darted my gaze at Kross and Reggie, who were jabbing and circling each other while the crowd tittered with chants of "get him, Reggie" or "knock him out, Rattlesnake." Just as I lifted my foot to take a step, the door to the main entrance opened. A gush of cold air swept in along with Alex, who was holding Raven's hand.

"Raven!" I screamed as I ran to her, scanning her body for any signs of bruises. Thank God I didn't see any.

She jumped into my arms. "Mommy." My heart faltered as her little hands locked around my neck.

I peppered kisses all over her as I held her tightly to me, tears rushing out. I inhaled her baby scent and suddenly, my pulse slowed. No sooner had my heartbeat quieted than it ramped up again when I glanced at the ring. As if in slow motion, Reggie's fist connected with Kross's face. Kross fell backward.

Nooo!

The ref began counting.

I whipped my attention to Alex, wanting to unleash all my rage on her, but I just sneered. I didn't want to scare Raven anymore than she already was.

"She's not hurt," Alex said, sounding sorrowful. "I had no choice." Her long hair was a mess, and her cheeks were flushed as though she'd been running.

"Everyone has a choice." I had to get Raven away from her.

I was about to check on Kross when Trent stalked toward us. He had a scowl on his face as he fixated on Alex. He couldn't leave. Detective Rayburn had said he would be here. I wanted to stop Trent, but I had Raven in my arms. Well, I wanted to do more than stop him. Trent deserved to feel physical pain.

He pushed Alex out of the way. "Nothing but trash," he said to her. "Now you'll never know what happened to your sister."

The ref was still counting.

I started for the door when it burst open. Detective Rayburn stormed in with men in blue. Trent backpedaled, looking for another way out.

Detective Rayburn pointed at Alex. "Cuff her." A buff cop grabbed Alex's arm as her eyes pooled with tears.

The noise level died.

Detective Rayburn and two cops surrounded Trent. "Trent Baker, you're under arrest for the kidnapping of Raven Lewis."

The audience gasped.

With Raven in my arms, I rushed to see Kross. When my gaze landed on the ring, the referee was holding up Reggie's arm, while Liam was waving something under Kross's nose. Kross stirred, and Liam helped him to his feet. He blinked several times before zeroing in on Detective Rayburn.

Kross visibly slouched when his eyes landed on Raven and me.

"Take him," Detective Rayburn said to the two cops, his voice booming in the quiet gym.

The cops cuffed Trent.

"I still got my money," Trent said with an air of arrogance. "Thank you." His gaze landed on Kross then me.

Suddenly, the joy I had dulled. The asshole still got what he wanted. *Yeah, but the money won't go far in jail.*

Detective Rayburn walked up to me. "Is she okay?"

Raven lifted her head from my shoulder and smiled.

He smiled back at Raven. "I guess so. I'll be back in a few minutes."

"I want to talk to Alex," I said. I had to find out why she'd kidnapped my daughter.

"As soon as I'm done with her." Detective Rayburn strode off.

Then as if nothing had happened, the referee said, "The winner is Reggie Stockman."

My heart plummeted. Kross's career was probably ruined. But at the same time, my heart soared. Raven was safe and in my arms. Suddenly, my legs trembled. I found my seat next to Kade, Kody, and the rest of my new family. Immediately, Raven waved at Kelton. Then in a flash, she was on his lap. For the first time in a very long time, I laughed.

CHAPTER 30
KROSS

Dizziness consumed me as I stood in the ring, staring at Ruby and Raven—the best fucking picture of my life. How Raven had gotten there? No clue, although I suspected Alex. With the bright lights of the ring, I could barely see past the chairs to the main entrance.

So Trent believed he had won. Maybe he'd gotten his money, but I got my family.

Blood comes first.

The crowd was thinning out and heading for the exit. Gail was immersed in her phone. The ref was talking to Reggie, while Liam was trying to guide me to the stool in the corner.

"I'm cool," I said to the kid. Although when I set my eyes on Jay, cool went out the window.

A look of disappointment slashed his features, causing pain to constrict my chest. The last thing I'd wanted was to ruin my relationship with him. I wanted more than anything to run to Ruby and Raven, hold them, kiss them, and tell them how much I loved them. But Ruby and Raven were surrounded by my brothers, Norma, and Dillon. Considering they were safe, I needed to apologize to Jay. I prayed he would understand. Then again, I actually didn't throw the fight like Trent thought I had. I'd been buying my time, hoping Detective Rayburn would come through. If he hadn't, then I would have thrown it. But when Ruby had screamed Raven's name as if someone was committing bloody murder, I took my eyes off my opponent for a split second, giving him the upper hand, and he'd taken it. I didn't blame him. I would've done the same if the roles had been reversed.

I made my way over to Jay, replaying the conversation we'd had before Thanksgiving in which he'd reprimanded me. *"I know every underground fighting circuit in this city. If I catch you or get wind that you're at one again, we're through. You can find another coach."* Granted, I hadn't been at an underground fight since then, but the fact that I'd been dealing with someone like Trent Baker was the same in my book.

"I'm sorry for everything. I'll clean out my locker." It was futile to grovel. When Jay gave anyone a warning, he always stuck to his guns.

Jay diverted his gaze to Gail, who was watching us. She nodded at Jay or me. I couldn't tell which. I also couldn't decipher what was going through her head.

"Get your ass in my office," Jay said in a brusque tone.

"But—"

"Kross, I don't have any patience with you." He pinched the bridge of his hooknose.

I held up my hands. "I'm going."

"Oh, and don't stop to talk to anyone," he said. "Liam, make sure Kross goes straight to my office. Also, if you cover for him again, you will not have a shot at boxing for me."

Liam's brown eyes went wide. "Yes, sir."

Liam and I hopped out of the ring on the backside. Jay's office was behind the bleachers, completely opposite from where Ruby and Raven were.

On our way, Penelope swaggered toward us with a huge smile plastered on her face.

Liam swatted my arm. "You're not supposed to talk to anyone."

I didn't want to be rude to her. I also didn't want to jeopardize Liam's chances with Jay.

Penelope settled in front of us, losing her smile. "I'm sorry about your daughter. I'm also sorry about that night in the gym. I don't usually do coke, and with the two drinks I had, the combination did a number on me."

"Come on, man," Liam said rather nervously.

"No need to apologize," I said. "I'm just glad you're all right."

Her red lips split into a smile. "Always the gentleman, worrying about everyone. Anyway, my dad will be pleased to hear that Trent Baker got arrested."

"I'm sure he will. Look, I've got to run. I'll see you next week for training, right?" I wasn't so sure I would be training her anymore, especially if Jay fired my ass.

"Sure," she said then made her way to the exit.

Once in Jay's meticulous office, Liam whipped out a towel from his back pocket then threw it at me. "You have blood on your lip."

I had blood on my eyebrow, and pain seared my jaw. I didn't mind. In fact, adrenaline had helped me grow accustomed to the pain. Still, over-the-counter pain meds were essential after a fight. "You didn't have to cover for me with Jay before the fight." I dried the sweat and blood from my face.

He folded his young body into a metal chair. "I wanted to. So I overheard your brothers telling Dillon that you were going to throw the fight. Why?"

"Actually, I didn't. I'd planned on it, but I got distracted before I could follow through. In any case, to answer your question, family was the reason."

He swiped a hand over his brown hair. "That's your little girl out there. She looks just like you."

All I could do was smile. "She looks more like my mom than me."

"She's going to be a knockout. I pity her boyfriends when she gets older."

I did too, but I didn't want to think that far ahead. I could only think as far as the paternity test at the moment. Even that thought sizzled out when the door flung open. Jay, Gail, and Detective Rayburn ambled in.

I should have said that Jay stomped in. "Liam, out."

Liam scurried out as if someone was chasing him.

When the door closed with a thud, I set my gaze on Gail. She had her hands in her coatdress pockets, her expression unreadable.

"I was distracted, and it cost me the fight," I said. There was no sense in delaying the inevitable. "However, I really appreciate the opportunity you gave me. I'm sorry that I disappointed you."

"Detective Rayburn"—she pointed a red nail at him—"filled us in on why you were distracted."

"Jay, I've been a member here a long time," Detective Rayburn said. "You know I wouldn't screw you on anything. As I said on the way here, Kross wanted to cancel the fight, but we had a little girl's life at stake. He was operating on my orders."

"I'm more pissed that you couldn't share any of this with me." Jay glared at me. "You're practically my son for God's sake." Hurt flared in his dark eyes.

"I'm sorry." I berated myself for being a schmuck. I should've come clean with Jay from the very beginning when I'd found out about Ruby and Raven. He was right. He reminded me a lot of my old man. He'd given me advice, not only on boxing and the industry, but on how to be patient in and out of the ring. Boy, had I struck out with Ruby early on when it came to that bit of advice. "I couldn't risk you canceling the fight."

"Okay," Gail interjected. "Most of what I saw in that ring from you, Kross, I didn't like. I want to sign someone who will give me one hundred and twenty percent. I front a ton of money to back a fight. I can't sign someone who will throw my money away."

Jay sat down in his chair behind his desk as though he wasn't ready to hear the rest of Gail's speech. Detective Rayburn leaned against the arm of the couch. As for me, I stood facing Gail, ready to take the hit.

She scrutinized me as she angled her head. "With that said, I also didn't like that Reggie was easily persuaded to jump into Mr. Baker's corner. Your reasons as to why you did what you did far outweigh the reasons for Reggie aligning with a criminal. I empathize with you, Kross. I have children of my own. If anyone ever kidnapped them, I probably would've done the same as you."

I held my breath.

"I did like how skillful you were in knocking Reggie out. I don't see footwork like yours, and I certainly haven't seen the hunger you displayed earlier in quite sometime. Don't get me wrong. Reggie has a better record than you, but his cocksure attitude is not what I'm looking for. On the other hand, you take responsibility for your actions. You've apologized to Jay and me. That says a lot about you as a person. I also want to work with someone who has a quiet intensity about him. Therefore, I would like to sign you to a five-year contract."

I grabbed onto to the back of my head and recited a quick prayer. Then I blew out a breath. "Thank you."

"I'll have the contract sent over early next week," Gail said to Coach.

He nodded. Me, I couldn't move.

Gail extended her hand. "Welcome aboard."

I would have hugged her, but I was sweaty, so I shook her hand.

"We'll be in touch." Then she walked out.

I hung my head as the knot in my stomach loosened. To say I was elated would be an understatement. I wanted to run out and find Ruby and tell her the good news. Hell, I wanted to tell everyone, including my dad. I could now comfortably support my family, and that alone would make my dad proud.

Detective Rayburn clapped a hand on my back. "I'm sure you have questions about Baker's arrest and what we found. I'll be out there with your family when you're ready." He eyed Coach. "Sorry about the fight. I thought I could get to Kross before anything happened."

"By the way, I didn't throw it," I said. "Ruby screamed. Then I went down."

"I think we were all distracted when we heard her," Jay added.

"See you out there," Detective Rayburn said as he left.

"Jay," I started. "I'm so fucking sorry."

"I get it, Kross. I'm hurt you didn't confide in me. If we're going to work together, we have to have open communication. For fuck's sake, I have a daughter. I would've understood." He plastered on a smile. "You look like shit. Shower before you see your girls."

I flew out of his office and into the locker room. All I could think about while I showered were my girls. Ruby and Raven were mine. I kept repeating that while the hot water beat down on my tight muscles. I had a family—two beautiful girls that I couldn't wait to start a life with. But first, I had to get through lawyers, a paternity test, and a judge. Regardless of all that, I dressed then strutted out into the gym with a huge fucking grin on my face.

Alex sat in a chair next to the ring with her hands cuffed behind her back. Detective Rayburn leaned against the ropes across from her, texting on his phone, and Ruby was walking out of the daycare room. When she saw me, she ran and hopped into my arms like an expert Olympic jumper.

Before I could say anything, her tongue was in my mouth. I couldn't help but return the kiss until Detective Rayburn cleared his throat. She slid down my body, her breasts brushing against me, sending jolts of pleasure to my groin. My dick had a mind of its own. *Not now,* I shouted in my head.

"Is Raven inside the daycare room?" I asked.

"Your brothers, Norma, and Dillon are playing LEGOs with her," Ruby said.

"I need to get Alex down to the precinct," Detective Rayburn said. "Let's make this quick."

Alex's face was pale, and red colored the whites of her dark eyes.

I crossed my arms over my chest. "I only have one question. Why? Why would you get involved with kidnapping? Dillon told me that you were looking for answers on who killed your sister. Did taking my daughter get you those answers?" My voice was even.

Tears slid down Alex's cheeks. "Trent promised me if I did this one last task, he would give me the answers I'd been searching for on the death of my sister. I'm sorry. I'm not asking you to forgive me. What I did was awful and low and so out of my league. I'd always prided myself on helping people. That's why I helped Ruby and Norma. I couldn't bear to see them living on the streets like my sister. It was just a matter of time before they ended up like her." She glanced at Ruby. "I tried to keep you both shielded from Trent. If only you'd stuck to waitressing and not fighting."

Red spots colored Ruby's neck. "Are you saying it's my fault?"

Alex shook her head. "God, no. Look, I'm not a bad person. When I heard your message, something in me snapped. I realized that the mission to find who killed my sister wasn't worth hurting others in the process."

Ruby narrowed her eyes at Alex. "I appreciate you giving Norma and me a place to stay. From the first time I met you, I knew you were a kind person. I get your need for closure with your sister, but you put a little girl's life in jeopardy. You frightened my little girl. She might have nightmares over all this."

I draped an arm over Ruby. Granted, Raven wasn't physically harmed, but Ruby had a point. Raven's emotional stability could have been compromised. Regardless of her motives, Alex needed to pay for what she'd done.

I turned to Detective Rayburn. Lines fanned out from the corners of his eyes. "Can you shed some light on what evidence you had to arrest Trent?"

Ruby planted a hand on my stomach.

"We were about to serve a warrant to Trent when I got a call from Pete, the bartender at Firefly."

Ruby and I exchanged what-the-hell looks.

"Apparently, after you left Firefly, Trent showed up. Tommy confronted Trent about the kidnapping. Then they got into a heated argument. Trent said no homeless woman was going to screw him out of money, and that she would get her kid when he got his money. So Pete called his cop buddy, Roy, and filled him in. Now I have Pete and Alex to testify in court against Trent."

I barked out a laugh. "You are talking about that bruiser, Pete?"

"Yeah, dude. The same guy that beat your ass that night at Firefly." Rayburn smirked. "Roy told me what happened."

"Oh my God. I punched Pete in the throat." Ruby's voice was strangled. "I need to apologize."

We both did. Then I needed to thank him.

Rayburn walked over to Alex and gripped her arm. "Let's go."

She rose, trepidation written all over her ghostly face. "Again, I am truly sorry."

I couldn't bring myself to forgive her actions. Ruby clung to me, not saying a word.

"Oh, and one more thing," Rayburn said. "I got a call before you came out from the locker room. A Ms. Waters is on her way here to pick up Raven. Before you go ballistic, Raven is legally a ward of the state until you get your court case worked out."

No sooner had he said her name than Ms. Waters clicked her heels against the floor, the sound grating on me. Ruby's heartbeat ramped up, pounding against my side. Or maybe it was my own. I didn't want Raven to be taken away again.

"We'll be in touch," Rayburn said as he ushered Alex out of the building.

It was time for the next battle. Ruby and I met Ms. Waters near the daycare room. Her face was clear of makeup. Her smile was as tight as the bun twisted on top of her head.

"Ms. Waters, can't we keep Raven for the night?" Ruby asked in a wobbly voice.

She shoved her hands into her coat pockets. "I'm afraid not."

My throat constricted. "Ma'am, how are we supposed to trust that Raven won't get kidnapped again? It's clear Mrs. Santos was distracted at the Boston Public Garden."

"Mrs. Santos won't be taking Raven to the Boston Public Garden anymore, and with the kidnapper in jail, Raven will be fine," Ms. Waters said.

"Ms. Waters," Ruby said. "I would never intentionally put my daughter in harm's way. I hope you know that. I was trying to survive, and in the process, I screwed up. I'll take whatever punishment you deem necessary." Tears cascaded down Ruby's cheeks.

Ms. Waters pressed her lips together as pity flashed in her eyes. "I've witnessed just how much you love Raven. If the tables were turned, I might've made the same choices you did. But it's not up to me to decide how this case plays out. That's for a judge to decide. For now, my recommendation to both of you is to find a suitable home for Raven. Do anything you can do to show the court you're ready to be parents. I'm here to help."

Then our next move was to go house hunting.

CHAPTER 31

RUBY

The cold and sterile walls of the courtroom sent a chill down my spine. I found Kross's hand and gripped it so hard, I would have sworn I was sucking all his muscled strength into me. His lawyer, or our lawyer, Mr. Davenport, was sitting on the other side of Kross, flipping through documents. I'd met the gray-haired man three weeks prior when he called Kross into his office to share the good news that the paternity test was a match. He was Raven's father. Of course, I had already known that.

My nerves were quivering faster than a couple swing dancing, mainly because the judge could rule that Kross and I weren't ready to be parents. Or Ms. Waters could give us a bad recommendation. I didn't think she would. She seemed to be sympathetic to everything that I'd been through. Still, I'd put my little girl in a bad situation that could have cost her her life. I had to atone for my mistakes. If I didn't, then I would be a bad example to my child. When Raven learned our story years down the road, I wanted her to see that I'd paid for my mistakes.

"My heart wants to fly out of my chest," Kross said.

It was good to know I wasn't the only one freaking out. I always had a hard time deciphering Kross's moods except when we were about to make love. Then his blue eyes always seemed to darken with one long look that screamed, "I want to rip off your clothes."

244

"We checked everything off our list." I rubbed the back of his hand as I stifled a laugh at how the tables had turned. Normally, he would have been the one comforting me.

Lately though, I'd been the one to give advice to him and his brothers, especially Kelton. It had surprised the heck out of me that Kelton seemed worried. He'd said we were in good hands with Mr. Davenport. He'd also mentioned the same thing Ms. Waters had about how the family court system always returned a foster kid to her family as soon as they could, provided the family met the guidelines.

The door next to the judge's bench squeaked opened. In walked a man wearing a black robe. He had thinning hair and a stony face. I heard rustling behind us. The entire Maxwell family was there to support us, minus Kade and Kelton's girlfriends.

My heart sputtered as I began silently praying.

Kross squeezed my hand. "Here we go."

Suddenly, I had that stomach churning feeling as if I was sitting at the top of a rollercoaster, looking straight down, and anticipating the car flying down the tracks. The difference was that I knew what would happen once the car coasted down. Glancing at the judge, I couldn't gauge his decision or how he would rule.

"As I counseled," Mr. Davenport whispered, "no outbursts. Let the judge talk."

I wasn't sure I could have even spoken.

The nameplate on the judge's bench read Judge Garner. He opened a folder as he sat down then picked up reading glasses and set them on his nose.

We could have heard a pin drop. I held my breath and grasped the life out of Kross. Or maybe he was the one clutching me as though he was trying to crack open a walnut.

I tossed a look over my shoulder. Apprehension flashed in each member of the Maxwell family's eyes as they focused on the judge.

Judge Garner cleared his throat, removed his glasses, and honed in on Kross and me. "I've gone through the case files for both Kross Maxwell and Ruby Lewis. I've had a chance to meet Raven Lewis. Before I make my ruling, I have some questions."

I sat up straighter.

"Kross, your record indicates that you box for a living. Financially, will boxing support your family?" Judge Garner interlaced his fingers in front of him.

Kross held his chin high. "Yes, sir. I've recently signed a five-year contract with a boxing promoter. So I'll have a steady stream of income."

Judge Garner turned to me. "Ruby, you haven't exactly shown that you're a responsible mother. Your file has a list of infractions that lead me to believe you can't take care of a child."

I opened my mouth then closed it. *Don't rock the boat.*

"What I want to hear from you is what makes you believe you won't be homeless again next week or two months from now?"

I glanced at Kross then Mr. Davenport. They both gave me a cursory glance. I couldn't exactly blame the judge for his question. After all, in a matter of hours, my life had gone from cushy to harsh when my mom had been carted off to jail.

"Ruby, I'm the one asking. Mr. Davenport and Kross can't help you with this question," Judge Garner said, his voice commanding.

I licked the dryness from my lips, struggling to find an answer because there wasn't a definitive one. Could I be homeless again? It was possible. Kross could leave us for some reason or another, then it would be Raven and me again. "Sir, the possibility does exist for any one of us to be homeless. For me though, I've set goals for myself to make sure that Raven and me never live on the streets again. I have a job, working at Rumors Night Club two nights a week." After Kross and I had thanked and apologized to Pete at Firefly, he'd said he would put in a good word for me with Tommy. But I'd declined. My days at Firefly were over. "I've signed up to get my GED, and my long-term plan is to teach ballet." Even though I could have been good at boxing, my heart was in ballet. "I don't ever want my daughter to see me as someone who relies on others or can't take care of herself." Tingles pricked my hand that Kross was holding.

Someone was sniffling behind us. I would have put money on Mrs. Maxwell. She'd shed tears when she met me two weeks ago. I still couldn't get over how nice she and Mr. Maxwell were. More importantly, I had been speechless when I laid eyes on Mrs. Maxwell. The resemblance between her and Raven was uncanny. I couldn't wait for Raven to meet them. When the paternity test had revealed that Kross was in fact the father, Mrs. Maxwell insisted on meeting her granddaughter. But the timing hadn't worked out yet. Actually, Kross and I had only had two scheduled visits within the last three weeks due to Ms. Waters's schedule.

Nevertheless, Kross had mentioned that his mom was quite emotional. I understood. She was a mother after all. I couldn't fault her for her sadness or pity. Part of me welcomed her sorrow. I wasn't sure why. But right now, everyone had to know that I would give my life before I ended up on the streets again.

"What about living arrangements?" Judge Garner asked.

"Kross and I are living in a nice two-bedroom apartment in Boston, where Raven will have her own room." We'd found a place in the same building that Kross had been living in with Kade, Kelton, and Lizzie. Mr. and Mrs. Maxwell had offered their house, but Ashford was too far for Kross and me to commute.

As Judge Garner jotted down some notes, I prayed that today would be the day Raven would meet her paternal grandparents. That also would mean we could live together in our new home.

A giddy feeling zipped through me. It felt weird to say home. I hadn't had a home complete with family in years. I often thought of my parents. I wanted both of them with me. I wanted to be able to sit in a kitchen while Mom cooked Thanksgiving or Christmas dinner and just talk. I wanted to hug on my dad like I used to as a little girl and tell him I loved him. I wanted them to watch Raven grow up and open presents on Christmas and her birthday. Most of all, I wanted Raven to love them as much as I did despite where they lived and what they'd done.

For now, I had to take things one step at a time, although I had to pinch myself several times per day to make sure I wasn't dreaming. My life had changed so drastically. Instead of dumpster-diving, I was eating at a table. The soft mattress that I curled up on at night with the sexiest guy on the planet was a far cry from the wet, cold, hard ground of the dark and dirty alleys I'd grown accustomed to. We were safe from the likes of Trent Baker, who was in jail. Even his high-powered lawyer hadn't been able to get him out of the kidnapping charge, not with Alex's, Tommy's, Pete's, Kross's, and my testimony. When it came to Alex, as nice as her intentions had been to return Raven unharmed, she had to pay for what she'd done. Like Trent, she too would be seeing the four walls of a prison for quite some time. In all, I felt as though I'd won the lottery. I couldn't wait to tuck Raven into her own bed at night and read her a bedtime story.

"Kross," Judge Garner said. "I'd like to hear how you feel about being a dad. You haven't been part of Raven's life for four years. So tell me what makes you think you can be an instant father."

Kross briefly eyed his own father. "I'm not going to lie. When I first found out that I could be a dad, I about passed out. Actually, I puked." Kross glanced at Kody then back.

His brothers chuckled. As for me, I loved that Kross could admit his emotions despite how strong and powerful he was on the outside. In fact, two weeks ago, when he'd told Raven he was her daddy, he'd cried as she hugged him.

"I also worried that I wouldn't know what to do. But my parents have taught me the importance of family. Not to mention, my dad is one of the best fathers a boy could have and learn from. I might not know how to handle a sick child or what to do when Raven cries. But what I do know is that blood comes first, and for that, my love for Raven will guide me to be the best father she will ever have."

Tears streamed down my face as I absorbed the feeling spilling from Kross's words. I didn't think I could have loved the man any harder or deeper, but I'd been so freaking wrong.

"Based on Ms. Waters's recommendation and what I've heard, it is my ruling that Raven Lewis be remanded to Ruby Lewis and Kross Maxwell immediately."

Kross and I glanced at each other as though we hadn't heard the judge correctly.

A hand landed on Kross's shoulder. "Congratulations, son," Mr. Maxwell said.

It was then that all the air left me, followed by tears of joy. Kross pushed to his feet before he helped me to mine.

As though the courtroom was our stage, he spun me around then pulled me to him before holding my face delicately in his hands. He lowered his lips to within a hair from mine. "Marry me."

A weird sound escaped me, or maybe it came from Mrs. Maxwell. I wasn't sure, and didn't care. My heart was racing like a galloping horse through the Wild West. I wanted forever with this man. I wanted to spend every waking minute with him and the child we had created and make more babies.

"I love you," he breathed. "Let's show our daughter how much we love each other."

"Say something," the Maxwell family said in unison.

I would if I had been able to speak. The only thing happening was that salty tears were sliding into my mouth.

Kross brought his lips to my ear. "I'll properly propose later when we're naked if that's what you want." I could feel his grin against my ear along with a slew of tingles from head to toe.

"Yes," I said, sure and strong. Then I couldn't stop saying yes until I heard Raven giggling.

Kross and I turned. Raven was walking in through the door the judge had come through earlier, holding Ms. Waters's hand.

"Mommy. Daddy." Her little legs ate up the courtroom floor as she smiled, her pigtails flopping as she approached.

I didn't know she was even there.

Kross and I squatted down. Instead of running into my arms like she normally did, she stuck her hands on her hips. Then she twirled around in her soft yellow and white dress that brought out her jet-black hair. "I have a new outfit. Mrs. Santos wanted me to have one. She said I should look extra special today for my mommy and daddy."

"It's beautiful, bumblebee," Kross said.

She giggled, showing that lone dimple that matched Kross's. "I'm not a bumblebee. I like bumblebees."

"What?" Kross touched his lips with his fingers. "Turn around. Let me see if you have wings."

She twirled again like the little ham that she was.

"Yep. Your wings are right there." He tickled her then swept her up in his arms.

She giggled again.

Kross carried her over to his parents. "Mom, Dad, this is Raven."

Mrs. Maxwell's mascara was running. "She's precious."

"Raven, this is your grandma and grandpa."

She stuck her finger in her mouth as she appraised the elder Maxwells. "Did you know Kody, Kelton, and my daddy are triplets?" she asked so innocently.

Everyone laughed, even Mr. Davenport, who I'd forgotten was standing next to Kelton.

I blew out a long, much-needed breath as I hooked my arm through Kross's free one. We were a family, and I was getting married to the man of my dreams.

EPILOGUE

KROSS

With my hands in my pockets, I stared out over the lake as my stomach swirled with nerves. Wild flowers bloomed, the warm breeze caused the trees around the lake to sing, and the water glistened beneath the May sunshine. Five months had passed since Ruby and I brought Raven home. Since then, life had been a whirlwind of bliss. We settled in as a family with no awkwardness at all, which was surprising to me. Being a daddy came super easy to me for some reason. Before our court hearing, I'd lost countless hours of sleep, worrying if I would know what to do as a father. Surprisingly, I had slipped right into a routine easily, reading bedtime stories, wiping Raven's nose when she'd gotten a cold, eating cereal with her in the morning, and watching cartoons. The only part of being a father I didn't like was traveling. Several times in the last three months, I'd had boxing matches that had taken me to Vegas, LA, and Houston. The best part was coming home and walking into the arms of Ruby and Raven.

"Are you ready, Bro?" Kade asked as he sidled up on my right.

"Yeah, man," Kody said on my left.

"We need to get this show on the road." Kelton walked up and settled in front of me.

"I should ask if you guys are ready?" All three of them had gotten certified to marry Ruby and me. Ruby and I didn't want a church wedding. When she'd first gotten a glimpse of the lake, she'd immediately gushed about how the area would be a perfect spot for a wedding. I couldn't have agreed with her more.

The lake symbolized so much for our family. From the small, carved-out area across the lake, which honored my late sister, to parties, bonfires, the boathouse turned man-cave, turned funhouse, then back into Kody's apartment, and finally to a place that brought our family together.

Kelton whipped out a small piece of paper from his black pants. The attire for the wedding was simple—no tuxedos or elegant dresses. For the men, black pants and a white button-down shirt. The women had decided on sundresses, although I had no idea what Ruby would be wearing. She'd mentioned that she didn't want an elaborate wedding dress, but she did want something pretty.

"You didn't memorize your lines?" I asked Kelton with a smirk.

"I did, but I just thought of something I wanted to add," he said.

After our vows, we'd planned on a small dinner with everyone, then Ruby and I were off to spend two weeks in Turks and Caicos. I couldn't wait to get her all to myself for two long weeks. Alone time with her was hard to come by with our schedules. But living in the same building as Kelton, Kade, and Lizzie meant that we practically had live-in babysitters. Lizzie always jumped at the chance to take Raven for the night.

I tossed a look over my shoulder. "Is Dillon here yet?" Since my brothers were marrying us, I'd asked Dillon to be my best man. Just as I was turning my head back, Dillon appeared from around the garage, decked out in the same style of clothes as the rest of us.

His hair was tied back in a low ponytail, and for once, he'd shaven the scruff from his jaw. He smiled as he came over to join us. "Man, wait until you see your bride. You're one lucky bastard."

Mom, Lacey, Lizzie, and Norma had kicked me out of the house, which was cool with me. I'd wanted some alone time anyway, mainly to quell the butterflies I had. Regardless, when Dillon said "bride," those butterflies fluttered wildly inside of me.

Voices peppered the air as Lizzie, Lacey, and Norma made their way down to the lake. The ladies were dressed in sleeveless yellow sundresses. Yellow was Raven's favorite color. I smirked when my gaze landed on their feet. They were all wearing flip-flops.

"Do you like our shoes?" Norma asked as her shoulder-length blond hair blew in the breeze. In the last five months, she'd grown out her pixie style and had gained about ten pounds, making her look curvier and healthier.

All of us men laughed.

Lizzie lifted up on her tiptoes and kissed me on the cheek before she pinned me with her gray eyes. "Make sure you don't drool."

I pinched my eyebrows together.

"Don't listen to her," Lacey said. "Your mouth better be hanging open when you see your bride." She giggled, her green eyes sparkling in the afternoon sun. "I can't begin to tell you how happy I am for you. I always thought Kade and I would be the first ones to tie the knot, but I'm glad we're not."

Kade reached out to grab her hand.

I swung my gaze from Kade to Lacey. "Why is that?"

"Too much pressure," Kade and Lacey said in unison then laughed.

"Bro," Kade said. "I've been the older brother with the spotlight seemingly on me to do everything first. Marriage, grandbabies, blah, blah, blah. But with Raven, and now your nuptials, Lacey and I can breathe. We are so fucking happy for you."

"You know that won't last long," Kody piped in. "Mom will be asking when you two will be tying the knot. Or even Kelton and Lizzie."

"Let's talk about you, man," I said to Kody. "Mom and Dad will be on your back, asking when you're going to find a steady girlfriend." He'd only taken out our former teacher, Ms. Sharp, a couple of times, but it wasn't serious.

He grinned like an ass. "When I'm ready."

"Oh, yeah. How's the older women pool looking?" I teased.

Everyone quieted before Dillon spoke. "Older women know what they want."

Norma lightly punched him. "Hey, don't judge. Us younger gals are just as good."

Norma had a thing for Dillon, and although I hadn't seen him with any women for as long as I'd known him, I knew Norma was definitely his type, especially with her blond hair.

Liam came running down. His brown hair was slicked back, almost sticking to his head. He'd accompanied me on some of my boxing matches when he could. Behind him, Jay strutted leisurely down.

"It's time," Liam said. "Your mom said to get into positions."

Mom stood near the garage, holding Raven's hand. Mom's hair was tied up into an up-do of sorts, and she was wearing a light-blue sundress. Raven had the same hairstyle and wore a yellow and white polka dot sundress. They both had flip-flops on too, sporting smiles.

My brothers scrambled into position with their backs to the lake. Dillon sidled up to me on one side, and Norma stood on my other side since she was the maid of honor. Coach, Liam, Lizzie, and Lacey all found spots behind me.

Dillon tapped me on the arm. "Turn this way."

I did and found my mom slowly walking down while Raven plucked flower petals from the small wicker basket she was holding and sprinkled them in front of her. Liam began filming the ceremony with my cell phone. Lizzie and Lacey were snapping pictures with theirs.

My heartbeat rammed and pounded against my chest as I kept switching my gaze between my mom and my little girl to the garage, where at any moment, my beautiful bride would emerge. Dad was giving her away. Ruby had cried last night, sad that her mom and dad couldn't be there. At least we would be able to send the video and pictures to her parents in jail.

When Mom and Raven were halfway between the garage and me, Dad and Ruby made their entrance. I faltered where I stood.

"Easy, dude," Dillon said as he grasped my elbow.

"I can't breathe, man," I whispered. I couldn't get enough oxygen in my lungs.

Ruby wore a strapless, cream-colored dress that hugged her body and draped to her toes. Her auburn hair was pulled up in a messy style with wisps of hair framing her delicate features. She smiled, and my chest clenched. That fucking smile was what had snagged me back in high school. Only now, it did more than snag me. My entire body was on fire.

As Ruby glided down like the angel she was, Raven tugged on my hand, breaking my concentration. It was probably a good thing since my groin had a mind of its own.

I met her dark-blue eyes. "Yes, bumblebee?"

"I love you, Daddy."

I swayed then smiled at the beautiful girl I'd created. It was still mind-blowing that I was actually a father.

"As big as the universe?" I asked.

"Bigger," she cooed then stepped behind me to hold my mom's hand.

Ruby and Dad then settled in front of me. Dad hugged me. "I'm so fucking proud of you," he said in my ear. "Treat her with the utmost respect."

Tears stung my eyes. I wasn't going to make it through this ceremony.

He joined my mom as Ruby hooked her arm with mine.

I ogled my stunning bride as she flashed her big blue-green eyes at me. We turned to Kade, Kody, and Kelton, both of us trembling.

Kade began. "Marriage may be the union of two people, but in my book, it is the union of family, growth, happiness, and a deep sense of love for each other, no matter the circumstances. Never forget that family is the most important thing in life."

Ruby and I squeezed hands as Kelton spoke. "Love grabs your heart. Love tickles your soul. Love is family. Love is friends. Most of all"—he glanced past us to no doubt Lizzie then back to us—"love is never-ending. Embrace life with love and respect, and never, ever lose sight of family."

A tear slid down Ruby's cheek.

Kody took over. "Today, my heart is filled with more love than I knew possible. I never imagined any of us getting married. Heck, it felt like yesterday when we were ten years old and causing trouble with girls. Now my brother has a family. I echo what Kade and Kelton said with one addition. Go and make more babies."

Okay, I wasn't expecting that. I figured Kody would've written us a song. But his sentiment was so much better. Regardless, Ruby and I weren't ready for another just yet. Our plan was to wait a year before we tried for another kid. We wanted Raven to have a sibling or two. Hell, I wouldn't mind having a boy.

Everyone laughed.

"Now your vows," Kade said.

Ruby and I turned to face each other.

She peered up at me with so much love in her eyes. "Kross Maxwell, thank you for being persistent in your pursuit to find me. I've never stopped thinking about you since the day we met at the academy. While I'm sad that we lost four years, I'm also beyond happy that we did. I believe we're that much stronger as a couple and as a family. I want lots of babies with you. I want to grow old with you. More than anything, I love you as big as the universe." She gave me one of her shy looks.

Yep, the blood was flowing heavily south.

I licked my lips as I searched her face. I didn't agonize over my vows. I knew exactly what I wanted to say. Nevertheless, I took in a deep breath of fresh air. "Star light. Star bright. You're the only star I see tonight. I wish I may. I wish I might. You're the only one I wish tonight. You're my angel, and I want to dance under the stars with you until death do us part." I leaned in and whispered in her ear. "Naked that is."

She shivered.

When I retreated, my brothers spoke in unison. "I now pronounce you husband and wife."

They had barely said "wife" when Ruby grabbed my face, plunged her tongue into mouth, and kissed me as though I was her last breath. I knew she was mine. Fireworks went off in my chest, my heart, and everywhere else in me. Our lives had just begun.

AFTERWORD

Dare to Dance was an emotional story to write. Several plot elements in this book are based on true events that have happened to me when I was young. I experienced some of Ruby's challenges of being homeless, albeit for a very brief time. But that one time led me to a man much like Trent. Thankfully, I was like Ruby and got the hell out of there.

However, I didn't have a night in shining armor. Instead, I joined the military the very next day. I was also Raven. My mom died when I was a baby, and my dad dropped into a deep depression. So I ended up in foster care for many years until my dad got his act together.

I struggled through my childhood and young adult years. Everyday, I thank God for watching over me. I'm grateful for the extended family I had who supported me, the friends who stood by me, and for the military who showed me the discipline to make it on my own.

My heart goes out to all the homeless and foster kids out there. I want say a huge thank you to all those families that take in foster children. One of my best friends did just that, and her now teenager daughter has a wonderful life and a future ahead of her.

With all my love, Susan

DEAR READER

I hope you enjoyed Kross and Ruby's story. If you would like to continue to read more about the Maxwell men, then check out the rest of the books in the series.

Other books in the Maxwell Series
Dare to Kiss - Kade and Lacey
Dare to Dream - Kade and Lacey
Dare to Love - Kelton Maxwell
Dare to Live - Kody Maxwell
Dare to Breathe - Final book on Kade and Lacey. Coming in 2018

Dare to Kiss and Dare to Dream should be read in order.

However, Dare to Love, Dare to Dance, and Dare to Live can all be read as a stand alone.

Dare to Breathe should be read after reading Dare to Kiss and Dare to Dream.

Also, if you have moment to spare, I would super appreciate a short review. Your help in sharing your excitement and spreading the word about the Maxwell brothers would be greatly appreciated.

TITLES BY S.B. ALEXANDER

To read samples and find out where to purchase all books visit:
http://sbalexander.com/books

The Maxwell Series:
Dare to Kiss - Book 1
Dare to Dream – Book 2
Dare to Love – Book 3
Dare to Dance - Book 4
Dare to Live - Book 5
Dare to Breathe - Book 6
The Maxwell Series Boxed Set – Books 1-3
Dare to Kiss Coloring Book Companion

The Vampire SEAL Series:
On the Edge of Humanity – Book 1
On the Edge of Eternity – Book 2
On the Edge of Destiny – Book 3
On the Edge of Misery - Book 4
On the Edge of Infinity - Book 5
The Vampire SEAL Collection - Boxed Set

TITLES BY S.B. ALEXANDER

A Stand Alone Novel
Breaking Rules

ACKNOWLEDGMENTS

I want to thank my fans, readers and bloggers. Without you guys I wouldn't be writing. You motivate me, you support me, and you encourage me. I'm humbled by all the reviews and messages I've received along the way. Hugs and kisses to each and every one of you for taking the time to take this journey with me and sharing your excitement.

To everyone in Maxwell Mania, I love the crap out of you. Thank you for loving the series, and the Maxwell boys. Most of all, thank you for spreading the word, your excitement means more than you know.

The team at Red Adept Editing is without a doubt the best editing team in the industry.

An enormous thank you to the talented Hang Le for her creativity and book cover design. You're absolutely amazing.

Marketing a book is one of the hardest aspects for an author, and I'm so lucky and overjoyed that I'd met Marissa at JKS Communications. She had a vision for Dare to Kiss, and she has an even bigger vision for the future of my books. To Marissa, Angelle and the entire team at JKS, thank you.

The publishing industry changes constantly, and without Katey Coffing's inspiration and coaching I wouldn't have come this far without her. Love you, girl.

Wendy Kupinewicz, you are a superb lady, a great friend, and poet. The poem you've written is perfect. Much love and thanks.

Kylie Sharp, thank you for all your support, feedback and advice. Love you.

Tracy Hope, you are my super fan. You've read my drafts and every line I've ever written, even when it was rewritten fifteen times. You're honest in your feedback when something isn't working. You kick me in the butt when I need it. And you've brought my books to life with your creative vision and superb producing skills of my book trailers. Love and hugs!

Finally, to the man who stole my heart. I love you more than you know.

www.ingramcontent.com/pod-product-compliance
Lightning Source LLC
Chambersburg PA
CBHW030656260626
47157CB00007B/2677